Undoing

An LA Lovers Book

JOURDYN KELLY

In case you missed it...

I n this book, Rebecca and Cass are married. If you missed the short story where the nuptials happened, here is the wedding scene from **You're Invited.**

"*Finally,*" Eve whispered in Lainey's ear. "*You look incredible. I can't wait to be married to you.*"

"*I love you.*" God, Lainey hoped her brain came up with something more profound than that when she said her vows. However, judging by the look on Eve's face, no other words were needed.

"Friends," Willamena began, pride and emotion tinging her voice. "Eve and Lainey have invited us here today to witness their union as a married couple. I was honored to be asked to officiate the wedding. What you can get on the internet never ceases to amaze me. Too bad it wasn't that easy to get my Ph.D." She paused for the spattering of laughter. "I have gotten to know Eve and Lainey very well over the past couple of years. When I received the call that they were getting married, I was delighted but unsurprised. They've both been through traditional weddings, which is why they've chosen something different today. Vows will be said, and rings will be exchanged, but they have also requested that this day be about more than just them. Eve?"

Eve nodded. "Love thrives when it is shared with those who believe in you. I have spent most of my life being closed off to everyone around me. I thought that was what I needed to do to survive. But that's all I was doing. Surviving. I wasn't living. In fact, I didn't start living until the day I met Lainey." She took Lainey's hands in hers. "You taught me how to open my heart. It hurt like hell, but the outcome is beyond anything I could have ever dreamed of. When I came to you with my idea for today, you didn't hesitate to say yes because *that's* the kind of person you are. You are a giving, loving, incredible human being who is more than willing to share your happiness with others."

When Eve paused, Lainey wiped tears from her eyes and took her cue. Neither of them discussed what they wanted to say today but were so attuned to one another that continuing Eve's thought was second nature for her.

"You often credit me with bringing heart and soul to your life, but it was you who brought breath to my life. I never knew how strong I could be until you showed me. I never knew the capacity of love I had in my heart until I found someone who loved me enough to allow me to open myself up. And it's because of you, Eve, that I'm now surrounded by people who support and care about me. It's for that reason that when you came to me with your idea of how you wanted this day to be, I was more than happy to say yes." She reluctantly let go of Eve's hands and reached for both Rebecca and Cass.

"Rebecca and Cass. When you should have been basking in the joy of your engagement, you unselfishly postponed the celebration when those around you were hurting. When there were those of us who doubted we could ever find happiness, you held onto hope and encouraged us to keep fighting. You helped guide Hunter and Ellie, are loyal to Patty and Mo, and advocated for Eve and me. This day is as much yours as it is ours. That's why we asked Willamena to be here. Not only so she could officiate for us, but for you two as well."

Rebecca's jaw dropped. "What?" She looked up at Cass, who was rendered speechless.

"For months, we've been asking you about your wedding," Eve said. "And for months, you would begin to plan only to be distracted by other people's issues."

"Or a demanding gallery owner," Lainey teased.

"Or that," Eve agreed with delight. "What you've always said, however, is you wanted it to be intimate." She spread her arms to indicate their surroundings. "You wanted your closest friends there." She gestured to their friends, who were just as shocked and emotional as

Rebecca and Cass. "And you wanted your aunt there." Eve pointed towards Willamena, who gave them a watery smile. "So, if you agree, Lainey and I would love to share this moment with the two of you."

"Yes!" Cass blurted out. "Uh, I mean, if Rebecca is okay with it, too."

Rebecca brought her misty eyes up to Cassidy's. "I want nothing more than to marry you, Cassidy. We have everything we need right here." She looked at Eve and Lainey. "Thank you so much for being so generous. We would love to share this moment with you."

The group clapped and whooped enthusiastically. When Eve and Lainey said they didn't want a traditional wedding, no one thought they meant this. However, it went along with how considerate they were.

"Rebecca?" Cass spoke up before anyone else could move on. "I tell you every day how I feel. I show you when I think you need more than just words. We may have met in unconventional ways, but that never diminished the strength of my love for you. I asked you once to let me be the risk you take. Thank you for allowing me to be a part of your life. Thank you for loving me."

"Oh, Cassidy. I'm the one who should be thanking you. You showed me that the only thing that matters in a relationship is true love. I fought what I felt for you because I didn't feel whole. I fought because of how much older I am than you. In the end, I fought *for* us because I can't imagine not having you in my life. I love you with everything I am, and I am so proud that I will be your wife."

"Well." Willamena cleared her throat and wiped away tears. "I believe the four of you have possibly given the most beautiful vows I've ever heard. Is there more, or would you like to continue?"

"Continue," the four said together.

Willamena smiled. She asked for the "I dos" and the exchange of rings. There was a moment of panic for Cass when she realized she and Rebecca didn't have rings. Willamena surprised them with the bands that Rebecca's parents used at their wedding. Rebecca's father's ring was a little too large for Cass's finger, but that could be easily remedied. The sentimentality of the rings meant the world to them.

"The only thing left to say is, by the power vested in me, and as witnessed by friends and family, I now pronounce you wife and wife. And wife and wife," Willamena laughed. "Kiss!"

Rebecca and Cass had no problem showing their affection towards each other. PDA, however, was new to Eve and Lainey. However, they buried their hesitancies and kissed deeply. Their guests cheered loudly, none as loud as little Bella. She whooped and giggled and launched herself into *both* her mothers' arms. Kevin and Darren did little happy dances and began hugging everyone in sight.

"Cake!" Bella yelled. With that loud announcement — or demand — she took off towards the house.

"I guess it's time for cake," Eve laughed.

"And mimosas!" Lainey announced. "It's time to celebrate!"

"Hear, hear!" the others agreed jovially.

"Eve, Lainey?"

"Thank you for agreeing to do this," Lainey said before Rebecca could continue. "We wanted to do something to show our appreciation for your continued support. Plus, you two needed a little kick in the ass."

Eve laughed and hugged Lainey to her. "God, I love you, woman."

"She's not wrong," Cass laughed, then sobered when she saw Rebecca's stern face.

Rebecca's fierceness lasted all of two seconds before the laughter began. "Leave it to you, Lainey, to be the one to give me a kick in the ass. Now that that's settled, let's go drink!"

Chapter One

"Hey, babe? Do you think we have too much sex?"

Rebecca poked her head around the bathroom door with a bemused look. Her body ached in all the right places from the sex she and her wife Cassidy just had.

"Excuse me?"

Cass held up her Kindle. "I was reading some reviews on that book from Joslyn Cohan. You know, the one that reminds me of us." Cass gave Rebecca a cheeky grin. "Anyway, there's a review here that says there's too much sex. I didn't think that would be an issue. And, um, we have a ton of sex."

Believe me, I know, Rebecca thought with a slight wince as she stretched her sore muscles. She couldn't help but laugh at the confusion on Cassidy's handsome face as she read more reviews. "Baby, why are you reading reviews?"

Cass glanced up and shrugged. "I dunno. I finished the book, and it took me here. I saw a one-star and was curious. Totally bogus review." She tossed the Kindle aside and hopped off the bed. Her naked, tattooed body on full display as she sauntered toward Rebecca. "They wonder when they worked or, you know, had time to do anything else. We manage just fine. Besides, do people really want to read about characters' bodily functions or boring day-to-day activities? I thought people read to get away from that stuff."

Rebecca feathered her pink fingernails up Cassidy's six-pack. "You're really taking this personally."

Cass shrugged again. "I connected with the androgynous character in that book. I guess it felt a little personal." She wrapped her arms around Rebecca. God, she loved the feel of Rebecca's body against hers. Where Cass's lean, tatted body was hard and muscular from working out, Rebecca was toned and voluptuous with smooth skin, one tattoo, and the sexiest belly ring Cass had ever seen. Cass towered over Rebecca's five-foot-two-inch frame, and in her mind — and heart — they were built perfectly for each other.

"You took it as a challenge, didn't you?" Rebecca guessed, lowering her hands to Cassidy's firm ass and squeezing.

"Maybe." Cass dipped her head, kissing Rebecca's full lips. "I have a mural to paint downtown, but I can spare a few minutes."

Rebecca laughed. "A few minutes? Be still my beating heart." She got on her tiptoes and kissed Cassidy again. "I have to take a shower. Your 'few minutes' will have to wait."

"Nope." Cass bent and grasped Rebecca around the back of her thighs, hoisting her up. She grinned when Rebecca automatically wrapped her legs around Cass's waist. "I can do what I need to do in the shower."

Rebecca frowned when Cassidy hesitated. "Did you change your mind?"

"No, I, uh, gotta pee." Cass gently set Rebecca back on her feet. "You get the shower going while I do my bodily functions."

Rebecca chuckled. "You're so weird," she teased as she walked to the shower, turning it on. Since Cassidy would be in there with her doing unimaginable things to her, Rebecca made it a bit cooler than usual.

"Yeah, but you love me," Cass called from the water closet.

"Yes, I certainly do," Rebecca muttered. She checked the temperature of the water, shivering slightly. *Cassidy better do an excellent job at heating me up in here*, she thought as she stepped in. She turned her face into the spray, allowing the pelting water to wash away the early morning brain fog.

If she didn't have a meeting this morning, she would have stayed in bed with Cassidy all day. Their time together had dwindled between Cassidy's work becoming more demanding and Rebecca being busier than ever with her consulting business. Yes, they had sex, made love, fucked — Mistress still dominated, but it was the little things Rebecca was beginning to miss. The lunches together or takeout on the couch while they watched cheesy TV shows were things Rebecca didn't think she needed but was quickly learning she did.

"Hey," Cass whispered in Rebecca's ear. She felt Rebecca jump slightly and held her tighter. "You okay?"

Rebecca turned in Cassidy's arms, wrapping her arms around Cassidy's neck. "Yes." She kissed Cassidy softly. "What time will you be home tonight?"

Cass heard the wistfulness in Rebecca's voice. "I can be home early if you need me to be, babe. Do you have something planned?"

"No plans. I don't want anything planned. I just want us to have a quiet night here at home. You," Rebecca kissed a tattoo on Cassidy's chest. "Me," another kiss on another tattoo. "Takeout," another kiss. "Movie," kiss.

Cass closed her eyes, allowing her body to feel each kiss Rebecca gave her. But even the sensation didn't detract from what Rebecca was saying. Cass knew they'd both been busy lately. After Eve Sumptor made Cass a featured artist at Sumptor Gallery, LA, Cass received more commissions than she could handle. She had to turn most of them down for lack of time, but the ones for hospitals or special events kept her busy now. Not to mention doing more canvas work for Eve. Was she neglecting Rebecca? Cass knew Rebecca had been busier than usual, too, but was that because Cass wasn't around?

"Becca?" Cass lifted Rebecca's chin with her fingertip. Rebecca's eyes were shimmering, but not because of the shower. "Am I neglecting you, baby?"

"No, of course not." Rebecca sighed. How could she feel neglected when they were constantly together? Rarely a day passed that they didn't fall asleep or wake up together. And, of course, everything in between those moments. So why did Rebecca feel this way? "I just miss... us, I think. We're too busy."

We're too busy, Cass thought with a bit of relief. Somehow, knowing it wasn't just her made it easier. They could work together to figure out how to make things the way they used to be.

"I know I've been doing a lot of work...."

"Charity, baby. I love what you're doing and why you're doing it. You take the jobs that mean the most. I need you to understand that I'm not upset with you. I'm busy, too. One night, baby. Just one night where we can be lazy and snuggle. I think that's what I need. A recharge."

"We can totally do that. How about I pick up some food on my way home? No later than five, yeah? Then we can veg out in front of the TV. I think we have a few shows to catch up on." Recharging for Rebecca meant Cass needed to keep it in her pants. As much as she loved making love to her wife, Cass loved just *being* with Rebecca more.

"Thank you, baby."

"I told you before, babe, I'd do anything for you. A recharge would be good for us both. Hey?" Cass kissed Rebecca's forehead. "I love you."

"I love you, too, baby. Now," Rebecca raised a brow. "What about that challenge..."

Cass's eyebrows shot up. "I thought you wanted to recharge."

"That's tonight. This morning, I could use a boost of endorphins."

"Oh, yeah? Did the boost I gave you earlier wear off?" Cass wiggled her eyebrows.

"No," Rebecca brought Cassidy's hand to her sex. "Just needs a little top-up."

Cass slipped a finger past Rebecca's lips to rub her swollen clit. She was sure Rebecca was sore from the pounding Cass had given her earlier. *Should have been gentler*, she thought as she sank to her knees. The only thing she hated about shower sex — besides the awkwardness of some positions — was being unable to get the full reward of Rebecca's intoxicating scent. However... Cass took Rebecca's clit into her mouth and sucked gently. She could still taste her.

"Mmm." Rebecca held on to the top of Cassidy's head with one hand, the other braced against the shower wall. God, Cassidy knew how to use that mouth. Cassidy also knew when Rebecca needed her to be tender with her.

Cass massaged Rebecca's ass as her tongue and lips did all the work. She lapped at Rebecca's clit with the flat of her tongue in a sensual, intimate kiss. Rebecca's hips moved to Cass's rhythm, granting her deeper access to that sweet nectar only Rebecca could offer her. Cass wanted to drape one of Rebecca's legs over her shoulder, but the slippery shower prevented much movement—another *con in shower sex*. Rebecca's hand fisted in Cass's short hair, and Cass knew she was ready.

"*Cassidy,*" Rebecca whispered. The noise of the shower nearly drowned out the reverent plea, but when Cassidy hummed against her clit, Rebecca felt her release travel through her body in slow motion. Rebecca knew from experience that it didn't matter if the sex they had was fast and furious or slow and steady; every orgasm threatened to bring Rebecca to her knees.

Cass slipped her tongue inside Rebecca just as she felt the orgasm ripple through Rebecca. Cass could live here, her face buried between Rebecca's thighs. She said it many times before. This was her heaven.

Rebecca sighed contentedly, floating down from the high Cassidy always gave her. She stroked a finger across Cassidy's jaw, hooking it under her chin to guide Cassidy up to her. Their kiss was as slow and passionate as what Cassidy just did to her.

"Thank you," she whispered against Cassidy's lips.

"Always my pleasure, baby." Cass picked up the loofah, dabbing Rebecca's favorite body wash and getting it sudsy. *Mmm, lavender.* "I always think of the first time we showered together."

"Why? That's not the greatest memory, baby." Rebecca recalled how broken Cassidy looked when Rebecca refused to kiss her. Just after that shower, Rebecca ran away, vowing never to see Cassidy again.

"Maybe not, but when I think about that, I see how far we've come since then." Cass rubbed the loofah over Rebecca's body as she talked. "I wanted to kiss you so much. I'd never had the urge to kiss someone like that, like my life depended on it. When you said no..."

"Baby..."

"No, Becca, it's okay," Cass smiled. "Because now I can do this." She lowered her head and kissed Rebecca like her life depended on it. "You're mine now. And I'm yours. If I find myself taking that for granted, I think about that day. That shower. When I thought I lost everything I didn't even know I needed."

Rebecca caressed Cassidy's cheek, brushing wet hair out of her face. "You're so sweet, Cassidy. Sometimes, I wonder if I deserve you."

"Oh, you deserve the very best of me, babe. And I," Cass rinsed

Rebecca's body. "Deserve the very best of you. I'm a lucky son of a bitch that you give me that best every day."

"You're going to make me late for my meeting, aren't you?"

Cass grinned. "Maybe a little. But *you* are someone people will wait for and say it's a privilege to do so."

Rebecca laughed softly and shook her head. "You charming devil. We're going to be so late."

"Five o'clock sharp," Cass said, handing Rebecca her briefcase. We have a date. I'm on food duty, and you are on drink duty."

"So, chocolate milk for you, Perrier for me. Got it."

Cass laughed. "Since we're being lazy tonight, I'll drink some Perrier with you."

"You don't like sparkling water, Cassidy."

Cass lifted a shoulder. "I'm warming up to it. As long as it's ice cold, I can handle it." She walked Rebecca to her Mercedes and opened the door for her. "Do you need me to stop and get anything else before coming home?"

Rebecca shook her head. "No, I think we have everything we need." She reached up and kissed Cassidy's cheek. "Thank you for listening to what I need, Cassidy."

"Always, babe. Always." Cass ushered Rebecca into the car and waited for Rebecca to start it and roll down the window.

"You know, the only thing that would make tonight even better would be if Mocha were home," Rebecca said with an exaggerated frown. "When does she get back from puppy boot camp?"

Cass *almost* rolled her eyes but thought better of it at the very last second. Yeah, she missed the cute little puppy that she gave Rebecca on Christmas, too, but a little training never hurt anyone. "It's not boot camp, babe. It's obedience school."

"Potato, potahto."

"She *ate* your favorite flog and chewed up a dildo!"

"Well, it wasn't her fault that *someone* left them out for her to get!" Rebecca argued, laughing.

"You're killin' me, babe." Cass absolutely loved this side of Rebecca. Mocha had brought out a maternal side that Cass wasn't sure she'd ever see from her wife. Too bad the pup couldn't stop chewing things up. They both decided it was good for their sanity if they sent her for some puppy training. However, neither knew just how much they'd miss the little bugger. "Mocha will be back before you know it, I promise. Now, get goin'. Be careful with my girl, yeah?" She leaned in the window and gave Rebecca a quick kiss. "I'll see you tonight, Becca."

"See you tonight, baby. I love you."

"I love you." Cass stood back and watched Rebecca drive off, giving her a quick wave. She checked her watch. She had a good three hours to paint today. It wasn't long, but Cass would do what she could in that time. She hopped in her truck and cranked up the tunes for her hour's drive to the location, a grin plastered on her face. This morning was blissful, so today would be a good day. And tonight would be a perfect night of recharging. Now... what was a good lazy night meal? Time to call Ellie.

Chapter Two

Rebecca knocked confidently on the office door. Despite her little shower rendezvous with her wife, Rebecca arrived precisely two minutes early for her meeting. She should have used the time to vet the client more thoroughly, but this should be an easy consultation to see how — she checked her notes — Mr. McEnroe wanted to move forward with his business.

Of course, she had the basics, including the company's profit margins for the last four quarters. But Mr. McEnroe had been less than forthcoming despite needing Rebecca's help. She'd see how this initial consult went and then do a full audit of the business and the man. She'd learned long ago that investigating the proprietors of a company is just as important as the numbers and business plans. If she wasn't comfortable with the type of person she'd be working closely with, Rebecca declined the endeavor.

"Yeah?"

Rebecca raised a brow. That was not a professional way of answering the door. Strike one. She wrapped her hand around the doorknob, took a breath, and let herself in.

"Mr. McEnroe?"

The man sitting behind the large — too large for the space — desk looked up at Rebecca, an arrogant smirk spreading on his lips.

"*You're* the consultant?"

Rebecca tilted her head, holding his gaze without a flinch. "I am."

"In the bedroom or the boardroom?" he snickered, undoubtedly patting himself on the back for the offensive joke.

"Excuse me?" *Strike two and three.*

"It was a compliment, sweetheart. With a body like that, you have my full attention." He gestured to the chair in front of the desk. "Take a seat."

"How did you get my information, Mr. McEnroe?" Rebecca asked, staying close to the door. She didn't think the man was a threat — just an asshole — but she wasn't stupid. She'd also decided less than one minute into the meeting *not* to work with this douchebag.

McEnroe raised his eyes from Rebecca's cleavage. "A friend. Apparently you... helped him. Now I'm wondering if we were talking about the same kind of help."

That smirk. Oh, Rebecca wanted to take a flog and whip the pretentious fucker into submission. That reaction surprised Rebecca enough to want to turn around and leave. If only her ego would allow her to. But no, she wouldn't give the pompous ass the satisfaction of thinking he got to her. She walked, shoulders back, with a confident stride, to his desk and laid a folder before him. She wouldn't work with him, but that didn't mean she couldn't dangle what he'd never have in front of him.

"I'm beginning to understand you a little more, Mr. McEnroe. In that file, you'll find a preliminary business solution that would have been perfect for getting your company back on track. If you..."

McEnroe pushed the file away. "Yeah, I don't think anything *you* show me will be better than what I've done with the place, Becky."

Rebecca's eye twitched, as did her hand. Her fingers curled into a fist, and she could feel the whip in her palm. "You may call me Mrs. Giles or Mrs. Cuinn-Giles. By the looks of your quarterlies, *anything* in that folder would supersede the piss poor job you've done with this *place*." She picked up the folder. "That being said, I'm definitely not the consultant for you."

McEnroe stood, his cocky attitude still locked in place. "So, bedroom? I bet you're a little freak in bed."

Rebecca's nostrils flared with anger. "I'm married. To a woman. And even if I was the straightest woman on the planet and you were the last man standing... well, I would turn gay just to get away from you.

You're a vile, immature little boy trying to play in the big leagues. Here's a tip for free. You couldn't handle me. I would make you run home to your mommy, crying the whole way." She leaned on the desk, closing the distance between them ever so slightly. "You have no idea how much of a *freak* I can be."

Rebecca watched his Adam's apple bob as he swallowed hard. There was intrigue in his eyes — who wouldn't be intrigued by a beautiful woman threatening their manhood? But what satisfied Rebecca was the lack of the bravado that had been there just moments before. This was a man who wasn't used to a woman standing up to him.

"Lose my number, Mr. McEnroe." *Just as you're going to lose your business.*

After that farce of a meeting, all Rebecca wanted was to go home and bask in Cassidy's optimism and love. But Cassidy was downtown, elbow-deep in paint, making a cancer ward in a children's hospital a little sunnier with a fun mural. Rebecca wouldn't take that away from those kids. However, she also didn't want to be home alone. So, Rebecca made a detour.

"What a fucking waste of time," Rebecca muttered, her heels clicking on the marble flooring of Sumptor, Inc. Her meeting had bothered her more than she cared to admit, which pissed Rebecca off. She was used to men dismissing her intelligence and expertise, but McEnroe was... different. He had no business sense at all. That, coupled with his wildly narcissistic attitude, not only gave Rebecca a massive headache but also made her wonder why in the hell he had called her at all.

Rebecca was also used to overtly sexual advances. Normally, she was able to dismiss it as tiny dick syndrome. The louder they were, the less they had to work with below the belt. The less they had, the faster they cried their safe word when Mistress showed them no mercy—years behind the mask taught Rebecca that. McEnroe's multiple sexual comments put Rebecca on edge for far different reasons than just being annoying. They reminded her too much of her past.

"Good afternoon, Mrs. Giles." Dorothea, Eve's assistant, gave Rebecca a kind smile. "Is Mrs. Sumptor expecting you?"

"No, sorry, Dorothea. Is she busy?"

"Never too busy for a friend."

Rebecca turned to the sultry voice and smiled. "I was hoping you'd say that." She accepted Eve's hug and kiss on the cheek, then followed her into the large office. "I didn't know if you'd be here or at the gallery. I took a chance." Rebecca sat on the plush couch, curling her legs up under her.

Eve sat beside her, turning her body to face her oldest friend. "Lainey and I are giving Lauren a little autonomy at the gallery. And, frankly, after everything that happened, we're a little more attentive here at Sumptor, Inc." Eve touched Rebecca's fidgeting hand. Rebecca Cuinn-Giles was not usually a jittery person. "Are you okay?"

"Hmm?" Rebecca saw Eve looking pointedly at Rebecca's hands. Immediately, Rebecca stopped tapping her fingers. "Yes, I'm fine."

"Becca?"

Rebecca rolled her eyes. "You only call me Becca when you're trying to butter me up."

Eve chuckled. "You came to see me, remember? Seriously, Rebecca. Are you and Cass doing okay?"

"Yes! Absolutely. I'm not here because of Cassidy, Eve. I just..." Rebecca blew out a frustrated breath. "I had a meeting today. A potential client. It didn't go well, and I feel a bit out of sorts."

Eve frowned. "I've seen you after a disappointing meeting. This isn't it. Did something happen?"

"He was an asshole. Nothing I haven't dealt with before."

"But?"

Rebecca shook her head. "I don't know, Eve. This time, it just rubbed me the wrong way." She wanted to discuss this with Cassidy before anyone else. Cassidy was her person—the one she wanted to turn to when she was feeling...off. As much as she loved Eve, that's not why Rebecca was here. "How would you feel about acquiring a wholesale warehouse? According to the quarterlies I've been given, it's well on its way to failing."

Eve laughed. "Well, you sure know how to sell it! Are you punishing me or the dickhead that made you feel this way?"

Rebecca grinned. "I know my business plan will work, and you have the resources to turn it around. More importantly, I want McEnroe to fail. Permanently."

Eve hesitated, bringing her phone out to text Lainey for her opinion. A few moments later, Lainey popped into the office.

"Hello, Rebecca." Lainey leaned down and kissed Rebecca's cheek. "Hard day?"

Rebecca raised a brow. "Do I look that bad?"

"No," Lainey smiled. "Eve mentioned it in her text. That and you want us to get into the wholesale business."

Rebecca glanced at Eve. "Do the two of you have some sort of shorthand? Because you couldn't have texted all that."

Eve lifted a shoulder, her mouth tilted up with a sly grin as Lainey sat on the arm of the couch next to Eve. "We do. But I also have fast fingers."

Lainey bit her cheek when Rebecca slanted a look at her. They all thought the same thing, but other than a knowing look, they let it go.

"Ahem." *Time to get everyone's mind back on business*, Lainey thought. "So, Sumptor, Inc. isn't in the market for wholesale, but that doesn't mean we can't take over the company and repurpose it. How big is the warehouse?"

Rebecca appreciated how Eve gave Lainey more responsibility in the company. Lainey had undoubtedly earned it. With a smile, she reached for her briefcase... which she had forgotten in her car. "Damn it. All the information you need is in my briefcase. Which I currently don't have. But I can email you all the details when I get home."

"And you're okay with us not keeping the business as is or using your business plan? You know we have the utmost respect and confidence in your work...."

"Lainey," Rebecca interrupted gently. "I honestly don't care if you burn the place down. I want that man to know what happens when I get pissed off."

"Burn it down it is," Eve teased. "Anything else you'd like us to do to him, Mistress?"

Rebecca playfully flipped Eve off. "I'll admit I imagined flogging the hell out of him, but Cassidy is the only one that gets the pleasure —and pain— of Mistress."

Eve chuckled. "On that note, why don't you just email the information? You should go home and get some of that frustration out."

Rebecca shook her head. "Nope. Tonight, Cassidy and I have a date with relaxation. Just... being with each other."

"Aww, I love those kinds of dates," Lainey cooed, stroking Eve's soft hair. "Sometimes just *being* is what we all need to recharge."

"I agree," Eve said. "Perhaps yours and Cass's busy schedules contributed to this meeting getting to you more than usual?"

"Maybe." Rebecca sighed. Her body and mind were tired. She was looking forward to doing absolutely nothing tonight with her favorite person.

Chapter Three

"Hello?" Rebecca tossed her keys on the table beside the door and set her briefcase down. She kicked off her shoes with a sigh of relief. She knew Cassidy was home since her truck was in the driveway, but no one answered. "Probably in the shower," Rebecca told herself. She was tempted to go and join Cassidy, but her fingers were still wrinkled from this morning's shower. Rebecca smiled. What a wonderful start to her day. If only it had stayed wonderful. If only McEnroe hadn't reminded her of someone from her distant past.

She checked the time and saw she had a few minutes to spare before her five o'clock date. And since Cassidy's enticing naked body was upstairs in the shower, Rebecca thought it best to stay downstairs and occupy herself. *Just send Eve and Lainey the business plan and shut down,* Rebecca ordered herself.

Rebecca frowned when she walked into her office. There was a faint scent she didn't recognize lingering in the air. She shook it off as she settled behind her desk, reaching for her trackball mouse. Her frown deepened when it wasn't in its usual place and her computer was on. Again, she shook it off. Cassidy probably needed something. *Doesn't explain the scent.*

"Babe?"

Rebecca looked up into Cassidy's bi-colored eyes. She was dressed in basketball shorts and a tank top, her feet covered in fluffy socks. It was such a ridiculous outfit. Rebecca couldn't help but smile.

"Hey, baby. Have a nice shower?"

Cass walked further into the office with a sly grin. "Not as nice as this morning. You were pretty far away just then. Everything okay?"

The bad meeting is still bothering you. Your brain is playing tricks on you, Rebecca. "Yeah, everything's fine, baby. Were you in here earlier using the computer?"

Cass shook her head. "Nah, I don't like touching your stuff. Well, I like touching your *stuff*, but not this stuff," she grinned. "Why?"

"You know you can, right? I don't care if you're in here. I have nothing to hide, and you won't hurt anything if you need to use my computer."

Cass walked over to the desk, propping her hip on it as she addressed Rebecca. "I know, babe. But I wasn't in here. I left my site around three thirty, stopped by Ellie's, grabbed some food, and high-tailed it home. Then I hopped in the shower to get the paint off me. Nothing I needed was in here until you came home. Is something wrong?"

God, she's so sweet. "No, not wrong. Do you smell that?"

Cass sniffed the air. "Sorry, babe. But I've either been wearing PPE or sniffing fumes all day, so don't trust my nose. What is it?"

"It's a perfume or something I don't recognize. And my computer was on. I could swear I turned it off last night before we went to bed. Or put it in sleep mode."

Cass's brows furrowed. Something was bothering Rebecca, and Cass didn't like that. She knew Rebecca wasn't secretive about her office. There wasn't anything the two of them didn't share. But Cass still asked for permission most of the time out of respect.

"Oh! The maid service was here today, right? Maybe one of them knocked your mouse while they were cleaning? That could explain the perfume in the air, too. Or maybe it's some cleaning stuff they used?"

Right. The maid service. They had only recently hired a service to keep up with the housework when they were too tired to do it themselves. Rebecca had forgotten they were scheduled today. She relaxed, chuckling at her paranoia.

"Sorry. I forgot they were here today."

"It's okay, babe, so did I. Did you check your computer? Is it still locked?"

Rebecca glanced at her screen. The lock screen was there, the cursor blinking in the box to input her password. "Still locked. I... I don't know why I got so bothered." Rebecca sighed. "That's not true."

Cass slipped off the desk and got to her knees in front of Rebecca. This was a far cry from the last time she was in this position. "Becca, something has you rattled. What happened today? You said you had a meeting. Did it not go well?"

Rebecca took Cassidy's face in her hands and kissed her. "Can we talk about this after I've changed and get some of Ellie's food in my belly? I think I'm a little hangry."

"Of course, babe. Do you want to take a shower while I get dinner set up? I'll make some flower tea, too. That always seems to help calm you."

"Yeah, that sounds wonderful. I will email the Sumptors and then shut down everything for the night. I'll only be a few minutes."

"He said what?"

Rebecca laughed softly at Cassidy's muttering about kicking his balls up into his throat.

"I made sure he knew I was married, baby. But that's not really what bothered me."

"Bothers me," Cass grumbled. Then she remembered to stop being a selfish prick and apologized. "What was it that upset you?"

"I'm not sure upset is the right word." Rebecca shook her head. "He was... arrogant."

Cass fed Rebecca a bite of banana cream pie before taking one herself. "You've worked with arrogant people before. In fact, you're one of the best at putting them in their place."

Rebecca wiped her mouth, swallowing the superb pie and immediately wanting more. She was stalling. Rebecca had felt this way before but didn't want to mention Samantha's name ever again, especially not in front of Cassidy. Nevertheless, they swore to be open and honest with each other. Good and bad.

"Something about him reminded me of... He was just so condescending. My ideas weren't good enough to even look at. Most of what he said focused on my looks or was sexual in nature. It's stupid to think, but it was like he called me for the sole purpose of trying to break me down."

Cass had set the pie aside the moment Rebecca said sexual, unable to stomach eating anything. What kind of fucker would speak to her wife like...

"Samantha," Cass managed, her throat tight with emotion. Rebecca nodded. "Shit, baby, no wonder you're on edge." Cass scooted closer, wrapping an arm around Rebecca's shoulders and pulling her into a loving embrace. "Baby," God, Cass didn't want to ask this question. "Did he... try something with you?"

"No." Rebecca sat up, looking Cassidy in the eye. "No, Cassidy. He was all talk. You know I would tell you if something happened. I've learned my lesson on keeping things like that to myself. Nothing physical happened...."

"But his attitude was enough like... *hers* that it was unsettling. Do you think that's why you were feeling a bit off in your office?"

Rebecca frowned. Was it? Did she make more of a simple situation? "Probably." She inhaled, holding it while she counted to ten, then let it out slowly. "I don't want to think of her. We've been so happy. I don't want to ruin that."

"Becca..."

"Wait. I've been keeping busy because I thought I needed to. But I think this is one area where our ages come into play." Rebecca held up a finger when Cassidy wanted to interrupt again. "I'm not saying anything negative, baby. Your career is just starting, and I'm so damned proud of you. You have no idea how proud I am. That being said, I've been working my ass off for more than twenty-five years. Almost as long as you've been alive. I'm tired, baby. I think today showed me just how tired I am."

"You want to retire?"

Rebecca's nose wrinkled in disgust. The same way it always did when they discussed their ages. "I'm not *that* old, Cassidy. I don't want to retire. Just... slow down. Our friends keep me busy enough. Ellie wants to expand, Blaise has her non-profit she's starting up, and Eve and Lainey will continue to buy the planet."

Rebecca rolled her shoulders, the tension headache she'd been feeling all day slowly beginning to fade as the idea of semi-retiring — that word still sucked — began to take shape. This conversation wasn't even on Rebecca's radar. Yet, here she was, making a case to get Cassidy's approval. Not that she needed it, nor would Cassidy ever tell Rebecca what to do with her life. But Rebecca would prefer to have Cassidy's support.

Cass drew random patterns on Rebecca's bare arm with the tip of her finger. "Babe, I'm all for you slowing down if that's what you want. And once this mural is finished —maybe in another ten days or so — I can slow down with you."

Rebecca looked back at Cassidy, her head resting on Cassidy's shoulder. "Do you really want to slow down on your art?"

Cass lifted the shoulder Rebecca's head was currently lying on, apologizing with a chuckle when Rebecca's head bobbed. "I want to spend more time with you. If that means slowing down, so be it."

"Baby," Rebecca sat up to face Cassidy. "That's not what I want. I..." She blew out a breath. "I mean, I *want* to spend time with you, but not at the expense of your career or art. Listen, I can pick up yoga again. Or learn a few dishes, so I can make us dinner... oh, Ellie is going to love me," she laughed. "My point is I can entertain myself until you get home. Then I can entertain you."

The smile that spread across Cass's face was beautiful and bright. "Yoga, food, and sex. Now *that* is my kind of retirement."

"Can you stop saying retirement," Rebecca scolded. "It makes me feel old."

"Sorry, babe. *Slow down.* Wait. That doesn't mean slowing down with me, does it? Shit, that sounded insensitive and selfish."

"Cassidy..."

"I hope you know I'm not with you just for the sex, Becca."

"Cassidy..."

"I love you with everything I am. And if you needed a break from sex, too, I would respect that...."

"Cassidy!"

"Yeah?"

"I think that by slowing down the stress of my outside world, I can give you more of my... inside world."

Another smile graced Cass's lips. "We should totally get a hot tub."

"Excuse me?"

"A hot tub! Picture it: I come home from a long day of painting, you're home after loosening up in yoga and cooking a wonderful meal, we slip into the hot tub to relax, we're naked, the hot water bubbling around us, oomph."

Rebecca slapped a hand over Cassidy's mouth. "I will agree to a hot tub if you stop talking. Tonight is about relaxing and just being. Think we can do that without marathon sex?"

Cass nodded her head, kissing Rebecca's palm. She took Rebecca's hand and removed it from her mouth. "We can totally do that. As long as I can snuggle with you and fall asleep with you in my arms, I'm golden."

Rebecca smiled. She leaned in to give Cassidy a kiss when her phone rang. "Rude," she muttered, glancing at her phone on the coffee table. "It's Eve."

"Get it, babe. I'll go heat up more water for tea." Cass kissed Rebecca's cheek as she popped up to go to the kitchen, taking dishes with her. "Tell her we're getting a hot tub!"

"Hello?" Rebecca snickered as she answered the call.

"Well, you sound much better than you did earlier," Eve said, a smile evident in her voice.

"That's what love does for you, right?"

"Don't I know it? I don't want to keep you away from Cass and wedded bliss for too long. We got your email. Rebecca, how deep of a dive did you do with this company?"

"I didn't do one at all," Rebecca confessed. "It was a last-minute meeting. McEnroe called, I asked for quarterlies, and I met him. I would have done my usual in-depth assessment if the meeting had gone better. Why?"

"Because we can't find any records of that company or...." Eve paused to flip through some papers. "Buck McEnroe."

"T-that can't be right. I was just there. I certainly didn't meet with a figment of my imagination, Eve."

"You went to his office?"

"Yes. His office that was at the warehouse."

"And you saw inventory?"

Why the hell was Eve interrogating her? Rebecca breathed in, calming herself. The damn headache she was just getting rid of was returning. "I didn't take a tour, Eve. I wasn't there that long. But I *was* there, in an office, with McEnroe, so I know they exist."

Cass returned at that moment, a frown plastered on her face. "What's up?"

Rebecca shook her head, taking the tea Cassidy handed her and pressing a button on the phone. "You're on speaker with Cassidy."

"I apologize for interrupting your night," Eve said softly. She hated upsetting Rebecca, but this could potentially be a situation if she and Lainey were right. "Becca, I had Jules look into this when Lainey and I couldn't find anything on this company. No public records, no state filings, nothing. And no one named Buck McEnroe is listed as a proprietor of such a business. I'm sorry, Becca, but I think someone deceived you."

Cassidy stood up to pace while Rebecca absorbed that information. "For what purpose?" she asked finally.

"We don't know, honey." This was from Lainey. "We're having Jules keep an eye on it. According to Reghan, there's nothing else we can do since lying isn't illegal."

"Can we at least find the prick and cut his nuts off?" Cass yelled.

"Cassidy."

"No, babe. I wanna know who gave him your number. The way he spoke to you? That's unacceptable. And it makes me think someone knows your, um, other business."

Unfortunately, what Cassidy said rang true. Rebecca grabbed Cassidy's hand as she paced by. "Sit with me, baby. Eve, Lainey? I would appreciate it if Jules kept an alert on this, but other than that, I'd like to forget about it." Rebecca held a hand up when Cassidy opened her mouth to argue. "*If* he contacts me again, we will deal with it."

"I don't like it, babe."

"I'm sorry. But I won't spend my... slowing down time worrying about this asshole. He's probably harmless."

"And if he's not?" Cass asked, her gaze never wavering from Rebecca's. Samantha probably seemed harmless at first, too. But if someone thought they could harm Rebecca while Cass had breath in her lungs, they were sorely mistaken.

"Ahem," Eve cut in carefully. "May I just say there were no criminal records found for Buck McEnroe, either? Believe me, Cass, I understand your concern. I promise you we will keep an eye on the situation."

"Fine," Cass sulked.

Rebecca rolled her eyes but still held onto Cassidy's hand. "Now that Cassidy approves, we're going to go. Thank you for calling. I'm sorry I wasted your time with this."

"You didn't waste anyone's time," Lainey said. "Jules loves using Sumptor, Inc. equipment to do things like this. And mine and Eve's lives have been so boring this past year. We could use the excitement." Lainey's sarcasm sparked a fit of laughter from her audience of three. "Get back to your night of relaxation, you two. Eve and I are going home to our kids. We'll talk to you soon."

Chapter Four

D ay one of 'slowing down' for Rebecca Cuinn-Giles. Rebecca blew her bangs out of her eyes, staring at her coffee cup in front of her. Cassidy had left a few minutes ago after promising to be home 'as soon as humanly possible.' Rebecca tapped her blunt fingernail on the cup.

"I should have eased into this slow down," she said to herself. Rebecca had checked her schedule for the week, canceling more than fifteen consulting meetings. She didn't like leaving those potential clients in a lurch, but Rebecca made sure to refer them to very capable business analysts. As for her friends' new ventures, everything was on track at the moment. So, Rebecca had the entire day to herself.

The first thing she needed to do was get out of her pajamas. Rebecca smiled as she remembered putting them on last night. It was very rare for either of them to wear anything to bed. But since last night was for relaxation only, the only way they could be that close to each other and not end up making love was by putting a barrier between them. Even then, it was quite difficult to keep their hands from roaming.

Cassidy, however, was a perfect gentlewoman. She never once pressured Rebecca for more than a cuddle. Cassidy was kind, tender, and loving. When Rebecca was jolted awake by a nightmare — one she hadn't had in so long — Cassidy was there to soothe Rebecca back to sleep. That nightmare, though. That was something Rebecca was going to have to call Aunt Wills about. She couldn't allow this uneasiness she had felt since yesterday to get too deep.

"Later." Rebecca got up and took her coffee cup to the sink to rinse it out. After a slight hesitation, she filled it with water. Unfortunately, with the nightmares came the headaches. Rebecca had woken up with one this morning, and if she planned on getting anything done today, that had to go. She opened the cabinet and grabbed the Tylenol. After downing a couple of tablets, Rebecca rolled her head on her shoulders to relieve some of the tension.

"I could really use a yoga class. And maybe to stop talking to myself." She snickered at herself. "Five minutes into your slow down, you're already going crazy." Rebecca grabbed her phone off the table to send Ellie a quick text.

Hey! I will literally pay you $1000 to get back into teaching yoga — and $1000 more to maybe give me a few cooking lessons.

"One thing on my to-do list checked off," Rebecca announced to... no one. Had she always had this much of a problem being alone? Was this what happened when you found someone who you loved and who loved you back? Time without them was lonely and ticked by so slowly?

Sweets, I will do all that for free. You and Cass come over tonight. You and I will stretch ourselves silly, and Cass and Hunter can sit out on the deck, drink beer, and talk about us in yoga pants. Then you can help me make a quick dinner, and we'll have those two drooling for a different reason: two birds, one stone.

Rebecca laughed out loud. Ellie Vale was the most unassuming, sweetest person Rebecca had ever met. No one would suspect she also had a wicked sense of humor and a fierce protective streak.

I love you! :D Is five-thirty too early?

Rebecca made a mental note to call Cassidy later to ensure she could be home in time to go to the Vales.

Five-thirty is perfect. Hunter should be home fairly early tonight. We'll see you then! And before you ask, don't bring anything — just your yoga pants and appetite.

Well, that was easy. Rebecca sent Ellie a kissing emoji and then checked the time. She had seven hours to kill. First things first, get dressed.

Cass whistled a light tune to try and keep her focus on her work. The night before had been replaying repeatedly in her mind, curbing her creativity. Oh, the time with Rebecca was wonderful. After Eve's call, they mutually agreed to let what happened yesterday go and enjoy the night. That's precisely what Cass did. She put the fucker that disrespected her wife out of her mind.

They watched shows, Cass gave Rebecca a massage, kneading out the stiffness in Rebecca's neck, and snuggled. It didn't matter if they were on the couch, on the floor, or in bed... they snuggled. When it came time to sleep, Cass insisted they wear some form of pajamas. It was a no-sex kinda night, and Cass respected that. But having Rebecca's naked body on hers would have made that incredibly difficult. The cute shorts and tight t-shirt didn't do Cass many favors, either. But she managed to keep her hands to herself. Mostly.

When Becca fell asleep, that's when Cass thought about McEnroe and how agitated Rebecca was. This douchebag had reminded Becca of Samantha. That was something Cass couldn't forgive or forget. Yeah, she knew her wife wanted to leave it alone unless something else happened. But what if that something else meant harming Rebecca? The fuck if Cass would allow that. She had contemplated going to Eve behind Rebecca's back but quickly vetoed that idea. Whatever happened, Cass would do it with her wife's permission.

Cass's resolve faltered when Rebecca was yanked out of a deep sleep, whimpering. The night terrors had stopped, and the past couple of years had been peaceful for Rebecca. She didn't even flinch anymore when Cass touched the scars on her back. Was this guy so much like that bitch Samantha that Rebecca had reverted? Maybe it was a good time to call Aunt Wills. Cass was snapped out of her thoughts by the sound of Siri telling her Rebecca was calling. Cass answered immediately.

"Hey, babe! How's... it going?"

"You were going to say retirement, weren't you?" Rebecca teased.

"Nope." Cass glanced around to make sure she was alone. "But if I do, will Mistress punish me?"

"Intensely."

"So? How's retirement?" Cass grinned at Rebecca's exasperated oath on the other end. "I'm kidding with you, babe. What's up?"

"Well, I'm learning I'm no longer good at being alone. I haven't found anything to occupy my time yet, and I miss you."

Cass's heart fluttered. Hearing Rebecca say she missed her made Cass want to pack up all her shit and hightail it home. *Kids. I'm doing this for the kids.*

"I miss you, too, babe. I think I'm going to make it a short day today. Maybe the rest of the week."

"Cassidy..."

"Just until you've gotten used to not having a ton of shit to do, babe."

"Cassidy, you're in a children's hospital. Watch your language."

"Oops. Sorry. But seriously. I'm ahead of schedule on this mural. I can afford to cut some time." Cass listened carefully to Rebecca's tone. She sounded a little better this morning. That was a good sign.

"That sounds good, actually. Do you think you could make it home in time to go over to Ellie and Hunter's tonight around five-thirty?"

"Yeah, of course! Were we invited over for dinner?"

"Well, I kind of invited us. Ellie will do some yoga with me, and then I will help her cook dinner. See? I'm already starting on my hobby list."

Cass laughed. "Does that mean we're going over there every night?"

"No, not *every night*, wise guy. I called Ellie before I called you. We decided she'd give me a routine and some simple recipes to do throughout the week. But I swear, if you say 'Ellie's is better' one time, I will take you into the playroom...."

"You just realized that's the perfect reason for me to say it, didn't you?" Cass joked.

"Yep. Will you be here by four, please, Cassidy?"

Cass checked her watch. It was just past noon now. If she focused, Cass could get a good chunk done by the time she needed to get home. Though...

"Yeah, but it only takes us like fifteen minutes to get to the Vale household. And it doesn't take me long to shower and get ready."

"Make it three-thirty," Rebecca said.

Holy fuck. Cass knew that tone. Her entire body began to tremble with anticipation. "Yes, Mistress."

"Thank you. Oh, and Cassidy?"

"Yes?"

"I ordered a hot tub."

With that, Rebecca hung up, and Cass sat there — mouth agape — for a good twenty seconds. She had wondered if Rebecca cutting back on her work was a good idea without a plan in place. But it seemed no plans were working out to be highly lucrative for Cass.

Cass burst into the house at three-twenty-three. She would have been earlier if she hadn't gotten stuck behind some stupid fender bender. The hours after Rebecca's phone call dragged so fucking slow. Cass constantly reminded herself that what she was doing at that hospital was important. She and Rebecca had the rest of their lives to be together. Some of these kids would never experience that. That thought helped Cass get a considerable amount done before practically running out of there, the image of Mistress seared in her brain.

"Babe?" She tossed her keys on the table and began peeling off her clothes. As she slipped her shirt over her head, she saw the yellow sticky note.

Take a shower, Cassidy. Then meet me in the playroom. Mistress.

The playroom was a recent addition, and one Cass was ecstatic about. They really were turning this house into *their* home. They had contemplated getting a new home, but Rebecca wasn't keen on losing the mermaid mural Cass had painted in the living room. Their compromise was doing some renovations — and additions. At first, the reno was small. They updated the kitchen with new appliances, which neither of them used regularly. Also updated was the downstairs gym area. Rebecca would join Cass sometimes when she was feeling particularly energized. Since Rebecca wasn't into weight training, Cass wanted to make the space more inviting for her wife. A nice, quiet yoga area and cardio equipment now took up half the space, and Cass was more than happy to divide her space with Rebecca. Now that Rebecca was getting back into yoga, maybe she would spend more time in there getting Cass's heart racing while stretching in her yoga pants.

Then came the playroom. Both wanted to keep their bedroom for their more intimate moments as a married couple. Mistress was fun, but there was always something a little more treasured when they were just Cassidy and Rebecca. After a few months of going to the club to get their Mistress fix, they decided to build an add-on.

"Best decision ever." Cass sprinted up the stairs. She was naked in the shower in less than three minutes. Granted, it was a lukewarm shower at best, but that didn't matter. Mistress was waiting for her.

Mistress was dressed in black today. The patent leather bra with a quilted design hugged her ample breasts like a lover. The waistband of the soft, silk-noil black bikini bottoms was trimmed with the same patent leather. An ultra-cropped leather jacket with the sleeves pushed up and opened to show Mistress's toned stomach completed the ensemble.

Mistress looked as badass as she felt. As the day wore on, Rebecca became more enamored with the idea of not working so much. The boredom wore off quickly as she began making a list of all the things she had wanted to do but never made the time for. An afternoon romp as Mistress with her sub-wife was high on the list. And Mistress was feeling extra spicy today. What a difference a night of relaxation and a change of pace can make.

She heard the rattle of the doorknob, and Mistress's heart rate doubled with anticipation. She nearly dropped her pink flog when Cassidy entered the room. Cassidy was barefoot, wearing faded jeans and an unbuttoned white shirt. Her torso tattoos and sleeves were on full display, causing Mistress to salivate.

"Come," Mistress ordered.

"Yes, Mistress." Cass walked to Mistress. She was trained well enough not to touch Mistress without permission. Oh, she wanted to touch her. Cass wanted to do so many things to Mistress, especially in that outfit. But this was Mistress's show. Cass would wait for any demand and eagerly obey. Her muscles twitched when Mistress ran her fingertips down her stomach.

"Go to the foot of the bed, Cassidy. Face away from me."

Damn. All Cass wanted to do was drink in Mistress. Visually and literally. God, she hoped Mistress wanted Cass's mouth on her today. For now, she followed orders and stood at the foot of the bed. She grinned when Mistress smacked her ass with the flog.

"Take the jeans off. Leave the shirt." Mistress stood back to watch the show as Cassidy — her back still to Mistress — unbuttoned her jeans and slid them down past her hips. Mistress's eyes focused on Cassidy's tight ass when she bent over to discard the jeans completely. They stayed there until Cassidy stood back up, and her shirt fell to cover it. Mistress blinked a couple of times to get her mind back in the game. *At least it's in the gutter where it should be.*

"Get on the bed, on your knees." Mistress waited until Cassidy was situated. "Arm," Mistress said simply. Cassidy raised her arm, and Mistress wrapped the cuff of the chain that dangled from the bedpost around Cassidy's wrist, tightening it securely. Then she repeated the action on the other side. Once Cassidy was strapped in, Mistress walked to her arsenal. This armoire resembled the one in her Pink Room and was similarly stocked. She chose what she wanted for this session and went back to Cassidy.

"You encouraged me to… slow down, Cassidy. I'm not used to having nothing to do, nowhere to go, no one to see. Do you know what happens when I don't have set plans?"

Cass shook her head. She hoped it meant that Mistress devised various ways to punish Cass. *Masochist,* Cass thought. *No, wait. I don't want anyone else to do this to me. I'm a… Mistresschist.* Cass nearly laughed out loud, then yelped when she felt the sharp sting of Mistress's whip on her thigh, one of the strands barely grazing her pussy.

"Answer me, Cassidy."

"N-no, Mistress."

"It means I get bored and wonder what I should do with myself when you're away from the house all day. So…" Mistress peeled off her jacket and then unhooked her bra. She let both fall to the floor, smiling when Cassidy's eyes were glued to her tits. *It'll get better, baby. Believe me.* She shimmied out of her bikini bottoms, exaggerating the shake of her tits for Cassidy's enjoyment.

Naked, Mistress climbed on the bed and faced her sub. Her lover. Her wife.

"Since you thought it was a good idea for me not to be busy all the time, you're going to watch what I wanted to do to myself. Idle hands and all that," Mistress muttered as she picked up a good-sized dildo.

Cass nearly moaned at the thought. Her pussy contracted just imagining watching Mistress pleasure herself. She squeezed her thighs together for a tiny bit of relief, but it didn't work. Cass hissed with pleasurable pain when Mistress's whip slashed across her covered tits.

Mistress reached over and opened Cassidy's shirt to see those beautiful, small breasts. She wanted to know how the bite of her flog affected Cassidy. Mistress wasn't disappointed when she was greeted with taut nipples.

"Do you know why I whipped you, Cassidy?"

"No, Mistress," Cass breathed. Had Mistress said something Cass missed because she was staring at her tits?

"Because you were squeezing your thighs together. Did I tell you you could have pleasure yet?"

"No, Mistress."

"Spread your legs further apart, Cassidy."

Cass obeyed, trying so hard to keep her hips from moving. She was so fucking wet she could feel it dripping down her legs, and Mistress hadn't even started. Cass all but gasped when Mistress laid down. It wasn't the view Cass expected. Instead of the sight of Mistress's legs wide open in front of her, Mistress lay with her head near Cass. No, not just 'near.' Mistress had positioned herself in a way Cass wasn't used to.

Mistress and Cass — and Rebecca and Cass — have made love, had sex, fucked in many different places and many different positions. The one position Cass had never had the pleasure of was the one happening right now. Cass almost jumped out of her skin when she felt Mistress's tongue on her clit. *Holy fuck!* Is this really happening?

Mistress glided the dildo across her clit and through her wetness as she tasted Cassidy. "Mmm," she hummed as she sampled Cassidy's soaking sex, sucking Cassidy's clit into her mouth. *She tastes so good.*

When Cassidy's hips bucked, Mistress flattened her tongue, allowing Cassidy to ride it.

Cass wanted to come. She *needed* to come. Feeling Mistress suck her, her hot tongue tasting her, was so fucking erotic that Cass struggled to last for more than two minutes. She didn't want to come yet. She wanted this to last forever. And she wanted to watch Mistress fucking herself as she came.

As though Mistress was listening to Cassidy's thoughts, she slipped the dildo inside her, her hips lifting off the bed to take it all inside. Cassidy's moaning filled her ears, her taste filled her mouth, and the dildo filled her pussy. Every sensation was rapidly bringing Mistress to climax. Then Cassidy bent slightly, granting Mistress better access to what she wanted most. She thrust her tongue inside Cassidy's dripping sex, fucking her as she fucked herself.

"Jesus fuck!" Cass gasped. Her arms strained against the cuffs, and her hips bucked as Mistress's tongue fucked her. Mistress's chin rubbed against her clit, and Cass knew she wouldn't last much longer. She watched the dildo plunging in and out of Mistress's pussy. Mistress's legs were bent, heels digging into the mattress as her movements became more frantic. Cass knew Mistress was close, too.

"May I come?" Cass panted. "Please, Mistress!"

Mistress reached her free hand back and squeezed Cassidy's ass cheek, her nails digging in as she latched on to Cassidy's clit again. She heard Cassidy's plea and the raggedness of her breath. On the verge of orgasm herself, Mistress patted Cassidy's ass, giving her permission as she moaned against her clit.

The vibration of that moan set Cass off. "Fuck! Fuck! Ahh!" Fucking hell! Cass's entire body shuddered against Mistress's face, yet Mistress didn't let up. Cass was about to beg her to stop when Mistress suddenly cried out.

Mistress pulled the dildo out, allowing her orgasm to erupt from deep within her. "Cassidy!"

"Yes, baby!" Cass heaved, forgetting their roles — hell, forgetting her own name after that fucking orgasm! She pulled against the restraints. Part of her — specifically her clit currently being fanned by Mistress's heavy breathing — didn't want to leave this position. Yet, it was the sight of Mistress's orgasm erupting just out of her reach that fueled Cass's desire to be released from her bonds and dive in.

Mistress, however, lay there for a full minute, licking her lips and trying to catch her breath. Having Cassidy come in her mouth was a potent aphrodisiac, and she fought her own internal war to cancel the plans they had and go for more. When Mistress heard the jingle of the cuffs she had put Cassidy in, she carefully — and reluctantly —scooted out from beneath her. Seriously, if she allowed herself to, she could have stayed there forever. Instead, she stood on the bed, wiped her mouth with a grin, and pushed her ample breasts into Cassidy's face as she unbuckled the cuffs.

Cass immediately took hold of a nipple and sucked it hard, whimpering when it was taken away from her. Then Mistress kissed her. Cass tasted herself on Mistress's tongue, and the actions from before came flooding back to her. Cass wrapped her arms around Mistress — Rebecca — crushing their bodies together. In that kiss, there was love and passion. And a gratitude Cass felt after every time Rebecca shared her passion. After every time Mistress shared her more provocative side. God, she loved each and every side of this woman, and Cass would spend the rest of her life showing it.

Chapter Five

Rebecca glanced at Cassidy, who sat in the passenger seat. "You're staring at me. Why?"

"You're beautiful," Cass answered simply.

Rebecca shook her head. "You've been quiet since the playroom, Cassidy. Did I do something you didn't like?"

Cass barked out a laugh. "Are you kidding me? I don't think I've ever come that hard in my life! And with *you*, that's saying something!"

Rebecca hid a satisfied — prideful — grin. "So, you're too tired to speak?" Again, Rebecca took her eyes off the road for a second to look at Cassidy. "And you're still staring. I know how you look at me, Cassidy. This look here," she said, waving a hand in Cassidy's direction. "Is questioning."

Cass shook her head. She opened her mouth to answer just as Rebecca pulled into the Vales' driveway. She took off her seatbelt, ready to get out to run around and open Rebecca's door.

"Stay, Cassidy."

Cass's hand froze on the door handle. "They're expecting us, babe."

"They'll wait. What's going on?"

Cass sighed. She fully admitted she was preoccupied while they cleaned up and got ready for their night with Ellie and Hunter. She had been contemplating how to ask Rebecca the questions swirling around in her head. Fuck, did Rebecca really think she didn't enjoy her time with Mistress?

"Y-you've never done that before," Cass said finally, nervous as hell. She didn't want to ruin the experience with questions that may upset

Rebecca. Cass didn't even know why she couldn't just be grateful and move on.

Rebecca tilted her head, studying Cassidy's apprehension. "I've never done what?"

Great. She's going to make me spell it out. "You know, what happened in the playroom," Cass stammered. Oh, sure. Every other time, she was plagued with a mouth with no filter. Now she couldn't form a coherent sentence.

"Me going down on you?" Rebecca guessed. She frowned. That wasn't true, was it? "I've tasted you before, Cassidy."

Cass groaned. "You saying things like that does things to my body, babe." She cleared her throat, squirming in her seat. "You've, um, tasted me from your fingers, but never like that. I-I always assumed it was something... like some kind of punishment. Before. And that's why you didn't..."

Rebecca used her extensive knowledge of Cassidy to decipher everything Cassidy was trying to say. It wasn't like her wife to be so... shy with her words. That meant she was afraid of hurting Rebecca.

"Punishment? From Samantha?" Rebecca guessed. Cassidy nodded. "N-no." Her eyebrows furrowed as she thought about her past. *And there was the headache that came along with it.* "I never... did that to her. Samantha was the true definition of a sadist when it came to me. Her pleasure came from my pain. I haven't done that to anyone except you...." She looked at Cassidy. "I've really never done that for you before?" Cassidy shook her head. "I'm sorry."

Cass took Rebecca's hand and kissed her palm. "No, babe, I don't want you to be sorry. Like I said, I always assumed you had a reason not to."

"No. I honestly didn't realize... I know your taste, Cassidy. I *love* tasting you. And I know I'm not exactly an expert, but if you enjoyed it, I definitely want to make that a habit."

"*If*?! Fuck, babe, it...I... Yes, I enjoyed it immensely. But, um..."

"But?"

"Do you have to be Mistress to do it? Does it take that kind of mindset, or...?"

Rebecca smiled. Cassidy wanted to share this new sensation in the bedroom with her wife. Not only in the playroom with her Domme. "I don't have to be Mistress to fuck you with my tongue, baby."

Cass threw her head back and groaned again. "Why, babe? Why do you have to work me up like that when we won't be home for like another hour?"

"Hour?" Rebecca laughed. "That's how long yoga is. Then we have to eat. And, of course, catch up. That's at least three and a half, four hours."

Cass growled. "It's not nice to tease me, babe."

Rebecca pulled Cassidy to her, their lips close. "But it's oh so fun," she whispered before crushing her mouth to Cassidy's. Out of the corner of her eye, she saw the porch light of Hunter and Ellie's house blink, and she couldn't help but laugh.

"What?" Cass pouted after being forced out of a passionate kiss. Rebecca nodded toward the house, and Cass glanced behind her. Sure enough, the porch light kept turning on and off. "Pussy-blocker," Cass muttered as Rebecca continued to laugh. Cass climbed out of Rebecca's Mercedes and trotted to the other side to open the door for her wife. "Laugh it up."

"I'd rather be lapping it up."

"Come on!" Cass whined. Great, she was going to be wet and uncomfortable all night. Maybe tonight was a good night to switch roles in the playroom, she thought as she placed her palm on the small of Rebecca's back and guided her up to the house. A little punishment was surely warranted after all the teasing. First, they had to get through socializing with their mean best friends. "Open up, Dad. We know you're in there flickering the damn porch light!"

The front door opened to a smirking Dr. Hunter Vale and her beautiful wife, Ellie. It was hard staying mad at such joyful faces. Especially since they were two of the nicest people Cass had ever known in her life.

"I apologize for my wife," Ellie chuckled. "She thought letting you know we could see you making out in the driveway would be funny." She kissed Cass on the cheek and gave Rebecca a fierce hug.

"Ha!" Hunter tsked at her wife as she welcomed their guests. "*She* wanted to turn the hose on the two of you! Hey, Becca," she said, kissing the top of the shorter woman's head. "Cass." She slung her arm around

Cass's shoulders. "Want to sit out on the deck and kick back with a beer?"

"I'd love a beer. But you know they'll be bending over a lot in those yoga pants, don't you? Does the view on your deck beat that?" Cass glanced over her shoulder and winked at Rebecca.

"Not even close," Hunter laughed and then lowered her voice conspiratorially. "But if I ever want to see my wife *out* of those pants again, we're not allowed to bother them while they're finding their zen."

"Leave your shoes at the door," Ellie instructed, her voice calm and inviting. "Then come and sit in front of me on your mat."

Rebecca wondered if she could get Ellie to record a meditation audio that she could listen to every night. Ellie's voice was so soothing. She slipped her shoes off and followed Ellie to a mat in the middle of the room.

"Your studio is incredible, Ellie. I always feel so serene when I'm in here." Rebecca sat and crossed her legs, mimicking Ellie's pose. But she couldn't help looking around. She wasn't lying about the tranquility of this room. Rebecca remembered when Ellie was designing it. Ellie had wanted a place where she could relax and work on her recovery after her devastating car accident.

What Ellie produced was a yoga studio with white walls that reflected the sun shining through floor-to-ceiling windows—the ocean view from those windows aided in quieting any chaos of anyone who walked in there. Ellie had chosen a holistic design, using earth-toned hues and textures that gave Rebecca a sense of freedom and mindfulness.

"I'm glad," Ellie responded with a gentle smile. "Are you ready?"

Rebecca nodded and took a deep, cleansing breath.

Ellie waited, observing Rebecca. There was a disturbance beneath the calm. But knowing Rebecca, Ellie would have to gently coax the clutter from Rebecca's busy — brilliant — mind.

"Let's begin with our grounding. Since we're already in Sukhasana, we'll stay here. Now let's do a gentle twist."

Rebecca placed one hand behind her with the other on her opposite knee, then twisted her torso.

"Straighten your spine, Rebecca. Sit tall." Ellie switched sides, knowing Rebecca would follow along. They went through four more stretches in their grounding before moving on. A gentle warm-up followed to prepare their bodies for more vigorous poses.

"How's your hip?" Rebecca asked as she performed cat/cow. *If Cassidy could see me now,* she mused with a small smile.

"It only hurts when it rains," Ellie joked. "Seriously, though, most days are good. It gets tired quicker than it used to, so I've shortened my days in the kitchen at the diner to appease Hunter's concerns." She stood up, gesturing for Rebecca to do so as well. "Ready for sun salutations?"

"Ready."

Ellie started their following sequence, going easy on Rebecca. She wanted Rebecca to stick with this so Ellie wouldn't scare her away with poses that were too difficult—even with Rebecca's experience taking Ellie's classes, the time away warranted a slow comeback.

As Rebecca positioned herself into the Tree pose, a wave of dizziness washed over her. She brought her leg down just in time to catch herself.

"Whew." Rebecca blinked a few times to try and clear her vision.

Concerned, Ellie went to Rebecca and helped her back down into a comfortable sitting position. "Are you okay?"

"Y-yes. Sorry. It's been a while since I've done this. I just need to find my balance again."

"Haven't you been utilizing your Zen area at home?" Ellie asked, rubbing Rebecca's back gently. She knew about the renovations to Cass's gym because Rebecca had requested Ellie to help her design it. Though not as big as Ellie's home studio, it did give Rebecca a peaceful place to practice.

Rebecca blew out a breath. "I haven't had much time to use it, unfortunately. But I'm going to have more time now. That's why I'm here. You're going to be so sick of me," she chuckled quietly, but even to her ears, it wasn't a mirthful sound.

"I would never," Ellie smiled. She knew now that she was definitely right about a disturbance within Rebecca. "Why will you have more time now? You seem to have more clients than ever these days. Including me, which, if you need to put me on the back-burner, I more than understand."

"No, no. I'm happy to help you — and anyone else in our group — expand. But I think our little group will be my only clients for the foreseeable future. I have decided to..." Rebecca shook her head. "I hate the word retire, but that's it essentially."

Ellie's eyebrows rose. "Retire? You're not old enough."

Rebecca reached over and patted Ellie's hand. "This is why you're my favorite."

She took a deep breath and noticed Ellie doing the same. She felt Ellie's fingertip tap the back of her hand. One, two, three, four, five. Then, a double tap and Rebecca let her air out slowly. One, two, three, four, five. Ellie had told her before that the way to a clear and untroubled mind is to purge the dam that blocked the ability to admit what was bothering you.

"I feel old, Ellie. And tired. I have been trying to top my latest great success since I was ten years old."

"Why? You must know your accomplishments are admired, but they certainly don't define who you are. Especially not to us."

"Oh, I think I know that deep down." Rebecca sighed. "When my parents died, I... spiraled. I thought if I'd just been better, if I hadn't talked back or made them worry, they wouldn't have left me. Their death was my discipline. At their funeral, I promised them I would do better. *Be* better. I wanted to make them proud. So, I worked my ass off. I graduated a year early from high school, double majored in college, and had CEOs of major companies seeking me out to build them a solid business plan *while* I was still a student. Then... I met Samantha, and I faltered. Despite my better judgment, I got involved with her and was punished again."

"Rebecca, you did nothing to deserve what Samantha did to you."

Rebecca would silently agree to disagree. She made the choice to be with Samantha and stay. That was something Rebecca had to live with.

"After that," Rebecca continued as though Ellie hadn't said a word. "I had to start over. I worked even harder this time. I needed to make my parents proud again. I turned a drowning club into the most successful members-only club in the city. My consulting business is thriving. And... I'm exhausted."

Ellie empathized with Rebecca. In many ways, they were as alike as they were different. "What I'm hearing is something had to give, and you didn't want that something — or someone — to be Cass."

Rebecca tilted her head, giving Ellie a small smile. "You would have made a great therapist."

Ellie chuckled. "I'll leave that to Aunt Wills. But, you know, being in the service industry for years, you learn how to observe. And being a mother, you learn that being proud of your child isn't contingent on how successful they are. When Jessie told me she wanted to attend medical school, I was so proud of her. Then, when she came to us and said she wanted to drop out because it was too much, I was even prouder of her."

Rebecca raised a brow. "Prouder that she dropped out?"

"That she had the courage to change something in her life that wasn't making her happy. And that she trusted us enough to come to us to talk about it." Ellie reached over and wiggled one of Rebecca's toes. "I think Aunt Wills is an extension of your parents, Sweets. And I don't think she could be any more pleased by the woman you've become. The trauma in your life could have easily been your undoing, yet you fought back. And now you're choosing a different path for your mental health and happiness. As well as Cass's."

Well, when you put it that way, Rebecca thought, her soul feeling a bit lighter than it did when she walked in here.

"With Cassidy's and my schedules, we barely have time for each other. And when we do, it's all about the sex. And that's entirely my fault, not Cassidy's. It's *my* insecurities that make me feel like I *have* to give Cassidy sex, or she'll find someone who isn't as used up as I am. Is that residual shit from Samantha? Probably." Rebecca scoffed. "I should be over my past by now. Cassidy makes me happier than I've ever been. And she makes me feel like I *can* slow down now. I have nothing to prove to Cassidy. She shows me that every day. It's time I show her I believe her."

"Thanks, Hunt." Cass clinked her beer bottle to Hunter's in a silent cheers, then took a long pull from it. The ice-cold bitterness of the pale ale hit the back of her throat, and she hummed with approval. "This is new."

"Yeah. Mo has found a new hobby. I was skeptical at first, but she isn't half bad at it. Of course, this is her fiftieth try at pale ale."

Cass laughed. "Fiftieth time is the charm. Not bad." She took another swig. Yep, she could get used to having a brewer in the group.

"How's it going with you, Cass? We haven't seen you two much lately." Hunter sat back in her glider, propping her feet on the matching ottoman. She'd never thought of herself as a rocking chair kind of woman, but Ellie certainly changed her mind about that.

"Yeah, sorry about that. Ever since the gallery opening, I've had commissions coming out my ass." Cass winced. "Sorry. That was crude. I'm, uh, trying to do better with that."

Hunter raised her bottle in a salute. "It's all good. We're proud of you. Our own renowned artist!"

"Ha! I don't know about renowned, but I sure as hell am busy." Cass frowned. "So is Becca — or was. We've been having trouble finding time to be with each other." Cass set her beer down and leaned her elbows on her knees. "We find time for sex, but I think we both need more, ya know? Sorry if that was TMI."

"Not at all. It's all part of being a best friend," Hunter smiled. "You said Becca *was* too busy."

Best friend. I like that. The two of them met through Rebecca and had become close. Of course, that was after Cass got over her stupidity of thinking Hunter and Rebecca had been a thing.

"Yeah, Becca has decided she wants to slow down a bit."

"Retire?"

Cass put a finger to her lips. "Shh. Don't let Becca hear you say that word! She hates it. But, yeah. Kinda." She lowered her head, contemplating how much to say that wasn't betraying Rebecca's confidences. "I think Becca deserves to slow down. She's worked hard most of her life, you know?" She looked up at Hunter. "She told me some asswipe said some awful shit to her yesterday during what was supposed to be a consultation. Of course, she put him in his place. That's Rebecca. But she shouldn't have to. And I think it upset her more than she lets on. So, yeah, I'm all for this new chapter."

"As a doctor, I highly recommend that Rebecca does whatever makes her happy," Hunter said after taking a drink of her beer. "But what about you? If Becca has all this time on her hands and you're still busy, how does that help?"

Cass thought about how it helped quite a bit before they had to leave to come here. Then again, that was the sex part. That was one area Rebecca and Cass had no problem with. Hunter was right. How would that sway their relationship if Cass was still busy while Rebecca wasn't? Would Rebecca eventually get tired of waiting for Cass?

"I'm an artist," Cass said finally. "I can work from home or anywhere Becca wants to go."

"But as I understand it, the work you've been doing lately has been for charity. You willing to give that up?"

"Hunt, I would give up everything if it made Becca happy. She's my world." Cass shook her head. Rebecca wouldn't be happy with Cass's decision to scale back with her, but hopefully, they'd find their balance together again.

Chapter Six

One week into 'slowing down' for Rebecca Cuinn-Giles. Rebecca scribbled in her journal, checking her watch to make sure she had the date right. Not being on a schedule severely skewed Rebecca's sense of what day it was, so she was taking Ellie's suggestion of writing a journal to keep her mind focused and busy while trying to transition into a life that didn't consist of business plans or crunching numbers. Rebecca wasn't the best at writing anything but business proposals, but she was giving it a shot since she wasn't good at being idle either.

"I shouldn't be long today, babe. I think I will check out pretty early today and tomorrow, then we can make it a long weekend." Cass kissed Rebecca on top of the head, squeezing her shoulders in a light massage.

Rebecca reached up and patted Cassidy's hand before standing to give her a proper kiss goodbye. "Cassidy, you don't need to rearrange your schedule for me. I can keep myself busy."

Cass wrapped her arms around Rebecca's waist. "I'd rather be the one keeping you busy," she winked. "Besides, our hot tub is coming on Friday, and I want to be here with you."

"Afraid I'll take advantage of the hot tub without you when they're done with the installation?"

"More like I don't want you here alone with the installers."

Rebecca scoffed. "I can take care of myself, Cassidy." She backed away, anger coursing through her veins. "I saw that."

Cass frowned. She had *barely* thought of Samantha when Rebecca said she could take care of herself. But apparently, Cass's face shouted it out, and now her wife was pissed at her.

"Becca..."

"No, Cassidy. You need to go to work now. I don't need to be reminded of my past for a second time in as many weeks. How dare you."

"Becca, please." Yeah, Rebecca's indignation was warranted, but usually, they could talk out their grievances without it going further than an annoyance. But now Rebecca was practically kicking Cass out.

"Please what? Please let you explain how you think I can't take care of myself because Samantha nearly killed me? Because I *stayed* with her, I'm essentially too dumb to stay out of trouble?"

Cass's eyebrows shot up in surprise. She couldn't remember a time when Rebecca was this mad at her. Mad enough to put words into Cass's mouth that Cass would never say or even think.

"Whoa! That's *not* what I thought, Becca. I never want to see you hurt again. I do *not* think you're weak or incapable of taking care of yourself, and I certainly don't think you're dumb. Part of my responsibility — my privilege — as your wife is taking care of you and keeping you safe. I don't want you mad at me, baby, but I can't apologize for wanting to protect you."

Rebecca rubbed her temples, trying to curb the threatening headache. Had she overreacted? She knew Cassidy would never entertain malicious thoughts about her. So why did this make her stomach hurt as much as her head?

"Fine. I'll see you later, Cassidy. Be careful."

Nope. I'm not leaving like this. "Becca," Cass reached for Rebecca's hands. "While I'm not sorry for wanting to protect you, I *am* sorry I upset you. I totally could have handled this conversation much better. But I can't leave this house while you're mad at me. I can't take the chance of something happening while my soul is in turmoil."

Rebecca sighed. First, Cassidy had been taking their joint yoga sessions seriously. Second, Cassidy was right. If she walked out and something happened to her while Rebecca hung on to her anger... well, Rebecca would never recover from that. Besides, Cassidy explained herself, which was a sweet explanation, as usual.

"I'm sorry. I don't know why I reacted that way." Rebecca wrapped her arms around Cassidy's waist.

"I do." Cass pushed a stray strand of hair out of Rebecca's eyes. "It all started with that douchecanoe last week. You've been restless at night, having nightmares. I should have been more sensitive to how you've been feeling."

"Don't do that, baby. Don't make this out to be your fault when I was clearly in the wrong." Rebecca stood on her tiptoes and kissed Cassidy gently on the lips. "I shouldn't have snapped at you the way I did. I'm not even going to blame it on whatever happened last week or my headache."

Cass kissed Rebecca's temple. "Another headache? Need me to stop and get you something a little stronger?"

Rebecca shook her head. "No, thank you, baby. I'm going to go downstairs and meditate for a while. Then, when the hot tub gets installed, we will break that in. A lot."

Cass grinned. *There's my girl.* "Well, until then, I will just have to give you massages to keep that tension at bay."

"You can massage me anywhere you want," Rebecca winked. "Now, get your cute butt out of here because you're going to be late."

"It's not a nine-to-five, babe. I make my own hours. However, if I wanna get enough done to take off the next three days, I have to scoot on outta here."

Rebecca slapped Cassidy's ass. "You best get to scootin' then," she teased. "If you're lucky, I'll make something hearty for dinner."

"Babe, as long as I'm coming home to you, I'm lucky. I love you." Cass gave Rebecca another kiss before tweaking her nose and walking away. She felt much lighter now that she and Rebecca were okay. A happy wife meant a creative mind for Cass Giles.

"I love you, too," Rebecca replied softly, her smile slowly fading as Cassidy left. What the hell was her problem? Rebecca's irritability had been running rampant lately, and she was having trouble reining it. That fucking consultation was messing with her head, and Rebecca was sick of it. "Time to work on my mood swings."

"Rebecca."

Rebecca opened one eye, annoyed at being interrupted during her meditation.

"Hello?" She listened for a few seconds, not hearing anything. "It's all in your head, Rebecca," she told herself. Closing her eyes again, Rebecca took a deep breath, blowing it out slowly. Ellie said that humming was one of the best ways to calm her nerves fast and effectively. Though it made her feel silly, Rebecca did it.

"*Rebecca.*"

"Ugh!" Rebecca clenched her hands into fists. *This* was not helping her relax. "Cassidy? Are you home?" She checked her watch. Cassidy had only left thirty minutes ago. Had she forgotten something and come home? Again, Rebecca listened for an answer and got none. She reached over and picked up her phone, turning off the melodic meditation music to make a call.

"Hey, babe! Miss me already?"

"Cassidy, are you here?"

"Huh? Becca, you just called me." Cass glanced down at her phone. *Yep, she called me.* "Are you okay?"

Rebecca frowned. "Yeah, I-I'm fine. I just thought I heard you...."

"I wish it was me. I'm stuck on the 405."

Rebecca untangled her legs from her lotus position and got up. Grabbing one of the bats she kept near every door, Rebecca stealthily made her way upstairs.

"Becca?"

Rebecca jumped at Cassidy's voice in her ear. "Yeah, babe, I'm here. Sorry to bother you. I'm downstairs meditating, and it's quiet, so I'm probably just hearing all the noises we tend to ignore all the time." She opted not to tell Cassidy about hearing her name. There was no need to alarm Cassidy while she was driving.

Cass, of course, was contemplating where to turn around and go home. Rebecca's meeting last week hadn't only affected Rebecca. Cass was also on edge. She had promised Rebecca to let it go unless the prick did something, but Cass certainly didn't want to wait until Rebecca was in danger before taking action.

"I'm going to turn around, babe."

"No, Cassidy. I checked the doors and windows. Everything is secure. Seriously, I think it was just too quiet in the house, and I'm not used to that. You know I need some kind of noise, even when I'm sleeping. This is probably why."

"You hear ghosts," Cass said softly. Those ghosts — one in particular — would always be with Rebecca. Cass would endure white noise at night to keep those ghosts away.

"I guess so." Rebecca shook off the chill that ran through her body. "Okay, baby, get off the phone so you can pay attention to driving."

"You mean sitting in this traffic? I would call it a parking lot, but cars move much faster in a parking lot."

Rebecca chuckled. "Just be careful, okay?"

"Will do, buckaroo! Call me if you need some noise to keep you company."

"What kind of noise will you provide?" Rebecca asked mischievously, then nearly dropped the phone when Cassidy let out a sexy moan. "Cassidy!"

"What?" Cass answered innocently. "You wanted to know!" She grinned to herself, knowing Mistress would file that one away for punishment later.

"Goodbye, Cassidy." Though her voice held authority, Rebecca was grinning from ear to ear. Leave it to Cassidy to cheer her up and take her mind off whatever was bothering her.

"Honey, I'm home!" Cass snickered at herself as she tossed her keys on the side table. She picked up her mail and sifted through it as she made her way toward the smell of food in the kitchen. Cass sniffed the air, frowning a bit when she smelled something burning. "Babe?"

Cass jogged to the oven and shut it off before grabbing a towel and fanning the smoke that poured out when she opened the oven door. She slipped on an oven mitt and pulled what looked like lasagna out, setting it on top of the stove.

"Becca?" Cass called out. She ran to the living room, then to Rebecca's office. There was no sign of her wife in either room. Cass took the stairs two at a time, slamming into their bedroom. "Rebecca?"

Cass was shaking with fear after looking in the bathroom, playroom, and Cass's studio without finding Rebecca. She pulled out her phone and dialed Grayson as she bound down the stairs to their home gym, promptly forgetting about pressing send when she saw Rebecca there in the middle of the room, lying on her yoga mat.

"Baby?" Cass fell to her knees, checking Rebecca for any injuries. "Becca? Baby, can you hear me?" She was on the brink of calling 911 when Rebecca stirred.

"Mmm, Cassidy," Rebecca smiled. "You're home."

"Are you okay?" Cass's hands were everywhere all at once.

"Cassidy!" Rebecca swatted at Cassidy's hands. "What are you doing?"

"Are you hurt, baby?"

"Why would I be hurt?" Rebecca sat up, looking around her in confusion. She must've fallen asleep while meditating.

"Becca, I've been calling your name and searching the entire fucking house for you!" Cass was so scared she was angry. Not at Rebecca. She couldn't be angry at Rebecca. But Cass never should have agreed to let this Buck McEnroe get away with whatever the fuck his game was. "I was about to call the damn cops!"

"Do not yell at me, Cassidy." Rebecca's tone was cold. "You don't *ever* yell at me. I will *not* go through that again." She pulled away from Cassidy's touch and stood up.

Cass knew better than to grab Rebecca, so she took half a second to calm down. "Becca, baby, wait. Please. I didn't mean to yell at you. I was just scared."

"Scared of what?"

Cass scrambled to get up, taken aback by Rebecca's attitude of late. She knew Rebecca was making a significant change in her life, but Cass sincerely thought Rebecca was doing what she wanted. That's why she didn't understand Rebecca's mood swings.

"Babe, I came home to find dinner burning in the oven and you missing."

Rebecca frowned. She inhaled, ready to tell Cassidy she was wrong, but the smell of smoke in the air confirmed Cassidy was telling the truth. But that didn't make sense.

"No, I... I was meditating, and I guess I dozed off."

"You were meditating again? Is something bothering you, Becca?" Hesitantly, she took Rebecca's hands in hers. "Baby, if there's something you need to be doing to be happy, please tell me."

"Oh, Cassidy." Rebecca pulled Cassidy close, kissing her. "I *am* happy." She sighed. "I haven't been sleeping well, and I guess it just caught up to me."

"I know, baby. And I think if we did something about this McEnroe guy..."

"Cassidy, we haven't heard from him since. This is my issue. I'll do better at not making it your issue, too."

"Babe, I'm your wife. That means we share the load." Cass kissed Rebecca's forehead. "I think maybe we should talk to Aunt Wills."

"You want me to start seeing a shrink again?"

"No, baby. I want *us* to talk to Aunt Wills to see if there's anything we can do to help you let go of the past again. You know I like exorcising your demons," Cass grinned. She hoped to hell she was saying the right things. With Rebecca's fluctuating moods, it was hard to tell what would set her off at any given moment.

Rebecca smiled. "Why don't you help me salvage what we can of dinner? Then you can exorcise all the demons you want." She kissed Cassidy again, putting passion and love behind it with full force.

"Sounds like a plan," Cass answered close to Rebecca's lips. Yeah, she noticed Rebecca didn't answer her about Aunt Wills, but Cass would let it go for now. If the restless nights and irritability continued, Cass would bring it up again. "But I think the lasagna is a goner."

"I'm so sorry, Cassidy. I wanted to have dinner ready for you when you got home. I screwed up. I'm sorry. Please don't be mad at me."

Cass watched in horror as Rebecca actually cowered in front of her. *Fucking Samantha.* "Baby, hey," Cass deliberately kept her voice soft and soothing. "Hey, hey, hey. Everything is fine. It's just lasagna, yeah?" She wrapped her arms around Rebecca, closing her eyes to hold back the tears as she felt Rebecca shake against her. "Baby, it's okay. I promise. We can get some take-out. No biggie. Becca, baby, you don't even like lasagna that much." She leaned back to look Rebecca in the eye. "You were secretly hoping we could get some tacos, weren't you?"

A tremulous smile formed on Rebecca's lips. "I like lasagna. I don't like ricotta cheese."

Cass chuckled. "You didn't have to put ricotta in there, babe."

"*You* like it. I was making it for you."

"Well, it just so happens that I like tacos even more," Cass said, wriggling her eyebrows. "Tacos are tasty."

Rebecca smacked Cassidy's stomach. "Fiend."

"Only for you." Cass's nerves calmed ever so slightly when Rebecca stopped shaking. If anyone walked in now, they would see the Rebecca everyone knew. Confident, sexy, flirty. A completely different woman than the one just moments ago. *Maybe I should just call Aunt Wills to see what she says.* "Tacos?"

"Make it a burrito, and I'm in. No wait. I want a taco, too."

Cass laughed. "Okay, we're gonna split a big ass burrito and get a couple of tacos, too." She pulled out her phone and opened the delivery app. "I want some queso, too, since I'm not getting any ricotta," she winked. "And, like, a tub of that special sauce they have."

"I have your special sauce right here, you bottomless pit."

"Oh, baby, you're dessert."

Cass kissed Rebecca's neck as she moved slow and steady inside her. Rebecca's soft moans in Cass's ear were like a balm to her troubled mind. Dinner went off without a hitch, but Cass couldn't get what happened before out of her head. She needed to talk to Rebecca about all of this. *Tomorrow,* she thought as she made love to Rebecca. *We'll talk tomorrow.*

"*Cassidy,*" Rebecca whispered in the ear close to her mouth. Cassidy nipped at her neck, rolling her hips as she buried herself deep inside Rebecca. "Look at me, baby."

Cass lifted her head, gazing down at Rebecca. The muscles in her arms strained as she held herself up. Her ass clenched when Rebecca dug her nails in, pulling her closer.

"I love you, Rebecca."

Rebecca's breath hitched, and she wrapped her legs around

Cassidy's waist. "I love you, Cassidy." She brought her hands up, cupping Cassidy's face and bringing her down for a passionate kiss. As the orgasm shot through her, Rebecca squeezed her eyes shut, moaning against Cassidy's lips. The kiss broke when Cassidy came as well, grinding out a guttural moan. "So much," Rebecca murmured reverently.

Chapter Seven

"Good morning, Mrs. Giles!"

Rebecca smiled at the enthusiastic greeting. "Good morning, Dani. Does Hunter have you answering phones now? Do I need to talk to her about working you too hard?"

Dani snickered. "Nah, it's all good. I'm just helping out in between sessions. Jonelle is still on maternity leave, so it's all hands on deck." Dani leaned in and dropped their voice. "I still have hands."

Rebecca snorted a laugh. "I'm glad you're here, actually. I wanted to tell you how proud I am of you, Dani. Physical therapist? That's impressive."

"Assistant," Dani corrected with a blush. "I have a long way to go if I want my DPT, but I've been really lucky getting to work with some great PTs, ya know? And, like, I couldn't have done it without... family."

Rebecca reached over the counter and patted Dani's hand. "That's what family is for. Keep up the good work! You think it's a long way to go, but you'll get there before you know it. Now, is the tyrant in?"

"Tyrant? I'll have you know I'm a very nice, *very* generous boss." Hunter winked at Dani and kissed Rebecca on the cheek. "Good morning, Rebecca. To what do I owe this pleasure?"

"Can we?" Rebecca gestured away from the front desk.

"Of course. Let's go to my office. Dani, could you let Mo or Patty know I'm tied up for the foreseeable?"

"You got it, Boss!"

Rebecca pushed Hunter as soon as they were in the hall and headed to Hunter's office. "Really? Tied up? Was that a Mistress joke?"

Hunter shrugged with a sly grin. "If the whip fits." She opened the door to her office and ushered Rebecca in. "Have a seat."

Rebecca settled in, crossing her legs as she looked around. Oddly enough, this was the first time she'd ever been in Hunter's office at the clinic. Sure, she had helped bring the clinic to fruition, but most of Rebecca's work can be done remotely. And since she had absolutely no idea how to outfit a medical clinic, she stayed behind the scenes and let the professionals handle the rest.

This office was definitely Hunter — with a bit of Ellie's touch. It was a corner office boasting a large window with a view of palm trees and mountains in the distance. A built-in made of balsa wood lined the wall behind Hunter, holding medical books that Rebecca couldn't fathom reading. The room itself was painted in a muted gray, offering patients a warm yet neutral environment.

"Approve?"

Rebecca brought her eyes to Hunter and lifted a shoulder. "Depends. Did you decorate, or did Ellie?"

Hunter quirked an eyebrow. "Ellie."

"Then it's perfect."

Hunter laughed heartily. "Have you always been this ornery?"

"Nah, it's getting worse as I age," Rebecca quipped.

"Lucky Cass," Hunter muttered playfully. She leaned her elbows on her desk and studied Rebecca when her joke was met with a frown. "I was just kidding, Becca."

"No, I know." Rebecca blew out a breath. "I *am* getting a little *too* ornery, Hunter. Cassidy told me she mentioned a meeting I had a couple of weeks ago to you."

Hunter nodded. "Yeah, I believe she called him an... asswipe."

Rebecca shook her head, a smile playing on her lips. "She has a new name for him every time she mentions him. The last one I heard was 'douchecanoe.'"

Hunter sucked in her lips, trying really hard to suppress more laughter. She picked up a pen and wrote the word down. "I'm going to use that one." She cleared her throat. "Anyway, back to you."

"The... encounter bothered me more than I want to admit. I'm moody and restless. I snap at Cassidy when she doesn't deserve it. I'm having nightmares again. Not every night, but often enough that I lie awake until I can't keep my eyes open any longer, which I'm sure is giving me headaches. I've tried taking Excedrin PM, but..." Rebecca shook her head. "I know I need to talk to Aunt Wills, but if I'm being honest, I just want to forget all this."

Hunter got up and walked around the desk to stand before Rebecca. She took a penlight out of her lab coat. "How bad are the headaches?"

"Not too bad," Rebecca answered. "They just linger." She squinted when Hunter shined a light in her eye. "Hunter, I'm not here for a physical. If you could just tell me what is a good, homeopathic way to get more sleep, I'm sure these headaches will go away, too."

Hunter replaced the penlight and hung onto the ends of her stethoscope. "You know, a physical isn't a bad idea. When we get to be a certain... age, it's always good to get that fifty-thousand miles service."

Rebecca narrowed her eyes. "Did you just call me old *and* compare me to a car?"

Hunter chuckled. "I did not call you old. But I do think you need a well-woman's check-up. Pap smear, mammogram, colonoscopy. I'd also like to do a quick MRI."

Rebecca blinked. "None of that sounds homeopathic."

Hunter sat in the seat next to Rebecca. "Most of that is routine, Rebecca. However, considering your past head trauma and the symptoms you've described, I would like to look inside that brilliant brain."

"Do you think something is wrong?" Rebecca's pulse spiked. This certainly wasn't what she expected when she came here to see Hunter. Maybe a high-powered melatonin or something.

Hunter took Rebecca's hand. "Listen, I'm a doctor who has fun toys thanks to our friendly neighborhood philanthropists. I can get all this done today. Well, except for the colonoscopy. The prep for that takes, um, a few days."

Rebecca raised a brow. "You didn't answer my question, Hunter."

Hunter swallowed hard. *That* was Mistress. And not a happy Mistress. "I don't mean to alarm you, Becca. What you're describing sounds like PCS or Post Concussion Syndrome. The trauma you endured from... the MRI will show me any abnormalities or scars that might be causing the headaches. Though it could most likely be from stress since it all began around the time you had the bad encounter."

PCS. Wouldn't that be fucking great? Why couldn't Samantha just go away?

"You're not going to do the pap smear, are you?"

Hunter's brows raised to her hairline. "I was your surgeon, Rebecca. It wouldn't be anything I haven't seen before."

Rebecca tilted her head and stared Hunter down. "My legs weren't spread wide in stirrups with your head between them, and you sticking things in my vagina, Hunter. Not only would that be embarrassing for me, but I think it would make our next barbecue extremely uncomfortable."

Hunter's eyes widened comically, and she reached over to pick up her phone. She dialed an extension and waited. "Dr. Okoro, are you available to do a woman's wellness exam today? It's a... friend of mine. I'll take whatever appointments you have for the next hour or so... Great, thank you!"

She hung up, wiping a bead of sweat that had formed on her forehead. "All set. Dr. Okoro is a wonderful doctor. She's very attentive and engaging, so if you have any other issues you'd like to discuss with anyone but me, I encourage you to do so. We'll also knock out your mammogram and MRI today."

"You really have all that stuff here at the clinic?"

Hunter grinned. "Like I said, friendly neighborhood philanthropists. When Blaise Steele and the Sumptors back your clinic, you get all the good stuff." She patted Rebecca on the knee. "I'm going to do you a huge favor and ask Patty to help you prepare for this instead of Mo."

"Hunter, I would have run out to my car for a flog if you'd suggested Mo." Rebecca hesitated. "I should call Cassidy and let her know I'm here."

"Want me to give her a shout?"

Rebecca shook her head. "I'll do it. If you call, she'll automatically think something is wrong. And I'd rather not tell her about the MRI unless... unless it's necessary."

"That's your decision, Rebecca. I'll go find Patty and give you some privacy."

Rebecca waited until Hunter closed the door behind her before taking out her phone. "Just a wellness exam," she muttered to herself. It was useless to worry Cassidy over something that was 'most likely' stress-related, she thought as she dialed Cassidy's number.

"Hey, babe! Great timing. I just sat down to eat my sandwich. What's up?"

A smile formed on Rebecca's face just hearing Cassidy's voice. It was so sweet and loving. Concerned and interested. There wasn't much Cassidy could hide from Rebecca as her face was too expressive, and her tone would change with her moods.

"Not much, baby. I was going to leave you a message, but I'm glad I caught you. I wanted to tell you I'm at Hunter's clinic."

"Are you okay?" Cass managed around the huge bite of sandwich she had just taken.

"Don't talk with your mouth full, baby. You're surrounded by kids, so don't teach them bad habits."

"Becca."

"I'm fine, worry wart. If you must know, Hunter said I'm due for my fifty thousand miles service." Rebecca heard a watery cough from Cassidy and laughed. "You just spit out your drink, didn't you?"

"Tell me she did *not* compare you to a car whose mileage just flipped to fifty k."

"She sure did. And now she wants to use all her fancy equipment on me. Probably so she can justify all her costly 'needs' to Blaise and Eve."

Cass snickered. "Probably. Hey, let me just clean up here, and I'll be right there."

Rebecca tightened her grip on her phone in a panic. "No, baby, you don't have to do that."

"I know it's pretty routine, babe, but it's still gonna be stressful for you doing all those tests. I want to be there for you."

Rebecca smiled. *She really is the sweetest.* "You just want to watch them smoosh my boobs."

"Guilty," Cass laughed.

"First, you can do your own smooshing when I get home. Second, I don't think they'll even let you in there. And third, this whole exam is humiliating enough, Cassidy. If you don't mind, I'd just like to get it over and done with, pick up some pizza, and veg out on the couch."

Cass was quiet momentarily as she thought about everything Rebecca had said. She'd never had any of these exams yet, but she knew what went on in them. She could respect Rebecca's need for privacy. "Yeah, babe, okay. But how about I pick up the pizza? It's the least I can do since you're... wait. Hunter isn't doing all this to you, is she? Oh fuck, is she going to see your... you know... down there?!"

A bark of laughter from Rebecca rang out in the office. "Down there? Everything we do, everything you *say* to me, and all you can come up with is 'down there'?"

"Well, I'm not going to say... *p-u-s-s-y* when I'm talking about Hunt! Or while I'm where I am. There are *kids* around!"

"Did you just spell pussy, Cassidy?"

"Shhh! Becca!"

Rebecca was having fun teasing Cassidy. She knew her wife was blushing and fidgeting on the other end. The good news was, they would use this later tonight when they were alone.

"You're crazy!" Rebecca snorted. "You *literally* just said fuck, but pussy is too dirty?"

"Baaaby!"

"Okay, okay. No, Hunter isn't doing the exams, Cassidy. A Dr. Okoro is."

"She?"

"Yes, she's a she. At least that's the pronoun Hunter used."

Cass let out a breath of relief. "Good. Me having to punch Hunter for looking at you really would have made the next barbecue awkward."

Again, Rebecca let out a belly laugh. "I told her that! Well, not the punching part, but the uncomfortable barbecue." She wiped the tears of laughter from her eyes, careful not to smudge her mascara. "I should go, baby. Patty will be here any minute to put me in one of those paper robes."

"Ooo, can you bring that home with you? I can play doctor and do my own exam on you."

"You're a perv, you know that, right?"

"Yep. But I'm your perv." Cass sighed. "Alright, I'll let you go. Will you call me when you're all smooshed out?"

"Yes, baby," Rebecca smiled. "I'll call you when I'm all smooshed out. I love you."

"I love you, too, Becca." Cass made kissy noises before hanging up, causing more laughter.

Rebecca had just put her phone away when the office door opened, and Patty stuck her head in. "Hey, Rebecca. Are you ready?"

"As I'll ever be."

"We're going to start with the MRI," Patty explained as she guided Rebecca down the corridor. "That way, Hunter can look at the results while you get... serviced."

Rebecca threw her hands in the air. "You too?! Is this a body shop or a medical clinic?"

"Technically, it's both," Patty teased. "You do have a body, and we're about to look under your hood."

"Patty!" Rebecca tsked playfully. "I expected that from Mo, but not you."

Patty shrugged with a grin. "Mo has been rubbing off on me."

"I'd rather not hear about you and Mo rubbing things. I have to get naked here. That's embarrassing enough."

Patty laughed, escorting Rebecca into a warm, inviting room. The lights were dim, the ambiance calming. A soft, melodic tune was playing over the speakers. This room was definitely decorated by Ellie.

"Okay, young lady. You're going to take everything off." Patty walked to a cabinet and brought out a white, fluffy robe and a pair of socks. "Put these on and have a seat in the massage chair. I'll come to get you when they're ready."

Rebecca took the robe, noting how warm it was. Heated cabinets? She made a note to hug Ellie the next time she saw her, convinced this was *all* Ellie's doing. Who else made such an effort to make others feel comfortable?

"No paper robe?"

"Do you really think Ellie would go for that?" Patty asked with a raised brow.

"Ha! I *knew* it! That woman is a godsend."

"Girl, you're not lyin'!" Patty walked to the door, ready to give Rebecca her privacy.

"Patty? What can you tell me about this Dr. Okoro?"

Patty's smile was genuine. "One of the best you'll ever see. She studied in Nigeria and came here to advance those studies. Her specialties are in women's health and LGBTQIA cases."

Rebecca held up a hand. "Your smile was all I needed, but hearing the rest, I'm sold. Thank you, Patty."

"You bet. Get changed and relax. This will all be over before you know it, child."

Chapter Eight

Patty led a fully-clothed, thoroughly examined Rebecca back into Hunter's office. "Have a seat on the couch," she instructed. "After all the poking and prodding you've endured today, you deserve to be comfy."

"What? No massage chair?" Rebecca teased.

"Ellie was afraid Hunter would never be home if she put a massage chair in here."

"I don't think Ellie has anything to worry about," Rebecca chuckled. "She has Hunter wrapped around her pie-making finger."

"That she does," Hunter said from the doorway. "I wouldn't have it any other way." She nodded at Patty, closing the door behind the nurse as she was left alone with Rebecca. Hunter sat next to Rebecca on the couch, Rebecca's charts in her hands. "How are you feeling?"

"Thoroughly humiliated. When will you develop a less invasive way to do those examinations?"

Hunter grinned that charming, lopsided grin. "Believe me, if there's a way... Sumptor, Inc. will probably find it," she laughed. "Okay, I have some results here for you." Hunter opened the folder. "Your mammogram looks good. Nice and clear. Your pap and HPV results will be a few days, but according to Dr. Okoro's notes, your genitourinary exam was normal."

"Oh, good. A normal vagina. Cassidy will be happy to know that it's still good to go even after excessive use."

Hunter coughed, choking on her own spit. *At least I wasn't drinking coffee.* "Right, ahem, moving on." She heard Rebecca snicker and rolled her eyes. "Your labs look good. Your CBC shows you're slightly anemic, but we can help that by eating iron-rich food. Spinach, red meat, shellfish…"

"Hunter?" Rebecca interrupted.

"Hmm?"

"You said everything looked great. Normal boobs, normal vagina, good labs. But I know you. I know your tics. What are you *not* telling me?"

Hunter sighed. This is why they tell you not to treat your friends or family. They know you too well. And it was incredibly difficult to tell them bad news.

"You could have let me keep going, Becca." Hunter reached over to the coffee table and picked up her tablet. "There was something on your MRI that concerned me."

"A scar?" Rebecca asked softly, feeling a bit vulnerable and scared now. Part of her wished Cassidy was here. A huge part of her. She couldn't understand the apprehension on Hunter's face. "You were prepared for that, right?"

"I was, yes. But this isn't a scar, Becca. It's a tumor. Now, I know this sounds scary, but …"

Rebecca saw Hunter's lips moving but couldn't hear anything over the ringing in her ears. Tumor. A *brain* tumor. "C-cancer?"

Hunter shook her head. "I'm not saying it's cancer, Becca. In fact, a large percentage of brain tumors are benign."

"How can you find out? When? Can you do it now?"

"Slow down, Rebecca. Do you want me to call Cass? We can discuss…"

"No. I don't want to worry her unless there's something significant…"

"Rebecca, this *is* significant. Benign or not, a brain tumor is serious. We need to get you with a neurosurgeon to discuss options. And, Rebecca, you need Cass there with you. Hell, she should be with you now." Hunter took Rebecca's hand in hers. "I'm one of your best friends, but even I know I'm not enough to give you the strength you need. Cass is."

"I don't know how to tell her this, Hunter."

"Then I'll help you. Look, Becca, I can't tell you what to do, but I can ask you this. What would you do if Cass was in your position and she decided not to tell you? Would you want to punish her?"

"That's low, Hunter."

Hunter shrugged. "I'm here as your doctor and your friend, Rebecca. One thing you know is I will always be real with you. And I'm being real with you now when I tell you you need Cass with you through this."

Rebecca inhaled deeply, blowing anxious air out slowly and methodically. "Fine. I'll tell her tonight. What are my next steps?"

"Talking to your wife is your next step. I'll get referrals…"

"No, I don't want referrals, Hunter. I want an appointment with the person you trust the most. Please make it as soon as possible because I don't want this looming over Cassidy and me. I suppose it's futile to ask you not to tell Ellie?"

"I won't —can't— if you don't want me to. Again, I'll use the 'what would you do' scenario. Would you have wanted us not to tell you when Ellie had her accident? Or for Lainey not to tell you when all that shit was happening with Eve?"

"You really play dirty for a 'best friend,' Hunter."

"I just don't want you to go through this alone when you don't have to, Becca. You have a family."

"Oh, god." Rebecca buried her face in her hands. "I have to tell Aunt Wills."

Hunter wrapped her arm around Rebecca's shoulders. "We're going to think positive, okay? Listen, more than seventy percent of brain tumors are benign. Keep that in mind when you're telling Cass and Aunt Wills. I'll make some calls and set up a consult for you." She stood and held a hand out to Rebecca, helping her up.

"Can you at least give me some insight into what I have to look forward to?"

"I'm not a neurosurgeon, Becca." Hunter sighed again when Rebecca just stared at her. "You'll discuss options with your surgeon when they have a better idea of what we're looking at. But they could include a biopsy and/or surgery."

"How much of my hair will I lose?" Rebecca rolled her eyes. "I'm aware that I sound extremely vain right now."

"Not at all. It's a genuine concern for a lot of patients, Rebecca. And the surgeon I'm thinking of has done many hair-sparing surgeries for patients who needed the extra mile to help with the emotional side of all this."

"Hair-sparing surgery," Rebecca repeated. "Is that a real thing?"

Hunter nodded. "I'll let the doc explain it to you when you speak with her. Do you want me to take you home? Patty can take care of things here."

"That's not necessary. I drove here. I can drive home." Rebecca hesitated. "I *can* drive home, right?"

"I'd feel better if you had someone with you." Hunter checked her watch. "It's Dani's lunchtime. Will you at least let them follow you home?"

Was this going to be her life now? Being a burden on others? Rebecca tried to shake that thought off. She was the first to tell her friends their group was a village. How hypocritical would she be if she pushed everyone away when she needed them the most? Still, Rebecca wasn't ready to be on the receiving end of everyone's pity.

"I will let Dani follow me if you promise to keep this between you and Ellie."

"Well, it's not for me to tell. And even Mo and Patty are bound by patient confidentiality."

"Damn it, I forgot about their access to this information."

"Hey," Hunter hugged Rebecca to her. "Just remember we're your friends first and foremost. We only want you to be healthy and comfortable." She guided Rebecca out to the reception area, calling out for Dani.

"Yeah, Doc?"

"Are you headed out for lunch?"

Dani nodded. "Yes, ma'am. Did you need me to do something first?"

"I was hoping you could follow Mrs. Giles home. She's too stubborn to accept a ride, so this was the compromise." Hunter let out an oomph of pain when Rebecca elbowed her in the stomach.

"The compromise was I would let you follow me home because this fusspot wanted to leave the clinic to take me herself when I'm perfectly capable of driving."

"*Fusspot*," Dani snickered, clearing their throat when Hunter glared at them. "I mean, I'd be happy to escort you home, Mrs. Giles."

Rebecca brought a twenty dollar bill out of her pocket and handed it to Dani. "Don't try to refuse it. This is interrupting your eating time. The least I can do is pay for your lunch."

Dani tipped their head shyly. "Thank you." They held their arm out to Rebecca. "Ready?"

Nope. I will never be ready to tell Cassidy this news. Rebecca slipped her arm through Dani's. "Ready."

Rebecca tossed her phone on the couch next to her, pinching her nose in frustration. She had spent the last hour and a half torturing herself by googling brain tumors and everything that went along with that diagnosis. None of it sounded good.

"Babe? I'm home," Cass called out as she hung her keys on the new pegs Rebecca had put up a week ago. It was one of Rebecca's 'slowing down projects' along with a mail organizer. Cass liked the new system as it was easier to find her keys in the morning, and Rebecca threw away the junk mail before sorting it. When Cass didn't get an answer from her wife, she forgot about the mail and went in search of her love.

She found Rebecca on the couch, a fluffy blanket covering her legs which Cass knew were curled up underneath her. But what caught Cass's attention the most was Rebecca's demeanor. Her eyes were closed, and her head was down.

"Babe?"

Rebecca opened her eyes, blinking against the light. Her head was hurting, and, unsurprisingly, she couldn't help but wonder if it was because she had a long day or the... tumor. Then Cassidy's face came into focus, and Rebecca smiled.

"Hi, baby."

"Hey." Cass carefully positioned herself next to Rebecca, kissing her softly on the cheek. "Are you okay?"

Am I? "Yes, just a little tired. As it turns out, getting poked and prodded all day takes a lot out of you," Rebecca joked, trying to make light of the situation.

"Poor baby," Cass cooed, stroking Rebecca's hair with a gentle hand. "Want me to carry you up to bed? I promise to only poke and prod you in pleasurable ways." She wiggled her eyebrows, causing Rebecca to chuckle.

"Maybe a little later."

"I'll hold you to that. What can I do for you right now? Do you need something to drink? Eat? How did everything go besides being exhausting?"

Rebecca smiled at her wife. "I ordered some pizza which should be here in about," she checked her delivery app. "Twenty minutes. Why don't you take a shower, get comfy, and we'll eat and discuss today?"

"Sounds like a plan. Sure you don't want to take a shower with me?" Another wiggle of the eyebrows brought on another giggle from Rebecca. Cass never felt prouder than when she could make a woman like Rebecca Cuinn-Giles giggle.

"I took a shower when I got home, baby."

Cass made a face. "Had to get the clinic air off of ya, hmm?" She shivered. "It's weird, isn't it? Hospitals and clinics — especially Hunter's — are probably the most sterile places to be, yet somehow I feel... icky every time I leave one."

"Icky," Rebecca repeated with mirth. "I guess you're right. It doesn't help when all your bits have been out for everyone to see."

Cass laughed. "I suppose that doesn't help mat... wait. Everyone?" She narrowed her eyes. "If Hunter copped a feel..."

"Don't be crass, baby," Rebecca snickered. "Hunter was the perfect gentlewoman and stayed away until it was time to give me results. Now, you've eaten up a lot of the time you had to take a shower before the food gets here. Get going."

"Yes, Mistress," Cass grinned. She leaned in and gave Rebecca a lingering kiss. "I'll be right back, okay?"

"Mmhmm," Rebecca answered distractedly. She could get lost in Cassidy's kisses. It was tempting to do just that. To forget about the food, the exams, the diagnosis, and make love to Cassidy all night long, pretending everything was fine. The only problem with that is nothing would be resolved. So, instead of getting up and joining Cassidy, Rebecca patted her on the backside as Cassidy got up. She watched as Cassidy did a happy little jaunt to the stairs.

I'm going to destroy that happiness, Rebecca thought sadly. She picked up her phone, immediately putting it down again. She was restless. A restless Rebecca was never good. Unless, of course, she could creatively release that pent-up energy with her wife. But Rebecca's libido wasn't on the same wavelength at the moment. All she could think about was how to tell Cassidy the news.

The sound of the doorbell brought Rebecca out of her trance. She looked at her watch and frowned. Twenty minutes had passed, and Rebecca hadn't come up with any answers. She flipped the blanket off her legs and padded to the door. She waited until the delivery person drove away before opening the door and grabbing their food. It smelled good, and Rebecca's empty stomach growled. She hoped she could scarf some of it down — and keep it down — while she and Cassidy talked.

Talked. "How the fuck do I say this?" She sat back on the sofa after setting the food on the coffee table. "Cassidy, I have... So, there's this little... Cassidy, baby, this is going to sound scary, but..." Rebecca groaned. "Come on, Rebecca. Just say it!"

"Just say what?"

Rebecca nearly jumped out of her skin. "Jesus, Cassidy! You scared the shit out of me!"

Cass winced, hiding a smile. "Sorry, babe. I thought you heard me coming down." That smile faded when she saw the look on Rebecca's face. "Becca? Something is up, babe. What is it?" Cass got to her knees next to the couch. Rebecca's day came crashing back into Cass's mind, and the cold fingers of panic grabbed ahold of Cass's heart. "Baby, did they... was there something on the mammogram? Should I call Vanessa?"

Rebecca's eyebrows furrowed. Why would she call Vanessa? And then it hit her. "No, no! No, Cassidy." She brought Cassidy's hands to her breasts, squeezing her fingers over Cassidy's in a very rudimentary self-exam. "See? All good."

Cass took a breath but couldn't shake the dreadful feeling in her gut. "Okay. What about the gyno exam? Did something come up there?"

"Nope. Apparently, I have a very normal vagina."

Cass snorted. "There ain't nothing normal about your vagina, baby. It's extraordinary." Another breath of relief still didn't quell the paranoia. "Okay, so tits and vag are good. What aren't you telling me, Becca? There's something wrong. I can feel it in here." Cass placed a hand over her heart. "I didn't even know you had an appointment today, and you didn't call me when it was over."

"Do you want to eat while the pizza is hot?"

"Becca. All I want right now is for you to tell me what you clearly don't want to tell me."

Rebecca was stunned by Cassidy's directness. She'd always been open and honest about what she was feeling. But it was usually in a cute yet flustered manner. This was... assertive.

"Alright, Cassidy." Rebecca scooted over and patted the couch, inviting Cassidy to join her. She foolishly hadn't expected her wife to be so intuitive. Cassidy *knew* Rebecca inside and out. "Are you willing to listen without interrupting me?"

Cass nodded. She didn't dare open her mouth to say anything because she feared she'd get sick. Fuck, she didn't like this, whatever *this* was. She wanted to bounce her leg or get up and pace. But instead, Cass sat there, waiting for Rebecca to explain.

"First, I didn't have an appointment. As you know, I've been having trouble sleeping lately because of the nightmares. So, I went to Hunter to see if she could give me some advice or maybe some potent melatonin or something. When I told her I've been having lingering headaches, she said she wanted to do an MRI because what I was describing sounded like maybe scar tissue on my brain from past... trauma."

Rebecca knew she was drawing this out far more than she needed to. But she couldn't bring herself to say the words. Not yet.

Cass gritted her teeth. *Fucking Samantha.* If anyone in the world deserved to be in hell, it was Samantha. "She's responsible for this?" Cass asked, hanging onto a single thread of calmness.

Rebecca inhaled. She wished she could blame this on Samantha. "No. It's not a scar, baby."

Cass sat back, relief washing over her. Then she replayed Rebecca's words in her head. It's *not a scar*. She sat back up, grabbed Rebecca's hands, and looked her in the eye. "It?"

The utter fear in Cassidy's voice and expression broke Rebecca's heart. Tears welled as she squeezed Cassidy's hands. "I have a tumor, Cassidy," she revealed quietly.

I have a tumor, Cassidy. The words were on a loop in Cass's mind, yet she couldn't grasp the concept.

"Cassidy?"

"A — a t-tumor. A *brain* tumor?" Cass watched as Rebecca nodded, and the sick feeling in her stomach intensified. "C-cancer?"

"I don't know, baby. They have to do a biopsy to determine that."

Biopsy. Cass sprang up from the couch and began pacing. She wrung her hands as she mumbled. Then she'd stop, rub her sweaty palms on her shorts, and start again. Cass went back to Rebecca's side, kneeling.

"Okay. What are our next steps?"

Rebecca had watched Cassidy go through the emotions of Rebecca's news. Judging by the mumbling Rebecca could decipher, Cassidy had gone through the five stages of grief in the span of thirty seconds. Of course, Rebecca knew this was the beginning of what could be a long, arduous journey, and Cassidy's emotions would ebb and flow with hers, but for now, Cassidy was on the 'do something' stage.

"Well, Hunter made an appointment for me with a neurosurgeon to discuss options."

"When?"

"Tomorrow morning."

"Yeah, okay." Cass took out her phone and opened her email.

"What are you doing?"

"Emailing the hospital to tell them I won't be there tomorrow."

Rebecca put her hand over Cassidy's phone. "Cassidy, no. This is just a visit to..."

"Stop, Becca. I'm going to be there. Did you really think I'd sit this one out? Just go paint while you see a freakin' *surgeon* about a brain tumor?"

"Cassidy..."

"No. I'm not a child, Rebecca. I don't need you to shield me from the hard things in life. I *want* to be there. I *need* to be there, Becca. Don't push me away on this when you know full well that if the tables were turned, you'd want the same thing."

Rebecca raised a brow. "You get this look when you dominate me. Determined. Focused. I've always found it sexy. Right now, I find it a little intimidating, and I can't say no to you."

Cass's lips twitched involuntarily. Imagine Mistress being intimidated by you. What a heady feeling. Cass just wished it was for more erotic reasons.

"I don't want you to say no." Cass plopped herself on the couch and pulled Rebecca onto her lap. "Tell me what you need, baby?"

"Just you. I don't know why I thought I should — or could — do this without you." Rebecca moved in and kissed Cassidy, cupping Cassidy's neck with her palm. She could feel the beat of Cassidy's heart beneath her touch, marveling at how it quickened when Rebecca's tongue slipped past Cassidy's lips. "How hungry are you?" she whispered through the kiss.

"For you? Starving."

With Rebecca secured in her arms, Cass stood — grateful she never skipped leg day. She cradled Rebecca, who nuzzled her face in Cass's neck. Her step nearly faltered when she thought about the tumor. It was going to be a long night, worrying about what it was they were up against. The only way Cass could get through it was to be with Rebecca. To hold her. Love her... Cherish her. And that's precisely what Cass planned to do.

Rebecca plucked the phone out of Cassidy's hands. Rebecca had insisted on freshening up and doing her nightly routine before any... extracurricular activity started. So, Cassidy was waiting for her in bed while Rebecca took her time. Of course, that meant Cassidy had time to Google.

"Hey! I was reading that."

"I know. I already went down that rabbit hole. Believe me, baby, it won't help. It only makes it worse." Rebecca put Cassidy's phone on the nightstand and crawled up on the bed to straddle her.

Cass's hands traveled from Rebecca's thighs, over her perfect ass, and under her tank top to feather over Rebecca's scarred back. She kept this sensual exploration going as she stared into Rebecca's eyes.

"I love you, Rebecca."

Rebecca smiled. "I love you, too, Cassidy." She lowered her head and kissed Cassidy, slowly letting the passion build within them. Tonight she wanted to savor every moment. Every touch. They had no way of knowing what they were up against in the future. But tonight, Rebecca knew all she needed to know. Cassidy loved her and wanted to be there through everything.

"Do you think we can forget about everything for tonight? Tomorrow will be here soon enough and I can't help the fear that things will change."

"Not between us, baby," Cass assured. "Whatever happens, we're solid, Becca. I'm here for the long-haul. But yeah. Tonight is just me and you. We'll keep tomorrow at bay for as long as we can."

Tears welled in Rebecca's eyes. She was grateful for Cassidy's understanding and profound devotion. There wasn't anyone else in the world she wanted by her side. "Lay down," Rebecca directed softly.

Cass waited until Rebecca moved off her and then did as instructed. No more words were said, but Rebecca's actions spoke volumes as she undressed Cass slowly before disrobing herself. Cass fully expected Rebecca to lay with her breast to breast, sex to sex. So when Rebecca flipped her position, Cass's body jerked with anticipation. Her mind — and body — went back to their last time in the playroom. The first time Mistress had tasted Cass in such an intimate way. It hadn't happened since that time, but Cass was a patient woman. Her patience was about to pay off with Rebecca.

Rebecca straddled Cassidy's face while she breathed in Cassidy's scent. Cassidy's arousal sent shivers through Rebecca's body. Her mouth watered at the thought of tasting her wife again. If she thought their time in the playroom was erotic, *this* was on a whole other level. There was something incredibly erotic about the position they were in, being savored while indulging herself.

Cassidy moaned against her clit and Rebecca countered by sucking Cassidy's clit into her mouth. At this moment, everything that happened that day faded away. The only thing Rebecca thought about was Cassidy. All of her senses were filled with Cassidy. She tasted Cassidy's elixir, smelled Cassidy's aroma, felt Cassidy's wetness on her tongue, watched Cassidy writhe beneath her, and heard Cassidy's excitement build with the looming climax.

Cass gripped Rebecca's hips, lifting her head and plunging her tongue deep inside Rebecca. Fuck! When Mistress used her mouth on Cass, it was fucking awesome. But this? Tasting Rebecca as Rebecca feasted on her? That was fucking heaven. She knew she said that frequently about being with Rebecca, but each time it was true. And Rebecca continued to surprise her. *This* was how Cass saw the future. Growing old, still head over heels in love, still being surprised, and still having mind-blowing orgasms.

Cassidy's hips lifted as the orgasm ripped through her. Rebecca felt her contract around her tongue while Cassidy's fingers dug into Rebecca's hips. Then she felt Cassidy's finger slip inside her ass and she exploded. She lifted her head from Cassidy, drawing in a sharp breath.

"Fuck! Cassidy!"

But Cass didn't stop the onslaught of licks, sucks, and nips. She held tight onto Rebecca's hips, refusing to let her wriggle away from the pleasurable torture.

"Please, Cassidy!" Rebecca had lost all concentration. She was now on her hands and knees, desperate to get distance from Cassidy's mouth — and, yet, wanting to stay right where she was for the rest of her life. She was panting, her heart racing as another orgasm came crashing down on her. "Fuck me!"

She collapsed between Cassidy's legs, barely able to breathe after that orgasm. Somehow between losing half of her bodily fluids and utter exhaustion, Cassidy had wriggled her way out from under Rebecca and started a bath. The next thing Rebecca knew, she was in Cassidy's arms being carried to the bathroom.

"Where are we going?" Rebecca asked sleepily.

"To get cleaned up, baby," Cass cooed softly. Her body was humming after Rebecca nearly licked her dry. The climax had the opposite effect on Cass as it did on Rebecca. While Rebecca was practically jello in Cass's arms, Cass was invigorated. She could have gone another few rounds. But since Rebecca seemed down for the count — understandably so with everything she'd been through today — Cass decided to use her energy in other ways. Like bathing Rebecca.

Being with Rebecca renewed Cass's determination that she would be strong for Rebecca no matter what they were told tomorrow. She felt ready — and willing — to fight any demon that had the audacity to come after her girl. Did she know how she was going to fight the worst-case scenario of this tumor being cancerous? Nope. But the fuck if she wouldn't try anything and everything to do just that.

Chapter Nine

Rebecca placed her hand on Cassidy's bouncing knee. "Stop, baby. You're making me nervous."

"Sorry," Cass mumbled.

They were sitting in a cold doctor's office, waiting for the neurosurgeon to come in. It had only been five minutes, but both were nervous enough to make it feel like an eternity. The only thing that kept Cass from storming around the entire office demanding to know where the doctor was was Hunter. Dr. Alita Lima came highly recommended by Hunter. That alone made the wait worth it. Rebecca and Cass trusted Hunter to send them to the best.

"My apologies for making you wait." A small woman with dark hair and a white coat came marching into the office. "I'm Dr. Lima."

Rebecca stood, wiping her hands on her jeans before holding one out. "Rebecca Giles. This is my wife, Cassidy."

"Cass," Cass corrected, shaking the doctor's hand amicably. The woman was shorter than Rebecca, yet held the same commanding aura. To Cass, that was a good sign.

Dr. Lima nodded a small smile on her serious face. "I understand you know Dr. Vale," she gestured to the door where Hunter stood. "She insisted on being here if you two consent to having a third party here."

"Yes, of course," Rebecca answered immediately, smiling gratefully at Hunter.

"Good. I feel having a doctor you trust to help you with decisions is beneficial. Please have a seat." Dr. Lima walked around her desk and sat behind it. She logged into her tablet and brought up Rebecca's MRI images. She pointed at a white spot near the front of Rebecca's brain. "This is what Dr. Vale is concerned about. It's about three and a half centimeters in size which I believe is causing the discomfort you've been feeling. Besides the headaches that Dr. Vale mentioned, what other symptoms have you been experiencing?"

Rebecca glanced at Cassidy. "Um, I've also been tired and restless." It was a difficult question for Rebecca to answer as she never thought of how she felt as 'symptoms.' Didn't everyone experience fatigue and headaches? Did having a tumor change the definition?

"She…" Cass gave Rebecca a questioning look, then continued when Rebecca nodded. "Rebecca had an episode a few days ago where she forgot she started dinner. I came home to burning lasagna in the oven and Rebecca asleep in our home gym." Cass fidgeted. It felt like a betrayal saying these things to other people. She just hoped Rebecca would forgive her for trying to be thorough and helpful. "And, uh, when I told her what happened, she was, um, afraid of me. I've never given her a reason to be scared of me. I can't help but think maybe this tumor is why?"

Dr. Lima wrote notes as Cass described Rebecca's behavior. She nodded absently as she finished, then looked up at Cass. "Changes in personalities, mood swings, memory loss can all be attributed to the tumor, yes."

"C-can you tell if it's…" Cass cleared her throat. She'd rather be doing fucking anything else in the world besides sitting here about to ask if her wife has cancer. "Can you tell what kind of, um, tumor it is?"

Dr. Lima brought up the image of Rebecca's MRI once again. "What I'm seeing here," she pointed to the screen near the mass, "is this mass has developed in the membranes surrounding the brain. In my opinion, we're looking at what is called Meningioma. Typically, this type of tumor is benign seventy-eight to eighty-one percent of the time. However, we can't know for sure what we're dealing with until we've done a biopsy."

Cass relaxed slightly. *Seventy-eight to eighty-one percent of the time, it's not cancer.* She had to remember that and chant it like a mantra to keep her thoughts from becoming morose.

Rebecca, on the other hand, heard the word biopsy and began to panic. She'd read what that entailed, and it didn't sound pleasant at all.

"The biopsy," Rebecca began softly. "You drill a hole in my head?"

"That's one procedure. That is called a needle biopsy. You would be under anesthesia and I would make a small hole in your skull, insert a needle and extract the tissue for analysis."

Rebecca paled. "Are there other options?"

Dr. Lima clasped her hands in front of her and leaned in. "There are options. There's a procedure called a stereotactic biopsy that is minimally invasive and highly accurate."

"I like minimally invasive," Cass stated for no particular reason than her own satisfaction. This wasn't her decision. But the less pain Rebecca went through, the better. Cass would always go for less is more in this situation.

Rebecca reached over and took Cassidy's hand. She gave it a slight squeeze before focusing on the doctor. "Which do you recommend?"

Dr. Lima glanced at Hunter. "Due to the symptoms you're already exhibiting, I would suggest going through with the surgery to remove the tumor. I would then send a sample out to be tested. It would save you having to have two procedures done."

"How risky is the surgery?" Cass asked. She read about the procedure even though Rebecca told her not to.

"Every surgery carries the risk of complications, but I've done thousands of these procedures. I know I'm a surgeon, however, I would never recommend surgery unless I was confident that the benefits outweigh the potential risks. *If* you decide this is the route you want to take, I will give you all the information you will need to educate yourself on potential side-effects or complications."

"I know this is an absurd question with everything that's happening, but how much of my hair will I lose?" Rebecca ran a hand through her long, blonde hair.

Dr. Lima smiled. "Dr. Vale mentioned you were worried about that. It's not absurd at all. You're already dealing with something very scary that you can't control. Any sense of normalcy can only help you in your recovery. I assume Dr. Vale told you I do hair-sparing surgery?"

Rebecca nodded. "Yes, but nothing specific. Like what that actually means."

"Normally, the area surrounding the incision would be shaved," Dr. Lima explained. "With this procedure, only a quarter-inch wide area where I'll be making the incision will be shaved. I'll then thoroughly wash the scalp to prevent infection."

Cass looked back at Hunter who hadn't said a word. She was merely listening very intently to the conversation.

"Hunt?"

Hunter glanced at Dr. Lima. She certainly didn't want to step on a colleague's toes by butting in.

Dr. Lima stood. "Why don't I give you some privacy to discuss this with Dr. Vale." She addressed Hunter. "Feel free to give them other options. I know people think surgeons will always suggest surgery. However, in this case, I do believe it's the best option."

With that, Dr. Lima walked out of *her* office and left them alone. Hunter blew out a breath. "I don't know if I'm comfortable giving you advice in another doctor's office."

"We're not asking for Dr. Vale's advice," Rebecca said. "What would you, *Hunter*, do if you were sitting in this chair?"

"Nah," Cass cut in. "What would you do if *Ellie* was sitting there?"

Hunter closed her eyes. She didn't even want that thought out in the universe. "I would go with the surgery. It's the most common treatment for brain tumors. It could potentially be the only treatment you'll need. If Dr. Lima is able to extract the tumor completely —which I believe she will be — and it's benign, that's it. You're done."

"And the risk is worth the reward?" Cass asked.

"Yeah, I think so," Hunter answered honestly. "As Dr. Lima said, every surgery has the risk of complications. We're dealing with the brain here. Some complications can be more of what you're feeling right now," she said to Rebecca. "But getting that tumor out should relieve those issues."

Rebecca looked at Cassidy. "What do you think?"

Cass dropped to her knees in front of Rebecca, taking her hands in hers. "I think I'll support you in whatever you decide, baby. But I can't be the one to make this decision. I just want you to be okay."

Rebecca slipped one hand out of Cassidy's and palmed Cassidy's cheek. "With you standing by me, I'll be okay." She looked back at Hunter but couldn't bring herself to form the words.

Hunter stood. "No decisions have to be made right now. Go home, talk about it, sleep on it. When you're ready, we can take the next steps."

"Yeah, let's do that, baby." Cass stroked a thumb over the back of Rebecca's knuckles.

Rebecca sighed. She wanted this thing out of her head as quickly as possible. But she owed it to Cassidy to agree to take some time to discuss it more.

"Okay." She watched the relief flood Cassidy's beautiful face.

"Why don't the two of you come over?" Hunter suggested. "Ellie can help you meditate, Cass will help me grill some burgers, and we'll relax. We don't have to talk about this at all if you don't want to. Or you can ask me anything you need to in order to help you make a decision. We could invite the others over and have a little party. What do you say?"

Rebecca looked to Cassidy, who shrugged. All Rebecca wanted was to curl up in a ball in her bed and never move again. The thought of socializing was giving her a headache. Or was that the tumor? Also, having to tell others made her feel sick. She knew her friends would support them both in different ways, but she wasn't ready for the pity.

"I'm sorry," Rebecca said with a forced smile. It wasn't fooling anyone, but at least she tried. "I'm just tired and would like to just go home and curl up with Cassidy. I know you mean well, Hunter, but I'm not ready to tell the others."

Hunter nodded and walked to the door, ready to get Dr. Lima to tell her Cass and Rebecca will need some time. She turned back, hand on the doorknob. "Maybe that's something you should think about, too? We're all here for you, Becca. *Both* of you."

"Thanks, Hunt," Cass saluted, effectively dismissing her best friend. She didn't want Rebecca doing anything she wasn't comfortable with. Even if she, herself, could use the emotional support. "Ready?"

Rebecca nodded. "We can go to the barbecue if you want, baby. I shouldn't have made the decision for you."

"Nah, babe." Cass stood, helping Rebecca up from her chair and kissing her on the forehead. "I'm good with your decision. I'm kinda draggin' myself. I see some leftovers, fluffy socks, and mindless TV in our near future."

"Sounds perfect."

Cass glanced over at Rebecca for the twentieth time since they began the drive home. Rebecca hadn't said a word since leaving the doctor's office. She sat rigidly in the passenger seat, holding Cass's hand. Occasionally, she would squeeze Cass's hand as though whatever she was thinking... scared her. Cass wished she could say or do something that would make Rebecca feel better. But all she could do was... be there.

"Do you need to go anywhere, baby?"

Rebecca jumped at the sound of Cassidy's voice. "What?"

"Do you need to go anywhere?" Cass repeated. "Want some ice cream? Coffee? A mound full of sushi?"

"Oh. No, baby, I just want to go home. Please."

"You got it." Cass held in a sigh. She felt helpless.

"Besides," Rebecca continued, clearly distracted enough not to notice Cassidy's moping. "I need to call Aunt Wills. I promised her I wouldn't keep anything from her again. I can't break that promise."

"Can you make that promise to me?" Cass asked suddenly. She pulled into their driveway and cut the engine, turning to Rebecca before getting out. "Were you planning on keeping this from me? Be honest, Rebecca."

"I-I don't know. I didn't want to worry you when Hunter suggested the MRI. Then, when she said it was a tumor, I...I thought it'd be easier if I could understand *what* it was before telling you. But I was wrong. The moment I saw you, all I wanted was for you to take me in your arms and tell me it would be okay. But that's not fair to you."

"Why? If it offers you comfort, I will do it all day, every day."

"You don't know if it's going to be okay. It's unfair to burden you with the possibility of lying to me."

Cass brought Rebecca's hand to her mouth and kissed Rebecca's knuckles with incredible tenderness. "Maybe it's not lying. Maybe it's manifesting. You know, putting it out there in the universe."

Rebecca chuckled. "You don't even believe that 'hippy-dippy' stuff, Cassidy."

"I will believe in anything I need to believe in, baby." Cass reached over and pushed a strand of Rebecca's hair behind her ear. "Promise me, Becca."

"I promise, Cassidy. I won't keep anything from you."

"Thank you. Now, it's getting a little toasty in here because I stupidly turned off the car, and the windows are still rolled up. You call Aunt Wills, and I'll make myself scarce."

Rebecca watched as Cassidy slid out of the car and jogged around to her side to open the door. She accepted Cassidy's helping hand, not relinquishing her hold when Cassidy closed and locked the car door.

"I don't want you to make yourself 'scarce,' baby. I want you to be there with me. I'm sure you have as many thoughts and concerns as I do. Let Aunt Wills help us both."

Cass grinned, touched at being included. She wrapped her arms around Rebecca, squeezing gently. "Everything's going to be okay, Becca." She willed those words out into the universe with all the belief she could muster. Cass made a mental note to ask Ellie to help her out in that area. "Let's call Aunt Wills. Maybe she'll bring us some goodies."

Chapter Ten

"Aunt Wills?"

Willamena lifted a finger, effectively cutting Rebecca off. She'd just been told that her niece — her dead sister's daughter — had a brain tumor. As a psychiatrist, Willamena knew how she *should* react. As an aunt/mother figure, all she wanted to do was cry. No, that wasn't true. After everything Rebecca had been through in life, Willamena was angry at the added heartache. She took a deep breath, counting to ten before saying anything.

"Did you get a second opinion?"

Rebecca glanced at Cassidy, who sat quietly next to her. "Well, technically, yes. Hunter found the tumor, and it was confirmed by Dr. Lima."

"Dr. Lima," Willamena repeated. "She's quite a renowned neurosurgeon."

"You know her?" Cass asked, breaking her silence. She couldn't imagine how Aunt Wills was feeling. She knew Aunt Wills thought of Rebecca as a daughter. After everything else Rebecca had been through, this couldn't be easy for Aunt Wills.

Willamena nodded. "In passing only. I've read some of the research she has published. Hunter chose well. What are the options?"

"Well, um..." Rebecca was a little taken aback by Aunt Wills's attitude. She had expected *some* kind of reaction. Shock, sadness...*something*. But instead, all Rebecca got was Dr. Willamena Woodrow. Professional and unemotional. "She seems to think surgery is the way to go. She wants to go in and remove the tumor because of the symptoms, then do the biopsy."

"Symptoms? What symptoms are you having?" Willamena sat forward, elbows on her knees. "Headaches? Dizziness?"

"Gee, *Dr.* Woodrow, should I schedule an appointment?" Rebecca asked sarcastically. It was silly to be upset by Aunt Will's response, but Rebecca didn't care. She was in her self-pity stage and wanted the people who loved her — who she loved — to feel sorry *with* her. Rebecca felt Cassidy's hand on her thigh and managed to calm down. A little.

Willamena sighed. Her need to keep her emotions in check had given Rebecca the insinuation that Willamena wasn't affected by the news. "I'm sorry if I made you think I'm not upset, my sweet girl." She reached over and took Rebecca's hand. "My go-to defense mechanism is to dive into the solutions. That's not what you need. You need me to be your aunt right now."

Rebecca squeezed Aunt Wills's hand. "No, it's not you, Aunt Wills. I'm feeling sorry for myself, and I think everyone else should too. It's selfish."

"It's human, babe," Cass reassured.

"Cass is right, Becca. And as your aunt, I should have given you my true feelings about this. I'm shocked and a little scared. I'll wait for the biopsy to gauge that fear. I'm also a little miffed that you didn't tell me you were having symptoms."

"*Miffed,*" Rebecca parroted. "I didn't *know* they were symptoms. I thought I was just stressed. I even..." Another glance at Cassidy. "Semi-retired because I was feeling overworked and overly tired."

"You must've suspected something was wrong if you went for an MRI." Willamena didn't know why she was giving Rebecca the third degree. Obviously, Willamena had residual guilt from not knowing Rebecca was being brutalized by her ex. This wasn't the way to express that guilt, but it was an honest response. Rebecca deserved that much.

"No, I went to Hunter to ask her for something to help me sleep." *Damn. I didn't tell her about the nightmares.* "I... anyway, Hunter suggested the MRI because of past... trauma."

"We'll gloss over why you were having trouble sleeping. For now." Willamena raised a brow and gave Rebecca a look she hadn't given her since Rebecca was a teenager. Then Willamena shook her head. "I've just realized what I'm doing. I'm focusing on everything except the actual problem because I don't know what to do." She felt helpless. Willamena had felt this way only three times before in her life, and she had hoped never to feel that way again. She took a moment to center herself. "Okay. When is the surgery?"

Rebecca got up to pace. "We haven't decided yet on what to do," she revealed. "I did a little research..."

"You Googled?" Willamena guessed.

"Yes. None of the options sound great. But surgery scares the hell out of me." Rebecca scoffed. "You'd think this would be a breeze with all the surgeries I've had."

Cass got up to intercept Rebecca, wrapping her arms around her. "This is your brain, babe. Of course it's scary."

"Speaking of, Cass, how does this make you feel?" Willamena asked, absolutely aware she had turned on her psychiatrist's voice.

"I... it's not about me, Aunt Wills."

"On the contrary. You love Rebecca."

Rebecca felt Cassidy's body tense. "Aunt Wills, this isn't a session. Cassidy..."

"It's okay, babe," Cass said softly. "I'm worried as fuck, if I'm being honest. I don't know whether to prepare for the worst or hope for the best. Or fucking both. It all happened so fast, and yet we don't know anything. I don't even know if that fucking makes any sense, but none of this does to me. Rebecca has been through too fucking much. This shouldn't be happening to her. If I could take her place, I would in a fucking second."

Cassidy was practically panting by the time she finished her little rant, and Rebecca rubbed small circles on her back to try and calm her down. She reached up with her other hand to cup Cassidy's cheek.

"Breathe, baby," Rebecca whispered.

Cass touched her forehead to Rebecca's, apologizing quietly for her outburst. She looked at Aunt Wills and repeated the apology.

"No, don't be. You said what you needed to say. And what I think we all feel. I encourage you to keep that honesty going."

"It's not what Becca needs," Cass disagreed. "She doesn't need the stress of my meltdowns."

"I think I can speak for myself on what I need, Cassidy. And I *need* that openness from you. Remember what I promised you? It goes both ways, okay?"

"Yeah, okay." Cass kissed Rebecca's forehead tenderly. "Are you hungry? You didn't eat anything for breakfast or lunch."

"Tattletale," Rebecca whined playfully when Aunt Wills gave her another look. "I am a little hungry. But nothing sounds appetizing."

"How about a turkey sandwich like I used to make you when you were younger?" Willamena grinned at Cass. "There was a time when Rebecca only ate turkey sandwiches with mayo, cheddar cheese, and exactly one slice of a tomato for a week straight. If I recall correctly, it was because she was upset she made a D on one of her school papers."

"C," Rebecca corrected with a scowl. "I've never made a D in my life. And that teacher was out to get me because I was smarter than him."

"I don't doubt you were, babe," Cass chuckled. "So? Turkey sandwich? I think we have a tomato."

Rebecca thought about it for a moment which caused her tummy to growl. "My stomach agrees. But only if Aunt Wills makes it. No offense, baby.

"None taken. Obviously, you gotta go with the pro," Cass winked. "You mind, Aunt Wills?"

"Not at all." Willamena stood from the couch and walked over to Rebecca. Cass still held Rebecca in her arms but immediately stepped back when Willamena approached them. Willamena took Cass's place, hugging Rebecca fiercely. "Do the surgery, sweet girl," she whispered in Rebecca's ear. "If Dr. Lima thinks she can remove the tumor completely, it's the best choice." She kissed Rebecca's cheek before hurrying off toward the kitchen.

"Think she's okay?" Cass asked worriedly.

"Yeah. I don't think this is what she imagined when we called to ask her over, but she adapts better than anyone I know." Rebecca turned to Cassidy. "But she's also the most vulnerable — other than you — when it comes to me. Be there for each other."

"Babe, stop talking like you're going to die. Please?" Tears welled in Cass's eyes. "I'm trying to do like Aunt Wills and wait until the biopsy to freak the fuck out, okay?"

Rebecca stood on her tiptoes and kissed Cassidy, deepening the kiss when Cassidy's hands settled on Rebecca's hips. "Everything is going to be fine," she said with conviction. Now if she could just believe it with her whole heart.

"Did you have enough to eat, baby?"

Cass tossed her t-shirt and boxers on the chair beside her nightstand and jumped onto the bed. "Yeah. I'm grateful your aunt stayed to make dinner, too. I'm getting kinda burned out on takeout."

Rebecca finished brushing her hair, taking a moment to look at herself in the mirror. Her silky blonde hair fell past her shoulders to the middle of her back. It had always been long. Even when she was young and tender-headed, she never wanted her aunt to cut her hair. Now she wondered what it would be like... what she would *feel* like if it was shorter. Would she feel as confident? Rebecca nearly laughed at herself. It was just hair.

She glanced back at Cassidy through the mirror. Her wife was currently naked, sprawled across the bed as she waited for Rebecca to join her. Cassidy's hair was short. Very short. Her confidence certainly wasn't. Rebecca gathered up her hair, creating a makeshift bob. She turned one way, then the other, trying to see if the look suited her.

"You could be bald, and I'd still think you were the most beautiful woman I've ever seen," Cass said, her eyes boring into Rebecca's through the mirror.

Rebecca let her hair fall and pushed away from the vanity. "Bald is a little too drastic for me." She untied her robe, letting it slip down her naked body. "But I'm trying to get to a place, mentally, where my hair doesn't define me."

"It doesn't, babe. Your ass does." Cass wiggled her eyebrows suggestively, sticking out her tongue for good measure.

Rebecca laughed. "Of course you would say that." She gave Cassidy a small glimpse of said ass before climbing into bed with her. "I...I'm going to do the surgery."

Cass's playful energy turned serious. "Okay."

"Are you? Okay with that, I mean?"

"It's your decision, babe. I support whatever you need to do."

"It's *our* decision. And if you don't want me to..."

Cass pulled Rebecca to her, trying not to let the skin on skin affect her brain. It was time to be an adult now. "I'm serious, Becca. I'm with you no matter what you choose. But if you need me to say it, I think surgery is the right choice. Let's get that fucker out of there. It needs to leave my girl alone."

Rebecca smiled. "Your girl could use a little... or a big... friend tonight. Care to volunteer?"

Cass raised three fingers in a salute, then added another one with a sly grin. "Come here, woman." She dragged Rebecca on top of her, then quickly flipped their position. She looked down into Rebecca's eyes. "I love you, Becca."

"I love you too, Cassidy."

The kiss started off slow. A mutual declaration of love and devotion. But the kiss became heated and needy as their bodies touched and their hands roamed. Neither would admit to craving the frantic connection because of fear of the unknown future. Instead, they would give in to it and let it guide them to whatever desires their bodies needed to fulfill.

Rebecca reached over the best she could with Cassidy's weight on top of her. She rummaged around the nightstand drawer until she found what she wanted. Rebecca pressed the dildo to Cassidy's chest. "Strap in, cowgirl. It's going to get wild."

Cass's eyes shone with excitement. "Cowgirl, huh?" She rolled over onto her back, spreading her legs. "Giddy up."

Rebecca got to her knees, smiling down at her wife. "Giddy up, indeed." She brought two fingers to her lips, licking them sensually as Cassidy watched. Then she lowered them to Cassidy's ready and waiting pussy. She circled her wet fingers around Cassidy's clit before pushing them inside her. "Just need to make sure you're ready."

"For you, babe, I'm always ready. I think I'm perpetually wet for you." Cass's hips involuntarily lifted when Rebecca brought the dildo close.

"Perpetually, hmm? I like that." Rebecca slipped the bulb end of the strapless strap-on inside Cassidy, shivering with gleeful anticipation when Cassidy sucked in a breath. "Feel good?"

Cass sat up, wrapping her arms around Rebecca in a tight embrace. "You feel better. I want to be inside you, baby."

"Good. That's exactly where I want you to be." Rebecca pushed Cassidy back into her prone position. Then Rebecca turned until her back was toward Cassidy and straddled her.

Holy fuck! Cass thought as she stared at Rebecca's perfect naked ass. *Reverse cowgirl. Yippie ki yay!* Her hands went straight to Rebecca's hips, guiding her right where they both needed her to be. But Rebecca had other ideas, and Cass's excitement nearly had her pumping her hips prematurely.

Rebecca smiled, knowing Cassidy was eagerly waiting. She touched herself, gathering the abundant wetness, then reached between her legs to take the dildo in her wet fingers. She stroked and pulled, knowing full well she was driving Cassidy wild. When she positioned the shaft between the lips of her pussy, gliding it along her saturated skin, Cassidy groaned.

"You're killing me, baby." Cass dug her fingers into Rebecca's hips as she watched Rebecca glide across her cock. She wanted to buck her hips. To slam herself inside Rebecca until Rebecca screamed her name. But Cass knew with *vast* experience that Rebecca's way of doing things *consistently* garnered more pleasure. So, Cass endured the throbbing of her own pussy and watched, captivated by the sheer sexiness of her wife.

Rebecca couldn't wait any longer, lifting her hips enough to guide the dildo where she wanted it. Then she sank down slowly, her head dropping back in ecstasy as Cassidy filled her in the most intimate way. How odd that she never thought she'd love anal sex, but that's what Cassidy brought out in her. Freedom from her inhibitions and fears. And a passion for giving Cassidy every part of her without hesitation or humiliation.

Cass watched the dildo move inside Rebecca. It was the most erotic thing, watching as you fuck the woman you love more than anything.

Knowing Rebecca trusted her enough to give herself to Cass this way meant the world. And she would wear that honor proudly for the rest of her life if Rebecca allowed her to.

No longer able to stay an idle participant in this carnal display of lust, Cass raised up, pressing her hard nipples into Rebecca's back. She reached around, cupping Rebecca's ample tits in both hands. Cass squeezed hard, causing Rebecca's breath to hitch. She peered around Rebecca, seeing their mating bodies reflected back to them in the mirror. Cass stared at the rapture in Rebecca's beautiful face. She snaked a hand down between Rebecca's legs, cupping her sex and slipping two fingers inside her.

Rebecca opened her eyes, catching Cassidy's stare in the mirror. She covered Cassidy's hands with her own, tightening the hold of one hand around her breast and pushing the other deeper inside her. Rebecca's hips moved faster as the orgasm fought to be released.

"*Cassidy*!" Rebecca closed her eyes as her hips bucked harder.

"That's it, baby. Let it go for me." Cass's breath was as hard and fast as Rebecca's movements. She was as close to coming as she knew Rebecca was. "Look at us, Rebecca. Watch us fucking. Watch as we both give each other what we need."

Rebecca's eyes went back to the mirror. She followed Cassidy's gaze as it moved from Rebecca's eyes to her tits, down to where Cassidy's fingers were buried inside her. She edged her hand under Cassidy's and massaged her clit as Cassidy fingered her. The sensations of getting her ass fucked, having Cassidy's long, strong fingers inside her, and touching herself proved too much to stave off the impending climax.

"I'm coming, Cassidy!"

Cass curled her fingers, gritting her teeth as the dildo collided with her clit with each move Rebecca made. "Come, Rebecca! Fuck yes!"

"Fuck!" Rebecca cried out as the orgasm crashed over her like a tidal wave. She fell forward onto her hands as the bed continued to sway beneath her. Was she still moving, or did that orgasm rock the entire house?

"You have to stop, baby!" Cass panted. "It's too much!"

Rebecca felt Cassidy trying to move away from the pressure on her clit and grinned. She sat back, rocking her ass back and forth. Yeah, it affected her just as much as Cassidy, but maybe Rebecca was a sadist — and a masochist — after all.

"Take it, Cassidy."

Cass's eyes flew open. Once again, her eyes met Rebecca's in the mirror. Only it wasn't Rebecca staring back at her. This was pleasure and pain in its most primal form. And Cass would take it all.

"Yes, Mistress."

Chapter Eleven

Two weeks had passed since Rebecca found out she had a brain tumor. Though she decided fairly early to have the surgery, the wait for the actual day was excruciatingly slow despite being busy. She had to do so many damn tests that she was ready to reach into her brain and rip the "fucker" as Cassidy called it out herself.

Between blood tests, ECGs, X-rays, and echocardiograms, Rebecca was over the whole thing. However, surgery day was finally here, and Rebecca was... scared. She suddenly found herself wanting to go back two weeks and endure all the tests over again.

"Hey, baby."

Cass sidled up behind Rebecca in the bathroom, embracing her and kissing her neck. She felt Rebecca's pulse beneath her lips and knew Rebecca was as nervous as she was. But Cass was determined to stay calm for Rebecca's sake. Or at least *act* calm. Was that going against their pact of not keeping things from each other? Cass's executive decision was no. Sometimes, it was better to just stay quiet.

"Are you ready to go?"

Rebecca leaned into Cassidy and sighed. "Would you think less of me if I said no?"

Cass turned Rebecca until they were face to face. "No. If you're not ready, I can call and reschedule, Becca."

Oh, she thought about it. It was on the tip of her tongue to say yes, but she didn't. "We can't keep wondering, baby. If it's malignant, it's best to get it out now. Even if it's benign, the headaches and nightmares are still there. I just want this over with. But promise me something, please?"

Cass held her breath as she nodded. God, she didn't want to hear Rebecca talking about dying. That's not the energy Cass wished to put forth today.

"After all this is done, promise we can ask Eve and Lainey to use their private island. I want to get away, lay on the beach, drink mai tais, listen to the waves with you lying next to me, and not think of one damn thing while we're there."

"Sounds like a dream, babe. I'm in. But, uh... I don't know how to make a mai tai. If you want a pina colada, I got you covered."

Rebecca chuckled. "I don't care what I'm drinking as long as you're with me."

"And then we'll make love in a hammock. I've always wanted to try that," Cass said as she guided Rebecca out of the bathroom. She picked up a duffel bag with some essentials Rebecca would need at the hospital. With luck, Rebecca would only be there for two days. Three at the most. Of course, Cass was hoping for the former. She wouldn't be leaving Rebecca's side, but a hospital chair isn't as comfortable as their bed.

"The way we make love? That hammock would be swinging upside down." Rebecca knew Cassidy was trying to distract her, and Rebecca loved her for that.

"Heh, yeah, it would," Cass smirked. "What a fucking ride it would be." They were downstairs and at the front door when Cass felt Rebecca hesitate. She kneeled and helped Rebecca put on her shoes. "I bet there's a pool. And a jacuzzi. Lainey sets these places up like a boss." She stood and took Rebecca's chin in her hand. "Pina coladas, sun, and fun, babe. You keep that with you today."

"I wish you could be with me."

"Me, too. Believe me. But look," Cass pulled out Rebecca's wedding ring that was on a chain around Cass's neck. Rebecca couldn't wear it during surgery and didn't want to risk losing it by taking it off at the hospital. "I have you right here with me. Hunter said she'd be in the OR with you. You got this, yeah?"

"Yeah." She stretched up and kissed Cassidy deeply. "I'm ready," she announced once the kiss ended.

I'm not, Cass answered silently. Outwardly, she smiled brightly and opened the door. *We just have to get through a few hours.*

"You'll stay in there with her the whole time?" Cass had yet to release Rebecca's hand even though they were about to wheel her away. The surgical team had already come in to introduce themselves and get Rebecca prepared. By then, things got very real for Cass.

"The whole time," Hunter reassured. "Dr. Lima is the best at this, Cass. I know you're feeling nervous after reviewing the paperwork and the possible complications, but we'll take good care of your girl."

"Her girl is lying right here," Rebecca said softly, reminding them that she hated being talked about like she wasn't in the room.

"Sorry, Becca," Hunter smiled. She stood aside when the circulating technician came in to get Rebecca. "Cass, it's time."

Cass gritted her teeth to keep from crying. She leaned down and kissed Rebecca gently on the lips. "You go in there and crack the whip," she whispered. "I'll be here waiting for you when you get out, okay?"

Rebecca nodded, unable to keep the tears at bay. They said their "I love yous," and Rebecca was wheeled away with Cass holding on to her fingertips as long as she could. She took a deep breath, gathering the strength she would need for the next three to five hours.

"Hunt?" Hunter stopped and turned to Cass. "You bring her back to me."

Hunter nodded. As a former trauma surgeon, she knew better than to promise anything. Too many things could go wrong. Especially when dealing with the brain. Still, she patted Cass on the shoulder and did just that before following Rebecca to the operating room.

"I'm going to get some coffee in the cafeteria," Ellie announced. She had joined Cass in the waiting room thirty minutes after they took Rebecca.

They were now an hour in, and Cass was pacing like a caged lion.

"Nah, uh, no. Thank you, though." Cass stopped pacing for a second. "Ellie?"

Ellie looked back, her eyebrows raised in question. "Change your mind?"

Cass shook her head. "I just wanted to thank you for being here. You know Rebecca didn't want anyone to know about this, so having your support helps a lot." She looked at her watch. An hour and five minutes in. Why was time going by so fucking slow? "Aunt Wills texted that she was on her way, so you'll have someone to help you with..." She gestured at herself. "This."

Because she suspected Cass needed it, Ellie came back and hugged her. "I'm not going for coffee because I can't handle you, Cass. I'm going because I'm nervous, and doing something as mundane as walking to the cafeteria helps me center myself."

Cass smiled. "I love that you're always honest with your feelings. It makes me less... scared to have my own. G'wan, and get your coffee. I'll keep the floor occupied until you get back."

Ellie patted Cass's cheek. "You'd think they'd learn to put treadmills in waiting rooms," she winked and took off for that bit of centering.

Cass resumed her pacing, looking at her watch every thirty seconds. That wasn't helping matters much. She tried waiting a little longer between each time check, but the farthest she got was another five seconds. She shook her arm as though that would make the time go faster.

"Cass?"

Cass spun around and frowned. "H-hey. What are you doing here?" Did Ellie or Aunt Wills call them? Oh, Rebecca wasn't going to be happy about this.

Eve raised a brow. "Jules pinged your phone here. You're not answering calls or texts."

Cass recalled seeing a text notification from Eve when they were taking Rebecca back but had forgotten to check it once she got to the waiting room.

"Sorry, I've been, uh, preoccupied. Was it important?"

Eve nodded. "I have news about this Buck McEnroe person."

Cass's brows furrowed in confusion. "Who?"

Eve glanced at Lainey, who was studying Cass intently. "Buck McEnroe," she repeated. "The person Rebecca…"

"Oh!" Cass interrupted. "The dude that was a douchecanoe to Rebecca." She shook her head. "I forgot all about him. It's been… kinda crazy lately. Um, I guess since you tracked me down, you have info. But can it wait?"

"That depends," Lainey said as she eyed Cass, noting the worry on her face. "Something's wrong. Where is Rebecca?" Cass didn't answer, but a quick look at the corridor leading to the surgical unit answered for her. "There's something you should see, Cass. And then maybe you could tell us what's going on."

Lainey took the tablet from Eve, who was growing more concerned by the minute. Lainey turned the screen to Cass and pressed play.

"Here is the warehouse Rebecca went to," Lainey explained. "In a second, you will see Rebecca pull up." As promised, Rebecca's car pulled into the vacant parking lot. She exited the car and walked up a couple of stairs to get to the door. Rebecca knocks, tries the doorknob, then shakes her head and returns to her car.

"As you can see," Eve took over. "No one was there. In fact, no one has been there for more than five years. It's abandoned. What happens next is what worries me."

Lainey continued the video. Rebecca gets to her car and stops. Cass could see her sway a bit before getting in.

"She sits there for forty-five minutes, Cass. The camera is too far away to see if she's on the phone or not, but according to Jules, it wasn't with anyone named Buck McEnroe. He doesn't exist. The company doesn't exist. At least not the one Rebecca described. Now, what's going on?"

Cass scrubbed her face, then ran her hands through her hair. Was this related to the tumor?

"Oh good!" Willamena walked into the waiting room with a strained smile. "You called in reinforcements. I'm sorry, Cass, I tried to get here earlier." She kissed Cass on the cheek and greeted Eve and Lainey amicably. "But I'm glad you have someone with you. Is Ellie here?"

Cass's brain took a moment to catch up. "Uh. Ellie is getting coffee. And..."

"And Eve and Lainey have no clue what's going on," Eve said stoically.

Lainey stepped between Eve and the others. "What Eve means is we just got here. We tracked down Cass to talk about another matter. However, it seems we've walked into something bigger. Did something happen to Rebecca?"

Willamena glanced at Cass apologetically. When Cass said nothing, Willamena took it as loyalty to Rebecca. She knew her niece. Having people know she was... impaired in any way dug into her confidence. A confidence she had spent years building after Samantha. However, Cass was now a part of Willamena's family, and she could use the support. They both could.

"Rebecca is having surgery at this moment," Willamena said finally. "To remove a brain tumor."

"Oh my god." Lainey reached for Cass's hand. "I'm so sorry."

"Don't be. She's going to be fine," Cass said with conviction.

"Why didn't you tell us?" Eve asked angrily. "She's our friend."

"And she's *my* wife." Cass stood tall, using her height as an intimidation tactic. She would probably look back at this and laugh one day, remembering how she seriously thought she, Cass Giles, could intimidate Eve Sumptor. "Rebecca asked me not to say anything, and I will *always* do what she asks of me. I'm sure you understand that."

Lainey felt Eve bristle behind her and turned to give her a look. That was all it took for Eve to stand down.

"Please forgive Eve. She gets a little... intense when she's worried. Look, I get it. I didn't want anyone to know what we were going through when Eve was being framed. But I am eternally grateful that you all were there for me. I don't think I would have survived otherwise. Technically, you're off the hook. You didn't tell us. However, I think Rebecca would understand better than anyone that we're family and need to lean on each other. So, you can stop with the aggressive posture. We know you're tall and strong. Believe me, I've heard it many times during girls' night."

Cass blew out a breath, her shoulders slumping slightly. "I don't know why everyone thinks Eve is the intimidating one."

Eve couldn't help but laugh. "That's what *I've* been saying!" She noticed Willamena watching the exchange closely. *Always the shrink.* Then again, Eve Sumptor was always Eve Sumptor. "I could have specialists here by the end of the day if needed. Who is Rebecca's surgeon?"

"Dr. Lima," Cass answered. Now, she wondered why they didn't utilize Eve's expansive resources. Of course, Cass trusted Hunter's opinion, and that meant she trusted Lima.

"Alita," Eve nodded. "You have one of the best, then."

Lainey smiled at Cass's confusion. "Eve is on the board here at the hospital."

"Right. Should have known," Cass grinned. She looked at her watch. One good thing about having friends around was the time went by a little faster. Fifteen minutes had passed. "Well, I'm going to get back to pacing. Uh, thanks for being here."

Willamena, Lainey, and Eve watched Cass pace and mutter to herself.

"Coping mechanism," Willamena said. "Let's leave her to it."

"Shrink," Eve muttered, receiving a light smack from her wife.

"I think I'll call Blaise," Lainey announced. She saw Cass stop in her tracks and look over at her. "Don't worry, you're still off the hook. I'll tell Rebecca it was all my doing."

"I already called her." Ellie came in with handfuls of coffee and snacks. "I saw the two of you coming in," she explained. "If Blaise knew everyone was here and left her out, I'd never hear the end of it." She held out the cup carrier with an offering. "The one on the right top is black coffee for Eve. Below that is tea for you, Lainey."

"Thank you," Lainey took the cups Ellie indicated, handing one to Eve, then turning back to Ellie. "Let me help you with that."

"Ah, ah. This is what I do. And I'm very good at it. Aunt Wills, this is an oat milk latte with agave for you."

"You are a saint!" Willamena took the cup and sipped from it carefully. "Perfect."

Ellie went to Cass. "Cass? I know you said you didn't want

anything, but I brought you some chocolate milk and a protein bar. You have at least another two hours of waiting. Keep your energy up."

"Yes, ma'am," Cass murmured a thank you and took her nourishment to a corner where she could be alone. She loved that her friends were there for her, but Cass just needed a minute to herself. Rebecca was going to be pissed at her. Yeah, Lainey was right. Cass *technically* didn't blab, but technicalities didn't count. It was okay, though. A mad Rebecca meant she was fine. Cass could live with that.

Chapter Twelve

"Cass?"

Cass looked up sharply. Her numb ass from sitting on the floor was completely forgotten when she saw Hunter. She scrambled up, wiping the dust off as she hurried to Hunter.

"Is she okay?"

"The surgery was a success. We got the tumor and didn't see evidence that it had metastasized, so..."

"Hunter!" Cass interrupted. "First things first, then you can go into all the medical mumbo jumbo. Is Rebecca okay?"

"Yes. She's headed to recovery." Hunter glanced over her shoulder, locking eyes with Willamena, who immediately came to Cass's side. "Now, it usually takes four to five hours for the patient to wake up after a surgery of this kind. However, we're going to keep Rebecca in a medically induced sleep for a little while longer."

Cass frowned. "What? Why? You just said she was okay."

"And she is. However, a piece of the tumor was in a challenging spot. While Dr. Lima was able to remove the entire tumor without damaging vital brain tissue, it did cause some irritation and swelling. The MIC is simply a precaution."

Cass was having trouble understanding all of what Hunter was saying. Mainly because the moment she heard "medically induced sleep," all she could think about was her wife being in a coma. This wasn't supposed to happen. Cass had been thinking positive thoughts all day. She wouldn't allow any negativity in. When she thought about what would happen after the surgery, it was Hunter coming to get her, telling her Rebecca was ready to see her. Of course, she knew about the potential complications. They'd gone over everything before the surgery. But Cass was so sure everything would be fine that this blindsided her.

"How long?" Willamena asked, allowing her doctor's side to take over for Cass's sake. The calmer Willamena was about this situation, the easier Cass would take the news.

"A day, maybe two. We'll monitor Rebecca closely, and if the swelling goes down before that, we'll wake her up."

"Aunt Wills?"

Willamena's heart broke for Cass. She looked so scared and lost. Willamena threaded her arm through Cass's and smiled up at her. "This isn't uncommon, Cass. The brain is delicate, and right now, Rebecca's is a little pissed off at being messed with. A little rest will do it good."

Cass stared at Aunt Wills, trying to gauge if she was telling her the truth. When she was satisfied that Aunt Wills wasn't too worried, Cass fixed her eyes on Hunter. "When can I see her?"

Hunter pursed her lips. She knew this wouldn't go over well, but she would put it out there anyway. "You should go home..."

"Did you?" Cass interrupted hotly. "When Ellie was in a coma, did you go home?"

Hunter visibly winced. That was still a sore spot for her. "Fair enough. How about this? I will let you back in recovery for ten minutes." Hunter lifted a hand to stop Cass's argument. "That's all I can do. Other patients are back there, and I don't want to disturb them. After that, you go and get some fresh air, maybe some food, and by the time you get back, Rebecca will be in her private room ready for you."

Cass contemplated that for a full minute. "Deal. Let's go."

Hunter nodded and turned to the others, surprised that nearly everyone was there. That certainly wasn't what Rebecca wanted. Then again, she couldn't fault Cass for needing friends to lean on. A support system was critical in times like these.

"Unfortunately, it's family only. I know we're all Rebecca's family, but she truly does need her rest. And if I learned anything from when Ellie was... here, it's that I'm not sure a coma is completely restful if there's a lot of activity around. Since Rebecca didn't want anyone to know about this, having you all fill her room is probably not a good idea. We don't need Mistress mad at us before she's even awake."

Cass's lips twitched at that. "I just need Becca to know *I* didn't say a word. I didn't tell them. *Technically*, Aunt Wills did. Can we go see my girl now?"

Cass squeezed Willamena's hand, ready to drag her along. But Willamena gently pulled away. "You go. Have your time with her. I'll wait until she's settled in her room. I don't want to overwhelm the situation."

"Are you sure?" Cass asked, not wanting to push Aunt Wills out of seeing her niece.

"Absolutely. Go see our girl and let her know we love her." She watched as Cass hurried off with Hunter, only *slightly* regretting her decision.

"Was it true?" Eve asked. "What you said to Cass about this not being uncommon?"

Willamena looked over at Eve. "Yes. I don't like it, but it happens."

Ellie sighed, her expression mirroring the worry in the others. "Right, well, we're not going to be too helpful here. Why don't we wait for Cass and then head to the diner? I'll cook us something comforting."

"You've been here for hours, Ellie. Are you sure you're up for standing at the stove?" Blaise asked. She had arrived about an hour earlier, dropping everything after Ellie's call.

"I'll be fine. You know cooking usually helps me keep my mind from veering off into negative thoughts. Besides, with your help, I should be fine," Ellie winked.

"I will help, too," Lainey chimed in. She slipped her hand in Eve's, giving it a slight squeeze. "Rebecca is one of the strongest women I know. As scary as this is, I have to believe she'll be okay."

"Hear, hear." Willamena touched her heart and looked up, sending a silent plea to her sister. "Thank you all for being here. I can't tell you how much it means to me that Rebecca has such caring friends in her life. She's always been so reserved, perhaps rightfully so. But I've never seen her so happy. That has everything to do with Cass and all of you.

When she wakes up, I think she'll be happy that we didn't listen to her and keep this private. She needs you all."

The small but mighty group formed a circle, each taking the hand of the woman next to them. They all knew what it was like to need the strength of others in their corner. They would give that strength to Rebecca — and Cass — now.

"Right through here," Hunter said, leading Cass towards Rebecca's bed in recovery. "Remember, only ten minutes, yeah? Then you go get some food. I'm sure Ellie has already made plans to have everyone at the diner. You eat, you relax a bit, then you can come back more refreshed for Becca."

"Yeah, I got it, Hunt. We made a deal. I'm not gonna back out of it." Cass stopped when Hunter did, trying not to look at the other patients in the area. She also tried blocking out the eerie beeps of various machines. She didn't like thinking about Rebecca in here. The faster she could get her wife home, the better for both their sanity. Cass thanked Hunter as she passed through the curtain Hunter held open for her. Then stopped and audibly gasped.

Hunter grabbed Cass when she swayed a little beside her. "Hey, she's okay. It's just a ventilator, Cass. It's helping her keep a steady breath while she sleeps. The other stuff is just monitoring her heartbeat and brain activity. Okay?"

Cass looked at Hunter, tears brimming in her eyes. She gave a slight nod before walking over to Rebecca's bed and taking her hand.

"H-" Cass cleared the worry and pain of seeing Rebecca like this from her throat. "Hey, baby. I hear you kicked ass in the OR. I had no doubts. They, um," Cass took another breath. "They said that you needed some rest, and me bringing my sexy self in here would blow your mind, so they're helping you sleep a little longer until you can handle all this androgynous sex appeal."

Hunter let out a low chuckle as she checked Rebecca's charts. She would have preferred giving Cass more privacy, but she was already bending the rules.

"They got it all, baby." Cass stroked Rebecca's pale face. "We'll worry about the other stuff later, but for right now, all we have to do is celebrate that that thing is outta here, yeah?" She sat there quietly for a while, just kissing Rebecca's hand and observing her as the ventilator caused a steady rise and fall of Rebecca's chest.

Hunter cleared her throat softly, signaling Cass that her time was almost up. It hurt her heart to see the two of them like this. Knowing how she felt when Ellie was in her coma, Hunter could all but feel Cass's distress.

"So, um, I made Hunter a deal, baby. I told her I would go and get something to eat while they moved you to your room. In return, I got to see you now for a little bit. But I gotta go for a minute now. I won't be long. I promise."

Cass backed away, her eyes never leaving Rebecca. It physically hurt her to leave her wife in such a vulnerable state. While she was grateful Hunter gave her this time, Cass resented being unable to stay by Rebecca's side as Hunter did with Ellie. *Not the same, Cass. Get a grip.*

"Ready?" Hunter asked quietly.

"No. So, drag me outta here, Hunt, because I'm having trouble leaving her."

A sad look crossed Hunter's face as she hooked her hand around Cass's arm and gently pulled her out of Rebecca's recovery area. "Go get something to eat, Cass. I'll keep an eye on your girl."

"Thanks, Hunt. I'm, uh, glad you're with her."

Chapter Thirteen

Cass's leg bounced as she pushed the food around on her plate. As much as she loved Ellie's cooking, her stomach was rolling too much to eat anything. Worry plagued her every thought, replacing the positivity she forced herself to have earlier.

"Cass?"

Cass felt a soft hand on her shoulder and looked up. "Huh? Sorry, El, I was just..."

"Worrying?" Cass nodded, and Ellie gave her an empathetic smile. "So are we. But you need to eat something."

"I just don't know if I can keep it down. My stomach is all in knots."

Ellie glanced at the uneaten sandwich — a turkey club, one of Cass's favorites — and decided to wrap it up for later. What Cass needed now was something lighter. Jessie got this way whenever she was particularly nervous or upset about something. The thing that always helped was soup. She picked up the plate and stopped when Cass's hand caught her arm.

"I promised Hunt I would eat. It's the least I could do for what she did for me."

"You will. But I think this is a little too much for you right now. Sit tight. I'll be right back."

Cass was sitting by herself despite the rest of the group being there. She chose that, and the others gave her the space she needed. She swiveled on the bar stool, unable to keep still.

"Friends help ease the pain, girl. Keep 'em close."

Cass blinked at the man. She'd seen him here many times but had never spoken to him. If she remembered correctly, Ellie had called him Big Al. "Sorry?"

"You're worried about your woman. This group... best around. Let 'em help."

Cass didn't know what Big Al knew, but the advice was sound. She could sit here and sulk alone or surround herself with love. She knew what Rebecca would want for her. "Thanks, um, Big Al."

Cass received a curt nod from the man, who then turned back to his... whatever the fuck he was drinking. Cass hopped off the stool and took a moment to breathe before making her way over to the group.

"Is there room for me?"

Blaise scooted over in the large round booth and patted the vinyl with a manicured hand. "Always room for you, mate."

Cass slid into the booth and sighed heavily. "This is freakin' torture." She winced inwardly because of who she was with. Cass was essentially 'preaching to the choir.' "How did you all not fall apart in the first five minutes with everything you've been through."

Eve reached for Lainey's hand. "Love. If you'd asked me no more than five years ago, I would have had a different answer, but that is the real answer."

"And not just the love of a partner," Lainey added. "I never knew how important it was to have friends who would stand with you, hold you up when you can't hold yourself up, and who will fight for you when your fight has left you."

"We all know this firsthand," Blaise provided. "When I was abducted, Ellie hired Grayson to find me. Despite the circumstances, she *knew* something was wrong."

"You already know what Lainey has done for me," Eve said.

"And Eve has pretty much helped everyone," Lainey smiled. "Rebecca has been a strong force behind all of us. She's a cheerleader, a confidant, and a powerhouse in every aspect."

"And you," Ellie continued as she came up and placed a bowl of soup in front of Cass. "You've done wonders for Rebecca. You've made her happy and..."

"And given her jelly legs for the past three or so years," Blaise teased with a sly grin.

Cass snorted with laughter. "I assure you, Rebecca gives as good... no, better than she gets. The woman is sixteen years older than I am, and she runs circles around me." Cass took a spoonful of soup, slurping it carefully. The hot liquid warmed her from the inside out. And it was freakin' delicious. "This soup is awesome, Ellie."

"Thank you. It's Jessie's favorite." Ellie pushed Cass closer to Blaise so she could sit on the edge of the booth. "I'm glad you decided to join us over here."

Cass nodded toward Big Al. "He told me it was where I needed to be."

"Big Al?!" Ellie and Blaise exclaimed at the same time.

"The Old Man is warming up to us," Blaise laughed. "Who can blame him? We are charming."

"She's going to be fine, right?" Cass asked suddenly, her spoon halfway to her mouth.

"Yes, sweets," Ellie answered. "This is Rebecca we're talking about. She is a fighter."

"That's just it." Cass pushed the remainder of her soup away and grabbed a cracker just to have something in her hands. "Right before all this happened, she told me she was tired. Rebecca has been fighting her entire life, El. This was supposed to be her time to relax. To enjoy life. Why did this have to happen? She's been through enough. It should've been me. Why couldn't it have been me?"

"I think we've all felt that way, Cass." Eve reached over and covered Cass's hand in a rare show of affection to anyone other than Lainey. "And every one of us would take Rebecca's place if we could. Unfortunately, the best we can do is be here for anything either of you needs."

Cass was temporarily taken aback by being touched by Eve Sumptor. That feeling quickly subsided as Eve's words sank in. These women loved Rebecca almost as much as Cass did.

"Thank you. All of you. I've been researching how to care for Rebecca when she comes home. I'm not great at any of the things she's going to require, but no one could love her more than me. I may need a little help in all the other areas, though."

"I have the food covered," Ellie smiled.

"I can have fresh flowers for Rebecca's enjoyment," Blaise

announced. "I'm working on a new line of arrangements that focus on serenity and peace."

"They're quite amazing," Ellie offered enthusiastically.

"Well, food and decor have been taken care of. Eve and I can provide specialists, physical therapists, or anything else you or Rebecca may need," Lainey promised.

"I imagine Hunter, Mo, and Patty will provide any medical services," Eve said in her no-nonsense boardroom voice. "Willamena would certainly be available to talk with you, I'm sure."

Cass frowned. "Where is Aunt Wills? I thought she'd be with you."

"She said she had a couple of things to take care of before returning to the hospital," Ellie answered. "She said she wouldn't be long."

"Oh. Okay." Cass checked her watch, then looked at Ellie. "Do you think I can go back to Rebecca now?"

Ellie patted Cass's thigh in a motherly manner. "Yeah, I think you can go. If Hunter has a problem with that, tell her to come talk to me."

Cass grinned. "She's scared of you, so I'll be good." She shimmied out of the booth when Ellie stood. She kissed Ellie on the cheek. "Thank you."

Willamena

"Hello, Gwennie." Willamena sat on the ground and dusted debris off her sister's headstone. "I'm sorry I haven't been to visit lately." She sighed. "This is going to sound odd for a psychiatrist to say, but not seeing your name with dates underneath helps me pretend you're still alive."

Willamena nearly laughed at the ridiculousness of that. Obviously, she knew her sister was dead. In fact, the thirty-fifth anniversary of the deaths of Gwendolyn and Declan Cuinn was fast approaching. That also meant an anniversary of a different sort for Rebecca.

"I guess you know what's happening with our girl. Gwennie, I need you to make sure Becca is okay. As selfish as this sounds, I can't lose another... anyone else. And poor Cass." Willamena smiled involuntarily despite the solemnness of the conversation. "You should see them together, sis. They would put you and Deck to shame." She glanced over at her brother-in-law's headstone. "No offense, Deck."

Willamena leaned back on her hands, toying with the green grass under her fingertips. "You would be so proud of Rebecca, Gwennie. Perhaps a little scared and more than a little unprepared for who she's become. Imagine our little Becca inducing fear..." Willamena's voice trailed off. "Maybe that wouldn't surprise you one bit. She's always been strong-willed. Until... Samantha." She inhaled, blowing the air out slowly. "I know you saved her that night. She should have died. The injuries Rebecca sustained that night could have easily killed her. But she lived. She thrived. Gwennie, she's so happy now. So I'm going to ask that you help her again. The brain tumor is out, but I'm concerned about why they're sedating her. She needs to be okay. *I* need her to be okay." She repeated. "We all do. I'm afraid Cass won't survive without Rebecca. Hell, I'm afraid I won't. Please, Gwennie."

Willamena closed her eyes, letting the gentle breeze caress her face. She imagined it was her sister answering her pleas. A tear rolled down her cheek, and a small smile played at her mouth. *Thank you for listening, Gwennie.* Willamena gave herself a few more minutes with her sister, then rose, brushed herself off, and set off to the hospital to face head-on what they were up against. Whatever it was, she would be there for Rebecca this time.

Chapter Fourteen

"It's been three days, Hunt."

Cass paced the corridor outside of Rebecca's room. Her patience was running out waiting for Rebecca to wake up.

"It's been forty-three hours, Cass," Hunter explained calmly. "Our goal was to begin waking her by forty-eight. I just looked at her charts, and I think we will make that goal."

Only forty-three hours? Cass frowned. It felt like weeks since she heard Rebecca's sultry voice. Months since she had seen Rebecca's incredible eyes. A lifetime since she had felt Rebecca's sexy body next to hers.

"So, the swelling has gone down?"

Hunter nodded. "Yes. And Rebecca's vitals are good. Dr. Lima will be here within the hour to examine Rebecca, and then we can wake Sleeping Beauty up."

"Okay." Cass blew out a breath. "Good. Can I be in there when she wakes up?"

"Sorry, Cass. You'll have to wait out here while all that is happening. But I'll come and get you as soon as I can." Hunter placed a hand on Cass's shoulder. "I'll be right there with her."

"Why is the party outside of Rebecca's room? Did we miss something?" Lainey asked as the group strolled in for their daily visit.

"Hunt says they're going to wake Rebecca up today," Cass announced with a toothy grin.

"Hunter says," Hunter began with her stern doctor's voice. "That

Dr. Lima will be here soon to make that determination. But I do believe today is the day we start weaning her off the sedation medication."

Ellie bumped Hunter's hip as she walked past her to kiss Cass's cheek. "How are you holding up?"

"Excuse me, ma'am," Hunter whined. "*I'm* your wife. Why didn't I get a kiss?"

"Because you're on duty." Ellie stood on her tiptoes and whispered something in Hunter's ear.

Cass laughed. "Dude, your face is beet red! What did our sweet little Ellie say to you?" She waggled her eyebrows at Hunter.

"Sweet little Ellie," Hunter muttered. "If you only knew." Hunter's lopsided grin told the group all they needed to know. "Oh, hey. There's Dr. Lima," she pointed out, taking the attention off herself.

Cass was suddenly nervous. She didn't know why. She'd been waiting for Rebecca to wake up for what seemed like an eternity. So why the jitters now? She looked around for Aunt Wills.

"Where's Aunt Wills? We have to wait for her."

"I'm here, I'm here!" Willamena came rushing up to the group, looking a bit disheveled. "Sorry! My session with Dani and Claire ran a little long. But I'm here now. What's the plan?"

"*My* plan is to examine my patient," Dr. Lima answered. She glanced at the group, recognizing them all. Eve, Lainey, and Blaise were on the hospital board. Ellie was Hunter's wife. Dr. Woodrow was a renowned psychiatrist. Patty and Mo were exceptional nurses whom Dr. Lima would welcome in her OR any day. But this wasn't the OR. "I appreciate how close-knit your friendship is with Rebecca. However, there will be no audience for this portion."

"I've heard that tone before in the boardroom," Eve grinned. "Dr. Lima received experimental surgical equipment using that tone. Anyone up for a coffee while we wait?"

"You all go ahead," Cass answered. "I'm going to stay. *Outside* the room," she clarified for Dr. Lima. "But I don't want to be too far in case Rebecca asks for me."

"Same," Willamena chimed in. There were two chairs in the corridor. Perfect for the two nervous Nellies to keep each other company as they waited.

"Be aware that this process can take hours or days. It depends on Rebecca's response to being taken off the sedation. There's also a chance that Rebecca will wake up feeling confused or agitated. Patients respond differently to this procedure, so we'll have a better idea once Rebecca is fully awake." Once she was done, Dr. Lima nodded and disappeared into Rebecca's room, with Hunter following close behind.

"She said a lot without saying anything at all," Ellie said with a frown. "Perhaps we should convene at the diner while we wait." Obviously, that was directed at everyone except Cass and Aunt Wills, as Ellie knew they weren't going anywhere for the foreseeable. "Call us with any news?"

Cass smiled up at Ellie from her seat. "Will do, buckaroo!" She waved enthusiastically at the others.

"You're nervous," Willamena stated. "Overcompensating with exaggerated excitement."

"Are you shrinking me, Aunt Wills?"

Willamena glanced at Cass. "I am. I'm sorry. *I'm* nervous, and I don't know why."

Cass turned in her seat to face Aunt Wills. "You feel it, too? I have, like, this weird feeling in my tummy."

"It's fear of the unknown. The tumor may be gone, but we still have to wait for the biopsy results. Plus, we both know Rebecca doesn't like being uncomfortable. She's not going to be a good patient," Willamena laughed. Neither of them spoke of the warnings Dr. Lima gave. It was enough to hear it once.

"True. But that's okay. She can yell, cuss, whip me, or do whatever she needs to do. I can take it as long as she's with me and recovering."

Willamena shook her head, hiding a smile. Cass was so in love with Rebecca that it made Willamena's heart swell with pride. This is what she wanted for her niece all along. Someone who loved her enough to endure her own discomfort to make Rebecca happy.

"We don't need to talk about Mistress whipping you," Willamena teased, knowing it would embarrass Cass.

"I... Did I really say that?" Willamena nodded, and Cass buried her head in her hands. "Sorry."

"It's okay," Willamena chuckled. "I've come to terms with who my niece is and who you are to her."

"Have you? Before Rebecca, I thought this whole..." Cass looked around and lowered her voice. "*BDSM* thing was bullshit. I couldn't imagine being submissive to someone or getting some kind of pleasure from pain. I certainly didn't understand how someone could like hurting another person for the sake of sex. But even when Rebecca is in hyper-Mistress mode, she's conscious of how she's treating me. I've never felt more cared for ...or more in control than when I give it up to her." Cass winced. "TMI?"

Willamena patted Cass's thigh. "You can't imagine the things I've heard as a psychiatrist. I think with Rebecca's past experience, she wanted to change the world she'd been thrust into. I believe the lifestyle is invigorating for her, but the way she was introduced to it... well, you know what happened there. She had to make it her own, and I think it helped more than just herself."

"It definitely helped me." Another wince. "What I mean is, I've learned to be more open and accepting. Even assertive. I don't automatically scoff at things I don't understand, you know? But I'm still not sure *BDSM* is the correct term for what Mistress offers. She's not a sadist. She doesn't want to see me in pain."

Well. Cass didn't think waiting for the docs to wake Rebecca would include a session with Dr. Woodrow. But talking kept Cass's mind busy enough to pass the time without too much restlessness.

"I wouldn't consider you a masochist either, Cass. Perhaps labeling what Mistress does isn't necessary. You both know what you need and want from each other. That's all that matters."

Cass smiled. "Yeah. We can keep the BD part, though."

"I am reducing the sedation," Dr. Lima announced as though she was giving a seminar. "Heart rate and vitals will be monitored regularly. We'll perform simple cues to gauge her response as the medication wears off."

Hunter remained quiet. She had worked with Dr. Lima before and knew the instructions were not for Hunter's benefit but a running commentary on Lima's next steps. In her silence, however, Hunter began thinking of all of the side effects this medically induced coma could produce. Her hope was that Rebecca hadn't been under long enough to suffer the worst of those side effects.

"Dr. Vale?"

Hunter blinked, focusing on Dr. Lima. "Yes?"

"I asked if your friends were going to wait out in the corridor the entire time."

Hunter smiled. "Probably. Rebecca is very much loved."

"By you as well, I see."

Hunter nodded. "Yes. We met at one of the lowest points of her life. I was there at the happiest point of her life. I'll continue to be there for Rebecca and Cass. That's why I brought you in. I trust your work."

"The side effects are not inevitable, Dr. Vale," Dr. Lima said, seemingly having read Hunter's earlier concerns. "However, you should prepare for the worst scenario. Rebecca is healthy, fit, and relatively young. Those factors rule in her favor."

Hunter glanced over at Rebecca, chuckling. "She'll love you for saying she's young. Relatively or not." She placed a hand on Rebecca's foot, squeezing gently. "Rebecca is strong. This is nothing compared to what she's survived before. I'll follow Cass's positivity vibe she has going."

"Very well. I'll be back in an hour to check on Rebecca. I've left instructions with the nursing staff to page me immediately if there are changes before I return."

�⚭

"If you don't take it easy, you'll end up in a bed next to Rebecca."

Cass dropped from the bar she was hanging from. It had been five hours since Dr. Lima reduced Rebecca's meds, and Rebecca still wasn't awake. Cass's restlessness got the better of her, and Hunter sent her to the physical therapy ward to work off some of that energy.

"What I wouldn't give to be in bed next to Rebecca," Cass panted, taking the offered towel from Ellie. "Thanks. Is she awake?"

"Hunter is in with her now." Ellie handed Cass a bottle of water. "She said Rebecca is coming around, so I came to get you from torturing yourself."

"Torture is not being with Becca." Cass sniffed her underarms. "Should I take a shower?"

Ellie sucked in her lips to keep from laughing. "I'm sure Rebecca will love seeing you whether you're stinky or not."

Cass's eyes shot to Ellie in shock. Ellie's cute little mischievous smile did more to calm Cass's nerves than the workout she just did.

"You're mean. But probably right," Cass grinned. "Is Aunt Wills here? I know she stepped out to get food earlier."

"Mmhmm. She got back about an hour ago."

"Shit, I've been in here that long?" Cass glanced at her watch. "That explains why my arms are like jelly."

"You know, you could have meditated with me. That probably would have been less stressful on your body."

"Nah, the physicality of weightlifting really helps my concentration. I mean, no offense to your yoga stuff. Rebecca gets me to do that occasionally, but I guess I haven't mastered how to do it. I can't get my brain to stop thinking stupid things while I'm trying to relax."

Ellie smiled. "People don't realize how difficult meditating is. Some believe it's just sitting there, maybe chanting here and there. But it is something you have to practice. You should keep at it with Rebecca. You'd be surprised how it can change your life."

Cass wrapped a sweaty arm around Ellie, chuckling when Ellie let out a soft 'ew.' "I will keep that in mind. I do know that yoga and meditation certainly help Rebecca in many different aspects of our lives together."

"Oh, I know. Hunter says the same about me," Ellie winked. "Now, let's go see your girl."

Chapter Fifteen

"Patient is responding to stimulation," Dr. Lima announced. "The ventilator has already been adjusted, and the patient is maintaining steady breaths without assistance."

"She's waking up," Hunter said when Rebecca stirred. She pushed past Dr. Lima, forgetting about protocol, and took Rebecca's hand. "Becca?"

"Dr. Vale..."

Hunter glanced at Dr. Lima with a raised brow. "You're a brilliant doctor, Alita, but this is one of my best friends. I'd rather she come out of the MIC and see a friendly face than someone treating this like an educational seminar. I'm sorry."

Alita frowned. "As am I if you thought that's what I was doing." She stood back and allowed Hunter to continue coaxing Rebecca awake.

Rebecca shifted, moaning softly when her body ached in return. Her brain was foggy, trying to remember where she was and how she got there.

"Rebecca?"

The muffled voice barely broke through the fog. Rebecca moaned again, trying to answer. Her mouth felt like it was filled with cotton, and her throat... hurt like hell. She lifted a hand to her mouth, and a tube met her fingertips. Rebecca's eyes popped open, and she began clawing at the tube.

"Hey, hey. It's okay." Hunter gently pulled Rebecca's hands away from the apparatus. "It was helping you breathe while you slept."

Hunter looked into Rebecca's wild, scared eyes. "We can take it out. Doctor?"

Dr. Lima walked to the opposite side of Rebecca's bed. She pressed a button that lifted Rebecca into an upright position. "Rebecca, I'm Dr. Lima. This will be a little uncomfortable for you, but we'll try to make it as smooth as possible."

Hunter gave Alita a look. That was the least clinical she'd ever seen Dr. Lima. "Just try to relax," she said to Rebecca. "First, we're going to suction out any debris that may be present." Dr. Lima performed that task while Hunter tried to keep Rebecca calm. When she got the nod from Alita, Hunter returned her focus to Rebecca. "Now, I want you to take a deep breath. As you exhale, Dr. Lima will extract the tube. Deep breath in."

Rebecca held vibrant blue eyes as she inhaled. When the order was given, she exhaled, wincing when there was a hiss before Dr. Lima pulled the tube out. Rebecca coughed, her face scrunching up with disgust.

"It's okay. That's just mucus that needs to be expelled." Hunter took the suction device and helped Rebecca clear her airway. "Your throat may be sore for a few days." She shifted so Dr. Lima could place a nasal cannula on Rebecca. "This is just supplemental oxygen to help you. Are you okay?"

Rebecca frowned but nodded.

Considering the side effects of an MIC, Hunter began her initial assessment of Rebecca's cognizance while Dr. Lima poured a cup of water from the pitcher next to Rebecca's bed. "Do you know your name?"

Rebecca cleared her throat. "Rebecca."

Good start, Hunter thought. "Do you know why you're here?"

Rebecca closed her eyes and frowned. When she opened them again, they were full of fear. "Beaten."

Hunter's breath caught in her throat. *No.* "Rebecca, do you know who I am?" She was met with a confused look.

"Here." Dr. Lima stepped in. She handed Rebecca the cup, placing the straw close to Rebecca's lips. "Take small sips to soothe your throat." Alita glanced up at a shell-shocked Hunter before returning her attention to her patient. "Better?" Rebecca nodded, tears pooling in her eyes. "Can you tell me what year it is?"

A tear rolled down Rebecca's cheek. She concentrated for a moment before looking at Dr. Lima. "2001. Is my aunt here? Has anyone called her? I want to see my aunt."

Hunter's heart sank to her feet. "I-I'll go find out." She nodded at Dr. Lima and smiled warmly at Rebecca.

Hunter took a moment, holding back her own tears, before breaking the news to Cass and the others. First, she had to figure out how to get Aunt Wills in the room and warn her without blurting out the situation in front of Cass. She needed to ease Cass into the issue. Hunter stuck her head out, a smile plastered on her face.

"Aunt Wills? She's asking for you."

Willamena looked up, a huge smile across her face. Until she saw the strain in Hunter's. *Something is wrong.* She grinned at Cass, who was getting up to go in the room, too. "She probably wants me to get her all prettied up for you," she told Cass, patting her shoulder. "Give me a minute with her?"

It took considerable strength to agree, but Cass nodded. "Sure, of course."

Cass was watching them too closely for Hunter to say anything to Willamena. Hopefully, Aunt Wills would forgive her for this. However, Hunter's focus was Cass. This was going to devastate her.

"How's she doing?" Cass stuffed her hands in her pockets, anxious to go in and see Rebecca.

"There's, um..." Hunter found Ellie's eyes, searching for strength to say the words. As always, Ellie knew something was wrong and fell in beside Cass for support. Hunter saw the others step forward as well. "There's been a development." *Coward.*

"A development," Cass repeated. "What does that mean?"

"It means... Cass, Rebecca is experiencing some disorientation and agitation. Both are common when waking up from a coma." *Stop stalling, Hunter!*

"Okay. Should I go in there and help calm her down? I know all of the techniques — clean ones — Rebecca uses when she's upset." Cass grinned, but it was tremulous. She could feel in her bones that something more was happening here than simple side effects. Whatever it was, Cass would fix it. She'd do anything for Rebecca.

Hunter stepped in front of Cass when she moved towards Rebecca's door. "She's confused about what year it is, Cass."

Cass heard Ellie gasp softly beside her but couldn't understand why that was such a big deal. "And? Come on, Hunt. Haven't you ever woken up from a deep sleep and didn't know where or when you were?"

Hunter sighed. Cass needed to hear the words. Hunter just wished she had the right ones to say. "Rebecca... thinks it's 2001 and that she's here because of Samantha."

Cass heard the words coming from Hunter's mouth. She heard the shocked murmurs from the friends that surrounded her. Still, she wasn't comprehending the meaning of those words. She let out a small laugh that held no joy.

"That... that doesn't make sense. What are you talking about?"

"It's early, yet, but Rebecca seems to be suffering from retrograde amnesia," Hunter explained gently. God, the look on Cass's face killed her. The heartbreak on the faces of the others heightened the emotion of the situation. "Her memory seems to be beginning at the time she woke up in the hospital after Samantha nearly killed her."

Cass looked around. Every face looking back at her held sorrow and pity. "But that was years ago. We met..." She shook her head. The ramifications of what Hunter was telling her were too catastrophic for Cass to accept.

"Cass..."

"Wait. Just..." Cass held a hand up, cutting Hunter off. "Y-you're telling me that the love of my life, my *wife*, d-doesn't know who I am?"

"I'm sorry." Hunter knew the words weren't enough, but at the moment, they were all she had.

"You're sor..." Cass scoffed and looked at the others with a sardonic smile. "She's sorry." Before she knew what she was doing, Cass reared back and punched Hunter.

"Hey, my sweet girl. How are you feeling?"

Willamena made a bee-line to Rebecca's side, taking her hand. She had noticed Dr. Lima's curious look but didn't take the time to analyze it. Willamena's first priority was Rebecca.

"I-I don't know, Aunt Wills. Everything feels... weird."

"Are you in pain?" Rebecca shook her head but didn't seem convinced by her non-verbal answer. Dr. Woodrow looked back at the other doctor in the room.

Dr. Lima stepped up, dropping her voice to speak directly to Willamena. "Rebecca seems to be suffering from retrograde amnesia following waking up from the MIC."

"*Amnesia?*" Willamena's voice wavered as she whispered the word. *That explained Hunter's look,* she thought solemnly. She turned back to her niece, pushing messy hair away from her face. "Can you tell me what the last thing you remember is?"

Rebecca began to cry. "I didn't want you to know. I didn't want you to be disappointed in me." She squeezed Aunt Wills's hand. "I wasn't strong enough to get away from her. I'm sorry, Aunt Wills."

"Oh, my sweet girl." Willamena gratefully accepted a tissue from Dr. Lima when it appeared seemingly out of nowhere and wiped at her own tears. She used a second tissue to dry Rebecca's cheeks. "I've never been disappointed in you. That vile woman is gone now, and you never have to worry about her again. In fact..."

Rebecca winced, and she pressed her fingertips to her temple. She moaned softly as another wave of pain hit her. The pain came whenever she thought about why she was here in the hospital. Something wasn't right, but she couldn't pin down what it was that was bothering her. Rebecca remembered Samantha's fists and feet hitting her. She could remember the pain and utter shock. She could remember barely being able to move, see, or breathe. Yet, as she lay here, the pain she thought she should have wasn't there.

Rebecca also knew Samantha was dead. Detective Chi said as much when Rebecca had called him for help. And judging by Aunt Wills's statement, the news of Samantha's death was out. So, where was the sadness or guilt? Shouldn't she feel *something* after letting Samantha just... die? Was this what it meant to be in shock?

"Dr. Lima?" Willamena called out when Rebecca groaned again.

Dr. Lima placed two fingers on Rebecca's wrist, timing the pulse she felt there. "Her heart rate is elevated from the stress." She turned slightly, catching Willamena's attention. "I know it's tempting to fill all the gaps in Rebecca's memory. However, I suggest taking it slow while she's recovering. Excessive stress can negatively affect any progress Rebecca makes during recovery."

"I'm still here," Rebecca muttered as she laid her head back on her pillow and closed her eyes. She was so tired, she just wanted to sleep. But being unable to hear what the doctor was telling her aunt was annoying Rebecca. It intensified the feeling that something was terribly wrong.

Aunt Wills chuckled. "Okay, my ornery girl. We're just discussing how to keep your stress levels down."

"Talking about me like I'm not here is not the way." Rebecca's eyes were still closed, her brows furrowed. Her mind was on a continuous loop of punches and kicks and death. When she tried thinking about something else — *anything* else — there was... nothing. Why did that make her heart hurt?

"We will need to sedate you if you remain agitated, Rebecca," Dr. Lima warned. "I'd rather not do that so soon after taking you off..."

A loud commotion sounded from the corridor, causing all three women to jump.

"What on earth?" Willamena exclaimed. "I'll go check..." Rebecca grabbed Aunt Wills's hand, a look of fear and confusion etched on her beautiful face. "Oh, Becca. It's okay. Nothing can hurt you now. I promise I'll be right back."

She hurried to the door. Having been preoccupied with Rebecca's memory loss, Willamena didn't stop to think about how this would affect Cass. *Oh no.*

When Cass's fist met Hunter's jaw, Mo jumped into action and wrapped her strong arms around Cass's waist. "Cass, stop!"

"You told me she would be okay!" Cass fought against Mo's hold, and Eve and Patty stepped in to hold onto Cass's arms to keep her from striking out again. "You promised me you'd bring her back to me!"

Lainey stepped between Hunter and Cass when Cass lunged again. She pressed a hand against Cass's chest.

"Cass, please. Don't do this."

"She lied to me!" Cass cried. "She took my wife away from me!"

Four women struggled to control a distraught Cass as she continued to yell and charge at Hunter, who merely stood there and took it. She wouldn't fight back when she knew Cass was only acting out of fear and sorrow. Pleas for Cass to calm down fell on deaf ears, and Hunter braced herself for another strike.

"Cassidy!"

Cass immediately stopped, looking around for Rebecca, as she was the only one who dared to call her that name. But she was met with an angry yet sympathetic Ellie.

Ellie stood in front of Cass, fists clenched at her sides. "I know you're devastated. I can't even begin to imagine how confusing and scary this is for you. But I will *not* allow you to keep coming after my wife!"

"It's okay, El." Hunter laid a hand on Ellie's shoulder, feeling the tension. She wanted to get Ellie out of harm's way if Cass lost control again, but Ellie stood firm.

"No, it's not. We are all shocked by the news, Cass, and we will stand by you every step of the way. But if you hit my wife again..." Ellie took a breath before continuing. She had been beyond shocked when Cass struck Hunter the first time. She wouldn't be silent... or frozen if it happened again. "This is not Hunter's fault."

Cass looked down at Ellie with anguish. "Then whose is it?"

"No one's," Willamena answered from the door. She came out into the hallway, nodding at the others to let Cass go. "Sometimes these things happen, Cass. No rhyme, no reason. Just a tragic bit of ill fortune that we must overcome. Together."

Willamena examined Hunter's bleeding lip. "Why don't you go take care of that," she said to Ellie. "I'll stay here with Cass."

Ellie nodded, wrapping her arm around Hunter. She shot a glance at

Cass as she walked by her. The others silently left as well, each finding the situation tragic and unimaginable.

Cass threw up her hands, gesturing toward Hunter. "I didn't mean..."

"She knows. I'm sure she understands where that came from."

"Ellie doesn't," Cass responded miserably. "Oh god." Cass slumped into the chair and buried her face in her hands. "I *hit* Hunter. My best friend. How the fuck could I do that?" Tears streamed down Cass's cheeks. "Rebecca would be so disappointed in me. I'm just like..."

"Don't even finish that sentence," Willamena ordered. "Your remorse shows you're nothing like that bitch." She gave Cass a defiant look when Cass peeked at her through her fingers. "I said what I said. Now, let's focus on what's important. Rebecca."

The tears kept coming. "It's true, isn't it? She doesn't remember?"

"I'm afraid so, Cass."

"H-how long will it last?"

Willamena sighed. "I wish I could give you definitive answers, but unfortunately, there's no way to determine that. You could walk in there right now and cause her to remember everything just by seeing you." She took Cass's hand. "Or, it could be hours, even days."

"But she will remember?"

Willamena was reluctant to give Cass too much hope in the early stages. On the flip side, she didn't want to *discourage* Cass too much, sending her into a depression.

"I believe so. Are you ready to go in and see her?"

Cass shook her head, eyes wide with fear. "I-I can't. If I walk in there and Becca looks at me like a stranger, it would kill me, Aunt Wills."

"Listen to me, Cass. Whether Rebecca remembers you or not at the moment, she *needs* you - your strength, your support, and most of all, your love. I know it will be so hard for you to keep the faith if she doesn't remember right away, but you have to try. *I'm* asking you, Cass, as Rebecca's aunt, please don't give up on her."

"I could never give up on her, Aunt Wills. But I may need some help with the faith part."

Willamena stood and held her hand out. "That's where the rest of our family comes in to help us both," she said when Cass took her hand. Aunt Wills pulled Cass up and into a hug.

"I fucked that up pretty good," Cass muttered sadly.

"Nonsense. We're all allowed to have moments. I think Ellie knows that better than anyone. We forgive and move on." Willamena stepped back, giving Cass a small smile. "However, you will have to grovel a little. Hunter will let it go easily enough, but Ellie will need a little more persuading."

Cass considered what she would do if the roles were reversed, and Ellie took a swing at Rebecca. Then, because that scenario was too far-fetched, she shook it off. "I totally get it. I'm holding a grudge against a dead woman I didn't even know." Cass closed her eyes and took a deep breath. "I'll fix it," she vowed.

"I know you will. Now, are you ready to go in?"

Cass would never be ready to face the love of her life and see those silver eyes staring back at her like a stranger. But Cass had often told Rebecca that she'd do anything for her.

"I'm ready."

Chapter Sixteen

Rebecca side-eyed Dr. Lima, who said nothing as she checked Rebecca's vitals. When Dr. Lima hummed and wrote notes in Rebecca's chart, Rebecca sighed.

"Is 'hmm' a good thing or a bad thing?"

Dr. Lima briefly looked up from the chart. "Neither. It's merely a sound."

"Ah. Thanks for the update," Rebecca responded with a slight attitude. She already had a headache and felt dirty, and if she didn't get a brush — hair and tooth — soon, things would get ugly real fast.

The stoic doctor's lips twitched ever so slightly. "Your vitals look good, Rebecca. We need to keep your stress levels down, and those headaches you're getting will start to fade."

"I could use a shower, and I want to brush my teeth. *That* would keep my stress down considerably."

"You'll be able to shower with assistance. However, I encourage you not to wash your hair until after the sutures..." Dr. Lima clearly saw the look of defiance on Rebecca's face. "Baby shampoo. Have whoever is assisting you wash *around* the incision. I realize this is frustrating, but you certainly don't want complications."

"Fine." Rebecca sighed again. "Sorry, I don't mean to be rude. I don't like being... dirty." She frowned, imagining someone in her life making a joke out of that, but couldn't picture who. Definitely not Samantha. Aunt Wills?

"I'm a surgeon who washes her hands hundreds of times da*ily*. I understand." Dr. Lima offered Rebecca a small, uncomfortable smile.

Sensing the doctor's discomfort with small talk, Rebecca changed the subject. Although she didn't want to discuss it, she needed to know.

"What's the extent of the damage?" She asked. "I don't feel as broken as I should with everything Samantha did. Am I on some pain medication?"

Dr. Lima's brows knitted together in confusion. "I'm sorry, I don't..."

"Knock, knock."

Aunt Wills popped her head around the door, and Rebecca smiled. That smile quickly faded into embarrassment when she saw the incredibly sexy woman with her. Rebecca pushed her greasy hair out of her face and then contemplated covering her face with it. *I look like an ogre, and Aunt Wills brings the sexiest woman I've ever seen in here.*

"You have a visitor," Aunt Wills stated unnecessarily.

Cass's heart beat painfully in her chest. God, Rebecca looked stunning. Of course, Rebecca was pale and a bit mussed after the surgery and coma. Even so, to Cass, no one could match Rebecca's beauty. And she was awake. Cass was grateful for that despite... everything else.

"H-hey, Becca."

Rebecca's brows furrowed. *Becca? Do we know each other?* "Hi. A-are you another doctor?" Rebecca shyly tucked her hair behind her ear, unable to look the handsome woman in the eye.

The pain of those words caused Cass's stomach to churn. "No. I'm, uh..."

What could she say? Aunt Wills had warned her that too much information could cause Rebecca stress. That's the last thing Cass wanted to do, so she looked to Aunt Wills for help.

Willamena's heart broke for Cass. Oh, she could see Cass trying to keep it together, but Willamena knew how those bi-colored eyes lit up when Rebecca was around. Right now, they were dull and sad.

"Rebecca, this is Cass. Do you remember her?"

"Cass." Rebecca's eyes traveled up Cass's body. *I'd like to get to know her.* "I'm sorry, I don't..."

"It's fine," Cass said quickly before Aunt Wills could say more. She could have never prepared herself for hearing Rebecca call her 'Cass.' It sounded... wrong. "I, uh, wanted to come see you and make sure you were okay. I'm just going to take off and let you rest." She turned to Aunt Wills, shaking her head slightly. "I'll call you later, Aunt Wills."

Cass's overwhelming need to touch Rebecca had her touching Rebecca's blanket-covered foot briefly before she rushed to the door. She had to get out of there before she lost it in front of Rebecca. She was pretty sure if she started sobbing right there in the hospital room, Rebecca would think she was crazy, not to mention that it would cause Rebecca unneeded stress.

"Aunt Wills? She calls you Aunt Wills? Who is she? Why did she look so sad? What is going on, Aunt Wills?"

Dr. Lima cleared her throat, and Willamena sighed. Rebecca was getting worked up. That certainly wasn't Willamena's intention, but obviously, bringing Cass in here so soon was a mistake for both Cass and Rebecca.

"I know you have questions, Rebecca, but..."

"No buts. I have this... sick feeling in my stomach." *It's more like my heart,* Rebecca thought silently. "That I'm missing something important."

Willamena saw the same dull sadness in Rebecca's eyes that she saw in Cass's. *Their souls miss each other.* It was unorthodox for a psychiatrist to believe, but Willamena did nonetheless. She glanced at Dr. Lima and received a slight nod. Willamena knew she'd have to tread carefully, so she would tell Rebecca the bare minimum until she thought Rebecca could handle more.

"Okay, sweet girl. We're going to make a deal, and I don't want you to argue with me. We will discuss everything you need to know, but we do it my way. You have to promise you won't jeopardize your recovery by getting upset if I do what I think is best for you. That includes not overwhelming you with an abundance of information all at once. Our first priority is your health. Can you agree to that?"

Rebecca stared into Aunt Wills's kind eyes. She saw the compassion she always saw there. But there was something else. Sadness? Fear? A mixture of both?

"I'll do my best." Rebecca held her hand up to stop Aunt Wills's protests. "That's all I can promise, Aunt Wills."

Willamena nodded, pulling a chair up beside Rebecca's bed.

"I'm going to excuse myself," Dr. Lima announced, reminding them she was there. "Rebecca has expressed the desire to take care of her hygiene needs. Are you able to assist her, Dr. Woodrow, or shall I call in an orderly to help?"

Willamena knew Rebecca wouldn't want a stranger helping her. "I can do it. Thank you, Dr. Lima."

"Rebecca, to address your previous question before I leave, I want to keep you overnight to monitor your progress. If all goes well, we will review your at-home care procedures and medications before discharging you." With a curt nod, Dr. Lima left the room.

"She's... direct," Rebecca said after a minute.

"Yes, she is. But she's also very good at what she does."

Rebecca lifted her arm — the one she could remember being limp at her side when Samantha.... "I'd say so. My arm doesn't even hurt. Whatever these meds are, they're working. I have a headache, but the rest of me feels... fine."

Willamena took Rebecca's hand, clasping it between both of hers. "Rebecca, you're not here because of Samantha." Ugh, it made her sick to her stomach saying that name. She wished with every ounce of her being that Rebecca had forgotten this part of her life and not the part when she was finally happy.

Rebecca's face was the picture of confusion. "I don't understand."

"I know." Willamena rubbed the back of Rebecca's hand as she did when she was little and had nightmares about her parents' death. "I've been trying to think of an easy way of saying this, but nothing about this is easy."

"Aunt Wills, please." Rebecca hated this feeling- the unknown. She'd spent years with Samantha fearing the unknown, and she didn't want to live that way any longer.

Willamena closed her eyes briefly, asking Gwennie for the right words. Oh, her sister was good at things like this. But, even being a psychiatrist, when it came to her family, Willamena faltered with hard news.

"You're here because you had a tumor. A brain tumor," Willamena clarified. "You had surgery to remove it, and..."

None of this made sense to Rebecca, and Aunt Wills's stalling was not helping. "And?"

"There's been a complication with your memory, Rebecca. You have amnesia."

Pain seared through Rebecca's head, and she ripped her hand away from Willamena, pressing the heels of both hands to her temples. She whimpered as the pain continued.

Willamena stood abruptly, reaching for the call button.

"Don't!" Rebecca ordered. "Just give me a minute." She breathed in, holding it for ten seconds. She could hear a calming voice in her head counting to ten, but she didn't know whose voice it was. For some unknown reason, that bothered Rebecca. "Amnesia," she repeated when the pain became bearable.

"Yes." Willamena still had the call button in her hand, her thumb poised to push it if Rebecca's pain came back. "That's enough information for now..."

"Cass?" Rebecca asked softly. "I should know her?" Tears pooled in Rebecca's eyes when Cass's face popped into her memory.

Willamena hesitated. "Yes."

This time the pain wasn't in Rebecca's head. Her heart felt... empty. No, that wasn't the word. Lost.

"How long?"

Willamena put the call button back in its place. "How long?"

"How much time am I missing?"

"It's 2023, Rebecca." The dam burst, and Willamena held Rebecca as she wept quietly.

<hr>

"I can do this by myself."

"No, you can't. Rebecca, you had brain surgery. This is one of those times when you must trust that I'm doing what's best for you. Besides, I've seen you naked before, so you don't need to be shy."

Rebecca rolled her eyes. "Fine. Can I at least brush my teeth by myself?"

"If you behave." Willamena was gracious enough to turn her back while Rebecca got undressed, affording Rebecca a modicum of privacy. "Do you want a shower cap?"

"No. I need to wash my hair. Dr. Lima said it'd be fine if you avoided the stitches."

Willamena picked up a bottle of baby shampoo that a nurse must've brought in while Rebecca ate her dinner. "I'm guessing this is what I'm supposed to use." Her eyes raised to the mirror in front of her, and she caught a glimpse of Rebecca's bare back in the mirror, gasping in horror. Forgetting all about privacy, Willamena whirled around. "Is that what Samantha did to you?"

Rebecca turned her head, looking past Willamena in the mirror. She saw the scars and winced when she realized she must not have told her aunt everything.

"Rebecca, why? Why didn't you tell me how bad it was?"

Rebecca crossed her arms across her bare chest. She felt vulnerable enough being naked. Talking about the scars that marred her back only heightened that feeling.

"How?" She bowed her head, unable to look Aunt Wills in the eye. "How was I supposed to tell you about the mess I got myself into? I was ashamed, Aunt Wills. Ashamed that I fell for her bullshit. And ashamed that I was too weak to leave."

"You weren't weak, Rebecca. You were conditioned and manipulated." Willamena brushed past Rebecca to turn on the shower. She remembered how these conversations had gone in the past. The more Rebecca was pushed to discuss this subject, the less she did. The last thing Willamena wanted to do was pressure Rebecca, causing more stress. "What matters now is that it's over."

Rebecca frowned. It wasn't like Aunt Wills — or Dr. Woodrow — to give up so easily. Of course, she was clever in trying to coerce information out of Rebecca, always respecting Rebecca's boundaries. But she never just... quit.

"That's it? No asking the same question fifteen different ways?"

Willamena shook her head. "I told you, Rebecca. This happened to you more than two decades ago. I've been your therapist for just as long. This amnesia... I don't think it will last forever. And if you don't have to go through it all again, I'd be more than happy to spare you that pain.

However, I have to admit finding out you didn't tell me about the scars is gnawing at me."

"I'm sorry. I'm sure I had a good reason not to." Rebecca stepped into the shower, appreciating the hot spray of the water cascading off her body. "It feels like I haven't showered in years," she said with a satisfied sigh. Just then, Rebecca's stomach tightened as though *it* remembered something her mind couldn't. She shivered with a strange feeling of... pleasure.

"Rebecca? Are you okay?"

"Hmm? Oh, um, y-yes. Sorry." Rebecca took the soap from Aunt Wills. This part she could surely do herself. Her eyebrows furrowed when the loofah snagged on something at her belly. When she looked down, her frown deepened. *A belly ring? When did I get that?* Something else caught Rebecca's eye a little lower, and she ran her finger over the small tattoo. She shook her head. It was too weird not having any recollection of getting these things on her body. Maybe when she got home, she could concentrate more on all the pieces missing in her memory.

"Do you think I'll be able to go home tomorrow?" Rebecca stopped washing and frowned. "Where is home?"

Oh boy. "You... live with Cass."

"I—" Rebecca stared at Aunt Wills and shook her head. "Aunt Wills, I can't put this burden on a woman I can't remember."

"Cass would gladly take that burden, Rebecca. She would do anything for you." *She loves you deeply.*

Again, tears filled Rebecca's eyes. What was it about this Cass that made Rebecca feel so emotional? Obviously, if Rebecca lived with her, they were serious. But how serious? How much could Rebecca give of herself after Samantha? Especially when she didn't feel worthy enough for someone like Cass. Because even if Rebecca didn't remember her, she knew in her soul Cass was special.

"That may be true, but I just can't do that to her. Or to myself. I already feel bad enough that I don't remember her. But I don't know if I can move to New York with you either."

Willamena was still thinking about Rebecca's admission of guilt about not remembering Cass that she almost missed that last part. "Oh, sweet girl, I live here now. Can we talk about why you feel bad about Cass?"

"Um, no. I want to talk about why you live here. Since when? You always said New York was your home."

"And it was. Until it wasn't."

"Did you do it because of... me?"

"Of course I did. You're my family. However, to ease your mind, I only moved here a few years ago. Now sit here so I can wash your hair." Willamena scooted a shower chair closer to Rebecca, chuckling at the face Rebecca made at it. "Stop being so stubborn. If you want me to wash your hair, you have to sit."

"I'm not an invalid."

"We're not going to argue about what you can and can't do, Rebecca."

Rebecca rolled her eyes, mumbling something about her aunt being mean. But she sat and allowed herself to appreciate her aunt's help, especially when her headache dissipated as Aunt Wills massaged the shampoo in her hair.

"Can I stay with you, Aunt Wills?"

Willamena paused her careful scrubbing. "If that's what you want, yes." Cass would be devastated, but Willamena hoped she would understand Rebecca's dilemma. With any luck, Rebecca would regain her memory before too much damage was done to Cass's heart.

Chapter Seventeen

Cass walked into the dimly lit bar, scrunching her nose up at the depressing odor wafting through the air. She hadn't been here in years but didn't remember it being this... dreary. Perhaps it was just her own dismal attitude being thrown back at her. Whatever the case, it was the perfect atmosphere for Cass.

"Shit! Look who the cat dragged in!" The bartender slapped the bar with her towel, smiling like a lunatic.

Cass slid onto a barstool. "Mickey." Cass couldn't believe Mickey was still here behind the bar. Back in the day, all Mick would talk about was opening her own bar and getting out from under Nadia, the bar's owner. Of course, back then, being under Nadia wasn't the worst thing in the world. That was way before Cass knew the wonders of Rebecca Cuinn.

Mickey grabbed a glass and cheap whiskey. "Your face looks like you need a stiff drink or two. If you're gonna be drinkin' your sorrows away, best to go with the cheap stuff."

Cass clenched her jaws. "Still playing therapist, eh, Mick? I can't imagine that's gotten better over the years."

Mickey shrugged. "Never know. You spend years behind a bar getting the ladies drunk, and you hear all the drama."

You probably caused most of the drama by giving the pretty ladies free drinks. "Not here for the cheap stuff," Cass muttered.

"'Kay. What can I get ya?"

Cass frowned. It was on the tip of her tongue to say a shot of Fireball, but she stopped short. It reminded her of the first day she met

Rebecca. God, her wife would be so disappointed in Cass if she could see her now. Even so, Cass couldn't go home to an empty house and couldn't go back to the hospital to the woman she loved because the confusion on Rebecca's face was too difficult to bear. So, she was here.

"Club soda."

Mickey scoffed. "Seriously? You used to laugh at the dipshits that came in here and ordered a pussy drink."

Cass merely raised a brow, staring at Mickey until she got her club soda. Thankfully, Cass's poor attitude kept her from having to engage in small talk with Mickey. The last thing she wanted to do was talk about the fucking past.

"Well, well, look who's back. If it isn't Cassanova." The good-looking brunette sauntered to the bar, too close for Cass's comfort. "I never thought I'd see you again after hearing you got married. Guess the honeymoon is over."

Cass was wrong. *This* was the last thing she wanted. "You don't know what you're talking about, Nadia. I just want to be left alone."

Nadia nodded at Mickey, and the bartender left them alone. She perched herself on a stool next to Cass. "You look upset. Most people end up alone in a bar in the middle of the day because things are bad. Girl trouble?"

Nadia tilted her head in question, but it didn't affect Cass as when Rebecca did it. Cass sipped her club soda, scooting away from Nadia to the opposite edge of her stool, putting one foot on the floor as though she would have to make a break for it at any given moment.

"No," Cass said simply.

"Come on, Cass. We were friends once."

Nadia touched Cass's arm, and Cass jerked away like she'd been burned. "Is that what we were?" Cass thought back to the handful of times she and Nadia were together. There wasn't much talking. Perhaps that's why they didn't last very long. Neither were interested in getting to know just how compatible they really were.

"It certainly wasn't for you."

Cass took another sip, wishing she could feel the burn of whiskey sliding down her throat. "Sorry."

"Don't be. You were always upfront with what you were looking for. I wasn't delusional enough to think we could be more. In fact, I was surprised when I heard you had gotten married. I didn't think that was your thing. Rebecca, right?"

Cass's chest tightened at the mention of Rebecca's name. "Yes. And it wasn't my thing until I met Rebecca. Now, I can't imagine my life without her."

"Then why do you look like you want to cry?" When Cass didn't answer, Nadia continued. "I hear it helps to talk."

The realization of the truth of that statement hit Cass square in the chest. "You're right." She dug money out of her pocket and slapped it on the bar.

"Where are you going?" Nadia asked when Cass stood up.

"No offense, Nadia, but you're not the one I want or need to talk to right now. Thank you for reminding me this isn't my life anymore." Cass turned away, then hesitated. Her words came out far harsher than she had intended. Nadia hadn't deserved Cass's lousy attitude. Maybe they weren't friends, but they certainly weren't enemies either. She turned back.

"What happened here, Nadia? I don't remember this place being so... depressing."

To Cass's surprise, Nadia let out a small laugh. "Neglect and disinterest. I know we didn't talk much about our lives, but I was a bartender here, Cass, sleeping with the owner. When she died, I found myself with a bar that bled more money than it made. I tried in the beginning with the limited business experience I had. As I got older, I changed, but the clientele didn't. I lost the urge to keep trying, and now I don't know how to get it back to its former glory. Or update it."

Cass pursed her lips in thought. "My girl," her voice hitched. "She's, uh, a pretty brilliant businesswoman. Things are hectic at the moment, but I bet she could help you get this place the way you want. Just something to think about, Nadia. Take care." With that, Cass took off to see the one person she hoped could help her stay positive.

Nadia stood there for a moment, watching Cass's retreating back. "Well, that was weird."

Mickey grabbed Cass's glass, dumping the nearly full contents in the sink. "Think that has anything to do with the crap Miranda pulled?"

Nadia looked over at her bartender. "I don't know. But I've never seen someone as confident as Cass Giles look so... lost."

Cass's hand shook as she pressed the doorbell, shuffling her feet as she waited. She practiced what she wanted to say the entire way here. But now that she was actually here, all of those words left her. The door opened, and Cass wasn't sure if it was good or bad luck when it was Ellie staring back at her.

"Please don't slam the door in my face," Cass said hastily.

"I wouldn't," Ellie answered calmly. "But if you're here to yell at my wife — or hit her again — you can turn around and walk away."

Cass shook her head. "I-I'm not. God, Ellie, I don't know what came over me. I can't apologize enough."

"It's not me you should be apologizing to. I'll go get Hunter."

"Wait! Please?" Cass blew out a breath. "I'm... not ready to face her yet. I know how cowardly that is, but my emotions are off the charts, and I just need to get a handle on what's happening here." Cass gestured to her heart and head.

Ellie couldn't help but feel empathetic for Cass. She knew first-hand what it was like to be unable to control her emotions. She lashed out at those she loved the most, and luckily they forgave her.

"Would you like to come in?"

Cass shook her head. "I thought, um, maybe you would go for a walk with me? Just a short one!" she clarified quickly, not wanting to piss Hunter off even more by tiring out her wife.

She needs to talk, Ellie thought silently. "Let me put my shoes on and tell Hunter where I'll be." Ellie stepped back to let Cass in, but Cass didn't move.

"I-I can meet you down there," Cass pointed towards the beach behind the Vales' house.

"You're going to have to face Hunter sooner or later."

"I know." Cass lowered her head in shame. "I will, I promise."

Ellie nodded. "I'll see you down at the beach." She closed the door as Cass took off.

"She still mad at me?"

Ellie turned to her wife, wincing at the bruise forming on her cheek. "I don't think she ever was, love." She touched Hunter's cheek softly. "She's scared and embarrassed by her actions. Just give Cass a little time. You two will be drinking beer and grilling burgers again in no time."

Hunter gave Ellie a small, sad smile. "Not if Rebecca doesn't fully recover."

"Is that a possibility?"

"It depends on why it's happening. I don't want to speculate…"

Ellie sensed Hunter's uneasiness. "Then don't. I know this is affecting you almost as much as it is Cass. Rebecca is one of your dearest friends."

Hunter touched her forehead to Ellie's. "It hurt when she didn't recognize me. I can't imagine how Cass felt. I don't blame her, you know. If you didn't remember me, I'd probably go a little insane, too. Don't be too hard on her, please?"

Ellie smiled and leaned in for a quick kiss. "I won't. However, if it happens again, I won't be as forgiving. I'm going down to the shoreline to talk to her. I'll be back in a bit."

"'Kay, babe. I'll pretend not to watch you from the window."

Ellie laughed. "Do you think Cass is going to hurt me?"

"Nope. But if she says the wrong thing, I can't be certain you won't hurt her." Hunter kissed her wife again, swatting her lightly on the ass as she walked away.

Cass felt an arm wrap around the crook of her elbow, and for a split second, she thought it was Rebecca. She looked down and saw Ellie's honey-blonde hair. On the one hand, it hurt her heart that it *wasn't* Rebecca. On the other hand, this was a good sign that Ellie really did forgive Cass for her stupidity.

"I don't know what to do," Cass began, tears not even taking the time to threaten, just freely falling. "If this was Miranda or some other douchcanoe trying to hurt Becca, I could help. I could physically protect her. But this? How do I fight this, El?"

"Sometimes fighting isn't the answer. Protecting Rebecca can mean many things. Like continuing to love her even when she doesn't know she loves you."

"That's not a problem. My fear is... that her memory won't come back, and I'll lose her. What happens then? If she doesn't remember me or our life together..."

"Then you make her fall in love with you again," Ellie answered after a moment's pause. She couldn't fathom a life where Cass and Rebecca weren't together. It just seemed... wrong. "You did it before and quite fast, if I remember correctly."

Cass smiled, then frowned. "But she's not the same Rebecca. I'm not saying I feel differently about her," she said quickly. "I'm saying she had years to get over what that fucker..." Cass winced, remembering who she was talking to. "Sorry."

Ellie bumped Cass with her shoulder. "I don't know why people think I don't use that word or that it embarrasses me. Say it all you want. Especially about the woman who hurt Rebecca."

Cass nodded distractedly. "The point I was trying to make was it took Rebecca years to become confident again. And *that's* the woman who fell in love with me. What if this version... can't?"

Ellie stopped walking and plopped down in the soft sand, patting the spot next to her for Cass to join her. "Have you ever heard of the term muscle memory?"

Cass dusted sand off her hands, bringing her knees up to lean on them as she considered Ellie's question. "Yeah. It's like when you do something over and over, and your muscles just sort of remember the motions."

"Mmhmm. Did you know that the heart is a muscle?" Ellie rested her head on Cass's shoulder, hoping she could help ease Cass's fears. "I'm not a doctor, so I can't give you all the scientific... what did you call it? Mumbo jumbo? However, I do know Rebecca quite well. She loves you so much, Cass. Not even brain surgery could change those feelings that are so deeply ingrained in her. I truly believe that."

Cass sighed as she stared at the crashing waves of the incoming tide. "Even this less confident Rebecca?"

"Even this one."

"How?" Cass glanced over at Ellie. She knew Ellie was aware of how Cass and Rebecca had met. It was much easier to get someone to fall in love with you when you were giving them incredible orgasms. Unfortunately, Cass didn't think that would be an option this time around.

"You're worried that without sex, you can't win her over?" When Cass nodded, Ellie knew she had guessed perfectly what was plaguing Cass's mind. "Believe it or not, when Rebecca talks about how she fell in love with you, she doesn't talk about the sex. *You* won her over, Cass. Who you are and *how* you treat her. It's knowing everything you know about her and still thinking she's perfect. It's *you*, Cass. All you need to do is be yourself." Ellie hesitated a split second, then said, "And be as persistent as you were before."

Those ever-present tears refused to stay put again, sliding down Cass's cheeks unchecked. "Even *this* Rebecca?" she asked softly.

"Any version of Rebecca Cuinn-Giles will fall for you every time, any time."

Cass's lips twitched, and a smile threatened to form, but sitting here talking about Rebecca and being unable to be with her hurt Cass's soul.

"I should be there with her," Cass said aloud. "I know she has Aunt Wills, but it should be me. Instead, I went to a fucking bar."

Ellie sniffed near Cass. "You don't smell like alcohol."

"I didn't drink. I wanted to, but I thought about how disappointed Rebecca would be if I did. She doesn't think drinking solves problems," Cass explained. "I get that after what she went through in her past."

Ellie stretched out her legs in front of her, trying to relieve the pressure on her bad hip. She would sit there as long as Cass needed her to, so she found a comfortable enough position and settled in.

"She told us that once at a girls' night. One of us was having a bad day, and Rebecca suggested we do something other than drink to sort it out. She said drinking to get rid of a problem only creates another problem. We ate cake instead," Ellie chuckled.

This time, Cass did smile. "That's my girl. I left the bar and came straight here for guidance." Cass touched Ellie's hand briefly. "I'm glad I did. I know that if Rebecca doesn't regain her memory before being released from the hospital, she's not going to come home with me. *That's* my girl, too. She never wants to be a burden on anyone, though I would carry her burdens for the rest of my life if I had to. Going home and her not being there? God, that's gonna suck so bad. But I think you've helped me hold onto hope that she and I will be together again."

"You're very sweet." Ellie wrapped her arm around Cass's back. "If that happens, make your presence known as often as you can. There will always be a reason for you to go and see her," Ellie grinned. "Persistence, Cass. Just like before. Memory or not, Rebecca won't be able to resist you."

Chapter Eighteen

Rebecca snuggled into the soft blanket as she lay on Aunt Wills's couch. With the headache she had after leaving the hospital, she didn't dare argue with Aunt Wills when she insisted Rebecca rest while she made dinner. At least the couch was comfortable. Yet, as comfortable as it was, Rebecca still felt... out of place.

"Are you sure you're okay with me being here?" Rebecca called out. Thankfully, the home was an open-concept design, and Aunt Wills was only a few feet away in the kitchen.

Willamena shook her spatula at Rebecca. "Don't make me come over there. You are my family, Becca. My home will always be open to you."

"But what if you have a... friend over? You gave up your life to take care of me before. You shouldn't have to do it again."

Willamena moved the food off the burner, switching it off before going to Rebecca. She sat on the edge of the couch and tugged Rebecca's ponytail. "Now you listen to me, young lady. I didn't give up my life. After Gwennie died, you *were* my life. I wanted to take care of you then, and I want to now. If you're not ready to go home yet, this will be your home for as long as you need it to be."

Home, Rebecca thought. She tried to remember it... and Cass. That's all she'd been doing since meeting Cass. There was something about the woman that made Rebecca feel... well, she felt a lot of things around Cass. But the one thing that stood out the most was a deep connection.

"It will come back, right? My memory." Rebecca desperately wanted to remember Cass but couldn't understand that desperation.

"I believe so. *If* you rest and take care of yourself, it could be back sooner rather than later."

Rebecca narrowed her eyes at her aunt. "Are you trying to manipulate me?"

Willamena's eyes widened with feigned innocence. "Moi? Never." She patted Rebecca's shoulder. "Now, relax while I finish dinner. I've already fixed up your room for you, so if you get too tired, you can go up and take a nap."

Rebecca nodded. "Thank you, Aunt Wills, but I'll be fine here. I can even help you cook if you want." Despite wanting to be rebellious, Rebecca yawned.

Willamena laughed. "You're a brilliant woman, Rebecca, but cooking isn't really your strong suit. Leave the cooking to me. I know you hate being idle, but maybe you can use this as a chance to learn how to slow down."

Rebecca frowned. "In my mind, all I've been doing is waiting for a chance to do something more with my life. Will you tell me what I've been up to these past few years?" She said few as though she wasn't missing two decades of her memory.

Willamena pursed her lips. "I'm hesitant to say too much before we've given your memories a chance to return. I don't want to influence those memories. Does that make sense?"

Not really, Rebecca thought, but didn't want to argue with her aunt. "I guess so. I suppose I could be patient."

Willamena snickered. "We'll see how long that lasts," she winked when Rebecca stuck her tongue out at her. "Okay! Back to dinner. I hope you're hungry." Rebecca nodded. "Good. How does pesto fettuccini with chicken sound?"

Rebecca's stomach growled. "Apparently, that sounds perfect," she smiled. "Thank you, Aunt Wills."

"You're welcome, sweet girl." Willamena touched Rebecca's cheek. "Can you wait to take your pain meds with your food?"

"Yeah, I'm okay for now. Maybe some hot tea?"

"You got it."

As happy as Willamena was to have her niece here, she felt horrible for Cass. When she had called Cass earlier to explain that Rebecca wouldn't be coming home right away, Willamena could hear the pain in Cass's voice when she said she understood. The faster Rebecca's memory came back, the better. Not because Willamena wanted her space but because Cass needed Rebecca as much as Rebecca needed Cass. Until then, Willamena would do her best to take care of Rebecca as well as keep Cass from spiraling into a depression.

"This should be interesting," Willamena whispered to herself.

Cass's heart pounded in her ears. She'd been standing on Aunt Wills's front porch for three minutes, trying to will herself to ring the doorbell.

"You have a legitimate reason to be here," she told herself. Cass squared her shoulders and rang the bell, trying not to fidget as she waited for Aunt Wills to answer. But when the door opened, it wasn't Aunt Wills.

"Hey, Ba... Becca." Cass couldn't stop staring. Rebecca wore baggy sweats and an oversized sweatshirt, her hair up in a ponytail, and her fresh face completely makeup-free. She looked incredibly beautiful, and it took every bit of strength Cass had not to reach out and scoop Rebecca up and kiss her.

"Cass! Hi," Rebecca blushed slightly, knowing she looked like a total slob at the moment. God, was she ever going to look good when Cass saw her?

Cass did her best to hide her disappointment at Rebecca calling her Cass. All those years of hating being called Cassidy changed when Rebecca said it. Now, she longed to hear it again.

"I'm sorry to just, um, show up like this. I thought that..." Geez, was she a freakin' teenager? *Get the fucking words out, Cass!* Cass cleared her dry throat and tried again. "I understand you're not ready to come... that, um, you're more comfortable staying here right now. So, um, I thought you might like a few of your things. Some essentials, you know?"

Rebecca looked down at the bag that Cass held. As cordial as Cass was, Rebecca couldn't help but notice Cass's hand shaking or the hitch in her voice when she spoke. Hurting this woman — no matter how unintentional — made Rebecca want to cry.

"T-thank you. You're very sweet."

Cass looked up abruptly, searching for any sign of recognition in Rebecca's eyes. But there was none. She shrugged self-consciously. "It's the least I can do."

They stood in awkward silence for a moment, just staring at each other. God, how Cass wanted to hold Rebecca in her arms. Her body ached to touch Rebecca. It had been nearly five days since she last kissed Rebecca or heard the words that fueled her soul every day. *I love you, Cassidy.*

What was it about those intriguing bi-colored eyes that made Rebecca feel so... safe? The way Cass looked at her sent chills down Rebecca's spine. But not in the same way as Samantha. No, these chills weren't fear and loathing. This felt... good. Yet, Rebecca couldn't shake the feeling that she was missing something important in her life when she thought of Cass.

"I-I should, um..." Cass jerked a thumb over her shoulder. She didn't want to go, but the last thing she wanted to do was make things more complicated for the woman she loved more than anything.

"Cass? Is that you?"

Cass peered around Rebecca and smiled. "Hey, Aunt Wills. I hope I'm not interrupting anything."

Rebecca held up the bag Cass had given her. "Cass brought some of my things over."

"Ah, that's nice." Willamena had noticed the slight wince when Rebecca called her Cass. She also caught the slight slump in Cass's shoulders. "Rebecca, why don't you let the woman in? We were just about to sit down for dinner. Join us."

"Oh!" A light blush blossomed on Rebecca's cheeks. "Right. I'm sorry, I should have..."

"No, no, it's okay." Cass reached out but stopped just before touching Rebecca. "Honestly. I just wanted to make sure you had your things before it got too late. I don't want to impose."

"Nonsense! Ellie texted to tell me you might be stopping by, so I made plenty." Willamena hid her smirk when Rebecca gave her an exasperated look. "Come in."

Still, Cass hesitated. She mentally thanked Ellie for cluing Aunt Wills in, however... "It's up to you, Becca. If you're not up for company, I can totally go."

Totally, Rebecca repeated silently. She ignored the small tingle she felt in her tummy, focusing on her answer and the kind eyes that watched her carefully.

"You went out of your way to bring me some of my things. The least we could do is feed you."

Cass chuckled. "With my appetite, I don't think the deed was worth the reward." She patted her thighs. "Hollow legs, remem... uh..."

Rebecca bit her lip to hold in her laugh. Cass really was sweet, and a flustered Cass was priceless. "Please, come in. I'll never hear the end of it from Aunt Wills if I'm impolite."

"She's got that right," Willamena called out as she returned to the kitchen. This was a start. She didn't want to overwhelm Rebecca, but having Cass here could be beneficial to Rebecca regaining her memory. Besides, Ellie told Willamena about some of Cass's fears. Ellie's suggestion of making Rebecca fall in love with Cass again wasn't a bad idea. The romance of it tugged at Willamena's heartstrings.

"Can I do something to help?" Cass asked gently.

Willamena jumped slightly at the sound of Cass being so near. *The woman is a ninja!*

"You could set the table if you'd like," Willamena answered with a pleased smile.

"Hang on. I've repeatedly asked if I could help, and you refused!" Rebecca stood by the counter that separated the living room from the kitchen, her hands firmly on her hips and a perturbed look gracing that beautiful face.

"To be fair," Cass began, "I didn't just have brain surgery. How are you feeling, by the way? Sorry, Becca, that should have been my first question when you opened the door."

Rebecca wanted to hang onto her annoyance with Aunt Wills, but Cass's genuine concern squashed that pretty quickly. "I'm... okay, thank you for asking." She contemplated ending her answer there but felt compelled to be more open with Cass. She attributed that to the relationship they had. The one Rebecca's brain wouldn't allow her to remember. "I've had a dull headache that doesn't want to go away, and I get dizzy if I move too quickly. But, other than that, I feel fine. At least fine enough to set the table," Rebecca pointed out with feigned indignation.

Cass snickered when Aunt Wills threateningly whacked the wooden spoon on the counter. However, as with any other day, Cass was Team Rebecca, so she handed the cutlery and napkins to Rebecca.

"Thank you." Rebecca smiled at Cass, fascinated by the slight blush that graced Cass's face. She placed her items around the table and then went for glasses. "What can I get you to drink, Cass?"

There it is again, Rebecca thought silently. Every time Rebecca said Cass's name, Cass winced, and Rebecca could see the sadness in her eyes.

"Uh, I'll take some sparkling water if you have some." Cass needed to learn how to school her emotions. She had noticed Rebecca eyeing her curiously after calling her Cass. The problem was Cass had no control over the hurt that hearing Rebecca call her that name caused.

Again, Rebecca smiled. "That's my favorite, too."

It was on the tip of Cass's tongue to say, "I know," but for once, she refrained. Cass only started drinking sparkling water because Rebecca always had cans of it in the fridge. It became a good alternative to soda when Cass needed that bite of carbonation.

"Soup's on!" Willamena announced, hip-checking a mesmerized Cass out of the way. If she followed Cass's line of sight, she would see her looking at her niece's derriere. "Why don't you sit here at the head of the table, Cass?"

"Oh, uh, yeah. Okay." Before sitting, Cass pulled Rebecca's chair out for her, then hurried to Aunt Wills's side to do the same for her.

Rebecca's heart beat a little faster at Cass's politeness. She was the polar opposite of Samantha. Rebecca's interest in Samantha had been purely physical. She had been intrigued by the sheer power the woman exuded. Unfortunately, she was in too deep when she realized it wasn't power. It was control. Samantha needed control of everything and everyone in her life. And if you challenged that control, you were severely punished.

Cass, however, had this peculiar and intoxicating mix of confidence and... humility. Not to mention Cass's tendencies to be chivalrous and thoughtful. Even after knowing Cass for only a few hours — in Rebecca's brain — Rebecca could see what drew her to Cass. But there was also this fear inside Rebecca that she didn't deserve someone like that. Not after everything she went through... and did with Samantha. And since that thought made Rebecca sad, she put it out of her mind and focused on nothing but dinner. Dinner was safe.

"So, Cass?" Willamena began surreptitiously eyeing her niece and trying to read the expression on her face. It kept changing, which concerned Willamena. Rebecca was at war with her feelings, but Willamena suspected Rebecca couldn't understand *why* she was at war. At least not entirely. "How is the mural at the hospital coming along?"

Cass frowned. Aunt Wills knew she had finished the mural before Rebecca went into the hospital. When she received a glance from Rebecca and a slight nod from Aunt Wills, Cass caught on.

"I finally finished," Cass answered with a smile. "I keep getting texts with pics of the kids in front of it, so I think it's a hit."

"Mural?" Rebecca inquired. "Are you an artist?"

Cass wiped her mouth to hide the disappointment. "I paint," she said vaguely. "I did some charity work at the children's hospital."

"Oh! That's... I keep saying sweet when it comes to you." Rebecca pursed her lips. "I'm going to need to find different adjectives." *Like sexy, hot, attractive...*

"It wasn't much. Those kids have to deal with so much with their illnesses. I just thought brightening the place up would be nice for them."

"Don't let her downplay her talent," Willamena tsked. "Her work is in Sumptor Galleries."

Cass bowed her head, slightly embarrassed by the attention. Though if Rebecca was impressed, that was a plus.

"Sumptor Galleries? I'm guessing that's a good thing?"

Willamena bit her lip to keep from cursing. Of course Rebecca doesn't remember Eve and Lainey or Sumptor Galleries. With Rebecca's memories stuck in 2001, she and Eve had never met or worked together.

In fact, Eve would have been — Willamena quickly did the math in her head — thirteen.

"It's a very good thing," Willamena answered for Cass, who looked like she was about to cry. "Sumptor Galleries are some of the most prestigious in several countries."

Impressed, Rebecca looked at Cass. "Wow. Sounds like something I'd be interested in." Cass hadn't even looked up to acknowledge the praises Aunt Wills was handing out. She just continued to stuff her face with pasta. *Humility.* Rebecca glanced at Cass's plate and noticed the vegetables had been pushed to the side. And, since Cass seemed uncomfortable with the compliments, Rebecca decided to change the subject. "You should try the squash," she murmured.

Cass looked up sharply. "What?" Rebecca constantly tried to get Cass to eat more vegetables despite Cass's aversion to them. She especially disliked squash, but Cass remembered trying them once before at Rebecca's request.

"The squash." Rebecca nodded at Cass's plate. "You push your veggies to the side. But Aunt Wills makes the best squash. You should try it."

Cass glanced at Aunt Wills, who lifted a shoulder. "'Kay."

Chapter Nineteen

Cass flung herself on the couch, wrestling the pillow from under her and hugging it to her chest. Dinner had been as wonderful as it was painful. Spending time with Rebecca would always be Cass's favorite thing in the world to do. But sitting there needing to touch Rebecca, to kiss her, to just *be* with her how they were before and Rebecca not feeling the same way was a special kind of torture. And not the pleasurable kind Mistress gave her.

Tears sprang to Cass's eyes. "Mistress." The word was a whisper… perhaps a prayer. All Cass knew was she *needed* Rebecca back. The first time they met, it took them less than an hour to get naked and do things Cass had never even fantasized about. This Rebecca was reserved. Careful. Cass knew and understood why. Mistress didn't exist in Rebecca's mind yet. Samantha did, though. And Cass couldn't help but think that's what was holding Rebecca back. Obviously, Cass didn't expect Rebecca to jump in her arms and make mad, passionate love to her. But to be so… nervous around Cass? That hurt.

"Fucking Samantha!" Cass growled. She swiped angrily at her tears, sniffling when they wouldn't stop flowing. She and Rebecca were just getting started, and now… now that beautiful life was on hold for God knows how long. "Fucking tumor," Cass muttered through another round of tears.

Since Cass had nothing better to do with her life at the moment, she decided the best way to deal with her depression was with some ice cream and a mindless movie. She wasn't in the mood to watch anything, but the silence in the house was deafening. The need for any noise to keep her out of her head was building in her gut. If Cass didn't get a handle on this depression, she wasn't going to be any good for Rebecca when her memory came back. She certainly didn't want to risk resenting Rebecca when what was happening wasn't her fault.

Cass had just turned on the TV when she heard a knock at the door. She wiped her eyes dry before getting up to answer it. She wasn't expecting anyone, but with friends like hers, it could be anyone. Well, except Hunter. And maybe not Mo or Patty since they were probably on Hunter's side. Cass went through her list of friends, giving herself many different excuses why it couldn't be any one of them.

"How about you just answer the freakin' door?" she mumbled to herself. Cass was sure her friends would understand if she had a red nose and a tear-stained face. And if it wasn't a friend... well, then she didn't give a fuck what they thought. She stopped in her tracks right before she got to the door. What if it was her parents? *Shit.* Cass hadn't told them what was happening with Rebecca. Hell, she couldn't remember if she told them about the tumor. Everything happened so fast, and Rebecca was adamant that she didn't want anyone to know. "Please don't be my parents."

Cass took a deep breath and opened the door. That breath came out in a surprised 'whoosh' when she saw Eve standing there. "E-Eve! Hi!" *Calm it down, Cass. She's just a friend. And... your boss.* Cass glanced past Eve.

"If you're looking for my better half, she's at home with the kids," Eve smirked.

"Oh. Um... Becca isn't here. She's staying with her aunt until... for... well..."

"Cass, I'm here to speak to you." Eve had a plethora of empathy for Cass's bumbling sadness.

"Oh," Cass said again. *Eloquent, Cass.* "Listen, I know I owe you some canvases..."

"Do you think so little of me that you would assume I'm here because of work during a time like this?"

"No! I'm sorry, I just..." Cass sighed. "I'm sorry."

Eve offered Cass an understanding smile. "May I come in?"

"Yeah, yeah. Sorry... again." As she guided Eve in, Cass saw the heap of bedding on the couch and cringed with embarrassment. *Great.* "I, uh, apologize for the mess. I wasn't expecting company, and I..." Cass exhaled sharply. "How'd you do it?"

"Do what?" Eve scooted a pillow off the chair next to the couch Cass was clearly using as a bed.

"Cope without Lainey when you were... away," Cass answered as she pushed blankets and pillows to the side in a failed attempt to tidy up.

"I didn't," Eve said honestly. "I had many panic attacks. I'm not good with small spaces, and without Lainey, those spaces tend to close in on me much faster."

Cass was silent for a moment. That's the first time Eve Sumptor had been so forthcoming with a weakness of hers. "Sometimes it's easy to forget that you can be as vulnerable as the rest of us."

Eve raised a brow. "I'm not a robot, Cass."

"No, but, like Becca, you've built, like, an intolerance to bullshit." To Cass's surprise, Eve laughed. It was a sound that was... out of place in this house these days. "What do I do?" she asked suddenly. "I can't sleep upstairs in our bed because the room is too small and too big at the same time. I don't know if that even makes sense, but..."

"It does. Look, Cass, if you want words of hope and keeping the faith, I can call Lainey or Ellie for you. They're the best at that."

"And what are you best at?" Cass asked cautiously.

"The facts." Eve sat back and crossed her legs.

"Okay. The fact is, Rebecca doesn't remember me. Or you, for that matter. She's stuck in some god-awful time in her life, and I can't help but wonder why she remembers that shit and not me."

"I can understand how you'd be upset by that," Eve said amicably. "As long as you keep in mind that it's not her choice."

"I know." Cass scrubbed her face irritably. "You have to be kinda pissed that she doesn't remember you, don't you? Haven't you two known each other for, like, ever?"

Eve smiled. "You do realize that the time she's stuck in, I was thirteen. I still had my mother and a warped sense of hope for the future."

"Shit. I always forget you're only in your thirties. Not that you look old! You don't! You just have so much poise... I'm going to shut up."

Eve bit her lip. Lainey was going to enjoy hearing this story later. "Now that we have that sorted," Eve chuckled. "No, I met Rebecca about ten years later. Sumptor Galleries was doing quite well, and Sumptor Inc. was finding its niche. But I was ready to expand into areas I wasn't familiar with. So, I sought out the best, and that was Rebecca Cuinn. We bonded over our love of business and then... over our similar backgrounds."

Cass settled back onto the couch and listened to Eve's story. Not only was she learning more about Rebecca's past, but she was also learning more about the enigma that was Eve Sumptor.

Eve cleared her throat. She hadn't come here to get too personal, but she had already said way more than she expected to Cass. She felt a sort of... kinship with Cass. When she was forced to be away from Lainey, Eve nearly lost all hope that they would be together again. She imagined Cass had that same fear.

"The past isn't the issue here. It's the present and the future."

"Yeah, but it's the past that could hurt our future," Cass argued. "Rebecca isn't Mistress. She's... I don't know if the woman who barely escaped Samantha with her life could fall for me. It took her fifteen-plus years to get involved with someone else." A sick feeling washed over Cass. "What if this time that someone isn't me? What if I remind her too much of Samantha? Or even worse, I don't fit her needs because I'm *not* Samantha. If Mistress is gone, if she's not a Domme anymore, is she a sub? I know we role-play, but I don't know if I can always be that for her. Sorry if that was too much information."

"What's a little over-share amongst friends?" Eve smiled, then leaned forward to make sure she had Cass's full attention. "Mistress isn't someone Rebecca created, Cass. She *is* Rebecca. Always has been. Strength and confidence like that aren't learned. They're uncovered from deep within. Samantha needed to dim Rebecca's light because she was too afraid — too jealous — to let her shine. But you, Cass? You light Rebecca's soul. Those of us who have been there throughout the different stages of Rebecca's transformation noticed the real change when you came into her life. Rebecca no longer bears the weight of that guilt about Samantha, and according to Willamena, that's the big difference between then and now. Rebecca doesn't seem to be carrying that burden like she did back then. So, the fact is, you irrevocably changed Rebecca, and not even amnesia can take that away."

The tears didn't even threaten this time. They freely flowed down Cass's cheeks, and she wiped at them with the back of her hand.

"S-she's so timid around me."

Eve glanced around as if they weren't alone. "If you tell Rebecca I said this when she gets her memory back, I will call you a liar. But a little birdie named Willamena told me that it's not timidness but..." Eve lowered her voice almost to a whisper. "*Attraction.*"

Cass started to shake her head but then thought about the little interactions she had with Rebecca. The blushing, the tucking of the hair behind the ear. These are things Rebecca had done before when she felt particularly... enamored with Cass. If Eve was right, Cass had reason to hope.

"I thought you weren't into emotions and stuff."

"I'm not." Eve stood, smoothing out the wrinkles in her jeans. "Everything I just said was absolute *fact.*" A slow smirk formed on Eve's face. "Now, I have to go. Young Bella has organized a family date night." She paused, thinking about how Cass would be alone. "You're welcome to come, Cass. Bella would love to have you. So would we."

"Oh, uh, thank you, really. I wouldn't be the greatest company, and I have a lot of thinking to do. But, uh, could I ask a favor?"

"Of course."

"Our puppy, Mocha, is supposed to be coming home this week, but, uh..."

"You're not ready?" Eve guessed.

"I don't wanna half-ass it, ya know? I love that ball of energy, but my focus is on Rebecca, and honestly, I want her to be home when Mocha comes home." *They will* both *come back to me,* Cass vowed. If she kept saying it, maybe she would believe it.

"We can take Mocha in. I can't promise you that Little Miss Bella won't claim her as her own, though, and fight you for her."

Cass chuckled. "I'd probably lose that fight. But, hey, if it's too much, I can bring her home, Eve."

"No, no. I have to admit, puppy-sitting sounds fun. And it'll teach Bella a good lesson about responsibility. If she does well, maybe she'll get a puppy of her own," Eve smirked. "And by Bella, I mean Lainey. Ever since you and Rebecca brought Mocha over, Lainey has been hinting. But we've agreed we want to make sure Bella is ready, so you're actually helping us."

Cass knew Eve was trying to make her feel better about her decision, but she appreciated it. "Thank you. G'wan. Have a wonderful date night with your family."

Surprising both of them, Eve leaned in and hugged Cass. "Keep showing up," she whispered in Cass's ear. "That's how you won her over the first time."

"Thanks, Eve." Cass stepped back, giving Eve her space. "I really do appreciate you coming here to talk to me. And I know you didn't ask, but I'll get some canvases to you soon."

Eve shook her head. "You don't have to worry about that, Cass. Your prints at the gallery are doing well. And a little advice from one artist to another. Don't try to paint if your heart isn't in it. Art is an expression of your emotions, not a fulfillment of an obligation."

Cass respected the advice as she knew Eve was fully aware of the difference between painting your emotions and trying to paint without purpose.

Willamena stood at the doorway watching Rebecca read. It reminded her so much of when Rebecca was younger. Reading was how Rebecca used to cope with life after her parents died. She used to tell Willamena that escaping into books helped her not be so sad all the time. As Rebecca got older, the books became less frivolous and more academic. But she always found time for a good romance.

"Can I get you anything?"

Rebecca looked up from her book. "No, I'm okay, thank you. Unless you have more books from this author." She had been surprised, yet quite happy, to find sapphic novels on her aunt's shelf. Particularly the spicy ones. Since she couldn't do much else, a bit of light — or hot — reading would be a good distraction.

Willamena glanced at the title and smiled. She just so happened to have every book from Joslyn Cohan because of her niece. "I do. I know how you read, so I'll bring a couple up for you. On one condition."

"Which is?"

"You can't stay up all night reading like you did when you were a teenager. You have to get your..."

"Rest," Rebecca finished with an exaggerated eye-roll. "Yes, ma'am. Aunt Wills? How old is Cass?"

Oh boy. "Why do you want to know?"

"I'm just... wondering." Of course, Rebecca wasn't going to admit to her *aunt* that the book she was reading had Rebecca thinking of Cass in many different ways. And positions. *So weird.* Rebecca had never thought about anyone like this. Not even Samantha. Perhaps, especially not Samantha.

"Right. Does it matter how old she is?"

"That young, hmm? What was I doing with her?" Yeah, Rebecca had done the math. Adding twenty-two years to her age... "I'm old, Aunt Wills."

"I beg your pardon! If you're old, what does that make me?"

Rebecca smirked. "Old-*er*." She stuck her tongue out at her aunt.

"Oh, *that's* mature." Willamena came into the room and sat on the edge of the bed. "You're not blind, my sweet girl. I know you've seen the way she looks at you. If she doesn't care about your age, why should you?"

The way she looks at you. Rebecca felt butterflies in her stomach. "You're not going to tell me, are you?"

"It's one of those things you're just going to have to trust me on, kiddo."

"Fine," Rebecca sighed and held up her book, effectively changing the subject. Her aunt was far too stubborn to waste time arguing when Rebecca could be reading. "Have you read this?"

Willamena actually blushed, looking at the sexy cover. "Yes, I have."

"I have so many questions. One being, is there something you're not telling me?"

"Oh, child, there's a lot I'm not telling you. But I'm not queer if that's what you're getting at," Willamena chuckled. "But that doesn't mean I can't enjoy a good romance."

"Romance," Rebecca scoffed. "This book is full of kinky BDSM sex!"

"Ah, but behind the sex, there is a beautiful love story."

Rebecca couldn't deny that. The love that the characters had for each other practically leaped off the page. And the sex? *Holy. Fuck.* "It feels so... familiar. But nothing like what I had with Samantha. Was Cass my..."

Rebecca stopped. Did she want to know the dynamics of that relationship?

"Rebecca?"

Rebecca shook her head, which was beginning to throb again even after the pain meds. "I don't think I'm ready for that information yet. Do you mind if I just say goodnight now?"

"Of course not." Willamena kissed Rebecca's forehead. "Remember not to stay up too late. If you're lucky, I'll bring you breakfast in bed in the morning."

"Don't you have patients to shrink?"

"You make me sound like a mad scientist. But no. I'm mostly retired now. A few patients keep me on speed dial, but I have plenty of time to make my favorite niece some breakfast."

"Only niece," Rebecca corrected.

"Which means you're my favorite. Now, get back to your book. What chapter are you on?"

"Um," Rebecca opened the book to the marked page. "Just starting chapter seven."

"Ooh, that's a good one!" Willamena patted Rebecca's knee. "Have fun. Goodnight," she winked and laughed all the way out the door.

Rebecca snickered at her aunt's foolishness. Then she hunkered down and dug into chapter seven.

Chapter Twenty

K*eep showing up*. Cass sighed. Here she was, sitting in her truck, trying to muster up the courage to *show up* at Aunt Wills's front door for no reason.

"You have a reason, dipshit. Your wife is in there." Cass glared at herself in the rearview mirror. She was tired and cranky. *Sad*, she corrected silently. She was allowed to be sad, yes. But that didn't mean she had to stop trying. Stop showing up. So, she grabbed the small bag next to her and jumped out of the truck, trotting up to the door. She rang the doorbell before she could talk herself out of it.

Rebecca opened the door and was surprised — yet very happy — to see Cass standing there. *God she looks good.* The tight jeans and V-neck tee were indeed an appealing look for the tall, androgynous woman.

"Cass, hi," Rebecca smiled. She noted again the flash of disappointment, but Cass's return smile was genuine.

"Hey, Becca. How are you feeling?"

I stayed up way too late reading and fantasizing about you, so I'm tired. "I'm okay. I'm being waited on hand and foot by my aunt and sleeping a lot because she won't let me do anything else."

"I can hear you!" Willamena shouted from somewhere inside the house.

"I know!" Rebecca shouted back, then swayed when a wave of dizziness washed over her. She pressed her fingers to her temple, hoping it would help relieve the pounding.

Cass immediately closed in on Rebecca, her arms wrapping around her. "Are you okay?"

"Oh," Rebecca involuntarily breathed in Cass's intoxicating scent. "I-I'm fine. Note to self: do not shout at your overly doting aunt."

"Come on, let's get you inside." Cass bent and hooked her arm under Rebecca's knees, easily picking her up.

Fuck me. Rebecca buried her head in the crook of Cass's neck, hoping to hide her blush. *Please tell me I didn't say that out loud.*

"I-I can walk." *Shut up. If the woman wants to carry you, let that muscled body press against you.*

Cass's heart was pounding in her chest. Rebecca's arms were wound around her neck, and her lips were close enough that if Cass just tilted her head, she could...

Cass cleared her throat. "I know, but why walk when you can get a free ride?" she grinned. She gently deposited Rebecca on the couch and covered her with a soft blanket. "There, all cozy." Cass's fingertip grazed Rebecca's cheek as she pushed a strand of blonde hair behind Rebecca's ear. Their eyes were fixated on each other, but neither quite knew what to say.

"What happened?"

Ugh! Perfect timing, Aunt Wills! Rebecca barely managed to control her frustration. "Nothing happened. I got dizzy, and Cass helped me to the couch. End of story."

Cass stood faster than a teenager getting caught with her hand down her girlfriend's pants. "I-I probably should have called before I came over. I didn't mean to cause any undue stress."

Rebecca reached up and touched Cass's hand. "No, it wasn't your fault."

Willamena could have kicked herself for interrupting their moment. But she wouldn't gamble with Rebecca's recovery. She'd apologize to Cass later.

"You know you're always welcome here, Cass," Willamena said, noting that Rebecca was still holding Cass's fingers. "Did you need something, or were you hoping I had more pasta?"

Cass smiled. She, too, was painfully aware Rebecca was still touching her. Cass's body wouldn't let her try to ignore it. *It's fine. I'm fine. Everything is fine. Keep a cool head, try to stop the blood from traveling south, and we're good. All good.* "I will never turn down food.

Actually, I'm here because, uh, I forgot to pack Becca's favorite brush."

Now that she was standing here in this situation, Cass's reason for coming here sounded incredibly pathetic.

"Brush?" Reluctantly, Rebecca let her hand drop because she couldn't think of a good reason to keep holding Cass's hand. "I... have a favorite brush?"

"Totally." Cass grabbed the brush out of her back pocket, waving it around like a prize. "You use it every night. It makes your hair so silky and soft. I love running my fingers... I mean, uh..." Cass sputtered, not knowing whether to apologize or run away.

Rebecca absently touched her ponytail. Oh, what she wouldn't do to have Cass running her fingers through her. *Hair! Through your hair, Rebecca!* But her hair was neither soft nor silky at the moment. Still, something inside her itched for the chance to tease Cass.

"They tell me I have amnesia. How do I know this is my favorite brush?"

"Well, I..." Cass saw a glint in Rebecca's eyes. *She's teasing me!* That had to be a good sign, right? "I guess you'll just have to trust me."

"I guess so." Rebecca tried unsuccessfully to stifle a yawn. "Sorry! That is in no way a reflection on my present company."

"Someone stayed up too late reading even though they promised they wouldn't," Willamena scolded playfully.

Right. Reading. "Thank you, Aunt Wills." Rebecca caught Cass's eye and made a face. Her breath caught when Cass laughed heartily.

"What were you reading?" Cass asked, wiping tears of laughter from her eyes. Those were much more welcome than the tears of sadness she shed last night as she tried to sleep.

Rebecca pursed her lips. What would Cass think about her reading preferences? Samantha never allowed her to read 'trashy novels.' Once, when Samantha was high, she admitted it was because Rebecca didn't need to get any wrong ideas about what a relationship should be. Rebecca was a possession. A toy for Samantha's pleasure. No more, no less.

"Just a book I found on Aunt Wills's shelf. I thought it might keep me entertained while I was cooped up."

"You're not cooped up. You're recouping," Willamena countered, curious as to why Rebecca didn't tell Cass what she was reading. She assumed it had to do with Samantha. If so, Willamena was willing to help her niece by showing her she didn't have to be worried about telling Cass the truth. "She's reading a Joslyn Cohan book. One from her series."

Cass's eyes lit up, but Rebecca missed it because she was too busy glaring at her aunt. "The one with the, uh, interesting dynamic between the two main characters?"

"That's the one!" Willamena announced with a shit-eating grin.

Rebecca narrowed her eyes. "Don't you have food to prepare, woman?" Cass's words then registered in her brain. "Wait, you read Joslyn Cohan?"

Cass nodded. "Hell, yeah! They're freakin' hot! Well written, too. I don't wanna give any spoilers, though."

Rebecca smiled. "Thank you. I'm almost done, so maybe we can discuss it after I finish?"

She wants to see me again! "I'd like that." Cass smiled when Rebecca yawned again. "I should go and let you rest."

"You don't want to stay for dinner?"

Cass kneeled next to a disappointed Rebecca. "I do, but you can't stop yawning. My first — my only — priority is your welfare and recovery, Becca. I'm gonna go so you can take a nap. Maybe when you wake up, you can finish that book, and we'll have our own little book club about it."

Rebecca smiled sweetly. "I'd like that." She yawned again and laughed. "I'm so sorry."

"Don't be." Cass brushed her fingertips over Rebecca's soft cheek. "I'll see you soon, okay?"

Rebecca nodded. As much as she wanted Cass to stay, she was having a difficult time keeping her eyes open. "Soon."

Cass sat there, staring at a blank canvas. *Don't try to paint if your heart isn't in it.* Her heart was only a couple *of* miles away, though it felt further somehow. Tonight, however, gave Cass hope. Rebecca still may not remember Cass, but there was something there. That spark that lit Cass's fire the first time around burned a little brighter tonight. She could feel it. The way Rebecca touched and looked at her? It was familiar, yet new. And oh, so exciting.

Cass picked up her paintbrush, and with the feel of holding Rebecca still lingering, she made the first stroke. She had no vision, no plan for this painting. But her heart was there. Cass wasn't able to express her love for Rebecca verbally. Or even with the actions she had become so accustomed to. Had she taken Rebecca for granted? Oh, she had always shown Rebecca love and attention. But could she have done better with just *being* with Rebecca?

She didn't know if she deserved a second chance with Rebecca, but Cass sure as hell would fight for one. This time, she'd do it differently. She'd do it right. Rebecca would know without a doubt that Cass's life meant nothing without her. It wasn't about the sex — no matter how incredible it was. It was Rebecca herself that completed Cass. After years of being 'Cassanova' and never feeling the urge to be tied down with someone, Rebecca appeared seemingly out of nowhere and flipped Cass's world upside down. And sideways. And catawampus.

Cass chuckled, the low sound filling the silent air. "Catawampus. Maybe that should be my new safe word."

That made Cass think of Mistress. *Mistress isn't someone Rebecca created, Cass. She is Rebecca.* Cass hoped Eve was right. While there are things Cass would change about how she showed Rebecca love, the one thing she didn't want to change was submitting to Mistress. Giving herself to Rebecca fully was a true sign of trust for Cass. If Mistress really were a part of Rebecca, Cass would be more than happy to help bring that side out again.

"We just need to balance every aspect of our lives better," Cass told herself. That included work, home life, sex life, social life, and... family life. While Rebecca couldn't have kids, the discussion of adopting was never off the table. Cass wasn't sure that would be the direction their lives would go, but it was definitely something to discuss with Rebecca in depth to get a definitive answer. They had both been anxious to get Mocha back, though... Cass smiled. With Rebecca slowing down and

Cass determined to slow down with her, this had been the perfect time to see how well they did with having a full-time living being dependent on them. How would Rebecca react if Cass brought Mocha around to... reconnect?

Cass sighed and put her brush down. "Ugh! I'm overthinking this. We were great before the tumor. We'll be even better after. I'll get Rebecca and Mocha back and show them both I'm all in." She looked at her canvas and laughed. "And hopefully Mocha has learned that our toys are not hers."

"You're up late."

Rebecca bobbled the mug she had just taken down from the cabinet. "Please don't do that." She puffed out her cheeks and tried to regulate her heartbeat. It seemed that whenever Rebecca's pulse pounded, so did her head.

"Do what?" Willamena took the mug from Rebecca's trembling hands.

"Sneak up on me. And I was going to make some tea, so I'm going to need that."

"Sit. I'll make you some." Willamena waited until Rebecca complied with her request, then went to work on making that tea. "Just so you know, I didn't sneak up on you. *You*, however, were lost in thought. Care to share?"

"I was... trying to remember."

"Remember what?"

"Everything, Aunt Wills. But mostly... Cass."

Willamena smiled to herself. "You like her." *You love her.*

"She's sweet. Definitely different than..."

"Than what you're used to?" Willamena helped. She set Rebecca's mug in front of her, then took a seat, dunking her tea bag as she observed Rebecca as a psychiatrist. "Does that scare you?"

Rebecca raised a brow. "Seriously? You're going to psychoanalyze me now?"

"Perks of the job," Willamena teased. "You know, I happen to be pretty good at my job. But if you don't want to talk about this, I won't make you."

"Can I ask you something?" Rebecca said instead of acknowledging Aunt Wills's offer not to talk.

"Of course."

"Why did I choose Samantha? Did — or do — I know that answer? Mom and Dad didn't raise me to be weak. Nor did you. I don't understand why I would choose to be with a sadist like Samantha. And stay with her for years. H-how do I trust what I think I feel for Cass if I don't trust myself to make good decisions?"

Willamena reached over and took Rebecca's hand. "We have discussed this, and it took you years to forgive yourself for the choices you made. But I'll tell you now what I've always told you. You weren't the weak one. Samantha was. Rebecca, you have been pushing yourself since your parents died. It got to the point where all you did was work and study. Friendships suffered, and as a result, so did your confidence. Not in your abilities but in who you were. You had been called 'boring' so many times you needed to prove to yourself you weren't. Samantha was... exciting at the time. She introduced you to a world you didn't know you needed or wanted. Only, the way she did it nearly broke you."

"She did break me, Aunt Wills," Rebecca said, staring into her tea. Surely, Cass would see through whatever facade Rebecca must have been flaunting these past couple of decades.

Willamena shook her head. "I disagree. You are so different now." *Especially from the first time you woke up in the hospital after Samantha tried to kill you.* "You may have been knocked down, but you were never broken."

Rebecca frowned. "Is that what I'm doing with Cass? Finding something 'exciting' with someone who is clearly way younger than I am?"

"Absolutely not. You were way past finding who *you* were when you met Cass. She isn't someone you were looking for, but she's become someone you need. She balances you, Rebecca. And, more importantly, she makes you deliriously happy."

Rebecca sat back in her chair with a thud and a groan. "This not remembering shit is so frustrating!"

"I can imagine. But I think it's counterproductive to try and remember things you don't know you're supposed to remember. Don't look at me like that. It makes perfect sense. Let the memories come to you instead of you trying to get to them." Willamena patted Rebecca's arm. "Now, why don't you go upstairs and..."

"If you say get some rest, I swear I'm going to scream. That's *all* I've been doing!"

"Good," Willamena smirked. This stubborn side of Rebecca is one she hadn't seen in years. Well, that wasn't exactly true. Rebecca Cuinn-Giles was one of the most stubborn people Willamena knew, but it was the sullen pout that tickled Willamena's funny bone. It was one of young Rebecca's traits that Willamena wasn't sad to see go. Seeing a nearly fifty-year-old Rebecca do it was quite comical. "That's all you *should* be doing. Doctor's orders."

Rebecca narrowed her eyes. "Where did you get your degree again?"

"From a Cracker Jack box before they stopped giving anything but ridiculous stickers or tattoos."

Rebecca's eyes widened. "They don't give toys anymore?!"

"Nope. I'm probably one of the last ones to get a degree from there." Willamena stood, kissing Rebecca on the top of her head. "That means I have every authority to tell you to get your behind upstairs and..." she leaned down to whisper in Rebecca's ear. "*Get some rest.*"

Chapter Twenty-One

Rebecca blinked. She'd been staring at the TV for the past thirty minutes and yet had no clue what was playing. Per her aunt's advice last night, Rebecca was trying to allow the memories to come to her. She tried meditating, but the quiet was allowing her mind to wander into territories she couldn't quite navigate. The background noise of the TV gave her just enough of a distraction to space out without overthinking. However, she'd been brought out of her mini-trance by a different noise. And there it was again—the ring of the doorbell.

She glanced around to see if Aunt Wills was around to get the door but couldn't see or hear her. "Guess I'll get it. It's fine. I don't have anything pressing to do except sit on the couch and reflect on... whatever I'm supposed to be reflecting on." Rebecca realized then, halfway to the door, that she was having a full-on conversation with herself. "I'm going crazy."

She pulled open the door, her eyes moving up until she met the bi-colored eyes she was quickly being captivated by. Rebecca couldn't explain why this habit Cass had of stopping by every night made her incredibly happy. "Cass," she smiled. "You're a little early for dinner. Or did you forget to bring something else? Do I have a favorite toothbrush? Or maybe a favorite pillow you forgot to bring the first two times?"

Rebecca was teasing her, and Cass was here for it. Though it still hurt to hear Rebecca calling her Cass, seeing the playfulness in her eyes warmed Cass's heart.

"You do have a favorite pillow," Cass said with a grin. "But I'm kinda using it. Nah, actually, I was summoned today."

Rebecca tilted her head in question. Before she could ask what Cass meant by that, Aunt Wills came bustling in.

"Cass? Is that you?"

Cass peered past Rebecca to a smartly dressed Aunt Wills. She hadn't told Cass why she needed her here, but it didn't matter. As soon as she got the text from Aunt Wills asking if she could come over, Cass dropped everything and hightailed it over.

"In the flesh."

Rebecca's eyes involuntarily tracked over Cass's body. *Nice flesh.* "Ahem, what's going on, Aunt Wills?"

Willamena rummaged through her bag, searching for her keys. "I have an emergency session with a client," she said distractedly. "Ah! There they are!" Willamena held up her keys in triumph. "Anyway, I asked Cass if she could come over to..."

"To babysit me," Rebecca finished with a sour look on her face.

"No, Little Miss Sassy Pants," Willamena countered. She didn't waver against Rebecca's icy stare.

Cass snickered but immediately wiped the smile off her face when Rebecca glared at her. She couldn't help it! Aunt Wills just called Rebecca Little Miss Sassy Pants. How in the hell was Cass supposed to just let that slide by as though she didn't hear it?

"I asked Cass to come and keep you company." Willamena raised a brow. "Rebecca Aisling Cuinn G..." She stopped abruptly. Willamena hadn't told Rebecca that she and Cass were married yet. Was that going too far with the information? Perhaps that was a conversation for another time, not when she was rushing out the door. "You are only a few days out of surgery. You still have stitches, for goodness sake! I cannot leave you here by yourself. If something happened while I was gone, I'd never forgive myself. So, do an old woman a favor and just accept this. Please?"

Rebecca blew out a breath. "Fine. But I'm sure Cass has better things to do than be cooped up here with me."

"Nope," Cass shook her head. "I was just heading to the diner for lunch." She pursed her lips. "Why, uh, don't you come with me? It's a beautiful day. We could get some food, take a walk — a short one," she said quickly for Aunt Wills's sake. "I won't keep you out long, but at least you could get some fresh air."

Rebecca thought about it for a moment. A venture out of the house with the most handsome woman she'd ever seen? That sounded like a win-win. "Could you give me ten minutes to get ready?"

"I'll give you all the time you need, Becca."

Rebecca's breath caught in her throat. She was stunned for a good ten seconds, seeing the look in Cass's eyes. "I-I just need ten minutes. I'll be right back."

She headed for the stairs, turning back once to catch Cass's gaze on her. Amnesia or not, Rebecca couldn't remember a time when she felt so... beautiful. Even in her oversized sweats, that's how Cass made her feel.

"Smooth," Willamena winked.

"True," Cass corrected. Then she narrowed her eyes at Aunt Wills. "Do you really have a session? You usually do those over Zoom."

"Why would I lie?" Willamena handed Cass a bottle of pills. "Now, if a headache comes on, here are Rebecca's pain meds. She hates to take them, but it's better than her suffering. I'll be at least a couple of hours, but feel free to spend as much time together as Rebecca can handle."

"What am I not allowed to say to her?" Cass slipped the pills into her pocket, hoping Rebecca wouldn't need them. Aunt Wills was right. Becca *hated* taking medicine. It would be a chore just to get her to agree to one if Cass thought she needed it.

"I haven't mentioned you two being..." Willamena glanced toward the stairs. "*Married,* yet. That may be a subject for another day. But use your judgment, Cass. You love Rebecca. You *know* her. I think you'll do just fine. Okay! I'm off! I will see you in a few hours!" Willamena winked, patted Cass on the shoulder, and took off.

Willamena took out her phone and pressed the call button. "Blaise? Tell the girls that Operation Cassecca... Rebass..." She rolled her eyes. Ship names were *not* something she was good at. "Anyway, tell them Cass is here and taking Rebecca out to lunch. We're a go! I'll see you in ten minutes. Break out the mimosas!"

Willamena didn't even wait for Blaise to respond. She just shoved the phone back into her bag and trotted off with a smile fixed to her face. The more time Rebecca spent with Cass, the better. She loved her niece more than anything else in the world, but Rebecca wasn't Rebecca without Cass. It was time to get the memory gears turning.

Cass tapped her fingertips on her thighs — a nervous tic — and wandered around the living room as she waited for Rebecca. It was... odd being nervous with her wife, but then again, this whole situation was odd, to say the least. She eyed a book on the coffee table and wondered what Rebecca was reading now. Had she finished the Joslyn Cohan book she had been reading previously? Cass picked up the book, turned it over to see the cover, and smiled.

"Sticking with the author," she said quietly.

"She's quite talented," Rebecca said from the bottom of the stairs. She chuckled lightly when Cass bobbled the book before placing it carefully back on the table. "Sorry, I didn't mean to scare you."

"Nah, it's all good." Cass cleared her throat, studying the woman she'd known and loved for the past few years. Rebecca seemed... younger. Perhaps it was because Rebecca *thought* she was younger and carried herself that way. Or maybe it was the lack of stress in Rebecca's life. Without her memory, Rebecca had nothing to worry about except herself. No clients, no club... no Cass. "Did, uh, did you finish the other one?"

Rebecca tilted her head and merely stared at Cass for a good long minute. "What were you just thinking?"

Cass shook her head. "I was just thinking how beautiful you look." It was true. Rebecca was dressed in faded boyfriend jeans and a simple white t-shirt. Her hair was up in a ponytail, a usual occurrence these past few days. And her face was completely void of any enhancements.

"And that made you sad?"

Cass smiled softly. "I'd be lying to you if I said that you not remembering me doesn't make me sad, Becca. But I have to admit, you look very… refreshed."

Rebecca rolled her eyes. "That's because I'm not allowed to do anything except *rest*. I swear, if I rest any more, I'm going to go into a coma."

"Then we better get you outside and moving!" Cass chuckled. "Ready?"

"Totally." Rebecca bumped her hip to Cass's and winked. She slipped into her sneakers and made sure the front door was locked.

"You're going to love the diner. The food is crazy good!"

"Are you always eating?" Rebecca teased.

Cass tried to stop herself but failed miserably. Her glance floated down Rebecca's body and up again. "In one way or another." *Fucking word vomit.*

Rebecca blushed. She tried to stop it, tried to pretend Cass meant something other than the obvious innuendo, but failed miserably. She decided it was best to ignore the comment — and what it did to her insides — for now.

Cass thought about kicking herself the entire way to the car. *Smooth, Cassanova. Go ahead and run her off before she remembers who you are. Idiot.*

Cass disengaged the locks of a very sleek, matte black SUV that nearly had Rebecca salivating. She had no clue what kind of car it was, but it was almost as sexy as Cass. "Beautiful car."

Cass opened the passenger door for Rebecca, offering her hand to help Rebecca into the SUV. "It's, uh, yours." There was a slight hesitation before Cass held out the keys. "Would you like to drive it?"

Rebecca's eyebrows shot up. "Mine? How? Why?" She stopped and took a breath. "This is mine?"

Cass nodded. "You ordered it before the surgery, and I just picked it up this morning. You traded in your Mercedes."

"I… had a Mercedes?"

Cass winced. "This is too much, isn't it? Am I overwhelming you? Would you like me to take you back inside?"

"Cass, relax." Rebecca laid a calming hand on Cass's arm. Yeah, she was surprised by all the information. At the same time, she appreciated

Cass's being forthcoming — something Aunt Wills had been reluctant to do. "I'm fine. I'm just trying to catch up."

The buttery-smooth leather of the seats welcomed her as Rebecca sat back and waited for Cass to get the hint that she was fine in the passenger seat.

"You sure you don't want to drive?" Cass asked, the Aston Martin SUV purring to life when she pushed the ignition.

"I would love to, but..." Rebecca tapped her noggin. "I don't really recognize anything around here. I'd be lost."

Way to go, Cass. "Sorry, I wasn't thinking."

"You don't have to keep saying sorry, Cass. I'm sure this is as awkward for you as it is for me."

Cass glanced over at Rebecca. "I wouldn't say it's awkward. I still feel... right when I'm with you. It's just..."

"Awkward?" Rebecca said, filling in the momentary silence.

Rebecca smiled at Cass to soften the blow of reality. The truth was, she felt right with Cass, too. It was something she couldn't explain to herself, so she stopped trying, instead opting to see where it took her and her memories. She eyed Cass's arm resting on the console, her hand almost waiting for someone to take it.

"Do you drive all the time?"

Cass shook her head. "I think it's a fifty-fifty thing. You like to drive."

"Do we normally... hold hands?"

Cass's eyes flicked from Rebecca to her hand before bringing it to the wheel. *Yep, awkward.* "Uh, yeah." She stopped herself from saying sorry again. "Habit."

Rebecca reached over and brought Cass's hand back to where it was. Then she threaded their fingers together. *Yes, this feels right.*

"I hope this doesn't make you uncomfortable."

"Nope. Not even a little," Cass grinned, squeezing Rebecca's hand lightly.

Rebecca peered out the window, watching everything go by. Some things were familiar, but other things were completely different. It confused her how she could wake up one day having lost two decades of her life.

"She never let me have a car," Rebecca stated suddenly, knowing instinctively that Cass knew who she was talking about. She purposefully didn't look at Cass as she remembered why Samantha demanded Rebecca sell her car when they got together. "She said it gave me too much independence, and subs weren't allowed to have independence. I wasn't allowed to go anywhere without her."

Cass squeezed the steering wheel, forcing the hand that was holding Rebecca's to remain relaxed. "Is that why you're having a hard time being cooped up in the house now?"

Rebecca frowned. She hadn't thought of that. Or maybe she had subconsciously. "I don't know." She narrowed her eyes at Cass. "Have you been talking to my aunt, the psychiatrist?"

Cass chuckled. "I mean, I *have* talked to her in the past. Maybe I'm learning a few things? But it would make sense that if you're... stuck in that time, you'd be a little more anxious about your surroundings."

"Oh, you're good." Rebecca smiled sweetly and went back to watching her surroundings, thinking about what Cass just said. It made sense that Rebecca would be anxious, right? So why wasn't she when she was with Cass? After everything Samantha did to her, how could Rebecca ever feel safe in another relationship? And what type of relationship did they have? Was it normal?

They pulled into a parking lot after some time of quiet driving. Oddly enough, Rebecca felt comfortable in the silence with Cass. There were moments when Cass would gently rub her thumb over Rebecca's, which sent a shiver down Rebecca's spine. The touch caused Rebecca to wonder more about the nature of their relationship. Samantha had never been gentle with Rebecca. Not even in the beginning. They never held hands or acted as a couple. Rebecca was Samantha's sub, and that was the extent of the relationship. Had Rebecca gotten out of that lifestyle once she was rid of Samantha?

"We're here," Cass announced softly as she cut the engine. Rebecca seemed to be deep in thought, Cass hated to interrupt.

Rebecca looked around. Nothing felt familiar to her, yet she felt... at home. "This is quaint."

"Yeah," Cass agreed as she surveyed the area, trying to look at it through the eyes of someone who'd never been here before. "The shop owners pay for the upkeep of the surrounding area." Cass pointed to the store on the corner of the small strip of businesses. "Knight in Bloom donates the flowers and stuff for the landscaping. Sumptor Gallery allows some of the sculptures to be placed out here for the aesthetic."

Rebecca gestured to the diner that took up the opposite corner. "And that place?"

Cass grinned. "Ellie's provides the amazing smells that make people drool. Hang on just a sec." Cass hopped out of the car and jogged around to Rebecca's side, opening the door. "M'lady?"

Charmed, Rebecca took Cass's outstretched hand. "Why thank you." She stepped out of the car and allowed the warm sun and cool breeze to wash over her. "Beautiful," Rebecca whispered, her eyes closed.

Very, Cass agreed silently. She longed to take Rebecca in her arms and hold her tight. She missed feeling Rebecca close to her. It wasn't even the sex she missed. It was the closeness she had with Rebecca. She missed the love that flowed between them with a simple touch. And, oh god, she missed the happiness, passion, and adoration that shone in Rebecca's eyes when she looked at Cass.

"Ready?"

Rebecca opened her eyes and smiled sheepishly at Cass. "Yes, sorry." She didn't know how to explain to Cass that it had felt like forever since she'd felt this... free. Rebecca was convinced that it had more to do with how Cass made her feel than just the rays of sunshine.

Chapter Twenty-Two

Rebecca stopped in her tracks, inhaling deeply.

"Oh, *now* I understand what you meant about the drooling." Rebecca sniffed the air again, trying not to actually drool. "I think this is what heaven smells like." She looked up at Cass, catching her scent as well. This was definitely Rebecca's heaven.

Cass grinned down at Rebecca. She caught the spark in Rebecca's eye and knew it had nothing to do with Ellie's pies. No, Cass had seen that look before. It was one she missed desperately.

"C'mon," Cass murmured. "This place fills up around this time, so we'd better get a table." Out of habit — and the urgent need to touch Rebecca — Cass placed her hand at the small of Rebecca's back, guiding her to the booth they used often. Intrigued, she watched as Rebecca glanced around, that small space between her eyebrows puckered in concentration. Cass wished she could read Rebecca's mind. Did anything ring a bell in Rebecca's memory, or was this as new to her as... well, Cass?

"My aunt mentioned an Ellie," Rebecca began, distracted by her surroundings and aromas. "Is this who she was talking about?"

"Yep."

Finally, Rebecca's attention came back to Cass. "Are they friends?"

Cass nodded. "Ellie is a... family friend."

Before Rebecca could ask Cass to elaborate, a beautiful woman walked up to the table with a glass of chocolate milk and a mug in her hands. Then Rebecca was graced with a smile that caused her to feel inexplicably calm.

"Hello, you two! I was hoping I'd see you today." Ellie placed the chocolate milk in front of Cass, giving her a conspiratorial wink. She then set the mug in front of Rebecca. "Green jasmine tea with a splash of honey."

Rebecca's eyebrows shot up in surprise. That was her favorite, especially when she was feeling particularly stressed. All the new sights and sensations were definitely contributing to her anxiety. Not to mention, she wasn't sure she liked the familiarity between this woman and Cass.

"I — thank you. How?" Rebecca blinked in an effort to clear her mind of the hundreds of questions and focus on one. "I'm so sorry. Obviously, you know me if you know the way I drink tea. But I don't... remember."

Ellie laid a calming hand on Rebecca's shoulder. "I know, it's okay."

"Cass told you?"

Ellie's eyes flickered to Cass with sympathy. Oh, how it must hurt to hear Rebecca call her Cass. Again, she turned on the pleasant smile for Rebecca, not wanting to admit how much it hurt that Rebecca didn't know her either. "My wife is your doctor, Rebecca," she explained delicately. "And we're all very close."

Rebecca rubbed her temple. She didn't want a fucking headache, she wanted answers. She *needed* to remember. "My doctor?"

"Yes. I'm Ellie Vale. Dr. Vale is my wife."

Rebecca frowned, concentrating on remembering the doctors who were in the room with her when she woke up. "Tall. Dark hair. Piercing blue eyes. Nice bedside manner."

Ellie's smile grew. "That's her."

"Wait, *you're* Ellie? As in..." Rebecca gestured at the diner as a whole.

"That's me."

"You were not what I was expecting." Rebecca sucked in her lips, a blush of embarrassment creeping up her neck. "I... that's... that was rude, I'm so sorry."

Ellie chuckled. "I'm used to it. Most people think I'm a white-haired, little old lady." She shrugged. "It's fun seeing the reaction when they realize I'm not."

Rebecca shook her head. "This is all so... weird. Have you ever felt like you're missing out on life even though you're standing right in it?"

"Girl," Ellie scoffed. "I know very well what that's like, but I believe your memory will return sooner rather than later." She leaned closer, her eyes focused on Rebecca's. "This too shall pass," she said with a wink.

"You sound like a guru," Rebecca laughed. Oddly enough, she believed Ellie. But *when* would it pass? It felt like it's been a lifetime already.

"Ellie is like a yoga master," Cass chimed in. She had been happy — and intrigued — just listening to the two's conversation.

"I teach yoga," Ellie corrected.

"That explains why you have a calming presence," Rebecca laughed. "But if you could tell it to pass a little faster, that'd be great. Thanks."

"I'll work on that during my next meditation," Ellie joked. "Now, do you want to see the menu or...?"

"Do I have a 'usual,'" Rebecca asked curiously.

"You do."

"I'll take that, then. It'll be interesting to see what it is."

"Coming up. Also, don't look now, but..." Ellie placed her hands on the table and leaned even closer, lowering her voice to barely above a whisper. "Joslyn Cohan is over in the corner. *Writing*!"

"Did you ask what she was writing?" Cass asked, matching Ellie's silly stage whisper.

"Of course not! I don't want to interrupt her. All I'm doing is making sure her iced coffee is never empty."

Cass peeked around Ellie. Sure enough, their favorite author was huddled in the corner of the diner, typing away on her laptop. Cass squinted but couldn't make anything out on the screen. "Tell me you're getting a little look-see on what she's writing when you're doing the refills."

"I would never!" Ellie looked at Cass indignantly, then grinned. "I'll tell you later. Don't go over there!" With that, she was off to get the couple their food.

"Like I'd go over there and intrude," Cass puffed out a whoosh of air. She turned to look over her shoulder and saw Ellie staring back at her, doing the 'I'm watching you' thing with her hand. Cass held up her hands innocently and laughed.

"She seems nice. And funny." Rebecca sipped her tea. It was perfectly made, solidifying the fact that Ellie knew her very well. *'We're all very close.'* Rebecca had never had close friends before. Not even growing up. "I wish I could remember."

"Don't worry, babe... uh, Becca. You will."

"Everyone seems very confident about that. I wish *I* were." Of course, Rebecca didn't miss the 'babe' slip-up. How could she? It made her insides all... tingly. She watched Cass over the rim of her mug, curious about the chocolate milk. Rebecca couldn't remember when she last had chocolate milk. Not that that was saying much these days. "How old are you, Cass?" she asked suddenly.

"Nope." Cass stirred her chocolate milk with a straw. She always loved getting chocolate milk from here because Ellie made it with a milk chocolate bar instead of the powder. It was always topped with chocolate shavings, too, which was an added bonus.

"Excuse me?"

The words only held a fraction of Mistress's strength. Even so, Cass was happy to hear the bit of heat coming from Rebecca. It made her backside itch to be spanked, but they'd get there again. Hopefully.

"The age thing? We've been there before. You tried to use it as an excuse not to date me." Cass smirked. "I won. I ain't giving you a second chance to overturn the win!"

Well, if they'd had this discussion before, it would have meant Cass was way younger than Rebecca. That was a first for her. Samantha was older and more experienced, which was what Rebecca was used to. Then again, maybe that was why this relationship with Cass worked. At least Rebecca assumed it was working.

"Aunt Wills wouldn't tell me either. *That* in itself is telling."

Cass pushed her chocolate milk aside and leaned her elbows on the table. "I don't like saying age is just a number. I've kinda come to the understanding that saying that negates what everyone has been through. But think of it this way. In your mind, you're what? In your twenties now? You feel that age because you *think* you're that age. So, I guess to me, age isn't the issue. Your mindset is. My age doesn't matter, Becca.

What matters is we're two consenting adults who enjoy each other." *Quite a bit.*

Rebecca sipped her tea as she contemplated Cass's outlook on things. She supposed it was true enough. "Fine. No more about age."

"Thank you!" Cass laughed.

"They look like they're having fun. Rebecca is laughing." Ellie stood on her tiptoes and peered out the small window of the door that separated the kitchen from the dining area.

"Did she remember you?" Blaise positioned a rose into the arrangement she was trying to perfect.

"No. I'm not going to lie; it stung." Ellie smiled when she saw Rebecca's reaction to eating her lunch. "She still likes my food."

"She has amnesia, El, not... whatever it's called when you can't taste food."

"Ageusia," Ellie provided.

"How in the hell do you know that?"

"I'm married to a doctor. Ooo, I'm going to insist Rebecca has a piece of my banana cream pie. Gotta go!"

"Wait! Don't forget to scoot them my way when they're done there. I have a special arrangement just for Rebecca."

"Got it. See ya, sweets!"

"That was the most incredible food I've ever eaten." Rebecca patted her belly, sure that if she tried to put one more morsel in her mouth, she'd explode. She wasn't lying. The food at Ellie's Diner was to die for! Was that the silver lining of having amnesia? The ability to have that 'first impression' once again? Would she remember this when — or if— she regained her memory?

Rebecca was beginning to feel the same way about her time with Cass, too. She couldn't remember how or where they met. Hell, she couldn't remember how she *felt* when they went out on their first date.

Had she felt the same butterflies in her belly? The same thrill when Cass touched her? She must have. This was simply another chance to feel all of that again. It was the only good thing Rebecca could attribute to this god-awful amnesia shit. The one thing she could hold onto when her hope started to wane. Or when the headaches began to creep in and ruin her day.

"Your head hurt?" Cass asked softly.

"A little."

"Do you want me to take you home?"

Rebecca looked up at Cass, touched by the genuine concern in her eyes. "No, you promised me a walk. And after everything I just ate, I need it," she grinned.

Cass nodded with a smile. "You're right. But hey, I have some of your meds," she patted her pocket. "You tell me if you need them, yeah?"

"You're going to trust me?" Rebecca squinted her eyes suspiciously. Obviously, Aunt Wills gave Cass the medication because she didn't trust Rebecca to take them if needed.

Cass shrugged. "Why wouldn't I? You know what you're feeling better than I do. I also know you hate taking medication, so you'll wait until the pain is unbearable. Just do me a favor, Becca, please? Don't let it get unbearable. And don't let me keep you out if you're not up for it. Trust *me* enough to take care of you when you need it."

Rebecca couldn't resist touching Cass on the arm. "You are very sweet. And whatever my memory is or isn't, I *do* trust you. I think I have since the moment you showed up at my aunt's house."

Pride swelled in Cass's heart. That meant a lot, and it renewed her hope that Rebecca would remember her. She had to. "Good." Cass jutted her elbow out and waited for Rebecca to slip her hand through the crook of her arm. "Are you up for a couple of stops?"

Rebecca inhaled deeply, willing the headache to subside. She didn't want to take any medicine- not now. The pills made her sleepy, and she wanted more time with Cass.

"Are we going to see more people I should know?"

Cass glanced at Blaise's flower shop. Before they left the diner, Ellie 'casually' suggested they stop by next door, insisting Rebecca would love the flowers. Ellie wasn't wrong. Rebecca always loved the beautiful bouquets Blaise created. But if Rebecca wasn't up for seeing anyone, Cass had no choice but to skip it.

"Probably," Cass answered truthfully. "If you would rather not..."

"No, it's okay. Do they all know about..." Rebecca swirled her hands around her head.

"Yeah. They were there during your surgery. And when Hunter... Dr. Vale told me about the amnesia."

Rebecca loved how Cass didn't hesitate to tell her the truth. "So when Ellie said we were *all* very close, how many is all?"

"Uh." Cass closed one eye in concentration, counting her fingers as she muttered names to herself.

"That many!" It was difficult for Rebecca to comprehend having so many friends.

"Well, our group is growing, but our core... is about seven strong. Then we get into the kids, the strays, and the occasional supermodels..."

Rebecca's eyebrows shot up to her hairline. "Supermodels?" She shook her head and took another breath. "Okay, let's tackle one thing at a time. Knight in Bloom, that's where Ellie said to go?"

"Yep. That's Blaise's place."

"One of our 'core,' as you called it?"

Cass nodded. "She's Ellie's bff. They started the whole girls' night thing."

"Girls' night," Rebecca repeated. That was probably something else she should know, but nothing came to her. It was another thing she never imagined herself doing. Girls' night with a bunch of other women? Samantha would never allow that.

"Sorry, I'm bombarding you with information." Cass could kick herself for going too fast with the info. Rebecca already had a headache, and Cass was just making it worse. She was about to suggest taking Rebecca home again when Rebecca chuckled.

"It's not too much information, Cass. It's more of *what* the information is. I've never had friends before, so this is all very... odd." She tugged on Cass's arm. "Come on. Let's go meet Blaise."

Chapter Twenty-Three

"Do all the places smell this heavenly in this strip?"

Cass watched Rebecca breathe in the floral scents of Blaise's shop and smiled. "Well, this entire strip is owned by our friends, so I'm going to say yes."

"You better say yes!"

Rebecca watched with interest as another beauty came straight at them. *Cass did say supermodels,* she thought as she studied her. The woman's whiskey-colored eyes exhibited kindness, yet Rebecca could sense the mischief.

"You must be Blaise."

"The one and only." Blaise curtsied, a silly grin on her lips. "Also known as the token straight friend."

Cass snorted. "You're not a token anything, woman. We'd be lost without you."

"Don't I know it," Blaise winked. She noticed Rebecca discreetly rub her temple. "I know you can't stay long, but I have something for you." She gestured for them to follow her to the back. Aunt Wills was hiding back there, sipping her mimosa. But she insisted on seeing how her niece was doing, so Blaise was obliging.

Rebecca was in awe of her surroundings. She'd been in flower shops before, but this was... different. "These flowers are perfect."

Blaise glanced back at Rebecca. "Thank you. Those are for the customers. These?" Blaise pointed out a tabletop greenhouse. "The ones with the 'flaws' are my favorites. They pollinate the bees and feed the caterpillars, who turn into beautiful butterflies. What could be more delightful than that?"

"What an interesting way of looking at it! "Rebecca said, looking more closely at one of the roses near her. What she saw as imperfections before were now tiny bite marks from small creatures who needed the flowers to live. Weirdly enough, it did make the flowers more beautiful. "This is different."

Blaise peered over Rebecca's shoulder. "Ah, that's a cross-pollination I'm working on."

"You made this?"

Blaise nodded. "My background is in botany and floriculture. I don't just make flower arrangements," she grinned.

Rebecca shook her head, a small smile playing on her lips. "I'll be glad to get my memory back, but I have to say it's been quite a trip meeting people and learning things. I feel like this is only the tip of the iceberg."

Blaise draped an arm around Rebecca's slim shoulders. "Girl, I cannot imagine how weird this all is for you. But I am a firm believer that this memory thing is only temporary. Very soon, all our shit will be flooding back to you relentlessly."

Rebecca laughed. "You make it sound so enticing."

"We give that writer chick some competition. What's that saying? Truth is stranger than fiction." Blaise leaned close to Rebecca's ear. "It's probably why Joslyn Cohan is here and magically found her way to Ellie's. Our little group is ripe with ideas for stories!"

She nudged Rebecca back to Cass. "Here, these are for you," she said, grabbing a small bouquet of pink roses and handing them to Rebecca. "On behalf of Cass, of course. You are taking Rebecca next door, right?"

Rebecca sniffed the roses. They were beautiful. "Thank you for these." She didn't know if it was true that these flowers came from Cass, so she kept her eyes on the roses, which were a perfect shade of pink. The color made her feel... something. But what? "We were just at the diner. It was so delicious," she said distractedly.

"Oh, um, Blaise was talking about the gallery on the other side," Cass offered. She watched with interest as Rebecca studied the roses. A faint blush formed on Rebecca's cheeks, and Cass wondered what was going through her mind. "Are you okay, Becca?"

"Hmm? Oh, yeah... yes." Rebecca let out a small laugh. "I'm sorry, there's something about this color that makes me feel like it means something to me." She looked up at Cass. "Does that make sense?"

Cass's heart constricted painfully. "Y-yeah. Pink is, uh..."

Blaise stepped in when Cass faltered. "Your favorite color. Did you remember something?"

"No, not... really. I just got a weird feeling when I saw this color." Rebecca waved it away. Whatever *it* was. "But you said it's my favorite color, so I guess I'm just picking up on that."

"Has it always been your color?" Cass asked carefully. She never thought to ask a question like that before. It had always been evident since Rebecca wore it and had decorated a sex room in that color. Now, she wondered if pink came before or after Samantha.

Rebecca frowned. "No. But..." Her hand fluttered to her chest, resting over her heart. "I feel like it is now."

Blaise looked at Cass and gave her a thumbs up behind Rebecca's back. "Well, listen, I don't want to keep you. I don't need Aunt Wills all up in my crack for tiring you out." She said that last bit a little louder for Willamena's benefit.

It took precisely two seconds for Blaise's words to register in Rebecca's brain. Then she snorted out a laugh. "All up in your crack? Is that a... cultural saying?"

"Nah, it's a Blaise-ism," Blaise grinned. "Feel free to use it."

"I might have to. Aunt Wills gets all up in my crack when I'm not resting as much as she thinks I should be," Rebecca said, rolling her eyes.

This was the younger Rebecca shining through. It was such an odd sensation for Cass to see Rebecca like this. Her wife was poised and authoritative. God, she missed that part of Rebecca. Yet, getting to know *this* Rebecca was... interesting, too.

"Can we please stop talking about Aunt Wills being up people's cracks?" Cass asked, shuffling her feet uncomfortably. She scrubbed her face with her hands when both Blaise and Rebecca laughed at her. Despite the slight embarrassment, Cass was glad they stopped in Blaise's shop. Leave it to Blaise to bring levity to every situation.

"Go on before Cass tattles on me." Blaise pushed the couple towards the door. "Don't keep her out too late, Cass! Ta-ta!"

"You're up, baby cakes," Blaise announced when Eve answered her call.

"Baby cakes," Eve repeated with a laugh. "Great. You've just given my wife a new nickname for me. How is she?"

"Good. Other than the amnesia, she seems healthy and... happy with Cass. We had a moment when we thought she remembered something. Get this, the color pink wasn't always her favorite, but it gives her the tingles now."

"The tingles." For the life of her, Eve couldn't figure out why she constantly repeated what came out of Blaise Knight-Steele's mouth. Perhaps she was trying to see if it made any more sense coming from her own. "Rebecca said... tingles?"

"Well, no. That's my word. But it works, so don't knock it, *baby cakes.*"

Eve saluted even though Blaise couldn't see her. "You got it, sugar tits. I see them outside. I'll report back to the Cupid Squad later."

"Work your magic. I'm going to cut Aunt Wills off and call her an Uber."

"I've had one mimosa!"

Eve cut the call when Blaise and Willamena continued arguing. "Never a dull moment."

Lainey took Eve's hand. "I've done dull, my love. I never want to go back to that. However, if we could have *normal* every once in a while, I wouldn't complain," she smiled. "Here they come."

"That was..."

"Blaise," Cass laughed.

"Well, I was going to say interesting, but I feel like I've been using that word a lot today."

"Maybe we could go back to the diner and see if Joslyn Cohan is still there. Surely she has a thesaurus."

Rebecca hip-checked Cass. "We're not allowed to bother her. And is it a rule that we must call authors by their full name?"

"I think so." Cass's arm involuntarily wrapped around Rebecca's waist. "I mean, how else would you know exactly who I'm talking about?"

Rebecca burrowed into Cass's side without a second thought. "She is the only Joslyn I know." She frowned. "Right? Do I know another one?"

Cass cleared her throat to hide a chuckle. "No. And technically, we don't *know* Joslyn Cohan. So, it's probably best to keep calling her Joslyn Cohan."

Rebecca laughed heartily. It was the first time she could remember laughing since... well since her parents were alive. "Whatever you say."

Cass peered down at Rebecca with a grin and wiggled her brow. "Would you like to go in?" she asked, gesturing toward Sumptor Gallery, LA.

"Sumptor Galleries," Rebecca read out loud. "This is where Aunt Wills says your work is displayed."

Cass nodded. "Yeah. But Eve and Lainey showcase many talented artists from different mediums. It's almost intimidating being surrounded by art of that... caliber."

Rebecca frowned, stopping to look up at Cass. "Your work is in there, too, Cass. *You* are of that caliber."

"You haven't seen my work, Becca," Cass reminded her.

"I don't need to. *Something*," Rebecca said, her hand once again finding its place over her heart. "Something about you tells me you wouldn't waste time doing anything you didn't love. Which means you put your whole heart into it. Why would you think you don't belong here when clearly others do?"

Tears threatened, but somehow Cass held it together. "I, uh, it's imposter syndrome, I guess. I've been doing murals most of my life. Or, you know, sketches here and there. I never thought about doing canvases until..."

"Until?"

"You," Cass revealed. "You encouraged me. You introduced my work to Eve Sumptor. My work is here because of you. Well, and because Eve liked what she saw, I suppose."

"Me?" Cass nodded, and Rebecca struggled to remember even a morsel of what Cass spoke about. It frustrated her when nothing came to her. "Let's go in. Maybe seeing your work will trigger something." She tugged on Cass's arm, anxious to get inside the gallery.

Cass held open the door for Rebecca, inhaling the smell of art. As much as she loved food — and she *really* loved food — and no matter how pretty flowers were, *this* was what Cass loved. The aroma of paint — old and new — on canvas stretched expertly into frames that lent as much to the art as the art itself. Then there were the metal, stone, ivory, wood, and clay sculptures. All of it ignited Cass's inspiration to create.

"Oh, it's beautiful in here," Rebecca said appreciatively. "I don't think I've ever been inside a gallery before." She glanced up at Cass. "Obviously, I have, but I don't remember."

Cass offered her a small smile. "We practically lived in this one when Eve and Lainey were opening here, and I was the featured artist. C'mon..."

"Wait. Please. I want to look around without you guiding me." Rebecca's nose wrinkled. "Does that make sense?"

"Yeah." And Cass meant it. Rebecca wanted to come in here to see if anything incited her memories. Cass wouldn't get in the way of that, so she stood back and let Rebecca wander. When Cass saw Eve and Lainey in her peripheral, she motioned for them to wait. Lainey nodded silently, taking Eve's hand and disappearing in the back.

Rebecca strolled, taking in every piece of art that she went by, purposefully not reading who the artist was. There were moving black-and-white photos that elicited strong emotions. There were landscape paintings that made her feel free, practically feeling the wind in her hair. Everything she saw was beautiful and powerful.

Then, she came to a series of paintings that took her breath away. The one she was drawn to more than others stood out in brilliant reds, oranges, and blues. The focus of the painting was a couple holding hands. She felt... hope and an intense love while gazing at it.

"This is yours," Rebecca announced. Even though she hadn't looked at the name of the artist yet, it wasn't a question. It was a feeling.

Cass came up behind Rebecca. "Yes," she confirmed close to Rebecca's ear. "Did you remember or see my signature?

"Neither." Rebecca's eyes moved to the signature. It was an elegant swish of the paintbrush that Rebecca wouldn't have expected from the light-hearted woman. "It was more of a... feeling." Rebecca turned, not expecting Cass to be so close. She whooshed out a breath and debated whether to step back or get closer. In the end, Rebecca stood her ground. "I can see why your work belongs here."

"I would say you're biased, but..." Cass felt the pull she always felt with Rebecca. It took all of her strength not to crush Rebecca to her and kiss her senseless.

Rebecca's laugh was shaky as her pulse raced with the way Cass was looking at her. "Does it make you feel better knowing I still feel that way despite my... condition?"

"Better?" Cass thought about it. The first piece of work that Rebecca saw of Cass's was the mermaid mural in their house. That had been after they'd been intimate in the pink room. Yet, they were still just beginning to get to know each other. So, did it make her feel better that none of that was a factor in Rebecca's admiration of Cass's work? "I think I'd say it cements what I've always known. That you're genuine."

Rebecca cleared her throat. God, no one had ever looked at her the way Cass did. And had her body ever felt this... turned on? The answer to that was a resounding no. Not even once. Not even in the beginning with Samantha.

"Could we, um," Rebecca inhaled and immediately regretted it. Every other scent she had experienced today was suddenly overshadowed by the scent of Cass. It was a clean, woody fragrance with a hint of... citrus. Whatever it was, it made Rebecca's mouth water. If she didn't move away from Cass right now, Rebecca was going to make a fool of herself.

Cass closed her eyes briefly when Rebecca turned away from her. There was no way Rebecca didn't feel the electricity between them. But she couldn't rush things. Not with this Rebecca, who had yet to find her... inner Mistress. *Mistress isn't someone Rebecca created, Cass. She is Rebecca. Always has been.* Again, Eve's words echoed in Cass's mind.

"Cass?"

Cass blinked, focusing back on the here and now. Eve and Lainey had joined them without Cass noticing their approach.

"Oh, hey. Sorry, I was, uh..."

"Daydreaming?" Lainey teased. "Hello, Rebecca."

"Becca," Cass said before Rebecca could respond. "This is Eve and Lainey Sumptor."

"Hi." This must be the owners of Sumptor Galleries. Friends. And obviously lesbians. The world really *had* changed quite a lot from what Rebecca remembered. "Your gallery is exquisite."

"Thank you. We owe a lot of that to you," Eve revealed.

"Me?" The more Rebecca learned about her life now, the more frustrated she was that she couldn't remember.

"You helped us find this place, and you've been instrumental in the success of quite a few of my businesses."

"I — don't remember."

"We know," Lainey said softly. "But you will."

Rebecca scoffed playfully. "Everyone is so sure about that."

"We know you." Eve gestured to Cass's painting. "Beautiful, isn't it?"

Rebecca was momentarily stunned by the sudden change in topics. She was grateful for it, though, as she didn't know how to respond to Eve's declaration. But there was an easy answer to her question.

"Spectacular."

"How does it make you feel?"

Rebecca glanced at Eve. She was studying the painting, allowing Rebecca to gather her thoughts. "Happy," she answered finally. "After the photos at the beginning, this gives me... hope. That's not to say the black-and-whites were bad! They're thought-provoking but so... sad. When I got here, I was glad it affected me more positively."

Lainey smiled. "That's by design. Without the dark, you'll never fully appreciate the light. The photos allow you to open your heart to the pain instead of closing yourself off. Once your heart is open, you're more likely to allow the happiness and hopefulness in. And that's a big reason Cass was our featured artist for the opening. Her work is awe-inspiring and radiates everything you want to believe life can be."

Cass shoved her hands into her pockets, bowing her head. Eve and Lainey had always been generously gracious about her work, but she'd never heard them describe her paintings in such a profound way. Why did compliments from the likes of the Sumptors make her feel so awkward?

"What a brilliant concept." Rebecca scanned the rest of the gallery. Everything seemed to have a rhyme and reason in the way it was displayed. It was impressive.

She thought of the diner with the delicious food, the flower shop with flawless flowers, and now the gallery. All owned by women, and for the most part, *lesbian* women. Rebecca felt pride swell in her chest for these women and vowed that whatever happened with her memory, she would make an effort to get to know this group of women all over again if she had to. Rebecca was about to say as much when a flash of pain seared through her brain.

"Becca?" Cass's arms wrapped protectively around Rebecca as she swayed. "Can we get some water, please?"

Eve hurried off while Lainey went to find a chair.

"I'm okay," Rebecca managed, but she couldn't hide the grimace when another wave of pain hit her.

"I shouldn't have kept you out this long." Cass was mentally chastising herself. This was all too much too soon.

"Please don't do that. I wanted to do this."

"Here," Lainey said, pushing a chair close to Rebecca. "Have a seat."

Eve twisted the cap off the water bottle and handed it over to Rebecca. She looked at Cass. If Eve were to sculpt Cass now, she would call the peace Fear and Shame. "What else do you need?"

Cass glanced up and shook her head. She knew from experience that Rebecca didn't like being 'weak' in front of others. Not even her best friends. "Maybe just some privacy?"

Eve nodded. "You're welcome to use our office. Otherwise, we'll direct the patrons away from this section while you catch your breath."

Once they were alone, Cass kneeled beside Rebecca. "Tell me what you need, Becca."

"I think I need that pill now," Rebecca answered regretfully. This wasn't how she wanted this time with Cass to go. But the pain was becoming unbearable, and she promised Cass she wouldn't let it get to that. Rebecca smiled when Cass didn't even hesitate to hand over the medicine. "Unfortunately, that means we have to skip the walk. These make me a little drowsy."

Rebecca took the pill from Cass, popping it in her mouth and chasing it down with a long pull from the bottle of water.

"I'm so sorry, Becca."

Rebecca touched Cass's sad face. "Please don't be. Today is the first day since waking up at the hospital that I've felt... alive."

Chapter Twenty-Four

Cass eased to a stop in front of Aunt Wills's house. Rebecca had fallen asleep on the drive back, and Cass was reluctant to wake her. She cut the engine and found herself staring at her wife. Up until now, the day had been positive and fun. Cass could pretend that they were role-playing—a new couple, getting to know each other. Then, with Rebecca's pain, reality set in. She would take Rebecca inside, and Cass would go home. Alone. Her heart broke a little more each minute she was without Rebecca. If Rebecca's memory didn't come back soon, would Cass survive?

"Are we home?" Rebecca asked sleepily.

No. "Yeah, you're home. Becca?" Cass knew it was wrong to ask Rebecca for anything while she was under the influence of medication, but she was going to do it anyway.

"Hmm?"

"I, uh, know your follow-up appointment is coming up. I'd like to be there."

Rebecca's eyebrows furrowed in thought. Aunt Wills had mentioned an appointment before, but Rebecca was too sleepy to remember the details.

"I..."

"Hey, you don't have to answer right now." *You're an idiot for taking advantage of her state.* "I just wanted to put it out there, yeah?"

"Okay." Even through the drowsiness, Rebecca heard the warmth in Cass's voice. "I can call you with the date and time." She frowned again. "I don't have a phone or your number. I'll have Aunt Wills call you."

Cass smiled sadly. Rebecca didn't have a phone because *Cass* had it. Cass had put it in her pocket the day of the surgery, along with Rebecca's wedding ring. At night, she charges the phone and sends an 'I love you' text to Rebecca's number while holding the ring tightly in her hand. She'd have to ask Aunt Wills if it was a good idea to give the phone back to Rebecca with everything she was dealing with. The ring? Cass would hold on to that until Rebecca was ready to wear it again.

"It's okay, Becca. I know when it is. I can take you if you'd like."

Unfortunately, Rebecca had nodded off again before she could answer. Cass hopped out of the car and ran to the passenger side. With the gentleness of a woman in love, Cass scooped Rebecca up into her arms and carried her to the house.

Willamena opened the door, worry etched across her face.

"She's okay, Aunt Wills. Just tired from the meds."

"Bring her to the couch. I have the blankets ready for her."

Cass side-eyed Aunt Wills. "You knew we were coming. Did Eve call you?"

"I *may* have been keeping tabs on you both today. While having *half* a mimosa at Blaise's shop. And if she tells you anything different, she's a liar."

Keeping tabs. "You didn't trust me to take care of her?" Cass settled Rebecca on the couch, freezing when Rebecca stirred. Once she quieted down, Cass covered her with the blanket Willamena handed her.

"That couldn't be further from the truth, Cass. I trust you with my niece more than anyone else in the world. Maybe even myself. We were just curious how things would go with you two."

"We?"

"The gals and I," Willamena confessed. "I think you know my appointment was a ruse today. We wanted to give you and Rebecca some time alone to see if it helped her remember."

"It didn't," Cass said sadly. Deep down, she did know what Aunt Wills and the others were up to. It had all been too perfect. "Thank you, though. I appreciate you trying to help and giving me some much-needed time with her."

"Oh, I disagree. I think it helped. The small... tingly feelings, as Blaise called them? That is a step in the right direction." Willamena hooked a hand around Cass's elbow and pulled her away from the sleeping Rebecca so they could talk more freely. "Ellie said Rebecca was laughing. The only time she does that is when you're around her. Cass, the secondary reason for my slight... manipulation is Rebecca's mental state. Amnesia aside, being cooped up, no friends, no work? That's a recipe for disaster. She went down that road before, and I won't allow that to happen again. We've worked too hard to get her where she is. And I'm including *you* in that. You found a way to absolve Rebecca of her guilt, and I'll be damned if I let Samantha take up residency in Rebecca's head again."

Cass nodded. "Yeah, I get that. I sure as hell don't want that bit..., um..."

"You can say bitch in front of me," Willamena laughed. "Especially when you're speaking of that sorry excuse of worthless flesh."

Cass raised her brows and pursed her lips. "Tell me how you really feel, Aunt Wills," she teased. "But you're right. Why didn't you just tell me what you had in mind? I would've agreed to anything when it comes to Rebecca."

"I know, but we wanted your reaction — and subsequent invitation — to be genuine. Rebecca is very intuitive, so I had to be very careful with how I arranged this."

"Which included running out of here like your bra was on fire and not giving her a chance to question the validity of your appointment?"

Willamena laughed again, touching her forefinger to her nose. "Bingo."

Cass nodded, a slight smile lingering on her lips. It wasn't that this conversation wasn't entertaining. She always enjoyed talking to Aunt Wills with her quick wit. But as Cass glanced back at Rebecca softly snoring on the couch, she dreaded having to leave and go home alone.

"You can stay," Willamena said quietly, accurately guessing the reason for Cass's somber mood.

"I want to," Cass readily admitted. "But I don't want Rebecca to be uncomfortable. She's still trying to figure all this shit out. The last thing she needs is me hanging around 24/7. I do have one request, though," she continued before Willamena could argue.

"What's that?"

"I asked Rebecca if I could be at her appointment. She agreed, but she's also, uh, under the influence of excellent pain meds. I want to be there, Aunt Wills. I need to know what the results are, and I don't want to sit back and wait. I can't. I'm freakin' going out of my mind already."

"Cass," Willamena laid a calming hand on Cass's arm. "You're more than welcome to be at the appointment. The only person who can say no is Rebecca, and I have a feeling that won't happen. You ground her, Cass. Even now. Today was a good day, and if you don't stay like you want to, at least take that with you."

Cass nodded. As hard as it was to leave Rebecca, she was grateful for today. From now on, she was going to look at this situation as somewhat of a do-over. The way Cass met Rebecca was unconventional, to say the least. And Cass wouldn't change that for the world. But this was her chance to woo Rebecca in a way she deserved to be wooed. Today was a good start if Cass said so herself.

"Oh, uh, I have Rebecca's phone," Cass told Willamena. "S-should I give it to her?"

Willamena watched Rebecca for a moment, tears forming in her eyes. She shook her head and walked Cass silently to the door. It was only then she dared to speak the words swirling in her head.

"Samantha never allowed Rebecca to have a phone. The only phone she was permitted to use was the landline, and Samantha would check the phone bill every month to make sure Rebecca wasn't calling anyone she shouldn't be."

"Like you?" Cass guessed, rage burning in her belly.

"Exactly."

"So, when Rebecca said she didn't have a phone, she meant it. Not that she didn't know where it was."

Willamena nodded. "I'm not sure giving her phone to her now will help or hurt." She blew out a frustrated breath. "Have I mentioned how much I hate that woman who hurt Rebecca?"

"That bitch was no woman," Cass snarled. "But I'm right there with ya." Cass drew in air through her nose, holding it for a moment before letting it out slowly. The pause gave her time to calm her anger. Neither of the women in this room was who she was angry with, so lashing out didn't help anything. "I don't like keeping anything from Rebecca, Aunt Wills."

"I know. Nor do I. But we must make choices based on what's best for Rebecca right now."

"And deal with the consequences later," Cass finished. She kissed Willamena on the cheek. "If you need anything, give me a call. It doesn't matter what time it is."

Cass gave Rebecca one last longing look before she walked out.

"Aunt Wills?"

Willamena looked up from her book and smiled. "There she is. Hello, my sweet girl."

Rebecca rubbed her eyes, yawning and stretching the kinks out. "Where's Cass?"

Oh, that's a good sign, Willamena thought with excitement. "She went home, honey. She wanted to stay," Willamena continued when she saw Rebecca's disappointment. "But thought it was best to let you rest."

"Ugh! I'm getting really sick of that word."

Willamena chuckled. "I'm sure you are. Do you need anything? Food? Drink?"

Rebecca shook her head. "I'm still a little woozy from the meds. Give me a minute to wake up, and I'm sure I can find something for you to do for me."

"I'm sure." Willamena tossed her bookmark at her niece. "Dang it, I need that."

"Too late now." Rebecca stuffed it down the front of her shirt. "That'll teach you to throw things at an invalid."

"You are hardly an invalid," Willamena laughed. "To hear you tell it, you're perfectly fine."

Rebecca stuck her tongue out at her aunt. Despite the banter, Rebecca was discouraged by Cass's absence. She picked at invisible lint on the blanket, trying to remember how she got from the car to the couch. Had Cass carried her again? If so, Rebecca was sorry to have missed it. She'd never experienced anything hotter.

"What's on your mind, Rebecca?" Willamena asked, curious about the pink creeping up Rebecca's cheeks.

Rebecca froze. She should know better than to think such thoughts in front of a professional headshrinker. "Hmm?" *Oh sure, play innocent. That'll work.*

Willamena hid her grin. Her niece was thinking about Cass, which was the outcome everyone was hoping for today.

"How was your day?" Willamena asked instead of teasing Rebecca. "Did you have a good time?"

The smile that graced Rebecca's face was instant and beaming. "Yes. Cass was..." She hesitated, trying to find the right word for how Cass treated her. "Gentle. And funny and kind. Oh, and so talented." She laid her head back on the pillow, smiling up at the ceiling like a love-sick teenager. "Cass took me to Ellie's diner. Oh my goodness, the food was to die for. Then we went to Blaise's flower shop. Apparently, we're all really close friends. I wish I remembered that because I've never had that..." Rebecca waved that thought away. "Then Cass showed me her work at Sumptor Gallery. Actually, I picked it out myself. I just knew it was hers. I could... feel it. Wait! My flowers!"

Willamena listened closely as Rebecca gushed about her day with Cass. Rebecca had never been giddy as a teenager. Willamena attributed it to losing her parents at an early age and then taking on the weight of the world. Seeing Rebecca like this now warmed Willamena's heart. Could she look at this as Rebecca's second chance to be young? To see life differently? Yes, Samantha still happened in Rebecca's memory, but there was a significant difference between this Rebecca and the Rebecca from two decades ago.

"Cass texted me about the flowers. She found them in the car when she got home. She said she'd bring them to you..." Willamena paused, forgetting she hadn't yet asked Rebecca how she'd feel having Cass at her doctor's appointment.

"Were you going to finish that sentence, or am I supposed to guess when I'm going to see Cass again?"

Willamena raised a brow. "Do you often wonder when you're going to see Cass again?"

"Aunt Wills!" Rebecca whined.

Willamena laughed. "Oh my goodness. The last time I heard you whine like that, you were fifteen and wanted to visit the Berkeley campus."

"But you wanted me to go to NYU, so you kept procrastinating."

"I was not procrastinating. I was giving you time to make a sensible decision."

Rebecca smiled. "And I did. I went to Berkeley," she winked. "Now, can we get back to Cass?"

"You are smitten!"

"Aunt Wills!"

They both enjoyed a spirited laugh. Willamena enjoyed hearing Rebecca's carefree joy. Rebecca enjoyed feeling this free and effortlessly credited Cass for her lightheartedness. Today, Cass showed Rebecca an entirely different world. One where she could be happy. One where Rebecca was an equal and not just a... play toy. One where pain didn't have to be a part of her life.

"Fine, my girl, calm down. I just wanted to mention — or remind you in case you were too sleepy to remember — that Cass wanted to go to your appointment with you." Willamena leaned forward to observe Rebecca's reaction. "Are you okay with that?"

Rebecca's eyebrows creased in thought. "Right. She asked me in the car." She raised her eyes to Willamena's. "When I'm with Cass, I feel... safe. I don't think I've ever felt that before." Rebecca winced. "I didn't mean..."

"Oh, my sweet girl." Willamena offered an understanding smile. "As much as I wish it weren't true, there was always a part of you that was guarded with me. Until Cass came along, that is. And believe me when I tell you I understood. You always carried too much responsibility for things you had no control over."

Rebecca wanted to argue, but Aunt Wills was right. At ten years old, when her parents died, young Rebecca was reserved. She loved her aunt and was grateful Aunt Wills took her in. But, at the same time, Rebecca worried that she'd do something stupid again and lose another person she loved. Then Rebecca met Samantha and was forced to keep Aunt

Wills out of her life. *Forced and too much of a coward to do anything about it.*

"Cass seems to be good at making things better," Rebecca said, focusing on that tidbit from all that Aunt Wills said. "This follow-up. Is it just to get my stitches out?"

Willamena shook her head. "Dr. Lima will discuss the results of the biopsy as well."

Rebecca closed her eyes briefly and nodded. "The tumor. I think I want Cass there. Maybe she'll bring me good luck. Or she can console me if it's bad news."

"Console you, hmm?"

Rebecca rolled her eyes. "Don't make it weird."

Willamena snorted. "*I* made it weird?" She wanted to be there with Rebecca when she heard the results. But she loved Rebecca and Cass enough to step aside and let them bond. "This actually works out great. Cass can take you to your appointment while I go grocery shopping. That girl can *eat*, and I'm sure she'll be starving when she brings you home."

"Wait, you're not going?"

"I don't want to overwhelm Dr. Lima. It's fine, sweet girl. Cass will be with you, and you can tell me about it when you get home. Unless you want me there."

"I don't want you to think I'm cutting you out again."

Tears welled in Willamena's eyes. "I don't think that. Our relationship is stronger than ever, sweet girl." She got up and went to Rebecca, hugging her gently. "I'll text Cass and let her know she can pick you up to take you to your appointment."

Rebecca's smile lit up the room. "Thank you, Aunt Wills. And since you're being so generous, do you think you could make me a sandwich?"

"Ha! Nope. My generosity has run dry," Willamena teased with a wink. "Turkey?"

"With mayo, cheddar cheese, and one slice of a tomato, please?"

Willamena grinned and kissed the top of Rebecca's head. "Comfort food coming right up."

"Thanks. Oh, hey. When is my appointment?" Rebecca needed to know how long she had to prepare for whatever news she got from the doctor.

"Tomorrow morning," Willamena called out on her way to the kitchen.

"Tomorrow?!"

Chapter Twenty-Five

"I, uh, didn't mean to push Aunt Wills out," Cass took a quick look at Rebecca before focusing on the road again. "I can bow out if she wants to be there."

Of course, that's not what Cass wanted—or needed. No, she needed to be with Rebecca when the results were read. Yet, she couldn't help but feel bad.

"She insisted, Cass," Rebecca reassured. She was trying very hard not to feel nervous about today. It was such a weird feeling to be scared of something you didn't remember. "Besides, I'm the one who told Aunt Wills I wanted you there with me."

Cass's heart jumped at that admission. "Y-you did?"

Way to embarrass yourself, Rebecca. You might as well have just told Cass you were hot for her. Rebecca cleared her throat. "Yeah, I mean, you asked, and I..." She sighed, wondering why she was being so weird. "No, I meant it. I want you there with me. I may not remember everything — or anything. But you help me stay calm. I feel like I need that today."

Cass risked rejection by taking Rebecca's hand that rested on the console. "Thank you. I'm glad I can be a calming presence for you cuz I'm a freakin' bag of nerves," she confessed with an uncomfortable laugh. "I probably shouldn't have told you that."

Rebecca bit her cheek. God, she loved the way Cass said whatever came to her mind. *Loved? Do we... love each other?*

"I appreciate your candor, Cass," Rebecca chuckled. "I'm a freakin' bag of nerves, too, but I don't think I really understand why. I... forget about the tumor. I have the stitches, I get the headaches, but I guess I still blame the, uh, other thing."

Cass squeezed Rebecca's hand, thankful that Rebecca didn't pull away. "I can't imagine what this is like for you."

"The only way I can describe it is like I've time-traveled into the future without a roadmap from the past."

"That's..." Cass ran that analogy over and over in her head. "That gives me a better understanding, I think, by giving me a sort of visual of what it's like." She glanced at Rebecca again and winked. "Thank you for sharing that with me."

Rebecca smiled coyly. "I don't even know where that came from."

"Sometimes the answers come when we stop thinking about it so hard."

"Aunt Wills said something similar. But trying not to think about what you're not supposed to be thinking about is almost impossible."

Cass laughed. "You sound like me! Maybe that's why I totally understood what you just said." She pulled into the nearly empty parking lot, finding a place close to the front to park. "Note to self: nine am on a Wednesday is the time to come here."

"Mmm." Rebecca leaned forward to look at the building through the windshield. "Such a nondescript building to cause this much anxiety," she muttered.

"Hey. This is going to be good news. I can feel it in my bones."

Rebecca turned her head to look at Cass and smiled. "You can feel it in your bones?"

"Yep." Cass hesitated for only a second before bringing Rebecca's hand to her lips and placing a light kiss on her palm. "Whatever happens up there, Becca, I'm here. Always."

Rebecca's palm tingled where Cass's lips touched her. The emotions she felt each time she was with Cass made her desperate to remember their lives together.

"Let's do this."

Cass grinned. "That's my girl."

Rebecca flipped through an entertainment magazine and frowned. "Who are these people?"

Cass leaned over to see who Rebecca was looking at on the page. There were a bunch of young celebrities that were 'just like us' coming out of grocery stores, drinking Starbucks, or going for a run. Cass pointed at one. "That's Adele. She's a singer, and you dig her. The rest," Cass shrugged with a laugh. "No clue."

"So weird," Rebecca whispered as she continued turning the pages. "I guess people still care who's dating whom." She smiled when Cass merely grunted next to her.

"Mrs. Giles?"

Rebecca didn't even look up at the receptionist who was calling her name. *Because she doesn't remember,* Cass reminded herself. "Uh, Becca? That's you."

"Hmm?" Rebecca looked around.

"Mrs. Giles?" The receptionist called again.

Cass stood and held her hand out to Rebecca. "That's you."

Rebecca frowned but took Cass's hand and followed her. Her brain was still trying to catch up. Who is Giles?

Cass was freaking out. No one had told Rebecca they were married, and Cass had followed their lead even though her gut told her not to. As they walked the hallway toward an exam room, Cass desperately searched for an explanation she could give Rebecca without the shit hitting the proverbial fan. If *this* were what pushed Rebecca over the edge and caused permanent memory loss, Cass would fucking lose her mind.

Rebecca was still trying to figure out why they called her Mrs. Giles. She didn't even know a Gil... She stopped abruptly. "Is your last name Giles? Are we married?!"

Cass winced at the volume level of Rebecca's voice in the quiet area. She turned to look at Rebecca. "Yes. And yeah, we are."

"And you didn't think — *no one* thought — to tell me?"

"Um, if you two could go right in here, please," the young woman said timidly, trying to usher them into an exam room. "I'll tell the PA you need a couple of minutes." She hurried out, leaving Cass and Rebecca alone.

"Becca…"

"How long?"

Cass sighed. She hated seeing Rebecca pissed, especially at her. But even more, she didn't want Rebecca to stress herself out. "Almost three years."

"And… it's legal? We're really, truly married? I'm Rebecca Giles?"

"Rebecca Cuinn-Giles, yes. We are legally, *lovingly* married."

Lovingly. Rebecca studied Cass and saw nothing but sincerity. Still, Rebecca was beyond annoyed that this kind of information was kept from her. "Why would everyone keep this from me? Don't you think I deserved to know?"

"Yeah, babe, I did. God, I wanted to tell you." Cass scrubbed her face in frustration, then hoisted Rebecca up onto the exam table and stood in front of her. "I've told you before that my number one priority is your welfare and recovery, Becca, so I followed Aunt Wills's lead with how much I could say and when. Maybe I made a mistake. But I have no clue how to navigate something like this, so I'm doing my best."

"Y-you didn't fight for me. If we're married, why didn't you fight for me to go home with you?"

Cass's eyebrows raised in surprise. "Is that what you think? Becca, my heart fucking shatters every time I go into that house alone. But you didn't know me — you still don't, not really. And I wasn't about to force you to do something you weren't comfortable with. If I had done that, if I had treated you like *she* treated you… what incentive would you have to regain your memories?" She feathered her fingers across Rebecca's cheek. "I want you to remember me, Becca. To remember *us.* And I need you to know that showing up every single day with some lame excuse to be there *is* me fighting for you. That's me making sure you know I'm here and always will be."

Rebecca couldn't argue with anything Cass just said to her. Hell, she couldn't even be mad. How could she when this whole situation was fucked up? Besides, the feel of Cass's fingers on her skin, the look in Cass's eyes, and how close her lips were made Rebecca forget what she was supposed to be upset about. The close proximity compelled Rebecca to lean in. Unfortunately, that caused the paper on the exam table to crinkle, startling them both. One snicker from Rebecca set off peals of laughter from both.

Neither heard the knock at the door.

"Good morning, Rebecca." Dr. Lima rounded her desk and settled in. "Cass, it's good to see you," she said before turning her focus back on Rebecca. "How are you feeling?"

Rebecca's leg bounced with nerves, her hands fidgeting in her lap. Getting her stitches out was a piece of cake. Especially since all she could think was; *I'm married to Cass.* This was the hard part, though. Having to sit down with the doctor and hear the results of the biopsy.

"I'm good. Um, I still get headaches, but they're less frequent and don't last as long."

"That's a positive result."

Dr. Lima wrote notes as she listened. There wasn't much of an expression on her face, and that frustrated Cass. She didn't even look away when Dr. Lima caught her staring.

"And has there been any improvement with your amnesia?"

Rebecca glanced between Dr. Lima and Cass. Cass looked as though she was trying to read the doctor's mind. The doctor looked as though her mind was a steel vault. It was almost comical.

"Not really. My memory is... still gone."

Dr. Lima frowned. "That's not ideal."

"No kidding," Cass scoffed. She jumped slightly when she felt Rebecca's hand on her thigh. "Sorry. I didn't mean to be rude. Do we know what is causing the amnesia?"

"Hang on, please," Rebecca interrupted. "Could we start with the biopsy results? My head starts to hurt when I'm stressed, and this dread hanging over me isn't helping."

"Shit, I'm sorry, Becca."

Rebecca shook her head. "No, it's fine. I want to know the answer to your question, too. Let's just get this biopsy thing over with first. Dr. Lima?"

Dr. Lima nodded and pulled her keyboard closer. After a few

keystrokes, she nodded again. "The results of your biopsy came back negative. The tumor was benign."

For once, Cass was grateful for Lima's no-nonsense, straight-to-the-point attitude. If she had made them wait like some dramatic reality show, Cass would have gone a little crazy. She sat back heavily, the intense rush of relief nearly leaving her body limp.

Rebecca let go of the breath she'd been holding. "Benign," she repeated just to hear it again. "So, it's over?"

"I was able to remove one hundred percent of the tumor. The chances of it coming back are minimal. I will suggest that you come back in six months for follow-up care and an MRI."

"O-okay. That was quick and to the point." Rebecca sat dumbfounded for a moment. She didn't know what she was expecting. Perhaps a little more fanfare? Maybe some emotion from her doctor?

Dr. Lima looked at Rebecca curiously. "I thought that would be good news."

"It is, it's just…"

"Your delivery could use a little warmth," Cass finished for Rebecca. Her wife probably would have been more diplomatic, but Cass's nerves were too raw to be tactful.

"Cass," Rebecca scolded gently.

"Sorry, but…"

"I apologize for being abrupt," Dr. Lima interrupted. "If you would like someone more familiar with you personally, I could confer with Dr. Vale."

"No." Rebecca took a cleansing breath. "I like it when people get to the point and say exactly what's on their mind." She glanced at Cass who was looking at her intently enough to make her blush.

What a fucking day, Rebecca thought. Information swirled in her head. It wasn't even noon, and she was already exhausted. Married and cancer-free. All in the span of an hour. *Married for almost three years,* Rebecca reminded herself. She blew out a breath, fighting off the headache she felt coming on.

"Now that we have the results, can we talk about the amnesia? Why have I forgotten…" Rebecca looked at Cass again. "The good in my life?"

"Your tumor was located on your frontal lobe, which is responsible for many of your cognitive functions. Including memory. Your amnesia is most likely a result of swelling."

"Most likely," Cass echoed. "So you don't know if it was something you did or some normal side-effect?"

"Cass," Rebecca whispered harshly. But Cass's stare was relentless. There was something familiar about this scenario that tickled the back of Rebecca's brain.

Dr. Lima, however, never even flinched. "The other explanation for memory loss is the removal of cells responsible for memory during the craniotomy, which was not a procedure I performed. I am very good at what I do, Cass. But I am keenly aware that the brain is highly delicate, and as much as we doctors want to believe we know everything about the way the brain works, we still have so much to learn."

While Cass appreciated the doctor's honesty, it didn't help her situation. "Will it come back? When the swelling is gone, will Rebecca's memory return?"

Dr. Lima steepled her fingers in front of her and addressed Rebecca even though she didn't ask the question. "I wish I could give you a definitive answer. Memory loss isn't uncommon after a craniotomy, and the length of time it lasts varies. If you have not regained your memory by this time next week, I would like for you to come back for an MRI."

Next week! Cass just hoped she could survive another week without Rebecca by her side.

Rebecca nodded, but inside, she wasn't as calm. There had to be a way to speed up this process, and she might have an idea of how.

Chapter Twenty-Six

"Come in, Rebecca."

Rebecca poked her head around the ajar door. "How did you know I was out here?"

Willamena lifted a brow. "You're pacing and mumbling like you're deciding what to say to a room full of CEOs." She waved her hand, beckoning Rebecca to come in, and patted the space next to her. "Do you remember when you used to come into my room after a bad dream? You'd pretend like you weren't scared or sad but wanted to keep me company."

"I remember." Rebecca climbed onto Willamena's bed and settled in beside her. "But don't pretend *you* weren't crying yourself half of the time."

"You heard that?"

"Mmhmm. Oddly enough, it made me feel better." Rebecca rolled her head to the side to look at Aunt Wills. "Not better that you were crying, but that I wasn't alone with my emotions."

"You never are, my sweet girl."

They sat in silence, each of them lost in their own thoughts. For Rebecca, those thoughts replayed the entire day from when Cass came to pick her up until Cass left about an hour and a half ago. Dinner had been awkward because Rebecca felt betrayed by having the truth kept from her. However, the flip side of that coin was relief and happiness over the biopsy results. What a weird fucking day.

"I'm still mad."

"And I still stand by my decision," Willamena rebutted.

"You kept my marriage from me, Aunt Wills!"

"No, I made an educated compromise not to inundate you with information that could have possibly had a negative effect on your recovery."

Rebecca stared at Willamena for a full thirty seconds. "That was the most shrinkity shrink sentence I've ever heard."

Willamena's lips curved into an amused smile. "Shrinkity shrink is the most Cass sentence I've ever heard."

Rebecca laughed. "It is, isn't it? She's very... expressive with her words."

"Would you have done anything different had you known you two were married?" Willamena asked. She was sure she knew the answer but thought Rebecca needed to hear herself say it.

"I don't know. Maybe. We'll never know now."

"Rebecca Aisling."

"Fine. Probably not." Rebecca made a face at her aunt, causing her to laugh.

"Exactly. And I didn't keep Cass from you, just the true nature of your relationship. We're all navigating this together the best we can, Becca."

"Cass pretty much said the same thing." Rebecca fiddled with the sheet, appreciating the softness of it. "When did gay marriage become legal?"

"Here in California? I believe it was 2013. And then in 2015, it was legalized in all fifty states."

"Wow. We've come a long way."

"Hmm. I know you hate talking about politics, so I'll just say over the past few years, any step forward has been met with two steps back."

"You sound like Activist Willamena."

Willamena laughed and playfully slapped Rebecca's comforter-covered leg. "What do you know about her?"

"Mom used to tell me about all your little adventures: protests here, shutting things down there, and building things up elsewhere."

Willamena shook her head. "Gwennie always loved the dramatics. The *truth* is, I volunteered for a few humanitarian agencies, and when those assignments were over, I backpacked through Europe."

"Mmhmm. That doesn't explain all the arrests."

"One time! I was arrested once in Italy for a *peaceful* protest! It was all for show!" Willamena argued, surprised her sister would tell a young Rebecca about that.

"Ah-ha! I *knew* it! Mom never mentioned the arrest. You're such a rebel."

"And *you* are a brat!"

Rebecca wiped tears of laughter from her cheeks and rested her head back on the fluffy pillow. "Do you have any regrets?" she asked suddenly.

Willamena rolled to her side and propped herself up on her elbow. "About what?"

Rebecca shrugged. "Anything. The protests, backpacking... or giving it all up for me."

Willamena smiled sadly. "I have regrets, Rebecca. Some are much bigger than others. But the one thing I don't regret is taking you in after losing Gwennie and Declan. Taking care of you helped me cope with the loss of my sister, and you, my dear, are my family."

A tear slipped down Rebecca's temple and onto the pillow under her head. "I regret so much, Aunt Wills. The worst being getting involved with Samantha. And then staying with her." She hesitated, almost afraid to hear the answer to the question she had been asking herself for a couple of days now. "Am I sabotaging myself?"

Willamena reached back to get a tissue from her nightstand and handed it to her niece. "Sabotaging, how?"

"I sit here every day and struggle to imagine my life with Cass, especially after our afternoon together. But I don't know what to envision. As much as I want to, I don't remember. What if I'm delaying my memory by being too... scared?" Rebecca swiveled her head towards Aunt Wills. "Do you think I should be immersing myself in what my life was before this happened? Would it help?" She dabbed her eyes with the tissue, then turned to mirror Willamena's position. She propped herself up on her elbow and stared at her aunt. "I'm asking Dr. Woodrow for her professional opinion."

"Well, Dr. Woodrow, with her fancy degree, hasn't spent enough time studying amnesia to give a well-educated opinion. However, as your aunt, I do know you and Cass well enough to think it would be beneficial for you both to spend time together."

"Because you want your space back?" Rebecca teased.

"I will bop you in the face with my pillow."

"Go ahead. Maybe it'll knock my brain back into working order."

Willamena shook her head. Of course, she wasn't going to plunk Rebecca with a pillow even though her niece had been extra ornery today and *might* deserve it. "No, my sweet girl. Because I think you're hiding here out of fear that you've made the wrong decisions again. Maybe this will help ease your mind. Cass has never kept you from me. In fact, she will call me when she thinks you need time with your favorite aunt."

Rebecca's face blossomed with a smile. Everything she had learned about Cass was the complete opposite of what she was used to. Perhaps it was time to trust Cass and Aunt Wills, and most of all, it was time to trust herself. Rebecca hopped off the bed with excitement.

"Okay! I can be ready in fifteen minutes."

"Wait!" Willamena called out, still lounging in her bed. "You want to go tonight? It's the middle of the night!"

Rebecca raised a brow. "It's *barely* ten, Aunt Wills. Do you know I walked around this entire house looking for you before realizing you had already gone to bed?" A sly smirk formed on Rebecca's lips as she eyed the book on Willamena's nightstand. "Did I interrupt your... alone time?"

Rebecca squealed and ducked out of the room as a pillow torpedoed toward her.

"I think now is a great time to drive you back home," Willamena groused playfully. "Just so you know, I'm going like this—in my pajamas. I think I'll put my hair up and put on my collagen eye patches."

"Aunt Wills!"

"I wonder where my slippers are."

"We can wait until tomorrow!" Rebecca said quickly.

"No, no. You wanted to go tonight..."

"I need to pack. And I should probably get some rest. It's been a long day."

"Oh, *now* you need rest," Willamena teased, laughing at the look of horror on her niece's face. It was fascinating to Willamena how different Rebecca was now. Even as a child, Rebecca had been serious. Then, she went off to college early. Willamena hadn't gone through the mischievous teen phase with Rebecca. It seemed like Rebecca was making up for that now. Was that Cass's influence? The phenomenon was enough to make Willamena want to study more about amnesia and how specific experiences affected the brain.

"Hello? Aunt Wills?"

Willamena blinked, her niece coming into focus as she stood by the bedroom door. "Sorry, what were you saying?"

"Where were you just then?" Rebecca asked instead of repeating the question her aunt obviously didn't catch.

Willamena shook her head. "I was thinking about research. But that's not what you originally asked."

Rebecca narrowed her eyes. Though she was curious about what research Aunt Wills was interested in, Rebecca let the subject go. "I asked if you could take me to Cass..." She paused and took a breath. "Take me home tomorrow. Maybe in the afternoon? That would give me time to get my things ready and have a panic attack if needed."

"I encourage you to let your feelings flow. However, let's try to keep the panic at a minimum," Willamena smiled. "I can take you. Or I could call Cass to come pick you up if you wanted."

Rebecca shook her head. "No, I kind of wanted to surprise her. You know, show up at her door like she's been doing here. Do you think that's stupid?"

"I think that's a wonderful idea."

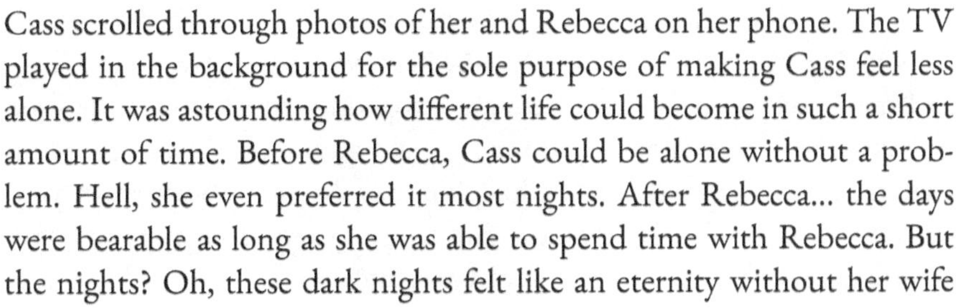

Cass scrolled through photos of her and Rebecca on her phone. The TV played in the background for the sole purpose of making Cass feel less alone. It was astounding how different life could become in such a short amount of time. Before Rebecca, Cass could be alone without a problem. Hell, she even preferred it most nights. After Rebecca... the days were bearable as long as she was able to spend time with Rebecca. But the nights? Oh, these dark nights felt like an eternity without her wife by her side. It was hard to see the light at the end of a seemingly never-ending tunnel.

Cass scrolled until she couldn't scroll any further. Then she'd start over, staring at each picture, remembering exactly when and where it was taken. She was driving herself insane by running through worst-case scenarios in her head. While everyone was trying to be encouraging, Cass was quickly running out of hope. The swelling should be gone by now, and everything she'd read and researched... Rebecca should have regained her memory by now.

Cass flopped back onto the couch with a heavy sigh. "Come on, Becca. *Fight*, baby." She chose a photo of Rebecca looking into the camera and smiling. They had taken a walk on the beach, wanting to get out and get some fresh air. Rebecca was barefoot, digging her toes into the sand and giggling when the waves lapped over her feet. It was a magical sight for Cass, seeing Rebecca so carefree and happy. That's when she snapped the photo of Rebecca. She had wanted to remember that day forever. Little did she know how precious that memory would be today.

Just as Cass closed her eyes to bring more memories to the surface, her doorbell rang. She groaned and thought about ignoring the damn sound and just burying herself under the covers and sleeping until Rebecca came back to her. But she couldn't risk the off chance this would be about Rebecca and forced herself to get up.

She glanced down at her shorts and ripped tee and shrugged. Whoever it was would have to deal with her bedtime attire since she wasn't expecting company, and it was past ten o'clock at night. And when she opened the door, she certainly wasn't expecting to see who was standing there.

"H-hunter. Hey."

Hunter discreetly took in Cass's appearance. Just as she suspected, Cass looked like shit. Everyone had been so worried about Rebecca — and rightfully so — that no one truly stopped to think about how Cass was dealing with everything. Hunter could admit she'd been avoiding Cass after what happened at the hospital. But that's not what this group of friends did. When the going got tough, they came together. So, Hunter put on her big girl pants, and here she was.

"Hey. Sorry, I know it's late."

"Nah, it's, uh, fine. Do you, um, wanna come in?" Cass started to open the door wider for Hunter, then stopped. "You're not going to punch me, are you? Not that I don't deserve it, but…"

"I'm not here to punch you, Cass," Hunter smiled sadly. "You're going through enough as it is."

Cass blew out a breath of relief. "C'mon in. Sorry about the mess."

Hunter spied the makeshift bed on the couch. "I'm sure you remember how I never went home when Ellie was in the hospital. So, I get it, yeah?"

Cass nodded. "Yeah. At least I'm taking showers," she teased, recalling how Hunter rarely left Ellie's side. Jessie had to threaten Hunter to get her to take fifteen minutes to shower and change.

"Thank goodness," Hunter chuckled. She took the seat Cass silently offered and wondered if she could trick Mo into coming over tomorrow to help tidy up. She vetoed that idea pretty quickly when she thought about how Mo cleaned by kicking things under anything that was remotely lifted off the floor. Maybe Ellie could help.

"Why are you here, Hunt? I can't imagine I'm your favorite person after what I did."

"I don't blame you for that, Cass. I was on my way home when El called to tell me the good news about Rebecca's results. Normally, I would have heard that from you." Hunter sighed. Man, she hated that she and Cass were on the outs. Especially now when Cass could use all the support she could get. "I wanted to apologize to you…"

"Whoa, what? What the fuck do you have to apologize to me for? I'm the one who sucker punched *you*."

"For good reason. I promised you I'd bring Rebecca back to you. This is exactly why doctors don't make promises. But I did, and I broke that promise. I'm sorry."

Cass bowed her head and lost the valiant fight she'd been fighting since she found out about Rebecca's tumor. She hid her face in her hands and began to sob. If it were anyone else but Hunter here, Cass would've been embarrassed by her breakdown. But she felt Hunter's arm suddenly around her shoulders and allowed herself to lean into the comfort of her best friend.

"I'm so fucking angry, Hunt. And sad. And… lost." Cass scoffed. "I used to think those saps who talked about love like it was a fucking lifeline were idiots. Why would you trust anyone enough to attach your entire happy existence to them? Now, I'm the idiot."

"You're not an idiot, Cass. You're in love. Love isn't a weakness. Your bond with Rebecca is a strength for both of you."

"So strong she doesn't even fucking remember me," Cass sniffled, grabbing a napkin from the pile that was accumulating on the coffee table and blowing her nose.

"I heard about your date. She remembers you, Cass. The Rebecca I knew back then would never have considered going out with anyone. Samantha did a fucking number on her ego, Cass. Despite your charisma, Rebecca wouldn't have allowed herself to be charmed."

Cass looked up. "That's right. You were there that day. Do you… do you really see differences between then and now?"

Hunter lowered her eyes. "I'm ashamed to say I haven't been by to see Rebecca since she left the hospital."

That surprised Cass. Hunter and Rebecca had been close for far too long for Hunter to avoid seeing her.

"Why?"

"Guilt."

"Look, Hunt, I should have never blamed you…"

"Not about that," Hunter reassured. "As you said, I was there. I saw Rebecca struggle, Cass. Especially that first year. Her self-esteem was fucking… non-existent. She was scared of her own shadow. I mean, Rebecca had enough in the tank to claw her way back and re-invent herself. But she was a completely different person than who you know today. I – I couldn't bear to watch that again. I feel guilty about what a fucking coward I am."

"Hunt."

"Cass, I'm not here for you to ease that guilt. That's mine to live with. That being said, from what I've heard from El, Rebecca is… confident. And flirty. She may not remember much, but it doesn't sound like she's lost the woman she became in the last twenty years. And *that*? That's all you, my friend."

Cass shook her head. "That's all Becca."

"Oh, I give Rebecca all the credit for undoing the shit Samantha did to her and becoming Mistress. But you, my friend? You brought back Rebecca."

Cass smiled through the tears still flowing down her cheeks. "Thanks, Hunt." She patted Hunter's leg awkwardly, now feeling uncomfortable after allowing her vulnerability to show. "I, uh, should have called after what happened at the hospital. Let me finish, please?" Cass continued when Hunter opened her mouth to argue. "I should have been woman enough to step up and apologize for my outburst. And I should have called you today to tell you the news. Not only are you Rebecca's oldest friend, you're *my* best friend. I really needed this. And I didn't know how much until I saw you standing at the door."

"Well, shit, woman," Hunter sniffed. "Way to turn me into a blubbering mess. Hand me one of those sandpaper napkins, will ya?'

Cass grabbed a stack of napkins and shoved them at Hunter, keeping a couple for herself. "Mo never hears of this."

Hunter laughed. "Are you kidding? We'd never hear the end of it."

Chapter Twenty-Seven

Rebecca fidgeted in her seat. She knew in her heart that this was the right decision, but she wished her head would catch up. The one thing she was sure of—somehow—was that she trusted Cass enough to make this leap.

"Are you sure about this, Rebecca?"

"That's the tenth time you've asked me that, Aunt Wills."

"And you've been a nervous wreck all morning. Rebecca Giles doesn't fidget, yet you can't seem to stop."

Rebecca Giles. While Rebecca never thought of herself as the marrying type or the type to take someone else's name, she had to admit that she liked the sound of it.

"My answer hasn't changed. I'm sure. But that doesn't mean I'm not nervous about it." Rebecca shifted in her seat. "Are you worried about me or Cass?"

"Both," Willamena answered honestly. "You're my niece, but Cass has become my family, too. When you didn't go home with her, it broke her heart. If you do this and change your mind, I'm afraid Cass's fragile heart will shatter beyond repair."

"Well, shit, Aunt Wills. No pressure." Rebecca sighed. "Look, I'm not planning on changing my mind. My focus is getting my memory back, and I truly believe being with Cass will help. God, the last thing I want to do, Aunt Wills, is hurt her."

Just the thought of Rebecca being the cause of pain for Cass was enough to bring tears to Rebecca's eyes.

Willamena nodded. "That's the best answer you've given so far. Way better than "yessss, Aunt Wills,'" she said, mimicking Rebecca's exaggerated whine.

Rebecca glared at her aunt. "You have gotten ornery in your old age." Willamena pulled to the curb, and Rebecca thought for sure she'd gone too far with the 'old' joke. "Uh, you're not kicking me out of the car, are you?"

Willamena laughed. "I have half a mind to say yes after you called me old." She pointed at a beautiful, modern home that sat far enough off the road to afford a good bit of privacy.

Rebecca's brows rose as she leaned forward to look out the windshield. "Is that Cass's... um, *our* house?"

"Yep." Willamena smiled as she watched Rebecca's awe. "It was Cass's home, then you moved in. Since then, it has changed a bit with the two of you deciding to make it uniquely yours."

"It's beautiful. So serene. So... different."

"Different than what you expected?"

Rebecca looked at her aunt. "When she was high, Samantha often accused me of sleeping with anyone that came near the house. Towards the end, she was high more often than not. Everything in the yard died. The house was becoming dilapidated. So when I say different, I mean it looks like a home and not a place where a soul dies."

Willamena reached across the console to take Rebecca's hand. "Your soul flourishes here, my sweet girl," she said, giving Rebecca a light squeeze. "Do you want me to pull into the driveway?"

"No, I..." Rebecca frowned when she looked up at the house again and saw an attractive woman coming out. "Maybe this wasn't a good idea."

Willamena followed Rebecca's line of sight, then shook her head. "Don't jump to conclusions, Rebecca."

"It's not that big of a jump, is it? Obviously Cass is familiar with that woman," Rebecca muttered grumpily.

"Yes, she is. So are you."

Rebecca frowned, squinting to get a better look. The brunette was shorter than Cass, though most of the people she'd already met fit that description. If she recalled correctly, Dr. Vale was tall with darker hair. No, this didn't look like anyone she'd met from their circle of friends.

"Who is she?"

"Her name is Lauren. She's the assistant curator at Sumptor Gallery. And as far as I know, she has a very close... friendship with a supermodel."

Rebecca exhaled sharply. "Shit. I just failed the first test, didn't I?"

"None of this is a test, Becca. You had a reaction based on past experiences. It's completely normal."

"You know what's not normal? You going all super shrink."

"That doesn't negate the fact that I'm right. In fact, I would venture to say that makes me right because I'm a professional."

"Professional pain in my ass," Rebecca mumbled.

"I will dump your *ass* right here on the curb, woman."

Rebecca snickered. "That's not much of a threat since I'm getting out here anyway."

"You really don't want me to help you?"

"It's two bags, Aunt Wills. I can manage, but thank you." Rebecca leaned over and hugged Willamena. "You're always saving me."

Willamena's smile faltered. "I will always be here for you, my sweet girl. Now, go on, get out of here."

Rebecca patted Willamena's hand. "I love you, too." She stepped out of the car, grabbing her stuff from the back seat. Her heart was pounding in her chest. What if...? Rebecca knocked on the window so Aunt Wills could roll it down. "What if she doesn't want me to move back in?"

"Child, I will sell my Cracker Jack degree on Marketplace if that woman turns you away. You have absolutely nothing to worry about. I promise you. Cass loves you and would turn the world upside down for you. If you remember anything, remember that."

Rebecca inhaled deeply through her nose and released it through her mouth. She then had a flash of doing the same thing with Ellie.

"Becca? Are you okay?"

"Hmm? Y-yes. I thought..." Rebecca shook her head. She didn't know if what she had was a real memory or something her brain generated because of what she had recently learned about Ellie. "Nothing. I'm good. I'll call you later. Uh, Cass will allow me to use her phone, right?"

Allow. "Rebecca, what you have with Cass is vastly different than what you had... before. You don't have to be afraid to ask for anything. And I know what I said about Cass's heart shattering if you changed your mind, but she would still understand. If you need to come back to my house for any reason, all you have to do is tell Cass, and she will drive you herself. She would do anything for you, even at the expense of her own happiness."

My first priority is your welfare and recovery. Rebecca was beginning to think Cass was *too* good for her. "Okay!" Rebecca stood tall and squared her shoulders. She looked confident to anyone on the outside, but in reality, she was trying to keep her lunch from making an appearance. "Wish me luck!"

"You don't need it. All you need is to be yourself and let things play out naturally. Don't rush this, Rebecca. No one has a stopwatch, and there's no timeline. Got it?"

"Got it," Rebecca winked and waved before making her way up the driveway.

Cass stacked canvases next to her easel. She felt a little lighter after handing off a few pieces to Lauren. They weren't typical pieces from Cass, and she was concerned they wouldn't be accepted. But Lauren was enthusiastic when she came to pick them up. Of course, they still had to pass Eve and Lainey's inspection. Whatever happened, Cass was proud of her work.

Art is an expression of your emotions, not a fulfillment of an obligation. Cass had taken Eve's words to heart. Though there were times when she had nothing to express because it was all too much for her, there were also moments when everything she felt flowed from the tip of the paintbrush. The work was chaotic at times, with bold colors contrasting against the white of the canvas in volatile patterns. Then the mood would shift, and Cass's art would shift with it. Canvases painted entirely black with muted colors calming the unrest in Cass's heart.

The one color she shied away from was the one that made her body respond the most. When Cass touched any shade of pink, her body burned with the need for her wife—for Mistress. Is that what Rebecca felt with her urges? When Rebecca came to Cass with needs that her body demanded, Cass couldn't understand. By talking more with Dr. Woodrow, they would both learn that Rebecca had been conditioned, that it was what her body was used to and that she could crave it at any given time. That's what the color pink did to Cass. It ignited her... desire.

Desire was something Cass wanted to stay away from these days. Her art helped. Painting kept her occupied for most of the day. Visiting Rebecca, oddly enough, helped as well. It reminded her how different things were at the moment. For the most part, Cass did fairly well keeping her brain and libido in check. But the night, when it was time to sleep, the dreams came. Dreams that were *full* of Rebecca/Mistress. They were so vivid that Cass considered staying asleep until Rebecca came back to her to 'feel' those hands, that body, and that mouth on her. One night, Cass woke up, stroking herself. Instead of feeling good, it felt like... cheating. After that, Cass vowed not to touch herself again until Rebecca came back to her.

Cass sighed and checked her watch. She had time to grab a quick shower before heading over to Aunt Wills's place. This time, though, she didn't have an excuse. Now that Rebecca knew they were married, Cass's only 'excuse' was showing up. She sure as hell wasn't going to let Rebecca ever believe Cass wasn't fighting for her. For them.

Cass had just made it to the bedroom, her shirt halfway off, when she heard the doorbell. "Gah, dammit," she muttered, trying to stuff her head back into her shirt, only to get it stuck in the armhole. She was in the process of getting unstuck when she ran into the doorjamb. "Son of a fuck. If this is someone wanting to sell me a car warranty..." Cass made it down the stairs without killing herself and finally got herself situated. She took a deep breath to calm her annoyance before opening the door.

"B-Becca?" Cass stared at Rebecca for ten seconds, then looked around. There was no car, and no Willamena. "How? Did you come here by yourself?"

Rebecca noticed Cass's disheveled hair and wrinkled shirt. "Um, Aunt Wills dropped me off. Am I interrupting something?"

"Huh?" Again, Cass looked around. "Dropped you off?" Eventually, Cass looked down and saw a couple of bags by Rebecca's feet. "I don't understand."

"Can I come in? Or are you busy?" Rebecca's heart was beating frantically. She saw Lauren leave, but that didn't mean there wasn't someone else here, right? Rebecca quickly shooed that thought away, choosing to believe Aunt Wills that Cass... loved her.

"Shit! Yes! I mean, no. I mean." Cass rolled her eyes. "No, I'm not busy. Yes, please come in." She stooped to pick up Rebecca's things, still confused by what was happening. All Cass knew for sure was that Rebecca was there, and that made Cass deliriously happy.

"Are you okay?" Rebecca stepped inside, allowing Cass enough room to close the door. She was nervous as fuck. So far, nothing felt familiar, and Cass didn't seem as happy to see her as Rebecca had hoped or imagined. She had to remind herself that Cass had no idea Rebecca would be showing up at her front door, luggage in hand, and that was probably throwing Cass off balance.

"Yeah!" *Stop yelling at her, dumbass! You're going to scare her.* "I'm so sorry. I was about to get in the shower, but then I got my head stuck in my shirt and ran into the wall. And now you're standing here, and I'm wondering if I hit my head a little harder than I thought, and maybe I'm really just passed out with my head stuck in my armhole and dreaming."

Rebecca's brows shot up, and she struggled not to laugh. "That... was a lot. But I can assure you, I'm really here."

"Yeah, well, that's something dream Rebecca would say."

"Dream Rebecca," Rebecca repeated merrily. Now she was glad she decided to surprise Cass. This little scene would never have happened otherwise. She stood on her tiptoes and kissed Cass lightly on the cheek, shocking them both. "I, um, I thought pinching you would be too harsh."

Cass touched her cheek in awe. "You're really here," she said, then her eyes grew wide. "Did you remember something?"

Rebecca hated having to burst Cass's bubble. "No. But I," she hesitated.

Her confidence was unpredictable. One minute, Rebecca thought this was the best idea she'd ever had. The next, she feared it would be too much for Cass, and she'd turn her away. Who needed this kind of burden in their life? *She loves you.* While it was still hard for Rebecca to believe someone besides Aunt Wills truly loved her, she held onto those words, allowing them to fuel her confidence once more.

"I thought maybe immersing myself in the life I don't remember would help. Does that make sense? I don't want to inconvenience you," Rebecca continued quickly. "And if this is a bad idea, please just tell me..."

"Becca? There's nothing I want more than for you to be here."

Rebecca blew out a breath of relief. "Good." She dug a bottle of pills out of her front pocket. "I'm supposed to give you these because I can't be trusted to take them myself, apparently."

Still dumbfounded, Cass took Rebecca's medication and absently stuffed it in her pocket. "I'm sorry. I should stop staring, I know, but I'm just so... surprised you're here."

"That was the point," Rebecca grinned. "I wanted to pull a Cass and just show up. That was probably a stupid idea."

"No, no. It was the best idea!" Cass laughed. "I was headed to the shower before I heard you at the door. Then I would have gotten ready to show up at Aunt Wills's."

"Beat you to it," Rebecca teased.

"You sure did." Cass shook herself out of her idiocy. Rebecca was going to turn around and walk out of there if Cass didn't stop acting like a fool. "C'mon. I'll, uh, put this stuff away in a bit. Maybe after you've gotten settled." She heard the muffled shake of pills in her pocket. "Do you need one of these, or can I put them away?"

"Definitely put them away for now."

Cass nodded. "I trust you to tell me if you need them, Becca." She emphasized her words by tossing the pills onto the entryway table. Obviously, Cass would get them later and put them in the medicine cabinet, but she wanted to do something symbolic to show Rebecca that she meant what she said. "Would you like a tour or...?"

Yes. But no. Fuck, why was she so nervous? Rebecca smiled warmly, knowing it was a little less self-assured than she'd prefer. "Could we sit down for a bit first? Maybe we could figure out how all of this is going to work."

"Of course." Cass would agree to anything as long as it meant Rebecca was home.

Chapter Twenty-Eight

"Forgive the mess," Cass said, setting Rebecca's stuff to the side and trying to clear a spot on the couch for her. "Maid's day off."

Rebecca inhaled sharply. Something about Cass's words tickled the back of her brain.

"Becca, are you okay?" Cass closed the distance between them in two strides, firmly holding Rebecca's upper arms to steady her. "Do you need the pain pills?"

Rebecca shook her head. "It's not a headache. It's more like..." She frowned, trying to find the right words. "Deja vu. I feel like I've done this before, but I can't..." She waved her hands around her head. "The feeling is there, but not the images."

"Hmm. Maybe being here is helping already," Cass grinned. "Here, have a seat."

"Is that my favorite pillow?" Rebecca asked, eyeing the bedding Cass had just tossed off the couch.

"Heh, yeah. It, uh, keeps me company down here."

"So, you sleep down here? Why? Do you not have a bedroom?"

"Yeah, we do have a bedroom. But it's too hard to sleep in there without you," Cass said, winced, and realized she needed to be more careful with her words. "Sorry, I shouldn't have said that."

"No, please. I prefer honesty—even awkward honesty," Rebecca laughed nervously. "Speaking of awkward honesty..." She took a breath and hoped what she was about to say wouldn't hurt Cass's feelings. "I really do want to try and take complete advantage of being here to help bring my memory back. However, I'm, um, not ready for intimacy yet."

Cass had never heard Rebecca sound so meek. It broke her heart. "Becca, I have never and *would* never force you to do anything you weren't ready for. I'm perfectly fine with staying right here on the couch while you take the bedroom."

"No, I couldn't... this is your house, Cass."

"It's *our* house. And I'm used to being down here. But your pillow stays with me," Cass teased. She had to do *something* to lessen the tension in the room.

Relief washed over Rebecca, and she smiled. "Fair enough. Thank you for understanding."

"Always." Cass sat back, propping her socked feet up on the coffee table. "Do you wanna talk about what changed about you being here? Why now? I mean, I hope that part of the decision was because you trust me."

"Oh, absolutely. That's the biggest reason I thought I could actually do this. Spending time with you has helped me see what kind of person you are and how you are with me." Rebecca tucked a strand of hair behind her ear. "As for what changed," Rebecca relaxed next to Cass, kicking her shoes off and bringing her feet up under her on the couch. "I get that I'm supposed to be taking it easy because of the surgery. But I was beginning to feel more... stagnant instead of relaxed. Please don't get me wrong, I love my aunt. Living with her wasn't the problem. It's just..." There was a slight pause while Rebecca found her words. "My brain wasn't relaxing. It kept trying to remember things it couldn't remember."

Rebecca frowned. She had tried to reiterate Aunt Wills's comment about not knowing what she was supposed to remember, but it came out even more confusing. "That made a lot more sense in my head."

Cass chuckled. She had been so preoccupied with Rebecca casually taking off her shoes and relaxing that she almost missed the very un-Rebecca-like explanation. Normally, Rebecca was capable of expressing herself eloquently, leaving the incoherent stuff to Cass. Oddly enough, Cass found it refreshing.

"Nah, I get exactly what you're trying to say."

"You do?"

"Yep." Cass changed her position, so she was facing Rebecca. *God, she's beautiful.* "It's like someone asking me to paint the scenery in the Canary Islands, yeah? But I've never been there, so I don't know what it looks like." She shrugged. "Still, I'm going to paint it how I believe it looks there, and whatever I come up with may be fine, but it wouldn't really be the Canary Islands, right?"

Rebecca tapped Cass's arm with excitement. "That's exactly it! Now that I'm here, my brain is able to fill in some blanks. At least, that's the hope." She looked around, taking in every little detail she could. Then, her eyes landed on the mermaid mural. How the hell had she missed that when she walked in?

Cass watched silently as Rebecca got up and walked straight to the mural. When Rebecca touched the mermaid's face, Cass's gaze fell on Rebecca's hand. The nails were unpainted and slightly longer than usual, but those slender yet strong fingers never failed to get Cass's blood pumping. Instead of squirming in her seat, she got up and joined Rebecca.

"You did this?" Rebecca asked quietly when Cass came up beside her.

"Yeah." Now, Cass was the one experiencing the deja vu.

"It's... me." Rebecca stared at the image. It was most certainly her, yet it was different. Cass saw her this way: beautiful, sensual, free. Was that how she was when she was with Cass?

"It is." Cass turned and leaned against the mural. She had been staring at the mural every night, but now Rebecca was actually standing in front of her. While she *could* stare all night, Cass didn't think Rebecca would enjoy that. "So, uh, it's too early for bed. Unless you're tired."

"Not even a little," Rebecca grinned.

"Good," Cass couldn't help but return the smile. "I could give you a tour of the place and get you settled in upstairs. Then, maybe, we could DoorDash some dinner and sorta veg out on the couch and talk."

"DoorDash?"

Stuck in 2001, you dolt. "Oh, right. Um, food delivery." Cass brought out her phone to bring up the app. "See? You browse a ton of different restaurants, and they bring you food. Here's Ellie's. But we can get anything you're in the mood for."

"Ellie's sound great. Can I...?" Rebecca gestured at Cass's phone.

"Hmm? Oh, uh, yeah." She swiped out of the app and handed Rebecca her iPhone. If Rebecca were stuck in 2001, she wouldn't have had one.

"I think this is what Aunt Wills has. I remember my last cell phone. It didn't look anything like this." Rebecca laughed, but it wasn't a happy sound. "It was a Nokia, I believe. It was a tiny little thing." She swiped the screen like she had seen Cass do earlier. She had no idea what any of the little squares were or what they did. Apps? Is that what Cass called it? They were colorful and plentiful, but Rebecca understood none of it, and that was frustrating. "I wasn't allowed…"

Cass frowned at the sadness in Rebecca's voice. She knew Rebecca was thinking about Samantha, and Cass didn't want tonight marred by memories of that bitch. Fuck, she wanted to run and get Rebecca's phone just to let her know she had free rein of everything she wanted. Was it the right thing to do? She pushed away from the wall to stand close to Rebecca.

"Wanna see something?" Cass scrolled to her photos app and opened it. Pictures of Rebecca and Cass popped up. She didn't know if *this* was the right thing to do, either, but she wanted Rebecca to think of more pleasant things than her time with Samantha.

Rebecca stared at each photo for a long time before going to the next. She looked incredibly happy with Cass. The laughter and light in her eyes was something Rebecca never thought she'd see again. She pushed the phone back to Cass.

"They're beautiful, Cass."

"But?"

"It's overwhelming right now. I'm so sorry."

"No, don't be. I shouldn't have pushed." Cass slipped her phone in her back pocket.

Rebecca touched Cass's arm. "You didn't push; you gave me… something to look forward to. Maybe tomorrow will be a better time to discuss *our* past. Tonight, I want to just sit with you in the here and now. I know that doesn't make much sense."

"Actually, it does. You need to get the lay of the land before you navigate it fully."

Rebecca laughed. "Why do you make it sound so easy to explain the unexplainable?"

Cass shrugged with a grin. "I've always seen things differently. Maybe that helps. Listen, why don't we take your stuff up to the bedroom, and you can get settled in while I go pick up some food?"

"I thought you were going to dash it here?"

Cass bit her lip. *Dash it.* "I was, but I thought I'd give you a little time to yourself. You know, just let you ease yourself into being here. Maybe take a shower, get into jammies and fluffy socks, look around." She lifted a shoulder. "We have all night to do nothing but sit around in the here and now."

"That sounds... perfect, actually."

"Cool," Cass smiled. "I'd, uh, run you a bath, but I'd prefer to be here for that. I meant," she blew out a breath, embarrassed by the innuendo. "I didn't mean... I just think it's better if I'm close, you know, in case something happens. I'm not making this any better."

Rebecca laughed. "It makes me feel better that I'm not the only one stumbling over my words."

Cass scoffed playfully. "Everyday occurrence for me, babe. Especially when I'm around you. C'mon, I'll show you where the bedroom is."

Rebecca sat on the huge bed, her feet swinging back and forth. Cass had left a few minutes before, and now Rebecca didn't know what to do with herself. This was her house, and she felt like a guest trying not to disturb anything.

Look around, Becca. Nothing is off-limits. It's all yours.

Those were the words Cass left her with. "So get up and look around, Rebecca. That's what you're here for," she told herself, finally hopping off the bed. She could take a shower, or she could snoop for a bit first. "Is it really snooping if it's your stuff? Also, you may want to stop talking to yourself."

She shook her head at her ridiculousness, pursing her lips in thought. Where should she start? The medicine cabinet? Nah, too cliche. She eyed the closet.

"Let's see what kind of woman Cass Giles is. Hell, let's see what kind of woman Rebecca Giles is. Also, you're still talking to yourself."

Rebecca snickered as she padded to the closet door. Why was she nervous about this? What did she think she'd find behind the door? After a deep breath, Rebecca opened the door and walked inside. The room was larger than she expected and much tidier, thanks to the drawers and shelves that lined it. Their clothes were color-coordinated, and their shoes were meticulously shelved. It was a far cry from what Rebecca was used to with Samantha. The more addicted Samantha became, the less she cared about neatness. It came to be too much for Rebecca to keep up, even more so when the abuse got worse.

Rebecca walked to the side of the closet that had more color. Since she'd only seen Cass in black, white, or gray, Rebecca shockingly assumed the more colorful side was hers. When had she embraced color into her life? Was this after Cass? As she rummaged through the outfits — impeccable and powerful outfits and lots of pink — she tried to imagine herself in them. Oh, she wasn't ready to try them on just yet, but an imaginary wardrobe change montage wouldn't hurt anyone.

There was also a spattering of jeans and casual wear. *So many clothes*, she thought, testing the quality with a fingertip. Before Samantha, Rebecca had cared about her appearance. To make it in the male-dominated world of business, a woman had to exude confidence and intelligence. By the end, Rebecca was lucky to get out of the house for more than five minutes. There were no dates and definitely no more working for Rebecca. Her wardrobe dwindled to skimpy lingerie Samantha had bought her. And, of course, oversized sweatpants and sweatshirts on those rare nights she didn't have to service Samantha.

Rebecca wanted those disturbing thoughts out of her head, so she went over to Cass's side. Touching Cass's clothes felt a little weird—almost perverted, especially when Rebecca leaned in to smell the white button-down shirt. That didn't stop her, though. She did, however, stop herself from actually wrapping the shirt around her. To keep the temptation at bay, Rebecca moved to the drawers. Was this an invasion of Cass's privacy?

"We're married," Rebecca murmured repeatedly. "This is totally normal. Besides, she brought you underwear. Why can't you see hers?"

Rebecca rolled her eyes and wondered if she could blame talking to herself on the side effects of the tumor. She drew in a deep breath and opened the top drawer.

Rebecca's eyes widened, and she quickly closed the drawer. "Nope. Not ready for that." Her piqued curiosity, however, had her opening it back up for a peek. "Just a little peek," she reassured herself. There was an array of sex toys, as impeccably organized as the rest of the closet. Dildos, flogs, cuffs, blindfolds... they were all there. Is this what kind of relationship she and Cass had?

Rebecca closed the drawer again, leaning against it for a moment to catch her breath. Her heart was beating so fast it was almost painful. Her body hurt. There was a need for... something, but Rebecca couldn't understand what that need was.

"Okay. In through the nose, out through the mouth." Rebecca did the breathing exercise a few times. When it didn't work, she decided getting out of the sex closet was the right thing to do. *Sex closet*, she scoffed. *It's one drawer. It's not like it's an entire room.* She narrowed her eyes as she scanned the bedroom. There was no other apparatus that she could see, so maybe that little drawer was just for "special times." That was the explanation she was going with. She'd worry about the nature of her and Cass's marriage later. For now, she had more exploring to do before Cass got home.

Chapter Twenty-Nine

Rebecca ran her finger across her name on one of the many awards that lined the shelf in the office. *Her* office. It didn't take a memory to know that much when her degrees hung on the walls, along with clippings of successful businesses. A tear rolled down Rebecca's cheek. Maybe Aunt Wills was right. Maybe Samantha *didn't* break her.

"Knock, knock." Cass kept her voice low, not wanting to startle Rebecca.

Rebecca looked back over her shoulder and smiled. "Hey, sorry. I didn't hear you come in."

"I figured. You were lost in thought there. Everything okay?" Cass kept her distance, not wanting to crowd Rebecca or make her feel uncomfortable.

"Mmhmm." Rebecca wiped the tear from her cheek before turning to Cass fully. "I really did all of this?"

"Sure did," Cass grinned. "And this isn't even the half of it. You're a brilliant businesswoman, Becca."

Rebecca lowered her eyes, blushing at the compliment. "Hopefully, I can still do it. I'll need to find a job at some point."

"We can talk about all that later," Cass said amicably. She wondered how this Rebecca would handle being retired—*semi-retired*, she corrected herself. "I got a ton of different finger foods. Actually, Ellie helped me pick some stuff out. I thought maybe we could have a little living room picnic." She noticed Rebecca hadn't changed her clothes. "If you're done exploring for the moment, maybe you wanna get comfortable while I get everything set up?"

"That sounds wonderful. I hope you don't mind that I looked around."

"Of course not. It's your house, Becca."

Rebecca bit her bottom lip. "I saw some of your paintings in the other room. I didn't touch anything," she said quickly. "But what I saw was beautiful. You're extremely talented."

Cass smiled. "Thank you. And seriously, there's nothing off limits in this house, Becca. If you want to go through paintings, papers, closets, or whatever, do it. I have nothing to hide, and everything in this house belongs to you as much as it does to me."

Rebecca tilted her head, studying Cass. "Why is the room down the hall locked?"

Cass's brows rose. *Well, shit. How the hell do I explain this?* "Oh, um, we have a service that comes out a couple of times a week. We keep that room locked so they won't go in there."

That was the dumbest non-answer in the freakin' world, but it was all Cass could come up with that wouldn't cause Rebecca to go screaming back to Aunt Wills.

"Hmm." Rebecca chewed her lip as she considered what Cass told her. This must be one of those things Rebecca wasn't ready to know. She trusted Cass enough to wait, right? As she looked into those kind, bi-colored eyes, Rebecca knew the answer. "I'll only be a few minutes getting changed. Then I'll help you with the food."

Cass released the breath she'd been holding. Rebecca obviously knew there was more that Cass wasn't saying about the room—their playroom—but she graciously let it go—for now. "Take your time. I got this," she grinned.

The flames of a low fire danced on the walls, beckoning Rebecca with their rhythmic swaying. She almost expected music to be playing, matching their motions. Instead, the TV was on, the sound muted, illuminating a massive blanket with delicious-smelling food spread out. The scene, with Cass as the focal point in shorts and t-shirt, was decidedly romantic. Oddly enough, that didn't bother Rebecca one bit.

"This is quite epic." Rebecca's eyes twinkled with delight.

Cass beamed with pride, gesturing to the empty space across from her. She twisted the cap off a sizeable green bottle that hissed as the pressure was released. Pouring clear, bubbly liquid into a wine glass, Cass glanced at Rebecca. "Perrier," she explained as Rebecca watched her. "I hope you don't mind. Alcohol was one of the items that should be avoided during recovery."

Ah, yes. Recovery. Rebecca was on the verge of forgetting about the tumor, the surgery, the memory loss, and recovery. Why couldn't this be a simple date?

"And that's the last time we reference anything about that," Cass announced. "Tonight is about the present." She lifted her glass. "Here's to a beautiful night with a beautiful companion."

Rebecca only hesitated for a split second before touching the rim of her glass to Cass's. How did Cass seem to always know what Rebecca needed? *She loves you.* Rebecca's eyes fell on Cass's full lips on the glass, blushing at the thoughts the sight conjured up. She drained her glass in one big gulp, holding it out to Cass for a refill.

Oh, Cass didn't miss *any* of that, including the desire in Rebecca's eyes. *Let it go, Cass. She's not there yet.* "So," she cleared her throat. "Did you finish the book?"

"Mmm, yes! It was intelligent, entertaining, and so *hot*!" Rebecca laughed as she picked up a sausage roll and popped it into her mouth. "This food is fantastic, by the way."

"Yeah, Ellie is freakin' awesome. You tell her what your plans are, and poof! The perfect meal to take your plans to the next level. Here, try this." Cass handed Rebecca a beef empanada. "Don't forget the chimichurri. Chef's kiss!" She emphasized the praise by kissing her fingers with an exaggerated 'muah!'. "And I totally agree with your assessment of the book! What did you think of the twist?"

"I did not see that one coming!" Rebecca answered, hiding her mouth full of food behind her hand. "But I'm reading one of the other books in the series now, and it seems like that's a theme with her books. I really like that little aspect."

"Yeah, me too. Are you on the third book?" Cass looked up from picking cilantro off the samosa she was about to devour and saw Rebecca nod.

"Mmhmm. It's so different than the last one in terms of the spice factor, but it still works, don't you think?"

"Totally," Cass readily agreed. "I like how Joslyn Cohan stays true to her characters' personalities."

Rebecca watched Cass pick at her food with amusement. "You don't like vegetables?"

Cass glanced up, poised to flick a bell pepper off a hummus phyllo cup, and grinned. "Nope."

Rebecca reached over, grabbed the offending bell pepper, and ate it. "They're good for you."

"Yeah, yeah, I know. I'm getting better, but bell peppers are a hard no for me. Ellie continues to put them on my food because you like them."

"Hmm. Good teamwork."

"The best," Cass said, handing Rebecca another bell pepper.

After another hour or so of food and conversation, Rebecca and Cass moved from the picnic to the couch to watch a movie. Cass was surprised and delighted that Rebecca chose to sit close to her, their thighs touching. Even so, Cass was careful with her movements and hand placement. The last thing she wanted to do was scare Rebecca, and really, this was all Cass had needed since Rebecca had surgery—just to be close to Rebecca again, to be *home* with Rebecca.

Rebecca stretched her legs out, aiming to prop her feet up on the coffee table along with Cass's. Yet her toes were the only part of her feet that touched the table. That was because she was flexing her feet as much as she could without cramping. She felt Cass's body shake, and she rolled her head to the side, narrowing her eyes.

"Are you laughing?"

"Me?" Cass shook her head, pointing to the TV. "I, uh, saw something funny on the TV."

"We're watching a drama." Rebecca playfully tapped Cass on the leg. "You're laughing at me because I can't reach the coffee table, aren't you?"

Cass's body shook again as she lost the battle to hold in the laughter. "I'm sorry!" she gasped. "You're scooting so far down on the couch, your ass is about to hit the floor." She observed Rebecca's position and laughed even harder when Rebecca stuck her tongue out at her. "You're gonna get a crick in your neck."

She sat up and pulled the table closer. It didn't matter that her own feet would now hang off the other side as long as Rebecca could sit more comfortably.

"Better?"

Rebecca snickered at the new dilemma. "Surely we have a more effective way of doing this that benefits us both."

"Well, yeah, but..."

"But?"

Cass hesitated. "You, um, kinda lay on me. Y-your head on my lap, I mean. With a pillow," she amended quickly, hoping to make it less awkward. It didn't help. She lifted a shoulder when Rebecca just stared at her.

Rebecca reached over Cass and plucked what she now knew was her favorite pillow from the couch's arm. She deposited it onto Cass's lap and proceeded to lie down.

"Oh, you're right. This is much better."

Cass smiled down at Rebecca before they both turned their attention back to the movie. It was easier to pretend this wasn't affecting them than to deal with emotions Rebecca didn't quite understand. However, Cass remembered that this position had two different outcomes. If Cass trailed her fingers across Rebecca's shoulder, their night lasted into the wee hours, doing incredible things to each other. But if Cass softly scratched Rebecca's head, Rebecca would fall asleep before whatever they were watching ended. She gently scratched Rebecca's head, carefully avoiding the area of the incision.

Sunlight filtered in between a small opening in the curtains, landing on Rebecca's face. She frowned, slowly opening her eyes only to close them against the brightness of the morning. *Morning?* Her eyes flew open, and she moved her arms out, fanning them as though she was making a snow angel. She was alone, in bed, and — she lifted the covers — still dressed in her sweats. That explained why she was hot but didn't explain how she got here.

The last thing she remembered was lying on the couch, her head on Cass's lap, and Cass's incredible fingers doing wonders on her head. No amount of meds had made Rebecca feel so relaxed. She obviously fell into a deep sleep in her thoroughly relaxed state since she had no recollection of coming to bed. Cass wasn't here, though. And while part of her was disappointed by that, her trust in Cass grew.

She rolled out of bed and cracked open the bedroom door to listen for any activity downstairs. When she heard none, Rebecca wondered if Cass was still sleeping or had left to run errands or do... whatever Cass did during the day.

Rebecca stopped in her tracks on her way to the bathroom. What did *she* do? She had been forced out of the business world when she was with Samantha. Had she gone back to it after? Did Cass allow her to work? Rebecca signed with frustration. She needed to stop thinking of Cass the way she thought of Samantha. Cass had already said Rebecca worked. But it was still frustrating that there was so much she didn't know. The only thing that kept Rebecca from crawling back into bed and throwing the covers over her head was the fact that she had taken the first giant step by moving in with Cass. Last night was wonderful with Cass, and Rebecca felt hopeful that this was the right decision. She wouldn't allow herself to screw this opportunity up.

Rebecca was determined to remember, starting today. Now that her brain knew what to envision, it was game on! She'd jump in the shower and put on something other than sweats. If she were lucky, Cass would be home, and they could have breakfast together.

Chapter Thirty

Cass looked at her watch with surprise. Nearly two hours before double digits meant it was way too early for Rebecca to be tooling around in the kitchen. At least it was for the Rebecca that Cass knew before the surgery. Was this another change? Whatever it was, Cass didn't want to scare Rebecca by sneaking up on her. The last time that happened... well, it wasn't something Cass wished to repeat. So, she made as much noise as she could while coming up the stairs from the gym.

Rebecca smiled when she heard Cass but continued with her task of making a rather large cup of coffee. The shower had helped clear the sleep fog from her brain, but her energy could use a caffeine boost. And she was surprisingly hungry after last night's absolute feast. As anxious as it made her, Rebecca wanted to cook for Cass. She just hoped Cass wouldn't mind.

Cass cleared her throat, giving Rebecca yet another warning that she was there. "Good morning."

"Good morning. Would you like to..." Rebecca turned, coffee in hand, and saw Cass in short shorts and a sports bra. Her skin glistened with sweat, and her abs... oh god, her abs. Rebecca's knees buckled at the sight of that sexy as fuck six-pack. "Fuck me. Eat me!" She exclaimed quickly. "Eat with..." Rebecca carefully put her coffee down with a shaky hand and pinched the bridge of her nose. "Would you like to eat breakfast with me?" she asked as calmly as her racing heart would permit.

Cass was torn between laughing at the situation and being irritated that she couldn't do anything about Rebecca's first suggestion.

"Yes. The answer to all of the above will *always* be yes."

Rebecca let out a sound she'd never heard herself make before. The crazy part about what had just transpired was that while she hadn't meant to say those things, she certainly *wanted* them.

"I'm so sorry. I... wasn't expecting you to come in here looking like that." *But now I understand why you can carry me so easily and why I'm attracted to you.*

Cass glanced down at her barely there workout attire. *Shit.* She'd been so distracted by the thought of Rebecca being awake and not wanting to startle her that Cass forgot about what she was wearing.

"I, uh, was downstairs working out." She grinned sheepishly. "I wasn't expecting you to be up so early."

That little space between Rebecca's eyebrows crinkled in confusion. "Am I not normally up at this time?"

Cass shook her head. "You're more of a double-digits kind of woman. You don't like getting up before double digits, and you don't like going to bed during double digits."

"And you allow that?"

Cass's brows shot up. "Allow? Becca, I'm your wife, not your keeper."

"But you're my... Domme."

Seriously, if Cass's eyebrows could go any further, they'd be resting on the back of her neck by this point. "Your..." She had to sit down before her legs gave out under her. "No. I'm, uh, not your Domme."

Those little crinkles deepened. "But I saw the, um, *activity* drawer. And I'm pretty sure that behind that locked door is more apparatus. I figured you didn't tell me last night when I asked because you didn't want to freak me out."

The activity drawer. Damn. Had Cass known Rebecca was coming home, would she have cleaned out that drawer? Probably not. She wanted to ease Rebecca back into her life, not lie to her. Or keep anything from her. *Yet, you still have her phone.*

"I – we... yes, we have an activity drawer, as you call it. But I'm *not* your Domme, Becca," Cass repeated. Funnily enough, something was holding her back from telling Rebecca *she* was the Domme.

"Then I don't understand."

"I know," Cass sighed with frustration. If she had been more convinced that throwing a ton of information at Rebecca wouldn't cause her stress or pain, Cass would be drawing maps, making spreadsheets, and showing PowerPoints right now.

Rebecca waited a beat, but Cass didn't continue. "You're not going to tell me?"

"Becca, it's not that I don't want to, it's just…"

"Just?" Rebecca rolled her eyes. "Please don't tell me Aunt Wills got to you with all this hoo-ha about not wanting to influence my memories."

"Hoo-ha," Cass repeated. Would *her* Rebecca have said a word like 'hoo-ha?' *This* is *your Rebecca!* "Ahem." She focused on the important part of what Rebecca said. "No, Aunt Wills hasn't said that to me. She was more worried about stressing you out with too much info. But, I mean, that makes sense."

"Does it?" Rebecca scoffed. "Because it sounds like hoo-ha to me."

Cass snickered. "I like when you say hoo-ha." She ducked when Rebecca threw a napkin at her that didn't even travel far enough to reach her. "Okay, okay. It makes sense to me because everyone's perception of an event is different." When Rebecca's blank look didn't change, Cass continued. "Aunt Wills wasn't there when we met, yeah? So, her version is what you or I have told her. My version is different than yours and vice versa because of how we came into the situation."

Cass could tell Rebecca was trying to understand, but perhaps not knowing the specifics was hindering that comprehension. Cass drummed her fingers on the table, thinking of a way to explain this.

"Hey, remember the gallery?" she asked suddenly.

Rebecca raised a brow. Was Cass changing the subject for her benefit or Rebecca's? "Yes."

"Don't look at me like that, babe. I'm not ignoring your question. I'm trying to answer it in my own Cass way."

"Fine. I'll be patient." Rebecca hasn't gotten used to that slight tingle she got when Cass called her 'babe.'

"Thanks," Cass chuckled. "We all experience art differently. And not just the paintings, photographs, and sculptures in a gallery; movies and music—anything that elicits reactions. Take a love song. Someone who just had their relationship turn to shit will listen to that song and hate it because it reminds them of their ex. However, someone who just fell in love will listen to that song over and over and love the fuck out of it because it reminds them of their relationship."

Rebecca narrowed her eyes, annoyed that that actually made sense. "What does the gallery have to do with this?"

"Oh, right," Cass grinned. "Remember my painting?" Rebecca nodded. "The way you explained to Eve how it made you feel? That was different than how you felt about it the first time you saw it."

"It was?"

"Yep. When you saw it in my workroom after I finished it, you said it reminded you of us. Happiness and hope were there, but what grabbed you the most was the intense love you felt looking at it."

Intense love. Rebecca had felt that at the gallery, as well, but had she equated it to her and Cass? Or was it a general feeling? Well, shit. Maybe Aunt Wills and Cass were on to something.

"I hate that that makes sense."

"Why? Because it means Aunt Wills was right?"

Rebecca tsked. "No, because now I can't badger you into just telling me everything. Aunt Wills being right is just salt in the wound." She dumped her now cold coffee out and poured another cup. "Do you want some? Or would you rather have chocolate milk?"

Cass looked up sharply. "How?"

"Don't get too excited," Rebecca warned. "I remembered that's what you drank at the diner."

"Oh. Yeah, um, chocolate milk would be great. It helps my muscles recover faster after a workout."

Rebecca's eyes traveled down Cass's body. Even in her slouched position, Cass was a specimen. *"Does the body good,"* she muttered as she grabbed a bottle of chocolate milk out of the fridge. She passed it to Cass and then sat across from her at the table. "Would you tell me if you were my Domme?"

Cass twisted the cap off the chocolate milk and chugged half the bottle before answering. The fucking way those words sounded coming out of Rebecca's mouth got Cass's libido all kinds of fucked up. Yeah, they had switched roles every once in a while, but being Rebecca's Domme wasn't what Cass desired the most. No, she needed Mistress almost as much as she needed Rebecca. Cass was addicted to that fierce confidence. At least, she thought she was. Being with the more tame version of Rebecca these past few days had taught Cass it wasn't just Mistress she was addicted to. It was every facet of Rebecca.

"Yes," she answered finally, wiping her mouth with the back of her hand.

"That's it? No elaboration?" Cass shrugged, and Rebecca sighed. She had a feeling she wasn't going to get answers about the locked room and drawer full of... stuff today. "Where did we meet?"

Cass lowered her eyes, picking at the label on her bottle. How would Rebecca feel about meeting at the club? Hell, how would Cass explain *why* they were both there without delving into all kinds of information she wasn't sure Rebecca was ready for?

"Seriously, Cass?" Rebecca asked, breaking the silence. Again, she saw Cass wince and curious sadness cross her beautiful features and pointed. "That! What is that look that you get when I say your name? Is that not what I call you? Are you lying about not being my Domme, and I'm supposed to be calling you... I don't know, Master or something?"

This time, Cass winced for a different reason. "Ew. Please don't ever say that again." Her entire body shivered with disgust. "I'm not your Master or Domme or keeper or whatever. I'm your wife." *And your occasional sub.* "But yes, you call me something different."

"Something you're not going to tell me so you don't 'influence' me, right?" Rebecca said sarcastically. "And is that the excuse for not telling me where or how we met?"

"I know you're frustrated, Becca..."

"You're damn right I'm frustrated! Do you have *any* idea what it's like to wake up one day and be thrust into the future without some kind of manual? I don't know what has happened in the last two fucking decades, but I *do* know that I'm missing *something*! I feel it here." Rebecca pressed a hand over her heart. "It hurts. Whatever my fucking brain can't remember is hurting my heart, and I can't take it anymore. So, please, give me *something*!"

"*Muscle memory*," Cass murmured.

"What?"

"I can take you," Cass said instead of repeating herself. "If you want to know where we met, I'll take you to see if it triggers anything."

"You will?" When Cass nodded, Rebecca stood. "How long do you need to get ready?"

"Hang on, Becca. We can't go now."

"But you said..."

"It's not open." Cass got up and walked toward Rebecca, careful not to crowd her. "I will take you tonight if that's what you want."

"It is."

Cass nodded again and hoped to hell she wasn't making the biggest mistake of her life. "It's a date," she said, forcing herself to smile. "What would you like to do until then?"

A date. That made Rebecca a little more giddy than she cared to acknowledge. "Well, I could use some food. I'm actually surprised you lasted this long without mentioning the breakfast I offered."

"You offered a few things," Cass cheekily reminded her. "All of which I'm open to. But breakfast will suffice."

Cass was standing too close for Rebecca to be thinking of those other things. "Great!" she exclaimed, a little overly excited. *Bring it down a notch, Rebecca.* "I'll just..." She jerked a thumb behind her, turning on her heel to get started before she did anything else embarrassing. She grabbed the eggs out of the fridge and took them to the counter.

Rebecca recalled seeing mixing bowls earlier when she was searching for the coffee mugs. Finding them again was easy; the hard part was how high up they were. She opened the cupboard, wondering what the odds were that Cass wasn't watching her. Rebecca got on her tiptoes and stretched as far as she could, and still, her fingertips barely grazed the bowl she needed. She gasped when she felt Cass's hot body pressed against her back.

"I got it," Cass murmured in her ear.

"T-thank you." Good lord. Her body had *never* felt this before. Whatever happened, whether Rebecca regained her memory or not, she wanted to stay with Cass. She wanted to get to know the woman she had married and explore her relationship with this dynamic woman. If Cass made her feel this way after only a few days and a few touches, Rebecca couldn't imagine what it would be like to be... intimate with her.

"My pleasure." Cass stepped back before she did something stupid like grab Rebecca and kiss her senseless. "Do you need help? I mean, I'm a shit cook, but I'm great at chopping and whisking."

Rebecca smiled. "I think I can manage."

"Are you sure?"

Rebecca paused in the middle of breaking eggs over the bowl. "Why do you sound skeptical? I assume I cooked for you before all this happened."

"We don't spend a lot of time in here, no. Every once in a while we get the urge to cook. Then we have to eat what we cook, and, well, we decide that takeout is much easier and tastier."

"I... *don't* cook for you?" When Cass shook her head, Rebecca frowned. "So, I didn't get over it?" she said more for her own benefit than Cass's. Then she looked up at Cass. "I used to love to cook. It made me feel normal. Then one day Samantha got mad at me and... you know this story, don't you?"

"Yeah. But you never told me you loved cooking."

"You said when we cook, it isn't that great. I stopped cooking after that episode, Cass. Maybe I never started up again." Rebecca leaned against the counter and sighed. "That makes me sad, actually."

"It's never too late to start up again if that's what you want, Becca. And if you do, know I will never *expect* you to cook, but I will always be grateful. And you'll always have me as a prepper."

The sentiment touched Rebecca. "Thank you. Let's see if I burn down the house first, then we'll go from there."

Though the lasagna incident popped into her head, Cass laughed. Rebecca's feelings were her priority, so Cass kept that memory to herself.

"I do the burning. That's why I'm relegated to prep work. Which I'm still totally willing to do if you need help."

"I would like to do this for you if that's okay."

"Yeah, it's definitely okay. I'll get out of your way and go take a shower. I'm, uh, gonna go upstairs to our bathroom, 'kay? I won't be long."

Rebecca nodded, trying and failing to keep from imagining the image of Cass in the shower. She was so focused on *not* undressing Cass in her mind that she forgot to ask how Cass liked her eggs. With a shrug, she went back to her task. If she knew anything about Cass Giles, it was that she would eat practically anything as long as it wasn't vegetables.

Chapter Thirty-One

It was difficult keeping your eyes on the road when your passenger looked freakin' awesome. When Rebecca asked Cass what she should wear that night, Cass picked out a few outfits and let Rebecca make the final decision. Her choice was perfection. The pale pink V-neck jumpsuit was as elegant as it was sexy, with the plunge of the V carefully framing Rebecca's cleavage. Cass knew exactly how soft that skin was, and her fingers itched to feel that delicate smoothness.

"You look beautiful," Cass said, chancing a quick glance in Rebecca's direction.

"That's the third time you've said that," Rebecca chuckled. "And each time, it's nice to hear, so thank you. I found this outfit in the closet. It's so unlike anything I've worn before, but I have to admit it's quite empowering." She took her time, drinking in the sight of Cass in her black jeans and a white button-down shirt. The shirt was unbuttoned enough to give Rebecca an exquisite view of Cass's tattooed chest. Tattoos spilled out from under Cass's rolled-up sleeves as well. Weirdly enough, Rebecca never thought of herself as someone who liked the tattooed look, but on Cass, it was intoxicatingly sexy.

"You look very handsome," Rebecca said finally, her voice a little breathless. Her heartbeat picked up its pace when Cass grinned at her. "May I ask you something?"

"Of course."

"I have a tattoo here," Rebecca touched low on her hip. "I don't remember getting it. Or my belly ring. Were they because of you?"

Cass's stomach clinched, thinking of Rebecca's tattoo. Don't freakin' get her started on the sexy as fuck belly ring. God, she wished they were because of her, but she shook her head. "Those were all you, Becca. I'm not sure when you got them, but it was way before we met and for a good cause."

"One that you're not going to tell me?"

Cass glanced over. "I can if you like. But it wouldn't be your version of the story." She paused, allowing that to sink in for a moment. "Becca, your memories are stuck in that time twenty years ago. Those feelings are fresh for you. Why do you think you got the tattoo?"

"You spend too much time with my aunt," Rebecca groused playfully. But it was a good question, a thoughtful one that allowed Rebecca to determine for herself what would make her want to get a tattoo. She closed her eyes, envisioning the ink on her hip—bird in flight. "It feels like freedom to me. I believe I would have gotten it when I felt free from Samantha's hold."

Cass nodded. Though Rebecca carried the guilt of Samantha's death until recently, she left behind the meek sub that Samantha had made her into.

"It's so weird," Rebecca began, turning slightly in her seat to look at Cass. "I don't feel like I thought I would."

"What do you mean?"

"D-do you know what happened with Samantha?"

"Yeah," Cass answered softly. She knew, and she hated Samantha for it.

"So you know what I did."

"I know what *she* did to you and what you survived."

"Cass..."

"No." Cass reached across the console to take Rebecca's hand. "I know for a fact that you did nothing wrong. I'm sorry, but this is one thing I won't let you relive, Becca. I proved to you that nothing you did caused Samantha's death, and I cannot let you live with that guilt again."

"You... proved it? How?"

"That's a story for another time, but maybe that's why you feel different than you expected. Because somewhere deep down, you know it wasn't your fault."

Cass had no idea if she was doing the right thing. Hell, this whole night could have been a terrible idea. She probably should have discussed this with Aunt Wills, but the important thing was that Rebecca wanted this, and Cass was most loyal to Rebecca.

"Maybe you're right," Rebecca said, interrupting Cass's inner meltdown. "Maybe there's something subconsciously directing my feelings. I'm not sad or angry. I thought I'd feel much more guilt. I'm really just... confused about everything. That's not the greatest feeling, but I suppose it's better than the alternative."

Cass hoped that feeling would last once Rebecca understood where they were going. Ugh, she *really* should have thought this through more. How would seeing the club affect Rebecca? Or her psyche? She was about to find out, and *that* wasn't the greatest feeling for her.

Rebecca looked out the window as soon as Cass turned into a long driveway and recognized it immediately. "Why?" Her heart began to race, and panic bubbled up inside her. "Stop the car!"

"Becca."

"Stop the car, Cass!" Rebecca pulled at the door handle, but it was locked. "Let me out, please!"

Cass quickly pulled over and cut the engine. She disengaged the locks so Rebecca didn't feel trapped. She got out when Rebecca did, and while she followed a visibly upset Rebecca, she kept a comfortable distance.

"Becca!"

"Why would you do this to me? Do you have any idea what it's like for me to be here?" Rebecca cried. She brushed a tear from her cheek, furious with herself for falling for Cass's 'nice girl' facade.

Cass jogged past Rebecca and stopped in front of her. "Becca, please stop." She sighed when Rebecca walked right past her. "You asked me to bring you where we met," Cass called out.

Rebecca stopped. That didn't make sense. She didn't know Cass's age but guessed Cass was significantly younger than her own. The math didn't add up.

"I don't understand. Why would I ever come back here? I don't want anything to do with Samantha or her club ever again."

"It wasn't hers, Becca," Cass reminded her softly as she stepped closer. "It's yours."

Rebecca shook her head slowly. Then remembered it was true. "I kept it? Why in the hell would I keep it?"

Cass took another step. She was close enough now to reach out to Rebecca if she felt it would be okay. "You told me before why you kept it, but I think there was another reason. I think you kept it so those scars on your back wouldn't be in vain."

Rebecca bowed her head in shame. "You know about those?"

"Yes, I do. Baby, this place," Cass pointed toward the club. "This is your triumph, not your tragedy. You built this club into something prestigious and sought after. From what you told me, I can only imagine what this place was before. It was *you* who came in and made it what it is today."

"You know what it was before? A sex club?"

"A BDSM club, yeah. And it's still one." Cass touched Rebecca's arm gently. "I fucked up, yeah? I should have warned you. Something in my gut wasn't sitting right about all of this, but I ignored it and did the one thing I never wanted to do. I hurt you."

The sincerity in Cass's eyes and words eased Rebecca's tension. She felt terrible for her knee-jerk reaction, thinking Cass was *anything* but pure and sweet.

"Hey." Cass bent her head slightly to look into Rebecca's eyes. "I probably don't deserve it after this, but I'm asking you to trust me. We exorcised the demons out of this place before. If I have to do it again, I will."

"I'm sorry I ran. And for yelling at you."

Cass smiled sadly. "It's okay. I understand." She held out her hand. "What do you say? Wanna give this another go?"

Rebecca inhaled, blowing it out slowly. She took Cass's hand, feeling stronger with that simple touch. Yeah, this was all very weird. "Let's go."

Rebecca's bravado faded slightly when they walked inside. Then, her eyes adjusted to the low light, and she truly saw the place. This was nothing like how the club was under Samantha. It was upscale, clean, and... sexy. The women didn't walk around with their tits out the way Samantha made them. The men wore silk pajama pants and robes instead of barely there bikini underwear. And the ones Rebecca assumed worked for the club all wore masks. The atmosphere was sexually charged, and Rebecca felt inexplicably powerful.

Cass felt Rebecca's grip on her hand tighten, and she pulled Rebecca closer. The one thing she did think to do before they got here was call ahead and warn the staff not to refer to Rebecca as Mistress. Cass had a feeling Rebecca needed to come to find Mistress within herself on her own terms. Not by someone throwing that name out there at her. There was no predicting how Rebecca would react to being in the Pink Room again. But there was one thing Cass did know, and that was that she'd be with Rebecca every step of the way.

"You okay?"

Rebecca looked up at Cass, smiled, and nodded. Was Cass one of the staff here? Is that how they met? She imagined Cass in silk pajama pants, a robe — because the bustier wasn't Cass — and a mask. The image certainly affected her libido, so she looked away.

"Do you work here?"

Cass pursed her lips. It wasn't a lie if she said no, right? She was a co-owner, but she didn't *work* here. Technically speaking, Rebecca didn't work there anymore, either.

"Um, no, I don't work here."

"But we met here?"

"Yep."

"So, you came here for...?"

"A bachelorette party," Cass offered. "And I wasn't happy about it. I didn't understand this lifestyle, so I disagreed with it. But I was here to support my best friend at the time."

She guided Rebecca to the VIP area, nodding at the waitress, who placed a shot of Fireball and two glasses of club soda on the table before leaving.

Cass handed Rebecca one of the club sodas, picking up the shot for herself. "I was sitting here convincing myself to be a good friend and stay when one of these came along. I didn't order it, but that didn't stop me from drinking it," she grinned, touching her glass to Rebecca's before slamming the shot back.

Rebecca couldn't say why the action turned her on. Perhaps it was the look Cass gave her right before. Or maybe it was the way it exposed Cass's long, tattooed neck. She drained the club soda in one long gulp just to keep from whimpering.

"So, I bought you a drink?" Rebecca asked, eyeing the other club soda. It had suddenly become increasingly warm in here.

"Mmhmm. Yet, you stayed elusive. I had gone back to contemplating the consequences of leaving when a pink card was left on my table, followed by the most amazing ass I'd ever seen."

A pink card? And was the ass mine? Rebecca hoped so. "I don't understand."

Cass gave Rebecca the second glass of club soda and took her hand again. This was it. She was about to take Rebecca to the room where they first laid eyes on each other. Man, if she fucked this up and stressed Rebecca out too much, Aunt Wills was going to kill her. *No turning back now, Cass. Keep moving forward and hope for the best.*

Cass led Rebecca down a hallway with different-colored doors. She remembered this: 'Each room will be a distinct color. Each color will represent the experience level of that occupant.' This was Samantha's grand idea for the club. Obviously, Rebecca kept it going, but why? She had hated it for what it represented, especially after becoming Samantha's sub.

As they neared the black door, Rebecca felt herself stiffen with tension. She barely resisted the urge to pull away from Cass and run again. But they didn't stop at that door. No, they went further down, finally stopping at a pink door. *More pink.*

Cass dug a pink card out of her back pocket and held it against the keycard door lock. When the light turned green, she pushed the door open.

"Good?"

Rebecca nodded. She blew out the breath she was holding, trying to prepare herself for what was inside. It was a fool's errand, as she had no way of knowing what to expect once she walked past the threshold.

Cass ushered Rebecca in, purposefully staying quiet. This was Rebecca's journey. Though Cass would fill in a blank here and there, she honestly didn't want to persuade Rebecca's memories in any way. At least, that was the plan. Rebecca's reaction once inside would dictate Cass's response. Influence or not, Cass wasn't about to let Rebecca suffer unnecessarily.

Rebecca walked in, taking in every detail. The furnishings were minimal but quite tasteful. And pink. Everywhere she looked, there was a different shade of pink, from the high-back chairs that faced each other to the colossal bed. Even the armoire was pink. What was it about this color? Rebecca never imagined she would feel... peace surrounded by this pale hue.

Cass sat in the chair she had sat in the first time she had been in that room and watched Rebecca's reactions closely. Her heart rate was through the roof, yet Cass put on a calm facade for Rebecca's sake.

Rebecca glanced back and saw Cass sitting quietly. Something about that felt familiar. Since she didn't know why, Rebecca continued her tour. She ran her fingertips across the soft blanket as she passed by the bed and headed straight to the armoire. She wasn't naive about what was inside. Samantha had a similar one. It had been black, and every time Samantha opened it, pain followed.

With trembling hands, Rebecca opened the cabinet. Her breath caught at all the apparatus hanging inside. *Pink*. Flogs, crops, ropes... everything that used to bring Rebecca pain was on full display. Only, for reasons Rebecca didn't understand, seeing these caused Rebecca's blood to heat.

Her eyes traveled down and landed on an assortment of elaborate masks in different shapes and colors. She chose a white mask with long silk ribbons to tie it on. Rebecca tilted her head, imagining the mask on Cass. But she couldn't. This wasn't Cass's style. No, Cass would wear a plain black mask and still make it the sexiest thing Rebecca had ever seen. But this mask... Rebecca lifted it to her face. The fit was perfect, as though it was molded explicitly for her.

Rebecca gasped as the realization hit her. "It's me," she whispered.

Rebecca dropped the mask and whirled around. "It's me!" she repeated for Cass's benefit. "*I'm* the Domme. I'm... *your* Domme!"

It wasn't a question; still, Cass nodded.

"Why would I do that?" Panic built up inside Rebecca. "Why would I become... *her*?"

Cass sprang up and went to Rebecca. "You didn't. You are the complete *opposite* of her, Becca."

Rebecca shook her head, tears threatening to fall. "I hurt you?"

Cass shook her head, taking Rebecca's trembling hands in hers. "Do you think I'd be here trying to win your heart, trying to help you remember if you hurt me? That's not who you are, Becca."

"Yet, here we are in a BDSM club where apparently I employ others to torture..."

"Stop, babe. No one is tortured here anymore. While you have rooms available for those who crave the hardcore stuff, you've completely redefined the way things work here. You scrubbed this place clean of toxic, so-called Dommes who get off on humiliation and manipulation. In doing so, you've taught me — and everyone else who comes in here — that submission and masochism are not synonyms, nor are sadism and domination. You've given subs back their dignity and the power to decide what happens to them. *That* is what a real Domme does."

Rebecca found it difficult to believe what Cass said. She certainly didn't *feel* like someone who could have pulled that off. She stepped away, unable to think clearly under Cass's intense stare.

"Were there others before you?" Rebecca asked softly. She wasn't even sure she wanted to know that answer. First, she didn't want to think about being anyone else's Domme. It was hard enough to think of herself as Cass's. And second, it made her feel... weird inside thinking about anyone else other than Cass. *Do you think I'd be here trying to win your heart...?*

"Not like me, no," Cass answered truthfully. "You had others in this room, but it was never about sex. It was about rebuilding your confidence and the reputation of this club."

Rebecca stood at the foot of the bed, erotic images of her and Cass flashing in her mind. Were they real or wishful thinking? Then came the comprehension of what Cass said.

"Wait, not like you?" *It was never about sex.* "A-are you saying you're the first person I had... sex with after Samantha?"

Cass nodded, trying to gauge how that made Rebecca feel. Would she want to explore her options now that she had what was essentially a do-over?

Rebecca exhaled sharply, leaning her elbows on the bed. A slow smile spread on her face. "She *didn't* break me."

Rebecca spoke soft enough that Cass wasn't sure she heard her right. "Sorry?"

"Samantha didn't break me," Rebecca repeated with more confidence. "The tattoo, the belly ring. Everything you've told me. All of it means that I became what Samantha said I could never be. Free, rebellious, in control." She looked up at Cass. "Loved. I could have easily fallen into a number of horrible situations or relationships that meant nothing, but I didn't. I waited for someone like you who wants to win my heart even though yours is breaking."

A tear rolled down Cass's cheek. "I thought I understood why you made the decisions you made, but I didn't until right now."

Rebecca went to Cass, reaching up to wipe the tear away. Her fingertips lingered on Cass's soft skin. God, she wished she could remember everything she felt and did with this woman. But even without those memories, Rebecca was drawn to Cass unlike any other.

"I'm so sorry, Cass."

Cass shook her head, placing her hand over Rebecca's. "You have nothing to apologize for."

Maybe I do, Rebecca thought. Of all the things she was learning, the one that stood out the most was how much she held back from Cass. Was that on purpose, or a defense mechanism she kept in place out of some irrational fear? She trusted Cass now when she couldn't remember anything. Was it Cass she didn't trust before — or herself?

"Are you okay, Becca? Does your head hurt?"

Rebecca blinked, her thoughts falling away at Cass's question. "A little," she confessed. She reluctantly backed away when all she really wanted to do was kiss Cass, to feel what it was like. "Ahem. So, we, um…" Rebecca looked at the bed. Dear lord, the images that flooded her mind then made her insides heat up. "We made love here for the first time?"

Cass was intrigued by the blush creeping up Rebecca's beautiful neck, but she wasn't about to lie. "No."

Rebecca's eyebrows shot up. "No?"

"We fucked in here," Cass answered bluntly. "You flipped my world upside down in this room and taught me that whatever I thought sex, desire, and passion were didn't even come close. You taught me that letting go of my inhibitions, fears, and biases would open up completely new sensations for my mind, body, and soul. *That's* what we did in this room."

"Well…" Rebecca swallowed, her mouth dry… other places, not so much. Unfortunately, the faster her heart beat, the more her head hurt. It was fucking annoying when she *really* wanted to explore what they did in this Pink Room more in-depth.

Cass could practically see the pain in Rebecca's eyes. "I think that's enough for tonight, babe. You're hurting, and I don't want to overdo it more than I already have."

"Shouldn't it be my decision on how much I can take?"

"Normally, it would be, but my priority is…"

"My welfare and recovery," Rebecca finished with a playful eye roll.

Cass chuckled. "You mock, but it's true."

"I'm not mocking, Cass. I think it's sweet. And I think you're probably right. As much as I would like to further… discuss what happened here, I'm getting a little tired."

She's flirting with me again. Cass grinned. "I'll discuss whatever you want to discuss when you're feeling better. I love long conversations. You know, the kind that lasts all night long."

Rebecca raised a brow, appreciating Cass's boldness. "It's a good thing I've been feeling better every day. A long, probing conversation could be exactly what I need."

Cass was the first to break when a small groan escaped from somewhere deep within. "I… we… uh…"

Rebecca giggled. Actually giggled. What an odd sound coming from her. Had she ever done that before? Rebecca linked her arm with Cass's. "Thank you for bringing me here. I may not remember still, but this helped me realize a few things." She hugged Cass's arm closer to her. "Let's go home."

Chapter Thirty-Two

ass held the door open for Rebecca, who stumbled slightly as she walked by. "Hey, you okay?"

Rebecca nodded. "The pain is manageable most of the time, but every once in a while, I get a sharp pain that takes me by surprise."

Cass touched Rebecca's temple with a fingertip. "Want me to get you some meds?"

"No." Rebecca inhaled, catching a whiff of Cass's cologne. *Yummy.* "I would rather not take any medication tonight. I think I could sleep it off." She swayed again when another sharp pain hit her.

Cass wrapped her arm around Rebecca and scooped her up. "I'll agree to no meds as long as it doesn't get worse, yeah?"

Rebecca didn't hear a damn word Cass said. She was too busy snuggling Cass's neck and taking long sniffs of that intoxicating scent.

"Becca? Do you promise to tell me if the pain gets worse?" Cass asked when Rebecca didn't answer. Her legs were beginning to shake. Not because Rebecca was heavy but because the feel of Rebecca's breath on her neck was wreaking havoc on her libido.

"Hmm? Oh, um, yes, I promise. I'm okay now if you want to put me down."

"Nope. This ride goes all the way to the bedroom." It was Cass who stumbled this time. Her arms tightened around Rebecca until she was sure she wasn't going to topple over. "I did not mean that the way it sounded."

"That's too bad," Rebecca teased. The power of that playful tease diminished marginally when she yawned. "Sorry."

Cass chuckled. "It's been a long day, Becca. You're allowed to be tired."

"Can you call me babe?" Rebecca asked sleepily. "I like that."

"Anything you want, babe," Cass smiled. Once upstairs, she pushed open the bedroom door with her foot. "Want me to run a bath for you, or do you just want to go to bed?"

Rebecca considered the bath as Cass deposited her onto the bed. While her mind was tired, her body was feeling... restless—almost painful.

"I think a bath might help." Of course, she wasn't going to tell Cass how being at the club and thinking of what the two of them did in the Pink Room had her all hot and bothered. No, Rebecca would take a bath, go to bed, and figure the other stuff out in the morning. And by other stuff, she meant these growing feelings she had for Cass. That was only natural, right? Obviously, somewhere deep down, Rebecca knew Cass. Her body *definitely* knew Cass. Now, if she could just connect all the dots...

"Okay. Sit here, and I'll go get it started."

Cass started towards the bathroom, and Rebecca's anxiety hit the roof. This scenario she remembered. The night she almost died, Samantha left her on the bed after shooting up and disappeared into the bathroom. That's when all hell broke loose.

"Wait! I – I can do it."

"I don't mind..." Cass saw the terror on Rebecca's face and put two and two together. "Hey, hey." She kneeled next to Rebecca, taking her trembling hand. "I know where your mind went, Becca, okay? But I'm not Samantha." Cass placed Rebecca's hand on her chest over her heart. "Feel that? That's my heart, baby. It beats for you and only you. I will never hurt you. Please, Becca, you don't have to remember me to know how much I love you. Just look at my face. Look into my eyes."

Rebecca did just that. She gazed into Cass's bi-colored eyes and saw nothing but love and compassion.

"I'm sorry."

"No need to be. Your emotions are valid, Becca. And I understand where they're coming from. Why don't you lay down for a while? If you still need something to take the edge off, come downstairs, and I'll get the hot tub fired up for you, yeah?"

Rebecca nodded, allowing Cass to take her shoes off. "I *do* know," she said suddenly. "I know you'd never hurt me. I don't know *how* I know, but I see it. I feel it. I wish I hadn't freaked out. I ruined your night."

"You did no such thing." Cass stood and moved away from Rebecca so as not to intimidate her with her height and proximity. "I'll leave you to change and get some rest, but I want you to know that I had a beautiful night with you, Becca. Every second I get to spend with you is... heaven."

Every second I get to spend with you is heaven. Cass lowered her head, her lips grazing over Rebecca's. The soft touch caused a fire to spread through Rebecca's body. Rebecca moaned when Cass deepened the kiss. God, she'd never been kissed like this before. She wanted to feel this sensation on every part of her body. Especially her...

Rebecca jerked awake with a gasp. The heat inside her wasn't just in her dream. She squirmed as the pain continued to intensify. Her hand snaked down the front of her pajama shorts to put pressure on her throbbing clit. This wasn't just arousal. It was too painful. Rebecca glanced at the dresser. Inside was an array of things that could bring her at least *some* relief. Rebecca slipped out of bed, determined to do something about this relentless discomfort.

Cass covered her eyes with her arm as she tried to will herself to turn off her brain and get some sleep. Unfortunately, her body was wide awake, aching for Rebecca. Not even the cold shower she took earlier helped. Cass scoffed. The only thing that shower did was wash away the tears Cass couldn't hold in any longer. Day after day, Cass hoped for Rebecca's memory to return. But it felt like that would never happen. The longer it took, the less likely it was going to happen, right? Cass increased the pressure of the crook of her elbow on her eyes to keep the fucking tears at bay.

She loved Rebecca, and that would never change. But would that magic still be there if Rebecca didn't remember their love? Could they recreate the bond they had?

"Cass?"

Cass sat up quickly. Rebecca was still in her pajamas, so Cass didn't think this was a hot tub moment. "Becca? Hey, are you okay? Is the pain worse?" She pushed the covers off, completely forgetting she only had boxers and a cut-off tank top on.

"Please don't get up," Rebecca said quickly. She'd already caught a glimpse of the rock-hard abs. "May I sit with you?"

"Yeah, of course!" Cass swung her legs off the couch, creating a space for Rebecca. Then she noticed the slight tremor in Rebecca's hands and the look in her eyes, and it hit Cass in the gut like a punch from a heavyweight champion. She knew this look very well, and her heart broke for Rebecca. "It's not your head that's hurting, is it?"

Cass's question startled — and embarrassed — Rebecca. Was her situation that noticeable? "N-no. I... my..."

"Your body hurts," Cass offered gently.

Rebecca's eyebrows shot up. "How did you know?"

"I know you, Becca. I understand why that confuses you, but I remember every nuance, every emotion, every look."

Rebecca lowered her eyes, which was a mistake because they landed right on Cass's strong legs. That certainly wasn't helping.

"So, why am I feeling this way?" she asked suddenly. Rebecca was in too much pain to care about humiliation anymore. She needed answers... or a solution.

Cass sighed. Going to the club was one thing. Doing what Rebecca needed when she got like this was something else altogether. Cass didn't think Rebecca was ready for that when, in Rebecca's mind, Samantha had only been gone a few weeks.

"How honest do you want me to be?"

Rebecca looked at Cass pleadingly. "Completely."

Cass nodded, turning to face Rebecca. It wasn't lost on her how

Rebecca's eyes kept sweeping down her body. No, she felt the heat of those looks down deep in her core.

"We learned that your body had become accustomed to the pain you used to get when... in your previous situation. When that happens, your body starts to ache, you feel restless, you can't concentrate. You feel like you're on pins and needles, and the only thing that helps is, um..."

"Sex?"

Cass shrugged a shoulder. "Yes, but not just sex. You need to feel the pain."

Rebecca squeezed her thighs together, but that did nothing to alleviate that ache Cass spoke of. "I don't understand. Do I make you... hurt me?"

"It's more like you submit to me. We switch roles. And I *only* do what you permit me to do. I never cross your limits and never give you pain without intense pleasure. But..."

"But?"

Cass shook her head, her heart pounding in her chest. What she was about to say went against everything inside her. She had an intense need to be with Rebecca, but not like this. "Please don't ask me to do that right now. When you explained this to me the first time, you were more than a decade removed from that life. From Samantha. But now? Becca, I want nothing more than to be with you, but I can't touch you like that and have you think of Samantha. I can't be *her* to you. It would kill me. There are," Cass's voice hitched as she tried to hold in tears, "things in the drawers upstairs that can help you."

Rebecca wasn't faring so well in the fight against the tears. Seeing Cass so sad hurt more than the aches. There was something about what Cass said about Rebecca's... condition that stuck with her.

"I considered the toys," Rebecca confessed. She mustered up enough courage to reach for Cass's hand. "They didn't appeal to me without you. Do we use them often? Do you use the..."

"Yes," Cass answered, saving Rebecca from having to say the words. This wasn't the Rebecca who had no issue with talking dirty or saying what she wanted.

Rebecca let that sink in for a moment while she mulled over what to do next. All she knew for sure was that she wanted to be with Cass, and she didn't think the way her body felt was the entire reason for this.

"What if it isn't the pain my body is craving? Maybe what I'm feeling right now is because my body misses... you. I don't feel as though I need pain, Cass. I think what I need is what I had with you." Rebecca's heart — and confidence — fell as Cass remained unconvinced, judging by the look on her face. Rebecca stood. She'd deal with this humiliation in private — maybe with a few toys.

"Becca, wait." Cass grasped Rebecca's hand lightly, trying not to startle her or appear too aggressive. She stood, towering over her petite wife.

Cass's height and proximity weren't intimidating for Rebecca. Quite the contrary, they were intoxicating. And when Cass tucked Rebecca's hair behind her ear with such tenderness, Rebecca nearly melted.

"I know this isn't ideal for you, Cass. And it's probably wrong of me to even suggest it. But maybe you could pretend that I'm the woman you fell in love with," Rebecca pleaded softly.

Cass's smile was gentle and loving. "I don't have to pretend, Becca. I know who you are." Was it wrong to want to be with your wife? Was it taking advantage of the situation? These are the things that ran through Cass's mind, battling her heart and body's needs and wants. Would Rebecca regret this in the morning? And if she did, would she forgive Cass?

Rebecca saw the desire and the fear on Cass's face. Desire, she understood. But why the fear? Was Cass afraid things would be different between them? Would the lovemaking somehow feel different because Rebecca was different? *Shit*. There was only one way to find out. Rebecca stood on her tiptoes, brushing a hand up Cass's chest and snaking it around Cass's neck.

"Kiss me. Please."

Chapter Thirty-Three

Holy fuck. Every nerve ending in Cass's body erupted at those three simple words. Yet, coming from Rebecca's mouth, they were anything but simple. Especially now. But Cass couldn't deny she needed this as much as Rebecca did. It didn't matter if it was for entirely different reasons. Cass lowered her lips to Rebecca's, her body tense from the effort to maintain her self-control.

Rebecca's knees were perilously close to buckling as Cass's lips got closer. She couldn't remember ever feeling this incredibly sexy and passionate. When Cass's lips touched Rebecca's, the past disappeared. There was only here and now. And the sensations Cass caused throughout Rebecca's body with a mere kiss.

Their tongues touched, and the electricity between them ignited. Rebecca's hands fisted in Cass's hair, and Cass's arms tightened around Rebecca's waist, crushing their bodies together.

Stay calm, Cass. Don't scare her.

Is this what this should feel like?

"If you need to stop at any point, babe, don't be afraid to tell me, yeah?"

Rebecca nodded, mesmerized by the way Cass looked at her. There was so much love in those bi-colored eyes it was almost frightening for someone who didn't know what to do with that kind of emotion. On the flip side, it gave Rebecca the courage to keep going without fear.

"Do you always look at me like that? Like you're about to devour me?"

Cass grinned. "Absolutely. Mostly because I am."

Rebecca's eyebrows slowly rose as the realization of what Cass said hit her. "As in... literally?"

Taken aback by Rebecca's question, Cass loosened her grip ever so slightly. Why did the thought of Cass going down on her surprise Rebecca? "Literally. Your scent and taste are aphrodisiacs for me, Becca."

A small moan escaped from Rebecca at the same time her pussy contracted. Cass hadn't even touched her yet, and Rebecca was sure she would explode at any second. "I don't mean to sound so... prudish. It's just that subs don't usually get that kind of pleasure."

Cass cupped Rebecca's cheek, stroking her thumb across the soft skin. "You're no longer a sub, baby, remember? You run the show. And I'm *privileged* to be the one that gives you that kind of pleasure. I enjoy the fuck out of it." She dropped her hands and hooked her thumbs in the waistband of Rebecca's shorts. "I can never get enough of you." She hesitated a beat. "May I?"

Rebecca felt the little tug at her shorts, and her heart rate spiked so high she was surprised she didn't have a heart attack.

"*Yes.*"

Rebecca greedily helped by slipping her shirt off while Cass kneeled and slowly pulled Rebecca's shorts down. The back of her knuckles caressed Rebecca's shaky legs the entire way. So many different sensations coursed through Rebecca that she was sure she couldn't feel any more aroused than she already was. Then Cass pressed her nose to Rebecca's sex and inhaled deeply.

"*Fuck!*"

Rebecca didn't know if that came from her or Cass, and at this point, she didn't care. She certainly didn't care who let out a guttural groan when Cass slipped her tongue between the lips of Rebecca's pussy.

"I'm going to fall," Rebecca warned breathlessly.

"I won't let you," Cass said, repeating the same words she had said to Rebecca the first time around. She took her sweet time getting to her feet, allowing her tongue a tasty journey on the way up Rebecca's body while keeping a firm grip on Rebecca's hips to steady her. "Do you want to go upstairs?"

Rebecca laughed softly. "I don't think I'll make it up the stairs. And if you pick me up while I'm naked like this..." She shook her head. "Same result, different reason."

Cass chuckled. "Couch it is. It's not like this couch hasn't seen its share of action." She gently nudged Rebecca down, then whipped off her clothes so Rebecca would feel less vulnerable. She was mindful of the first time they made love and how Rebecca reacted to Cass being on top of her. "Is it okay if I lay with you?"

Rebecca stared at Cass's naked body. If she got any wetter, they would need a few towels to help clean up. "Hmm?"

Cass sucked her lips in, biting her top lip to keep from laughing. She gestured to the empty space next to Rebecca. "May I lay with you?"

Rebecca nodded and scooted over to give Cass's long, hard, tattooed, sexy body more room. Thank god the room was cool with the amount of heat that radiated from both of them.

"I'm not being very sexy, am I? I don't know why I feel like this is my first time."

Cass linked her fingers with Rebecca's. Despite Rebecca's... needs, Cass didn't want to rush this for fear it might be too much for Rebecca to handle.

"The day you agreed to come home with me to be together outside of the Pink Room, I told you I wanted to make love to you."

"I – don't know how."

"That's what you said then. I offered to teach you just as you taught me to be your sub."

Rebecca made a face. "I'm not used to that yet. But you must've been a wonderful teacher if I married you."

"We both were. And we're still learning." Cass brought Rebecca's hand to her lips, softly kissing the knuckles. "You had trouble with me being on top of you that day. How do you feel about that now?"

Rebecca adjusted her position, laying on her back. "We won't know until we try." She was pretty impressed with herself. Here she was, naked with the most handsome woman she'd ever laid eyes on and having a full-on conversation as though they were sitting in a quaint cafe having coffee. She wasn't bashful about her lack of clothes. She wasn't embarrassed about her scars. In Cass's arms, she was safe, loved, and desired. Rebecca felt that in her soul.

Cass slowly rolled on top of Rebecca, bracing her arms to support the majority of her weight. She positioned her thigh between Rebecca's legs which meant her throbbing pussy was currently resting on Rebecca's soft skin. The last time she and Rebecca were together was the night before her surgery. That felt like an eternity ago. How Cass was able to stay calm and gentle said a lot about her true feelings for her wife. Love not only invited passion, but it also offered patience. It was Cass's job to know which one Rebecca needed at any given moment.

"Good?"

Rebecca breathed in, her hips lifting as she did so. "So good," she gasped, reaching up to tap Cass's arms. "You're shaking. You can put more weight on me, Cass. I'm okay."

Hearing Rebecca call her Cass reminded Cass just how delicate this situation was. If she made one wrong move, Rebecca could easily be triggered by a distant past that wasn't so distant to her.

"You'll tell me if it's too much?"

"I promise."

Cass lowered herself even more. Rebecca's pillowy soft breasts pressed against Cass's, their hard nipples competing for dominance. Cass's small breasts didn't put up much of a fight. They submitted to Rebecca almost as quickly as Cass had.

"*You feel so good. I've missed you, Becca.*" Cass's lips were a breath away from Rebecca's, waiting for another invitation.

"Would you believe me if I said I've missed you, too?" Rebecca trailed her fingernails down Cass's back to that firm ass. "I can't explain it, but this feels... right."

"Because it is." Cass dipped her head and kissed Rebecca again. She felt Rebecca's body relax beneath her, and that was enough of an invitation for Cass to deepen the kiss. They moved together in a familiar rhythm, even so, Cass could feel Rebecca's motions were still hesitant.

Cass moved to Rebecca's ear, nibbling and sucking. She paid keen attention to every breath, every sound, every move Rebecca made as Cass continued her journey of tasting every inch of Rebecca's body. Her tongue scorched a trail from that sensitive part of Rebecca's neck that always elicited a reaction to the swell of Rebecca's breast.

Oh, she would take her time here. Cass took Rebecca's taut nipple between her teeth, looking up at Rebecca as she did. The bites weren't enough to bring pain but just enough to make Rebecca writhe beneath her. Then she sucked the nipple into her mouth, flicking her tongue over it at the same time.

Rebecca's hips bucked, and her breath hitched in response. Since her hands had lost their resting place on Cass's ass, Rebecca fisted them in Cass's hair, urging her on. The feelings racing through Rebecca were overwhelming, as though every cell in her body was on fire. Cass's lips were so soft against her skin, contrasting the heat of her breath and tongue. Her hands were a study of how something so strong could be so incredibly gentle.

Cass spread Rebecca's legs, fitting her shoulders between them and wrapping her arms underneath Rebecca's thighs. This was her happy place. She knew she missed being with Rebecca, but the magnitude of what they had both been robbed of just hit her. She laid her head on Rebecca's inner thigh and took a moment to be grateful that even though Rebecca still hadn't regained her memory, she trusted Cass enough with this intimacy. She was well aware of how lucky she was that their separation was short in the grand scheme of things, but Cass and Rebecca were anything but ordinary. Hopefully, Rebecca would forgive her for prolonging this special moment.

"Are you okay?"

Cass looked up from her position between Rebecca's legs and smiled. "I'm in heaven." She lowered her head and kissed Rebecca softly, hearing a small gasp coming from her wife at the tender gesture. Cass had the opportunity to give Rebecca a second chance at a "first time," and Cass was determined to make it memorable. With her fingertips, Cass spread Rebecca's lips and dipped her head again to suck in Rebecca's clit.

"*Oh my god!*" Rebecca's body jumped at the contact, her hands contracting even tighter in Cass's hair. Had she ever felt something so exquisite? Obviously, she had with Cass. How in the fuck had she forgotten this? *This* was un-fucking-forgettable. She dug her heels into the couch, lifting her hips, desperate for more.

And Cass gave it to her. She didn't know if it was muscle memory or just instinct, but Rebecca was always good at demanding and pleading for more with her body than her words. Of course, Cass loved the words, but she could wait for those to come back as long as she could still feel the passion and desire. *And taste it*, she thought as Rebecca's essence filled her mouth. Rebecca was wetter than Cass expected, given the circumstances, which was a lovely surprise. She'd be lying if she said she wasn't just a little nervous about how *into* this Rebecca would be.

Cass maneuvered her right arm out from under Rebecca's thigh. By this time, the way Rebecca was writhing beneath her mouth, Rebecca — or Mistress — would be prompting Cass to use her fingers. So, going with her gut, Cass slowly slipped one finger inside Rebecca.

"*Mmm.*" Rebecca bit her bottom lip. She wanted to cry out, wanted to tell Cass she needed more, but Rebecca couldn't get the words out. Something was... blocking her voice. Whatever that hangup was, it wasn't affecting the pure pleasure Cass's mouth and finger were creating. *More!*

Cass felt Rebecca spread her legs even further apart and knew exactly what she needed. Still, she played it cautiously, inserting just one more finger instead of her usual three — or four if Rebecca was feeling particularly horny. Cass curled her fingers, hitting that one spot that always made Rebecca explode, using the flat of her tongue on Rebecca's clit at the same time.

Rebecca cried out, stunned by what was happening to her. It was all... too much. "Wait!" Cass immediately stopped, withdrawing her fingers. She started to move, but Rebecca stopped her. "No, don't leave, please," Rebecca begged. "I-I just need a second. What you're doing," she swallowed the lump forming in her throat. "It feels amazing." Rebecca scoffed at how ordinary that word was compared to the extraordinary things happening to her. "I don't know what to do or say," she confessed softly.

"What do you mean?"

Rebecca pushed Cass's hair back from her face to look into those beautiful eyes. "I feel so much, but when I try to tell you... I'm afraid."

Cass took Rebecca's hand, bringing it to her lips to kiss her palm. "When you said wait just then, what did I do?"

"Y-you stopped."

"Did I hesitate?"

Rebecca shook her head.

"Am I upset?"

Another shake of the head.

"You don't have to be afraid of me, baby. I won't hurt you." Cass kissed Rebecca's hand again to drive home that point. "As far as what to do or say, there's no script. There are no rules. All you need to do is let go. I'm yours, Becca. Give yourself to me."

Rebecca pulled her hand from Cass's and cupped her cheek. "*Taste me again*," Rebecca whispered. Cass didn't hesitate to oblige. "*Inside*," Rebecca murmured.

Cass slipped two fingers back inside Rebecca, adding a third when she heard Rebecca gasp for more. She continued savoring Rebecca, building that climax back up with ease. She knew Rebecca's body well enough to tell how close Rebecca was. She just hoped Rebecca could let go of the past and inhibitions long enough to surrender to Cass.

"Oh god!" Rebecca's hands took up residence in Cass's hair again, pulling Cass impossibly closer. She couldn't get enough. Rebecca felt the pressure build up inside her, and it took a lot of willpower not to stop. To allow herself to do as Cass asked and let go. *Give yourself to me.* Rebecca cried out as the orgasm slammed through her, curling her toes, contracting her muscles, and...

"You're the only one who's ever made me do that, Cassidy."

Chapter Thirty-Four

It took two point six seconds for Rebecca's words to register in Cass's brain. She was busy drinking the wonderful gift Rebecca gave her, so could you blame her for the delay? But then it happened. Cass replayed the words in slow motion in her mind just to make sure she heard right. Even then, she couldn't be sure it was her imagination playing tricks on her.

"W-what did you call me? W-what did you say?" Cass wiped her mouth, eyes wide, watching Rebecca carefully.

Rebecca smiled even though she felt like crying. At least this time, they would be happy tears. As she... flooded into Cass's mouth, the memories — *her* memories — came flooding back to Rebecca. It was like a tidal wave — in more ways than one.

"Cassidy," Rebecca repeated with such adoration it sounded more like a love letter than a simple name. She held her arms out, inviting Cass into them.

Cass scrambled up, nearly falling off the couch in her efforts to be embraced by Rebecca's loving arms. *Her* Rebecca. Only *her* Rebecca called her Cassidy. Cass's breath hitched with a sob as she forgot about being gentle and hauled herself on top of Rebecca, burying her face in Rebecca's neck.

"You remember?" Cass hiccupped.

"I remember, baby," Rebecca cooed, not even bothering to fight back her own tears.

Cass lifted her head to look at Rebecca, swiping at her tears and runny nose with the back of her hand. It was the most unsexy thing she could have done, but despite being naked on top of her wife, this wasn't about being sexy.

"Everything?" Cass sniffled.

Rebecca nodded. She brushed more tears from Cass's cheeks. "Everything." Rebecca pressed her finger to Cass's lips. "Before you start bombarding me with questions, I would like to finish what we started here."

Cass glanced between them. "I thought you did," she grinned. God, could she be any happier? *Her* Rebecca was back! And she knew it was her Rebecca because of the predatory look in her eyes. *That* was Mistress. *Fuck yeah.*

"Oh, that was just the beginning, Cassidy. Though, we're going to have to get this couch cleaned."

"Not the first time."

Rebecca chuckled. "Won't be the last. Hey," she lifted Cassidy's chin, holding her gaze. "I know we have a lot to talk about, but I've missed you so much. Do you think we could wait a little longer for all the serious stuff?"

"Does that include calling everyone to tell them you remember? And, uh, confessing to you about how I really handled all this?"

"Yes, including... confessing?"

Cass kissed Rebecca passionately, slipping her thigh between Rebecca's legs.

"Are you distracting me?" Rebecca panted once they came up for air.

"Is it working?"

"Only because I'm the one who suggested waiting for serious talks. But I *will* remember that. One more thing before you start kissing me like that again, and my brain melts."

Cass grinned. "Yeah?"

"Can we go upstairs to our bed?"

Cass popped up off the couch with ease. She gave the mess a fleeting thought before scooping Rebecca up into her arms.

"I hope you're ready for me, baby," Cass murmured in Rebecca's ear. "It has been a *long* time."

"For me, it feels like it has been twenty long years, Cassidy. I'm ready."

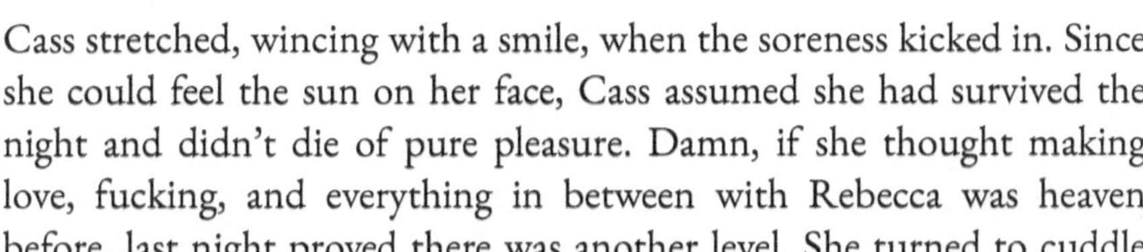

Cass stretched, wincing with a smile, when the soreness kicked in. Since she could feel the sun on her face, Cass assumed she had survived the night and didn't die of pure pleasure. Damn, if she thought making love, fucking, and everything in between with Rebecca was heaven before, last night proved there was another level. She turned to cuddle with her wife and was met with a cold, empty bed.

"Becca?" Cass listened for an answer or the sound of the shower and heard neither. She jumped out of bed, pulling on a pair of boxers and slipping a tank top over her head as she hurried downstairs. "Becca!"

The living room had been tidied up, yet Rebecca was nowhere in sight. Cass made her way into the kitchen, where a fresh pot of coffee was brewed but otherwise empty. She ran downstairs to the gym, hoping to find Rebecca meditating. Nothing.

"Becca!" Cass reached for her phone before remembering she only had boxers on without pockets and had left her phone upstairs. "Shit!" Cass took the stairs two at a time back up to the living room. Cass was about to go into full-blown panic mode when she heard a faint sound coming from outside. Out on the deck, Rebecca sat drinking coffee, seemingly without a care in the world. "Becca?"

Rebecca blinked, coming out of her pensiveness, and smiled at Cassidy. "Good morning, baby."

"What the hell, Rebecca? You can't just disappear like that!" Cass's body shook with adrenaline, but she couldn't determine whether she felt fear or anger.

Rebecca set her coffee on the table beside her, frowning. "I'm sorry. I didn't mean to scare you." She held her hand out to Cassidy, breathing a sigh of relief when Cassidy didn't hesitate to take it.

"Why are you awake?" Cass straddled the chaise lounge Rebecca was sitting on, draping Rebecca's legs over her thighs.

"I couldn't sleep." Rebecca tapped her temple. "My mind is going a mile a minute."

Cass caressed Rebecca's cheek. "Are you in pain?" When Rebecca shook her head, Cass continued. "Why didn't you wake me up?"

"You looked so peaceful. I'm guessing you haven't slept well since all this began. I didn't want to disturb you, baby."

Cass nodded but still felt a little unsettled. "You're not usually awake at this time."

Rebecca suspected Cassidy was scared that Rebecca's memory had gone away again. It would explain why Cassidy was so agitated when she found Rebecca out on the deck.

"I've gotten a little used to the peace during this time of the day. It's quite beautiful. Quiet, cool, calm." Cassidy was watching Rebecca with such intensity that it nearly made Rebecca squirm. She had to do something to put Cassidy at ease. "Do you remember The Great Thunderstorm of 2022 when we lost power for almost thirteen hours? It was chilly, but luckily, we had a gas fireplace, so we stayed downstairs in front of that fire the entire time. We talked, played games, and made love with the rolling thunder as our soundtrack," Rebecca chuckled. "We ate all the ice cream before it melted. Los Angeles was in chaos, but inside this house, we were living our best lives. I'll never forget it."

But you did. Cass didn't say that out loud, though. Instead, she smiled, relieved that Rebecca's memory was still intact. "I remember that night very well. Especially the part where you licked the ice cream off my body."

"Oh, yeah," Rebecca purred. "Best flavor of ice cream ever."

"It's available whenever you want it, babe." Cass stroked Rebecca's thighs with the pads of her thumbs. "What were you thinking about when I came out here?"

Rebecca inhaled and hummed as she let the breath out. "I was thinking about unretiring."

"I thought we weren't calling it that."

Rebecca rolled her eyes teasingly. "I was thinking about un-slowing down." She stuck her tongue out at Cassidy, who chuckled at her. "I can't help but wonder if the tumor was the main culprit in my fatigue. And, despite that last disaster of a meeting, I think I can handle expanding beyond our group of friends. Perhaps not as far as before, but enough to keep my mind busy."

Cass dropped eye contact for a moment. That last disaster of a meeting was the Buck McEnroe incident. Rebecca didn't know about that. She knew the dude didn't exist, but not why.

"Um, about that last meeting."

Rebecca raised a brow. "McEnroe? Did you find out who hired him to impersonate... an idiot?" She expected Cassidy to give her at least a courtesy chuckle for that, but her expression remained stoic. "Cassidy?"

God, she loved hearing that name come from Rebecca's lips. And the last thing Cass wanted to do was put a damper on Rebecca's day. However, one of the things they were adamant about in their relationship was honesty.

"Babe, Buck McEnroe didn't exist."

"Yeah, I remember Eve telling us that. But that wasn't my question. I asked who hired him."

"No one, Becca. When I say he didn't exist, I mean he wasn't real. Eve — or Jules — found surveillance of you going to that warehouse." Cass paused. "The tumor caused you to hallucinate, Becca. You believed you had an appointment. You even made up a business plan. Then you drove there, went to the door, then turned around, and went back to your car when it was locked." Cass leaned in, squeezing Rebecca's hands, offering as much strength as she could.

Rebecca frowned. "I—" She shook her head. The memory she had of "Buck McEnroe" was... off. Rebecca remembered speaking to Eve and Lainey about him. She recalled telling Cassidy what happened. But the actual *event* was... gone. "I made it up."

"No, the episode was a symptom of the tumor. To you, it really happened."

"And *you're* sure it didn't?" Rebecca felt the beginning of a headache and reached for the bottle of water she had brought out with her.

"Yeah, I saw the video."

"Well, so much for coming out of retirement," Rebecca scoffed. She drained almost half of her water, avoiding Cassidy's gaze. Making up some dramatic scenario? Tumor or not, it was fucking embarrassing.

"Why?"

"Are you serious? If clients found out that I..." Rebecca couldn't even finish the thought. "I'd be a laughing stock."

"Babe, you had a *medical* episode." Cass saw that wasn't making Rebecca feel any better. "Five people know, Becca. That's it. One is you, and the others are loyal to you. No one will ever find out, yeah?" Rebecca took a moment but finally nodded. "Good. Now, if you're serious about un-slowing down, I may have a job for you."

Rebecca raised a brow. "Are you opening an art gallery?"

Cass laughed. "And compete with *the* Eve Sumptor? I'm no dummy, babe. No, I stopped by an old haunt of mine recently. A bar over in West Hollywood. It's seen some better days, and Nadia is interested in fixing it up."

Oh, Rebecca didn't like the gross jealousy that slithered into her brain. "You went to a bar to see an old friend named Nadia?"

Something inside Cass snapped. That frayed string that held her emotions together these past few weeks since learning about the tumor finally broke. Everything Cass pushed aside in order to make sure Rebecca was okay came flooding back with a vengeance.

"Don't do that. Don't belittle my love for you by implying I would *ever* do something to hurt you." Cass lifted Rebecca's legs off of hers and stood. "*I* didn't forget, Rebecca. I went to that fucking bar because none of *our* friends would be there. Friends that were pissed off at me for what I did, so I didn't feel like I had a right to lean on them. I went there to get shitfaced and forget like *you* did. But I couldn't." Cass let out a humorless laugh. "No, I knew you wouldn't like that, and I didn't want to disappoint you because *I* remembered how much I love you. *You* remembered *her*!"

"Cassidy, that's not fair."

"You're right, it's not! *I* love you, Rebecca. *I've* never hurt you. I *never* would! So, why? Why did you forget me?"

Rebecca got to her feet, tears pooling in her eyes. Cassidy had never been this upset with her before. But it wasn't anger Cassidy was display- ing. It was anguish. And after everything that had happened, Rebecca couldn't blame Cassidy for those emotions. She knew Cassidy would bottle it up for Rebecca's sake. This was the conversation they needed to have last night, but Rebecca chose the physical first. And *that* wasn't fair to Cassidy.

"Do you think I wanted to? I would have given *anything* not to live through that time of my life again. It wasn't something I controlled, Cassidy. God, if I could have, I would choose you every single time."

Cass opened her mouth to apologize for her outburst but was interrupted by the chime of the doorbell.

"That's Aunt Wills. I'm so sorry, Cassidy. I texted her earlier, and she insisted on coming over. But I'll tell her to come back so we can talk."

"No, it's fine. I don't feel like talking anymore right now. I'll tell her you're out here."

"Cassidy, wait. Please."

The plea in Rebecca's voice caused Cass to hesitate. But she needed time to calm down. She'd already said too much and made Rebecca cry, which made Cass feel like shit. Maybe this distraction was a blessing in disguise.

"Sit and relax. Spend some time with your aunt. We can do this later." Again, Cass hesitated, but even upset, she loved Rebecca too much to walk away without some form of contact. So, she bent and kissed Rebecca quickly on the cheek before hurrying away.

Cass opened the front door, stepping aside for Aunt Wills to come in.

"She's out back," Cass announced, then shut the door and began to walk away.

"You took her to the club."

Cass stopped, her nostrils flaring with anger at the accusation in Willamena's tone.

"Yeah, I did."

"I thought we agreed to take things slow."

Cass whirled around. "What's wrong, Dr. Woodrow? Shouldn't you be happy that your niece got her memory back?" She stepped closer. "Rebecca wanted to go. She wanted to speed things up. And since she's an adult and my wife, who I'd do anything for, I did as she asked. It worked. Look, maybe you wanted to play it safe to give you a second chance at taking care of her instead of jetting back to New York like you did the first time. But I'm not going to play games with my wife's well-being to satisfy your guilt."

Willamena was stunned by Cassidy's words. That's not what she was doing at all. Was it? "If I wanted to keep Rebecca from remembering, I wouldn't have done everything I could to bring you two back together."

Cass shook her head. "There are two sides to every coin, Doc, but you need both for that coin to be valuable. You wanted Rebecca to need you again, but you knew she needed me, too."

Cass held her hands up, done with this conversation. She regretted everything she said. Hell, she didn't even know if she actually believed what she said. But Cass's emotions were getting the best of her, and they were too high and volatile to be in the room with anyone at the moment.

"I'll be in my studio. I'd prefer not to be disturbed."

Once again, Cass hurried away.

It took Willamena a moment to gather herself and go out to see her niece. What Cass said to her shook her. She would have to evaluate it later. Right now, she needed to see Rebecca and make sure she was okay. She opened the sliding glass door and stepped out.

"Hey, my sweet girl."

Rebecca lifted her head from her hands, wiping tears from her cheek. "Hey, Aunt Wills." She smiled tremulously.

Willamena pulled a chair close to Rebecca and sat down. "Are you in pain?"

Rebecca laughed sadly. "Yeah, but not in my head. Cassidy is mad at me."

Willamena sighed. She just had a taste of Cass's displeasure, and it wasn't fun. She could only imagine what Rebecca felt when this should be a time of celebration.

"Do you remember when you were six years old, your mom and I took you shopping for new clothes?"

Rebecca furrowed her brows, wondering what that had to do with

Cassidy being pissed at her. "I was six. I may have gotten my memory back, Aunt Wills, but it only goes so far."

"Fair enough," Willamena chuckled. "Well, I remember it very well. Gwennie and I were looking at cute little dresses for you. One minute, you were yelling no at everything we showed you, and the next, you were gone. We turned our backs for two seconds, and that was enough for you to disappear. We looked *everywhere.* We had the entire staff of the store looking. Oh, Gwennie was so scared. We both were!"

"Obviously, you found me."

Willamena nodded. "After twenty excruciatingly long minutes, your little smart butt jumped out from under a table of clothes yelling 'BOO!'. You laughed and laughed, thinking that's what had scared us. Gwennie was just so happy we found you, safe and sound, that she hugged you and kissed you all over your little face. But once things settled down, that's when the anger came. 'Don't you dare do that again, Rebecca Aisling Cuinn!'."

"'You scared me to death!'" Rebecca quoted, the memory of that day vaguely coming back to her. "Was that your long, drawn-out way of telling me that Cassidy is in her anger stage?"

"I'm saying she was scared of losing you, Becca. She was afraid you'd never remember how in love you two are. And now that she can breathe and feel something other than fear and loss, it's hitting her hard."

"What should I do?"

"Are you afraid of her?"

"No," Rebecca answered immediately. There wasn't an ounce of doubt that Cassidy would never hurt her.

"Then talk to her. What was it that you told me she did for you? Exorcise your demons?"

Rebecca nodded. "It's my turn to return the favor. Do you mind if we do this later? I don't want Cassidy to agonize over this any longer."

"Not at all. Let her talk, Becca. She needs to know she can be candid with you without losing everything." Willamena smiled, trying to appease the apparent anxiety in Rebecca. Every time there was discord within her relationship with Cass, Rebecca was thrown off-kilter. The quicker they get over this bump, the better. "Now, before I go, have you told the others that you've regained your memory?"

Rebecca shook her head. "You're the first. Could you tell them? I need to fix things with Cassidy. That's my priority right now."

Willamena got up, bringing Rebecca up with her and kissing her on the cheek. "I got it covered. Would you be opposed to having a little get-together?"

"As long as I can patch things up with Cassidy, I'm fine with whatever everyone wants to do."

"Cass in her studio. Could you give her a message from me?"

Chapter Thirty-Five

"Cassidy?"

Cass closed her eyes briefly. God, she didn't want to be angry with Rebecca. This should be a happy time. They were together, Rebecca remembered her, and the tumor was benign and fucking gone. So why did Cass feel so fucking crappy?

"I told your aunt I didn't want to be disturbed." *Fuck. I'm so going to get punished for my behavior.* Cass was afraid that the punishment wouldn't be the pleasurable kind. Rebecca wasn't going to put up with this attitude for long, so Cass needed to find a way to rein it in.

"My aunt?" Rebecca gritted her teeth. She understood Cassidy's mood, but that didn't mean Rebecca had to like it. They should be celebrating, not fighting. "My aunt has a message for you."

Great. Aunt Wills probably told on me, and now Rebecca was pissed off. "Yeah?" Cass tried sounding casual and bored, but it didn't quite work. Instead, she sounded like a little kid about to get a good butt whoopin' for being a brat.

"She told me to tell you that you're probably right but that it wasn't intentional. And she's sorry. Do you want to tell me what that's about?"

And now Cass felt like a dick. She vowed to apologize to Aunt Wills once she got her shit together. "Not really."

Rebecca blew out a breath of frustration. "Cassidy, I understand you're frustrated."

"Do you?" Cass interrupted hotly. "Do you know what it's like to take your wife, the woman you love more than anything in this world, to the hospital to have a fucking tumor removed, and then three days later, she wakes up and doesn't know who the fuck you are? That fucking killed me, Becca." Cass put her paintbrush down and stood up, but she didn't dare get closer. She was upset, but she certainly didn't want to intimidate Rebecca. "Then I realized that the woman I thought shared everything with me was holding back. I learned more about you as a stranger than your wife. The icing on the cake," Cass scoffed, "was finding out that even after three years together and being married, I'm still just a sub to you."

Everything Cassidy said ripped through Rebecca's heart, but she stood there and let Cassidy get it out. Rebecca owed Cassidy that much. However, it also brought on an intense fear that she and Cassidy wouldn't get past this if Cassidy felt this way.

"Is there more, Cassidy?" Rebecca asked calmly.

The cold fingers of panic wrapped around Cass's heart at Rebecca's lack of emotion. No, that wasn't exactly true. There was emotion, just not the anger Cass had been expecting. Would that change once Rebecca knew everything?

"Well, I guess you're going to find this out eventually. I slugged Hunter."

Rebecca wasn't expecting that. "I'm guessing that's what you needed to confess?"

Cass shrugged. Rebecca's demeanor didn't change even after hearing Cass had punched Rebecca's oldest best friend.

"Anything else?" Rebecca asked again. Cassidy shook her head, and Rebecca breathed in deeply. A lot depended on Cassidy's answer to Rebecca's next question. "May I say my piece, or would you rather I leave you alone? Or if you'd like to talk more about how this made you feel, we can do that."

Cass frowned. "Why aren't you mad? Why aren't you yelling at me or, you know, bringing Mistress out?"

Rebecca tilted her head. "Because I don't want to be like Samantha. I was reminded that I wasn't allowed to have emotions, Cassidy. I wasn't allowed to say no or to give voice to what hurt me." She gestured to an oversized chair on the other side of the room. "Can we sit?"

Cass nodded again. *Because I don't want to be like Samantha,* those words struck Cass. She never once thought Rebecca was like that bitch

Samantha. Oh god, what if her word vomit made Rebecca believe that? *Son of a bitch!* This wasn't what Cass wanted. She wanted to be honest, not fucking mean!

"Sit with me?"

Cass stopped her inner chastising long enough to do as Rebecca asked. Their legs touched when Cass sat down, and she took it as a good sign that Rebecca hadn't moved away.

"I-I said what I needed to say," Cass said softly. She wanted so badly to apologize. To fall to her knees and beg Rebecca for forgiveness. But Cass knew Rebecca hated it when Cass got on her knees in any form of submission.

"I don't want you to be afraid of me. I certainly don't want you to be afraid of Mistress. So, I would like to address the things you said to me. Is that okay?"

"Yeah, y-yes. Look, Becca, I shouldn't have said those things. I didn't..."

"Cassidy, you're allowed to have feelings. And I want you to come to me if there's something I'm doing that causes you unhappiness."

"I'm not unhappy, Becca."

"You think you're *just* a sub to me." Rebecca shook her head, not wanting to get ahead of herself. "Let me start at the beginning. You recently told me that everyone experiences the same event differently. I know what that means now more than ever after hearing your side."

Rebecca curled her leg up under her and faced Cassidy head-on. This change within her was freeing. The fear of Cassidy leaving her had dissipated because, despite everything that was said, she still saw the love in Cassidy's eyes. They've jumped hurdles before; they can do it again. Rebecca was determined to make this right.

"When I woke up, I was right back there in the worst time of my life. The weird thing is, now that I have my memory back, I can compare what I felt then to what I felt this time around. The pain, the fear, and even the guilt were gone. Instead, I felt confused and... incomplete. I knew that had nothing to do with Samantha, so I couldn't understand where that feeling was coming from. Then you walked into my room, and that feeling disappeared. Of course, I didn't realize why then because I was mortified that this incredibly sexy woman was seeing me in a hospital gown with messed up hair, no makeup, and bad breath."

Cass couldn't help but laugh at the face Rebecca made. "You were beautiful. You always are to me. All I cared about was that you were awake."

"And that I didn't know you," Rebecca reminded her. "But deep down, I think I did, which is probably why I was so open with you. Cassidy, those things I told you were on my mind because, well, that's where my mind was. Everything Samantha put me through was right there, front and center. But when we met five years ago, I was years removed from all of that and had spent countless hours trying to forget. Once you and I were together and I fell in love with you, I never had to hold anything back. I could let them go. *That's* the gift you gave me. And listen, we've only been together three of my forty-four — almost forty-five — years on this earth. We still have so much to learn about each other."

Well, when Rebecca said it *that* way, Cass's worries seemed unjustified. She bowed her head only to have Rebecca raise it with a fingertip.

"As for this assumption that you're just a sub to me, Cassidy, you *never* were. Not even when you came into the Pink Room the first time. It hurts me that you feel that way."

"It hurts me that I don't know if you gave me that kind of pleasure because of the tumor or not," Cass confessed, deliberately using Rebecca's own words.

Rebecca dropped her gaze for a moment. "It wasn't the tumor, that much I know."

"How?"

"Because I remember exactly how I felt that day. I thought we had this conversation already. Why is it bothering you again?"

Cass shook her head. "You told me you never did that to... her because she was a sadist. Last night, you said it was never done to you because you were a sub, and subs didn't deserve that kind of pleasure. Which one is true?"

Rebecca tilted her head and raised a brow. "Is there a reason that both can't be true?"

Cass opened her mouth, then closed it. No, there wasn't a reason. And now Cass felt even more like a dick. "No, but if they're both true, why wouldn't you tell me that the first time?" *Oh, sure. Double down on your dickness.* Fuck, Cass wanted to punch herself at this point.

Rebecca sighed. "It had nothing to do with you and everything to do with how I felt about my... arrangement with Samantha. I'm not proud of who I was back then. I sometimes wonder how I ever allowed myself to fall for her bullshit. But what it was is *nothing* like what you and I have now. There was no mutual respect, no love. Hell, there was nothing but pain and sadness. God, I hope I don't make you feel that way."

"You don't," Cass reassured Rebecca. She hung her head, berating herself for even starting this with Rebecca. After everything they'd been through the past few weeks, this could have waited. Or Cass could have forgone the idiocy altogether. "I'm so sorry, Becca."

Rebecca took Cassidy's hand, relieved when Cassidy didn't pull away. "I think the stress of the tumor and the memory loss has affected both of us. I don't think you would have felt this way had I not forgotten you. Or us."

"I know that wasn't your fault. It was so stupid to blame you." Tears threatened again, and Cass wondered if the two of them would ever recover from this. Would they be Rebecca and Cass again? Or Mistress and Cassidy? Or would this conversation become the wedge that breaks them apart?

"And it was stupid and irresponsible of me to insinuate you would ever cheat on me. Or hurt me in any way," Rebecca admitted. "We didn't handle this very well, did we? If this was a test, we made a solid D at best."

Cass's lips curled in a slight grin. "Eh, I give us points for not letting it stew and being honest with each other." She paused. "Okay, I give *you* points. I ran away like a little pussy."

Rebecca's lips twitched. "I like it when you say pussy." She stroked Cassidy's blushing cheek. "You know, I believe there's a silver lining to all of this."

"Yeah?" Cass leaned into Rebecca's touch. "Care to share?"

"I got a second chance," Rebecca answered simply.

"Second chance?" Cass sat back, beckoning Rebecca to join her. She was delighted when Rebecca snuggled into her side. "What do you mean by that?"

Rebecca's body relaxed when Cass wrapped her arms around her. "Let's see if I can explain this. Despite my embarrassment by my appearance when you visited me at the hospital, I was so smitten with you that I was sad I might never see you again. Those types of emotions were so foreign to me that I equated them with how a teenager might feel with her first serious crush," Rebecca laughed. "I thought about you constantly and asked about you. Then you showed up at Aunt Wills's all sweet and charming, and, oh, the butterflies in my tummy went crazy." She laid a hand over her belly, remembering how she felt seeing Cassidy standing at the door. "That night, I was reading in bed and kept imagining your face as the main character."

Cass smiled, captivated by Rebecca's story. "You're always the main character, baby. But I'm happy to play the role of the love interest."

Rebecca shook her head. "Nope. In my mind, you're the hero. You proved it that day I almost passed out, and you picked me up and held me in your arms." Rebecca over-exaggerated a sigh, fanning herself as she dramatically melted into Cassidy.

Cass tightened her arms around Rebecca, laughing at the theatrics. "I would put on my shining armor for you, but it's being polished at the moment."

"Darn!" Rebecca intertwined her fingers with Cassidy's. "We're going to revisit that one day, though." She brought both of their hands up to her head and gently tapped her temple. "Making a mental note to find shining armor." Then she hugged Cassidy's arms around her waist again, appreciating the feeling of safety it brought her. "You know, I wouldn't change the way we met because that story is uniquely ours. But I don't know. I kind of love not having to wonder what it would have been like if we had met before I hardened myself as Mistress. That's my silver lining, getting to meet you all over again as Rebecca without the not-so-subtle undertones of sex hanging in the air between us. That's not to say I wasn't attracted to you because I *definitely* was. But I felt... courted. I felt normal. You took me on a date," Rebecca said with a wide smile. "Once again, you gifted me something I'd never had before. You kept showing up, and even though I know how much it must've hurt, you left me each night with a smile that promised I would see you again."

Rebecca laid her head back onto Cassidy's shoulder, closing her eyes when Cassidy buried her face in Rebecca's neck.

"They say everything happens for a reason," Cass began, her voice thick with emotion. "As much as it did hurt to be here in this house without you, I can't deny how extraordinary it was to meet Rebecca before Mistress."

"Hmm." Rebecca thought about that for a moment.

Cass took Rebecca's sudden quietness as a sign that Cass had said something to offend her wife. "T-that's – I didn't mean that the way it sounded."

Rebecca patted Cassidy's arms so she would release her grip from around Rebecca's waist. "I know what you meant, baby." She straddled Cassidy's lap and wrapped her arms around Cassidy's neck. "I must say, Rebecca allowed herself to fall for you much quicker than Mistress did. Though, she was also twenty years younger in her mind."

Cass smiled up at Rebecca. "I'm glad you're not twenty years younger. I think dating an older woman is fucking hot."

Rebecca bent her head and bit Cassidy's bottom lip hard enough to cause a yelp. "That's for calling me an older woman." She dipped her head again and licked Cassidy's lip before kissing her gently. "That's for implying I'm hot."

Cass poked her tongue out to lick the sore area, smiling the entire time. Rebecca's playfulness and discomfort about her age were *really* good signs. "Can I ask you a question?"

"Have I ever said no to you?"

Cass pursed her lips. Was she going to give a smart-ass answer and risk being punished? Hell, yeah, she was. "I can think of a few times. Need me to list them for you?"

Rebecca's eyebrows shot up. "You're feeling a bit cheeky, aren't you?"

Heh. Cass's hands snaked down to grab a handful of Rebecca's ass and squeezed. "Now I am," she grinned.

"What is your question, Cassidy?" Rebecca playfully tugged on Cassidy's hair yet still pushed her ass back into Cassidy's touch.

"Is Mistress... gone? I mean, I know that becoming Mistress helped with undoing everything Samantha did to you. But with this second chance, do you... need her anymore?"

Rebecca thought about what Cassidy said about being just a sub to her. "Do you want Mistress to go away?"

"No! I mean, uh," Cass blew out a breath. "I love what we have, babe, but I don't want to make you be someone you're not. If this tumor and everything that's happened has changed something within you..."

"Baby, Mistress is a part of me. I think she always has been. And as long as you feel safe with her, she'll always be with us." Rebecca pushed Cassidy's long bangs out of her face. "I'm no longer afraid of giving in to Mistress, you know. Having this memory of being a sub so fresh in my mind, I think I understand more what it means to be a dominant and the balance of control for each."

"Another silver lining?"

"There will never be a silver lining for what Samantha did to me. But it was certainly a learning experience. So, as long as you want Mistress, Cassidy, you have her."

"Forever," Cass said immediately. "I want you both forever. Just *please* keep calling me Cassidy." She cupped Rebecca's face in her hands. "Cass sounded wrong coming from you, and I didn't like it."

Rebecca scrunched her face. "Yeah, that *felt* odd coming out of my mouth. Why didn't you introduce yourself as Cassidy?"

Cass shrugged. "I don't know. But I'm kinda glad I didn't because hearing you say it while coming in my mouth was fucking incredible."

Rebecca's nostrils flared as arousal coursed through her body. "We have a *lot* of missed time to make up for, *Cassidy.* Shall we get started?"

"Fuck yeah, we shall." Cass scooted up, making sure to keep a firm grip on Rebecca's ass. "Better hang on, darlin'."

"Darlin'?

Cass grinned. "Sounded good in my head." She stood, loving how

Rebecca wrapped her legs around her waist. Cass paused, peering up into Rebecca's silver eyes. They were dark with arousal and clearer than they had been in a long time. "Are we good, baby?"

"We're better than good. We're Rebecca and Cassidy. Now, I have a question. Where the hell is my dog?"

Epilogue

Rebecca stood in her office, gazing out the window and avoiding the crowd that was amassing in her house. This was precisely why she told Cassidy she wanted the "Welcome back, Rebecca" party at their home—so that when she felt overwhelmed, she could hide. Rebecca loved her friends dearly, but holy hell, there were a lot of them, and Rebecca was still trying to find her groove. Well, she and Cassidy had undoubtedly found their groove—multiple times. But Rebecca was taking her time with everything else. She should have taken more time with this get-together. Yet, she knew as soon as Aunt Wills began letting everyone know Rebecca's memory was back, this little party was inevitable. They all meant well, and the mutual love between everyone in the group is why Rebecca agreed to it less than a week later.

She could hear the bustle of people outside her office door. Ellie, Blaise, and Eve were preparing dishes in Rebecca's kitchen. Cassidy, Mo, Grayson, and Hunter were out on the deck grilling. Lainey, Patty, and Aunt Wills were on kid duty — including keeping the bigger kids occupied and out of the way. Even Mocha was in on the fun, barking and playing with Bella, who did an excellent job at dog-sitting. And Rebecca... was hiding. The good news was they were the most understanding friends anyone could have. This meant that Rebecca could hole up in her office for as long as she needed to without judgment. Yeah, she loved her friends dearly. Even...

"Hey, babe?"

Rebecca looked back over her shoulder and smiled at her wife. "Hey."

"You okay?" Cass walked over to Rebecca and wrapped her arms around her.

"Yeah, just..."

"Overwhelmed?"

"A little." Rebecca scoffed. "Or a lot."

"You don't like being the one everyone is here for, do you? When others need help, you're the first one there, but when it's you..."

"Are you analyzing me, Cassidy?"

Cass turned Rebecca to face her. "No, ma'am. I'm telling my wife what I honestly see. We do that now, right?" she grinned.

"Mmhmm." Rebecca had to chuckle at Cassidy's failed attempt at innocence. "You're right."

"I'm sorry, what?" Cass tugged on her earlobe. "I think I heard what you said, but I'm not sure. Could you repeat it?"

Rebecca narrowed her eyes at her lover. "You are just itching for a spanking, aren't you?"

"Baby, you have no idea." Cass wiggled her eyebrows and thrust her pelvis into a giggling Rebecca. "Unfortunately, we have a house full of guests. One of which would like to talk to you if you're up for it." When Rebecca nodded, Cass called out. "Hunt?"

The slight smile on Rebecca's lips faded when Hunter walked in.

"Hey, Becca."

"Hello, Hunter."

Cass didn't miss Rebecca's look. That look was Mistress, and a very annoyed Rebecca all rolled into one.

"I, uh, I'm just gonna..." Cass kissed Rebecca quickly on the cheek, patted Hunter's shoulder, and high-tailed it out of there.

Hunter cleared her throat. "How are you feeling? Have the headaches diminished?"

"Oh, I see. You're here as a doctor." Rebecca crossed her arms and turned back to the window.

"Becca, I know you blame me for what happened."

Rebecca whirled back around. "Is *that* what you think? That I blame you for losing my memory? Wow, doctors really do have God complexes."

Hunter sighed. "I don't have a complex, Rebecca. I'm just saying I understand. If I had suggested an alternate solution and not made you get the surgery..."

"Made me?" Rebecca scoffed. "No one makes me do anything, Hunter. You found the tumor, you found me the best doctor in the country, and you offered your opinion on the remedies. I took all of that information, talked to my wife, and made a decision based on what was best for me and those I love."

"Then," Hunter frowned, "why are you pissed at me? Cuz I'd rather you punch me than give me the cold shoulder."

"Cassidy already did that." Rebecca shook her head and paced away. "Where were you, Hunter? Hmm? You're my oldest friend, the one who was there for me when I woke up from nearly being killed. But this time?" Rebecca threw her hands in the air. "I saw Blaise and Eve and Lainey. Hell, I even saw Ellie. Where were *you*? Where the *fuck* were you?"

Hunter sat heavily in one of the chairs in the room. "I fucked up, Becca. I'm a fucking coward. I watched you go through that once, and I – I couldn't do it again. Especially because I blamed myself for what was happening."

"So, you just stayed away. Cassidy and I were there for you when Ellie was hurt. We're there for *all* of you. Even if you couldn't be around me, why in the *hell* weren't you there for Cassidy when she needed you?"

"Hang on, babe." Cass popped into the office and shut the door behind her. Geez, if Ellie knew Rebecca was tearing Hunter a new one, who knew what the fuck would happen. "Hunter was there for me. Yeah, I was eavesdropping," she explained when Rebecca raised a brow. "I saw the look on your face when Hunt came in here. I've put her through enough. And I think she's put herself through the wringer."

Cass stood close to Rebecca but didn't touch her. She knew her wife well enough not to try to placate her or distract her from the truth.

"Everyone was there for me despite what I did to Hunter. Ellie sat with me, talked to me, and gave me hope that even if you didn't get your memory back, you could fall in love with me again. Eve stopped by and spoke to me about... the facts." Cass leaned in and lowered her voice to a whisper. "She even hugged me."

Rebecca bit her lip to keep from laughing. She was still annoyed with Hunter, but Cass's recounting of their friends being there was beginning to thaw the coldness in her heart.

"And Hunt?" Cass laid a hand on Hunter's shoulder in support and gratitude. "I didn't deserve your forgiveness. No matter what I was going through, I should never have hit you. Being married to who I'm married to, I should know that better than anyone else." She looked at Rebecca. "*I* blamed Hunter, yet she showed up at my door and sat there with me as I bawled my fucking eyes out without an ounce of judgment. The others, including your aunt, came up with that little scheme of theirs to get us to spend the day together so I could charm you. Hell, even Mo sent me a case of her new beer. Then Patty sent flowers and said she was sacrificing herself to keep Mo from coming over and drinking the beer herself."

Rebecca finally lost her battle with the laughter and snorted. "That sounds like Mo." She became serious again as she thought about everything Cassidy just told her. She hadn't known about the crying or the loss of hope. "Why didn't you tell me any of this?"

Cass scratched her head and shrugged a shoulder. "Not sure. I think maybe I was afraid to tell you just how weak and needy I was. The point is, though, everyone did their best in the situation we were in. You didn't know any of them, babe, so I can only imagine they had a hard time trying to figure out what to do and how to help. But I need you to know they showed up for me. And for Mocha. Bella may never forgive us for taking Mocha back, but that's a bridge we must cross at another time."

Rebecca glanced at Hunter, who covered her mouth to stifle a laugh. She walked to Cassidy, standing toe to toe with her, and looked up. "You're so weird, baby."

Cass grinned down at Rebecca. "You still love me."

"That I do." Rebecca lifted herself onto her tiptoes and kissed Cassidy's lips. "Thank you." She looked at Hunter again, who had been very quiet the entire time Cass spoke. "And you. I will forgive you on one condition." Rebecca pressed a finger on Cassidy's lips when she began to argue, her gaze never leaving Hunter.

"Anything," Hunter said sincerely.

"I'll forgive you if you forgive yourself. None of this was your fault, Hunter. If anything, you helped me by being persistent about my having a physical that day. You couldn't have known the outcome. So let yourself off the hook."

Hunter stood and nodded. "I promise to try. I should've been there for you, Rebecca."

"You were there for the one who needed you the most, Hunter. And for that, I'm eternally grateful." Rebecca hugged Hunter tightly. "Thank you."

"Yeah, um, ahem." Hunter thumbed towards the door. "We should get back out there. Mo is manning the grill."

"Grayson is out there, too," Cass reminded Hunter.

"Uh, do you remember what happened with the hot dogs the last time Grayson was in charge?"

Cass's eyes widened. "Shit. I was scraping hot dogs off the grill for days. How the hell do you explode a damn hot dog?" She shook her head. "Head on out, I'll catch up with you."

Hunter saluted, winking at Rebecca with that lopsided grin that won Ellie over. Once they were alone, Cass took Rebecca in her arms.

"You sure you're okay?"

"Yes, baby. I'm going to take five minutes to do some breathing exercises that Ellie taught me, and then I'm going to stop being a rude hostess and go out there to be with my friends. Maybe we'll watch you studs grilling and... talk."

"Yeah?" Cass grinned down at Rebecca. "Gonna tell them how I'm the only one who has ever made you sq..."

Rebecca pressed her lips to Cassidy's to shut her up. "If you say anything like that in front of our friends, I will be forced to tell them about the anal beads fiasco."

"Fucking hell, babe!" Cass's entire body shivered. "I was nervous! When you're nervous, you clinch! I think we're good with keeping some things to ourselves."

"That's what I thought," Rebecca winked. "Now, go on. I don't want to smell hot dogs for the next three weeks."

Cass pulled a Hunter and saluted. "Love you, babe."

"Love you, too, Cassidy." Rebecca slapped Cassidy's ass as she walked away. Cassidy looked back and gave Rebecca a look that buckled her knees. Good lord, she really did love that woman. Rebecca inhaled, trying to focus on relaxing instead of what she wanted to do to Cassidy. *That* wasn't easy.

"Can I help?"

Ellie looked up from her task and smiled at Rebecca. "Absolutely. Grab a knife."

"Welcome back," Eve said, setting aside the bowl she was mixing veggies in and giving Rebecca a hug.

"Thank you. I heard you were giving these away," Rebecca grinned, relaxing considerably since she walked in. This was friendship, she thought. When you could walk in a room and no matter whose house you were at, everyone looked like they were home.

"Only to those who deserve it," Eve winked. "Since you're late, you're on onion duty with Blaise."

Rebecca nodded but stood there for a moment. "I wanted to say thank you for being there for Cassidy. All of you are in love with your soul mates, so I know you'll understand when I say that means more to me than anything else you could've done. I also know this situation was... weird for lack of a better word. But you never let Cassidy fall too far out of hope. I owe you so much for that."

"You don't owe us anything," Ellie said, sniffling and dabbing at her eyes with a paper towel. "We're family and that's what family does."

"Truth!" Blaise offered. "Now stop making Ellie and Eve cry."

"You're crying, too!" Ellie laughed.

"I'm cutting onions!"

Oh, how Rebecca missed this! "You're wearing goggles, you goof. Don't..." Rebecca stopped mid-sentence and looked at Blaise again. "You're wearing goggles."

"Yeah, and?"

"She doesn't like the way the onions sting her eyes," Ellie explained. "So, the only way she'll cut them is if she has goggles."

Blaise held up a pink pair. "Got another pair here with your name on them!" She tossed them at Rebecca. "These yahoos aren't going to do the dirty work, so put those on and get over here."

Rebecca laughed enthusiastically. God, she felt like she hadn't laughed like that for years. "Ladies, I love the fuck out of you!"

Eve, Ellie, and Blaise joined in on the laughter. "We love the fuck out of you, too!"

One Week Later.

"Are you sure about this?"

They sat out front of Nadia's bar, the car still idling while Cass tried to think of a way out of this. It was stupid since she was the one who asked for Rebecca's help. But now that they were there, Cass was nervous as fuck. What if Nadia said something to piss Rebecca off? That wasn't Nadia's style, but it sure as fuck was Mickey's. This is exactly why Cass never wanted to bring Rebecca here. It used to be her playground, but now it was just a distant memory. The only reason she offered Nadia help was because they had somewhat of a history.

Rebecca watched Cassidy drum her fingers on the steering wheel. She reached over and took Cassidy's hand. This was the first time she'd ever been to one of Cassidy's old hangouts. She had to admit, she was curious to see what it was like.

"Why are you so nervous about this?"

Because of what I used to do here. Cass shrugged. "I just don't want you to be uncomfortable."

"And you think being at your old stomping grounds will do that?"

Another shrug.

"I'm good, baby. In fact, I'm kind of excited to see where you used to hang out. I feel like you gave up so much when we got together. Including your friends. I never meant for that to happen."

"I didn't give up anything, babe. My only real friend was Miranda, and we both know how that ended. This was just a place I'd go to, uh... find companionship for the night. Once I met you, I didn't need anything or anyone else."

Cassidy was so loyal and loving that it was difficult for Rebecca to imagine this different side of her. "And Nadia? Was she a friend with benefits?"

Cass looked away with embarrassment.

"She must've been special to you if you want to help her now." Rebecca wouldn't pretend that there wasn't a tiny bit of jealousy behind that thought. But she trusted Cassidy implicitly.

"No one was special, babe. And that was a two-way street. They all had bets on who could tame 'Cassanova.' It was a game. And maybe it was like that for both parties, but at least I was honest with what I wanted."

Rebecca was silent for a full ten seconds. "I'm sorry... Cassanova?" She bit her lip. "Is that what they called you?"

"Oh fuck," Cass groaned. Who the fuck needed Micky spouting off shit when Cass could do it herself? She was never going to live this down. "You're gonna tell Hunter and Mo that aren't you?"

Rebecca feigned indignation. "I would never!" A smile slowly formed on her lips. "Ellie and Patty, maybe. And Eve and Lainey."

"Babe!"

Rebecca laughed. "Yes, Cassanova?"

"Baaaabe!"

The laughter increased with Cassidy's whining. "I'm just kidding, baby. Though, I will be calling you that as punishment when you deserve it."

"Can I use my safe word for that?" Cass pouted.

"Nope. Now, let's get this over with so we can go home. I have plans on how to conquer Cassanova."

Cass opened her mouth to argue, then thought of all the possibilities. *Heh.* "Yes, Mistress."

What the mind forgets, the heart remembers. True love will always find a way.

Acknowledgements

Oh my goodness! Besides Eve and Lainey, Rebecca and Cass are my most asked-about characters. Well, I have to put Willamena in there, too. One day, you all will hear more about Willamena, but first, let's talk about Undoing. This book started out as something else entirely. A foe was going to return and wreak havoc on their lives. However, Rebecca and Cass had other ideas. They told me in no uncertain terms that they would never let a person – friend or foe – come between them. If anything was going to separate them, it would have to be something huge. Something they couldn't predict or change. I think I subconsciously chose this 'foe' because of my experience with my momma's Alzheimer's. It worked for Rebecca and Cass because it gave me the opportunity to give them a second chance at romance. Something I don't think either of them really had in their lives. It provided me with really sweet, deep, and, at times, funny scenes that they needed to have despite how perfect they are for each other.

Thank yous

Daisy – As always, I could never do what I do without your support. Thank you for being my rock and making life fun!

Melissa – When I asked you if you wanted to do the cover for Undoing, you jumped at the chance! And it's perfect! Thank you for being Rebecca and Cass's biggest fan! And for being an awesome BFF!

Ami, Nellie, Tascha, Sarah, Vanessa, Karen, and Janice – You were ALL excellent beta readers! When writing, sometimes you get the feeling that it's not going the way you thought it would. You second guess your decisions, wonder if you're any good, and finally decide you're not doing anything right. However, you all gave me the encouragement and inspiration to keep going by letting me know what reading the book meant to you. And what Rebecca and Cass mean to you. Thank you!

To my VIP Patrons and those who support me on Ko-fi – Alice, Ariel, Arleen, Debbie, Angela, Chris, Diane, Elizabeth, FHTF81, Kim, Lisa, Paula, Sharon, Tamara, Tammy, Renate, and Kay – I'll never be able to express how honored I am to have you all in my corner supporting me. Thank you!

Thank YOU, the reader! I don't put out as many books as I wish I could, and yet you all stick around, excited about what's next! Your loyalty to my merry band of characters makes me giddy! It is especially hard to keep track of everyone in a series, but I love doing this series (and Eve and Lainey) because of the love you give to these characters! You all even help me when I forget a little something here and there. These books and these characters are a labor of love. And as long as you love them and continue to read, I'll continue to write. Just one more chapter...

About the Author

Jourdyn Kelly lives in Houston, Texas, with a beautiful zoo of pets ranging from furry to aquatic. Jourdyn attributes her passion for writing and sharing stories to the love of the written word she inherited from her mother, who always surrounded them with books. After losing her mother from Alzheimer's complications, Jourdyn started her own company, Jaded Angels, as a tribute to her and the strong women who have inspired Jourdyn throughout her life. A portion of the proceeds goes to alz.org in her mother's memory. Jourdyn collects Grogu merchandise with startling avarice, paints 3D printed models as a hobby, is a Dim Sum fanatic who loves going to the movies, and, of course, penning her novels.